IN THE RED

DINA SANTORELLI

Praise for *In The Red*

"Five stars! Dina Santorelli has done it again! Relatable characters. Dark intrigue. A mystery that feels personal. A book you just can't put down."

—Michael O'Keefe, crime fiction author and retired NYPD detective

Praise for Dina Santorelli's Baby Grand Trilogy

BABY GRAND
#1 Political Thriller on Amazon Kindle
#1 Kidnapping Thriller on Amazon Kindle
#3 Best Seller on B&N Nook
Top 30 Paid in Kindle Store
Runner-up, Shelf Unbound Best Indie Book Competition
Honorable Mention, Genre Fiction, Writer's Digest Self-Published Book Awards

"A perfect thriller from Dina Santorelli—heart-stomping, emotion-packed, and utterly surprising.... A terrific read!"

—Ellen Meister, author of the mystery novel *Love Sold Separately*

"Dina Santorelli has the gift of a natural storyteller, and *Baby Grand* sweeps along at a frantic pace . . . It's very human, very exciting, and absolutely engrossing."

—Chris Nickson, author of the Richard Nottingham series of historical mysteries

Also by Dina Santorelli

Fiction
Baby Grand
Baby Bailino
Baby Carter

Nonfiction (Author)
Daft Punk: A Trip Inside the Pyramid

Nonfiction (Collaborator/Contributor)
*Good Girls Don't Get Fat: How Weight Obsession Is
    Messing Up Our Girls and How We Can Help Them
    Thrive Despite It*
*Bully: An Action Plan for Teachers, Parents, and Communities
    to Combat the Bullying Crisis*
I, Spy: How to Be Your Own Private Investigator
*Raising Men: Lessons Navy Seals Learned from Their
    Training and Taught to Their Sons*
*Become an American Ninja Warrior: The Ultimate
    Insider's Guide*

Publisher's Cataloging-In-Publication Data
(Prepared by The Donohue Group, Inc.)

Names: Santorelli, Dina, author.
Title: In the red / Dina Santorelli.
Description: Massapequa Park, New York : eLuna Media LLC, [2019]
Identifiers: ISBN 9780997719192 (paperback) | ISBN 9780997719185
   (ebook)
Subjects: LCSH: Accountants--New York (State)--Long Island--
   Fiction. | Murder--Investigation--New York (State)--Long Island-
   -Fiction. | Man-woman relationships--Fiction. | High technology
   industries--New York (State)--Long Island--Fiction. | LCGFT:
   Thrillers (Fiction)
Classification: LCC PS3619.A586 I5 2019 | DDC 813/.6--dc23

dinasantorelli.com
elunamedia.com

Cover design by Alexis Castellanos
Interior design by Wooly Head Design
Production management by Stonesong Digital

For my dad

IN THE RED

DINA SANTORELLI

1

Kirk Stryker stared out his office window at the two little girls holding hands and skipping along the village sidewalk. The evening sky was a deep red, with swirls of color soaking the large canvas of clouds and casting both a beautiful and an ominous glow on their freckled faces and auburn hair.

All along Lake Shore Avenue, Gardenia was closing up for the day, the shopkeepers sweeping their storefronts and depositing the day's trash at the curb for the morning rounds. It had been a mild winter, following a devastating hurricane last fall, but those days of no electricity and lengthy gas station lines had been long forgotten as the days passed and the temperatures rose. Spring was in the air once again on Long Island, light jackets and baseball caps replacing the parkas and wool hats, lengthier conversations replacing the quick hellos and good-byes. Stryker could see the proprietor of the fruit market down the way chatting amiably with someone walking a dog, and Mayor Barbara Gottlieb having a heart-to-heart with a few constituents as she descended the steps of Village Hall.

Unlike those of his business neighbors, Stryker's night was far from over—another sign that spring had arrived.

Tax season was in full swing; he hadn't made it home before 10:00 p.m. in weeks. *Such was the life of a certified public accountant,* he thought. April was the cruelest month.

His eyes settled on the stone building across the intersection where Marty Benning had opened his accounting practice two years earlier, waltzing into Gardenia like a gunman into an Old Western town with his eye on the stagecoach. The firms faced each other like boxers about to square off in a ring. A young couple strolling down Lake Shore peered inside the dark windows of Benning's building. The guy hadn't been around lately, which was both strange and bad business.

"What are you up to, Benning?" Stryker mumbled as the red, white, and blue pennant flags in front of his building caught the evening wind, tangling themselves around a streetlamp. He imagined them wrapping their laminated nylon around Benning's neck.

He stepped away from the window. The stacks of papers on his desk rose like skyscrapers. Once upon a time, those stacks had been much taller—a trend he wished he could blame entirely on Benning, but he couldn't. Nowadays, a generation of do-it-yourselfers preferred to muddle their way through a tax form than pay someone who actually knew what he was doing. *Millennials.* No wonder most of the accountants Stryker knew were going out of business. If the industry were a spreadsheet, it would be insolvent; the debits were far outweighing the assets.

He pulled out his desk drawer, revealing the pack of cigarettes and lighter he had hidden behind the boxes of staples. He stuck a butt in his mouth, lit it, and took a slow drag, blowing the smoke across the room and watching it circle beneath the room's smoke detector. He was glad he had Hugo Lurch dismantle the thing after the village banned smoking on the public sidewalks. The government seemed to be cracking down on everything—drinking, smoking. A man couldn't even comment on how a woman looked these days. It was getting harder and harder to have a little fun. Still, Stryker enjoyed the sneaking around. *The secrets.* He took another drag of his cigarette.

He sat down at his desk and leaned back in his chair, his thoughts turning again to Benning. In two short years, the guy had managed to charm an entire incorporated village. How? Benning was new and handsome, and people liked new and handsome, plus he was a Manhattanite, which most people on Long Island viewed as royalty. Since his arrival, Benning had been elected chamber of commerce president, named Merchant of the Year, and given the Consensus Civility Award from the mayor, who seemed taken with the village's new wonderboy and his magical powers of deduction.

Stryker picked up a pen, wrote *B-E-N-N-I-N-G* on his desk planner and stared at it, as if trying to decode a message, his pen point pressing into the letter *G* like the end of a blade. There was talk that Benning was setting the stage for some kind of run for political office. *Carpetbagger.* Stryker couldn't imagine a place as conservative as Gardenia electing a liberal like Benning, no matter how handsome he was, but stranger things had happened.

His cell phone rang, and he looked at the caller ID. It was Gloria, probably wanting to know when he'd be home—as if tonight would be any different from the night before and the night before that. He sighed and let it go to voice mail.

He wiggled his mouse, which lit up his computer screen, and opened his email to compose a quick note. As he typed, he felt a twinge in his groin and smiled. He pressed *Send,* and as the words disappeared from his screen, there was a knock on his office door. Stryker jammed his cigarette into the paperweight on his desk and tossed the butt onto the plastic floor guard below.

"Come in," he said, waving his hand at the smoke and crossing his legs to hide his bulge.

The door opened, and Paulette stuck in her head. "I'm leaving, Kirk. Colby file's done. I left it on Eva's desk." She shook her head. "That thing was a mess as usual. Half the financial statements were missing, and after six years of coming to us, he still doesn't know how to itemize, or the difference between *equipment* and *supplies*."

"That's why he has you, Paulette," Stryker said with a smile.

"Lucky me." She leaned against the doorframe. "Anyway, everyone else is gone besides Sandy and me. Need anything? I can order from the Chinese place before I go."

"Nah, I'm only going to stay for a couple of hours."

"All right then, I'll see you in the morning."

"Thanks, Paulette. See you tomorrow." He leaned across his desk so he could see Sandra picking up her handbag from her desk in the outer office. "Good night, Sandy." She waved.

Paulette shut off the light in the main office, turning the entire second floor dark, except for Stryker's office, which was illuminated by a small desk lamp. He bent down and picked up the mangled butt he'd dropped on the floor. The ash was still lit, and he blew on it until it burned brightly and stood again next to the window. Downstairs, the tops of two heads appeared and bobbed their way across the street toward Stevie's, the overpriced pub where Sandra and Paulette grabbed a nightcap most evenings.

Hiring Paulette eight years ago was the best business decision Stryker had ever made. She was smart, confident, well-liked. Stryker knew Benning had been wooing Paulette since he opened for business, which made sense. Paulette was Stryker's most requested tax advisor and alone probably pulled in a third of the firm's income. It was time, he knew, to make her a partner. He couldn't hold off any longer, not with Benning around.

Stryker turned the page of his desk planner. He had a meeting with Colby first thing in the morning, and taxes were just the tip of the iceberg of things they had to discuss. He crossed the room to collect the Colby file from Eva's desk in the outer office but was startled by the silhouette of a person standing in the doorway. Before his eyes could focus in the semi-darkness, he heard a pop and felt a searing pain in the center of his chest.

"What the . . . ?" he yelled, lashing out, but his body convulsed, and he fell backward, slamming his head onto the corner of his desk.

❂

The streetlights outside the office window swam around the room, a light haze following them like the tail of a meteor as Stryker's eyes fluttered open. He was still on the office floor, a stale cigarette smell, buried deep within the carpeting from years of secret smoking, made him feel nauseated.

How long had he been lying there?

He looked around but couldn't see anything—his desk lamp had been turned off—and his body burned, as if tiny fish hooks were ripping into the flesh of his torso. He ran his hand along his midsection and found the buttons of his collared shirt and trousers undone, the skin of his abdomen raw and wet.

He tried to lift himself from the floor, but scorching pain forced him back down with a grunt, and he curled into a fetal position. A noise caught his attention at the far end of his office, and he remembered the figure from before, the one standing there in the dark, and he lay still, his eyes searching the room. Something small was floating near the window, a tiny dot that glowed bright and then dimmed again, and Stryker realized it was the lit ash of a cigarette—was it *his*?—and that someone was smoking it.

"Who's there?" he coughed, the action making his chest ache.

No answer.

"I know you're there," he said.

The ash, which hung in the darkness like a twinkling star, began to change color and shape, and suddenly with a sizzling *whoosh*, it burst into a bright orange, and he realized, with horror, that the window drapery had caught fire.

Stryker flipped himself onto his stomach, shouting in agony as his skin grazed the shag carpet. He reached for the molding of the doorframe when the sting of a kick forced him to retract his arm, and he curled his body again into a tight ball.

The figure was hunched and rummaging inside Stryker's closet, tossing things out—cardboard boxes, pillows, blankets, a raincoat, articles of clothing. Then it hit him: *The safe.*

He did a quick tally—stock and bond certificates, assorted business papers and media, and somewhere in the neighborhood of fifteen thousand dollars in cash. A feeling of satisfaction overcame him.

"You'll never open it," he yelled with a sneer. "The hardplate is drill resistant. The door is three inches of indestructible steel. The thing's bolted to the ground." He coughed, the pain of his midsection intensifying. "And I'm not about to give the keypad combination to some lowlife who would rather steal from a hardworking man than earn his own living, so go fuck your—"

The bullet pierced Stryker's chest, and he fell back onto the floor, clutching at the wound just below his clavicle and feeling the warm spurt of blood. Above him, the fire shot across the wood-paneled ceiling as the small office filled with smoke. Over the crackle of the flames, the faint sound of fire truck sirens echoed in the distance.

"I hear them. They're coming," he whispered, sucking in the last of the smokeless air as the door to his office opened and closed, and he realized the intruder had gone.

The burst of fresh air fueled the flames, which were licking the bottom of the disarmed smoke detector. Stryker kicked his feet in an effort to move toward the exit, but the pain was too excruciating, and he couldn't catch his breath. Instead, he reached over his head, his fingertips grazing the raincoat the intruder had tossed onto the floor. He managed to curl his fingers around the belt and pull the item to him, burying his face beneath the fabric, which he hoped would conserve some air until help arrived. The sirens were louder now, and the red light of the engines created a flashing bull's eye along the perimeter of the small office. The firefighters were right outside.

Stryker pressed his shattered shoulder into the floor to stem the bleeding, which had soaked the carpet below him. Shouts ricocheted outside his window now, and he tried to call back, but every inhale burned his insides, and he was beginning to feel lightheaded.

He pulled the raincoat down, forming a fabric tent over his body and hoping that would buy him some time. He laid his head as low as possible to the floor and peered through a tiny space between the raincoat and the carpeting.

"Please, hurry," he murmured as the blaze bore down on him, illuminating the glass eyes of a teddy bear lying on the floor.

Where did that come from, he wondered, and a new fear seized him. His eyes searched the bottom of his closet and landed on his safe. To his relief, it was still intact, but then he realized, to his horror, that the safe's indestructible and drill-resistant three-inch steel door was hanging wide open.

2

Three and a half months earlier

The small waiting room was packed with people. With only a half hour until closing, Muriel wondered how the doctors were going to get through everyone and still give her time to get home, feed the kids, and grade twenty-five test papers before passing out in bed.

"How much longer is the wait?" asked a tall, middle-aged brunette. She was drumming her fingers across the office counter.

"Dr. Stowe will be with you as soon as he can," Muriel said.

"You said that an hour ago." The woman's fingers curled into a fist.

"I know it's been a long wait, Mrs. . . ." Muriel scanned the sign-in log.

"Bernstein," the woman said, rolling her eyes.

"Yes, Mrs. Bernstein, but, look, see here"—she held up the log—"you're next. So it shouldn't be much longer."

"It better not be," Mrs. Bernstein said, reclaiming

her seat in the waiting room next to a young lady who looked as if she'd rather be anywhere else than a cosmetic surgery office.

"What a bitch," Samantha whispered, lowering her head so that she couldn't be seen by the patients in the waiting room. Muriel playfully kicked her under the table.

"Bella Connor?" Samantha said, standing up and taking hold of a file. "Bella Connor?"

"That's us, thank God," said a woman in the center row who had a little girl no more than six years old in tow.

"I thought you said we were next?" called Mrs. Bernstein, daggers shooting from her eyes.

"You are," Muriel said. "You're seeing Dr. Stowe, not Dr. Warnell."

Dissatisfied, Mrs. Bernstein returned to her magazine but not before rolling her eyes again; the young woman next to her slunk further down in her seat.

"Come right this way, Mrs. Connor," Samantha said, ushering the woman and little girl into the narrow hallway that led to the examination rooms. The white fluorescent lighting made even the soft, delicate features of the girl look haggard. Muriel prayed the appointment was for the mother.

"Excuse me, where's the bathroom?"

The young woman who had been seated with Mrs. Bernstein stood before the office counter. She was playing with the string tied to the pen of the sign-in sheet.

"Right that way, sweetie," Muriel said, pointing to the left. "Down the corridor, first door on the right."

"Thanks," she said and disappeared from view.

Muriel scanned the sign-in sheet. With the Connors

gone, that meant only four, five, six patients left, she counted, although there was double that in the waiting room, since most patients had spouses and/or children accompanying them.

"This is fucking insane," muttered Samantha when she sat back down beside Muriel. "We're never going to get out of here." She wiped a spattering of crumbs from her workstation into a garbage pail. "Are you going tomorrow night?"

"Yes," Muriel said, trying not to sound too excited about the practice's annual Christmas dinner, but it had become one of the few nights Muriel had an excuse to get dressed up and drive into Manhattan. "You?"

"Not sure yet," Samantha said, half-interested, as she swiped her phone's screen. Muriel imagined a twenty-three-year-old had plenty of options for a Friday night rather than spend it with a bunch of coworkers who were twice her age.

"Well, I hope you do," Muriel said, picking up a stack of brochures and ducking out of the office. "It would be nice to have someone to talk to."

In the small alcove next to the waiting room, the young woman who had been with Mrs. Bernstein was browsing the practice's display of brochures on her way back from the bathroom.

"Hi, sweetie," Muriel said, refilling several spots in the rack. The young lady reached out and picked up one that Muriel had just set down that read *Healthy Inside, Healthy Outside.*

"What's your name?" Muriel asked, sticking the last of the pamphlets into an empty slot.

"Christine. Christine Bernstein," she said with a shrug of her shoulders.

"What a pretty name. I almost named my daughter Christine because she was born around Christmastime. Why are you here today, Christine?"

The young lady glanced at Mrs. Bernstein in the waiting room who was reading her magazine. "I'm here with my mom. A nosejob, I guess."

"For whom, your mom?"

"No," she said with a tiny smile. She put the brochure back in its slot. "For me."

"Really? I think your nose is quite lovely. And, trust me, I've seen all kinds here."

Christine rolled her eyes in the way Muriel had seen Mrs. Bernstein do more than once. "It's big and ugly."

"Who says?"

"Everyone."

"I don't."

"Okay, well, not *everyone*," Christine said in the way teenagers do. "But a lot of people. Some kids at school . . . They call me stuff."

"Like what?"

"Like, I don't know . . . Beaker. Pinocchio. Or Jimmy somebody, I forget his name."

"Well, kids are mean and stupid," Muriel said, "and it amazes me how nothing has changed in the thirty years since I went to middle school. You go to middle school, right?"

Christine nodded.

"I mean, it's crazy. Same taunts. Same insults. My kids come home with the same knock-knock jokes. You know, *orange you glad I didn't say banana*. It's completely unimaginative."

Christine smiled.

"But let me ask you this: Is there anyone older than fifteen who calls you those kinds of names?"

Christine thought for a moment. And to Muriel's amazement, she nodded.

"Seriously? Well, whoever it is, I feel sorry for them. Obviously, they are shallow, immature, and someone I suggest you refrain from being around. You're a lovely young woman. Anyone with eyes can see that. And those kids who call you names? In ten years, they'll be asking you either for a job or out on a date."

"I guess," Christine said. She reminded Muriel so much of Ellie, the way her eyes searched for acceptance. "Well, I'd better get back. My mom will think I've drowned. Nice talking to you," she said before hurrying back to the waiting room.

By the time Muriel returned to the office, Samantha had checked off three more patients—all for Dr. Warnell. Muriel glanced at Mrs. Bernstein who looked as if her head was going to explode.

One of the examination room doors opened, and a young woman whose face was etched with Sharpie marks stepped toward the counter. Samantha hid her phone behind her computer and grabbed the appointment book to schedule a follow-up.

"Mrs. Bernstein, you're up," Muriel said, waving the patient file in the air.

"Finally," she huffed, and she and Christine followed Muriel into an examination room.

"Good luck," Muriel said, winking at Christine, who smiled as Muriel closed the door. It always amazed Muriel how such a beautiful girl could feel so ugly. She thought again of Ellie.

Samantha ushered another patient into a room, which meant there was only one patient left. *At this rate, I may even have time for a hot bath tonight,* Muriel thought, when the front door opened, slapping that annoying little jingle bell that Stowe had placed there for the holidays.

In the front office, Samantha was bending over and brushing her hair with one hand while applying lipstick with the other.

"What are you doing?" Muriel asked just as a rolled-up newspaper landed on the counter, and she looked up to see Marty Benning staring back at her.

"Hi," he said. He was wearing one of those caps that reminded Muriel of Ellis Island immigrants in sepia-toned photos. His cheeks were red from the cold, and his collar was pulled up so that his ears were covered and his five-o'clock shadow was partially hidden. "Cold out there."

"Hi," Samantha gushed, standing beside Muriel and dropping the lipstick and brush to the floor. "Nice to see you again, Mr. Benning."

Oh, brother, Muriel thought.

"Is he here?" Benning asked.

Muriel nodded. "Yes, he's—"

"You can wait in Dr. Stowe's office," Samantha said. "He told us to send you right in when you got here."

"Thank you," Benning said, his eyes crinkling as he smiled and left the window.

Muriel was about to ask Samantha why she didn't put on her tiara when her cell phone vibrated in the pocket of her sweater that was draped on her chair. She looked at the caller ID and swiped the screen.

"Is everything okay?" Muriel asked, putting the phone to her ear. "Yes, that's fine. I should be home in about . . ." She looked at the wall clock. ". . . an hour. Can you make sure Zack does his homework? No, that doesn't mean you can boss him around. . . . Thank you. See you later, sweetie."

"Who's that, your boyfriend?" Benning asked, startling Muriel. He was leaning against the door to the small office.

"My daughter." Muriel stuck the phone back into her pocket. "Did you forget the way to Stowe's office?"

"No, I have a good memory," Benning said.

"Good, maybe you can help Stowe find his reading glasses that he claims he doesn't need. He can't seem to find them."

"I'll try my best," Benning said.

"He'll be with you in a few minutes, Mr. Benning," Muriel heard Samantha chirp from the hallway as Benning left the doorway. Muriel gathered up the day's patient files and returned them to their places in the cabinet.

"Are you crazy?" Samantha whispered when she returned. "Do you want to get fired? It's *Doctor* Stowe. You called him *Stowe* again. You have to stop doing that. Especially to Benning."

"I couldn't help myself. Benning is an *asshole*," she said, glancing at the last remaining patient in the waiting room, a Mrs. Dokter and her daughter, Allison, who, thankfully, were sitting in the back and out of earshot. "It shouldn't be long," Muriel called to them with an apologetic face and was relieved when Mrs. Dokter smiled.

"Maybe, but he is so freakin' gorgeous," Samantha said.

"Who? Benning?"

"You've got to be kidding, Muriel," Samantha said, putting on her hooded sweatshirt. "Tell me you don't think Benning is the finest creature you've ever seen—I mean, for, like, an old guy."

Muriel took a Windex wipe from a drawer and cleaned her computer monitor. "I hadn't noticed."

"Impossible. Do you think he's had work done? By Stowe? I mean, he's got to be, like, at least fifty years old, right?"

"Who cares?" Muriel stacked the files with Post-it notes on them for the nurses who would be in the next morning. She was thankful she didn't have to deal at all with the insurance companies; part-timers got all the breaks.

Stowe stuck his head into the office and handed Muriel a file. "Schedule a rhinoplasty for the Smith girl next month," he said. "She wants to get it done and have it healed before her sweet sixteen."

"How about we schedule it for her when she's in her thirties?" Muriel said.

"Funny, Adams," Stowe said. "Benning here yet?"

"Yes, he's in your office," Samantha said as she waved for Mrs. Dokter and her daughter to come into the back with her.

"Tell him I'll be with him in a few minutes," Stowe said to Muriel.

"I'll tell him. I'm going that way anyway," Samantha said, rounding the corner.

"Of course, you are," Muriel said with a smile.

"Did you offer Benning some coffee?" Stowe asked Muriel.

"Coffee? We're leaving soon. Everything's been cleaned and set up for the morning." Muriel sat on her seat and reached underneath her desk for her handbag. "And, besides, isn't coffee for *after* a hangover?"

"Those laugh lines really stand out when you're sarcastic," Stowe said. "You know, I can fix those."

"So I've heard."

"Did you ever think that was why your husband left you?"

Muriel stopped herself from reacting. Stowe was a dick. She knew it. He knew it. But he seemed to go out of his way to remind her anyway. "Because of my laugh lines?" she asked. "Obviously, you don't know anything about being married."

"Not much vanity?"

"Not much laughing."

Samantha returned and checked out several of Dr. Warnell's patients who were leaving the examination rooms. She scanned the empty waiting room. "Looks like that's it."

"Sammy, sweetheart, can you get Marty a bottle of water?" Stowe asked, returning down the corridor.

"Already did."

"See that, Adams?" Stowe called. "Someone's on the ball."

Muriel was about to yell something she would probably regret when Samantha put her hand on her arm. "You know he just says that to push your buttons," Samantha said, slipping a new sign-in sheet onto the clipboard.

"Doesn't it irk you when he calls you 'Sammy' and 'sweetheart'?" Muriel asked. If anyone had talked that way to Ellie, Muriel hoped she wouldn't stand for it.

Samantha waved a dismissive hand. "Nah, he's old. And harmless. He doesn't mean anything by it."

Muriel wasn't so sure. As far as she was concerned, Stowe was single-handedly doing his share to fan the flames of the Me Too movement on Long Island.

"Hey, check this out," Samantha said, examining the issue of the *Gardenia Gazette* Benning left on the counter. On the front page was a photo of Stowe and Benning and several other men and women.

"Look at them," Samantha said. "Two peas in a pod. They both look pretty hot here, though. Who's that other guy?"

"What guy?" Muriel said as she finished straightening her work station.

Samantha skimmed the caption. "Annual holiday luncheon for Gardenia chamber of commerce . . . blah blah . . . Ben Stowe, Marty Benning and, oh, Kirk Stryker." Samantha looked closely at the photo. "I think I know that guy. My mother is friends with his wife. They went to high school together, like, a hundred years ago. And look at Benning's date."

"Do I have to?" Muriel asked, as Samantha pulled her toward the newspaper.

"Who?" Muriel asked. "You mean that babysitter Benning calls a girlfriend? That Stryker guy is the only one there with a woman his own age."

"You think she's that young?" Samantha said, straightening her sweatshirt. "You think Benning is into women in their early twenties?"

"I think Benning's into anything that moves," Muriel said.

"Well, he can move any way he wants with me." Samantha giggled. Her phone buzzed. "Shit, my mom's here to pick me up. I'll tell her it'll be a few minutes."

"Nah, you go ahead. I'll finish things up here."

"Really? You're the best, Muriel," Samantha said, grabbing her coat from the side closet and hurrying toward the front door.

"Hope to see you tomorrow night," Muriel called.

"Tomorrow? Oh, yeah, right, I'll try," Samantha said, which, Muriel knew, was young person speak for *I probably won't be there.*

Muriel straightened the chairs of the waiting room. Her cell phone beeped in the office, and she fished it out of the pocket of her sweater and looked at the screen. It was a text from Roxanne.

Stowe overworking you again tonight?

Muriel typed:

What else is new?

Another text came immediately.

Dick.

Muriel typed:

Asshole.

Another text:

Misogynist.

Muriel typed:

Egotist.

Another text:

Eunuch.

Muriel laughed out loud and then typed a row of smiley

faces. No matter the day or the circumstance, Roxanne always managed to put a smile on her face. She imagined that's what best friends were for.

She replaced her phone and walked toward the bathroom, checking the rooms, and wiped a paper towel along the sink before turning off the bathroom light. She ran her hand along the rows of brochures on her way back to the office, where she was startled by Benning, who was sitting in Samantha's chair.

"What happened to Stowe's office?" Muriel asked. She grabbed her winter coat from the closet and placed it over the back of her chair.

"I was getting lonely," Benning said.

"Oh, well, wouldn't you be more comfortable in *there*?" Muriel motioned to the empty chairs. "After all, it is a *waiting* room?"

"Would *you* be more comfortable if I sat in the waiting room?"

"Doesn't matter to me," Muriel said. "Here's the remote control." She handed it to him. "Go crazy."

A door opened, and Muriel braced herself for another verbal go-round with Ben Stowe, who, when he got together with Marty Benning, was even more frat-boy annoying than he was when he was alone, but Dr. Warnell ambled into the office. His kind face immediately put her at ease. How he and Stowe were colleagues—let alone friends—astounded her.

"Muriel, please schedule a follow-up appointment for Mrs. Connor," Warnell said, placing a chart on the counter and handing a lollipop to Mrs. Connor's daughter. "Have you been a good girl this year, young lady?"

The little girl nodded.

"I'm sure you have," Warnell said, mussing the little girl's hair.

As Muriel finished up with the patient, Warnell spotted Benning. "Well, what do you know?" he said, clasping Benning's hand. "Gearing up for tax season, my friend?"

"One doesn't gear up for tax season," Benning said. "One dreads it."

"I hear ya. I assume you'll be taking my business partner away for another night of debauchery."

"Something like that."

"I admire your energy," Warnell said. "After the day I had today, I want nothing more than to sit home and watch television, right, Muriel?" Muriel smiled politely and pulled her cell phone from her sweater pocket.

"Now, if you'll excuse me," Warnell said, "I have one more patient waiting."

"Take care, Alec," Benning said with a wave. He picked up the remote control and clicked off the television in the waiting room. "So is that what you'll be doing tonight?" he asked.

"What?" Muriel asked, pretending to scribble a note to the morning nurses. She was hoping she could treat Benning as she would a bee—ignore it in the hopes that it would go away.

"Sitting home and watching television?"

"If I'm lucky," she said.

A door opened, and this time Stowe poked his head into the office. "Mrs. Adams, can I see you for a moment, please?"

"Sure," she said. Stowe had called her *Mrs. Adams*. Usually that meant the matter was professional.

"Excuse me," she said to Benning and followed Stowe down the hallway to his office. Inside, Mrs. Bernstein and Christine were seated in two chairs in front of Stowe's oversized desk. Christine looked mortified, as if she had been caught making out with a boy on the living room couch. Mrs. Bernstein stood up.

"Just who do you think you are?" Mrs. Bernstein demanded of Muriel as soon as she stepped into the room.

"I'm sorry?" Muriel felt her cheeks redden as Stowe took his place behind the desk.

"Are you a psychologist?" the woman asked.

"A what? No." Muriel shook her head.

"A trained social worker?"

"No." She looked at Stowe, who kept his eyes trained on Mrs. Bernstein.

"Did you tell my daughter that she didn't have to get cosmetic surgery?" Christine was sitting behind her mother inspecting her hands.

"We were just talking," Muriel said. "I asked her why she was here."

"Why do you *think* she's here?"

"I don't know," Muriel said, restraining her sarcasm. "That's why I asked her." Stowe cautioned Muriel's tone with his eyebrows.

"Did you tell my daughter that she shouldn't be around me?"

"Shouldn't be around you? Why would I . . ." And then Muriel remembered the conversation she had with Christine, about anyone over the age of fifteen thinking she had an ugly nose: *Obviously, they are shallow, immature, and someone I suggest you refrain from being around . . .* Muriel had no idea they had been talking about Christine's own mother.

"This is a misunderstanding," Muriel said.

"Mrs. . . . Adams, is that your name, Adams? Mrs. Adams, do you have children?"

Muriel instinctively got defensive. "Yes," she said. "I have two."

"Well, do you think you know what's best for those children?"

"Yes, I do." At this point, Stowe had a faint smile on his face. He seemed to be enjoying this.

"Well, so do I. I'm the one who's drying the tears every night and hears her cry about how all the other girls are being asked out, while she's sitting home on a Saturday night—"

"*Mom*—" Christine said, turning red. She looked down at the floor.

"—how she's not getting the lead in the school play, how the popular girls won't talk to her . . ."

"Mrs. Bernstein, I'm sorry if you think I was out of line, but—"

"Out of line? That's an understatement."

"I was just showing your daughter our brochures and—"

"If getting a new nose is going to increase her self-esteem, I don't think it's any of your damn business."

"Well, frankly, in my opinion, a new nose isn't going to increase your daughter's self-esteem," Muriel said, crossing her arms. "But maybe a mother who thought her daughter was beautiful just as she was *might*."

"Mrs. Adams," Stowe warned.

"Really?" Mrs. Bernstein said, crossing her arms in kind. "That's hilarious coming from you." She looked Muriel up and down. "How are *you* even allowed to work here?"

"I'm fine with the way I look."

"Really? I think you might be the only one."

"Okay," Stowe said, standing up. "It seems we have gotten to the bottom of this . . . misunderstanding. Mrs. Adams, please leave us."

Heat flooded through Muriel, and words circled around her head—like where, exactly, Mrs. Bernstein could shove her nose job—but, *crap*, Muriel needed *this* job. She spun on her heels, trying to hold her tongue and her head high and, as she turned the corner from Stowe's office, slammed right into Marty Benning.

"Sorry," he said, startled. "I didn't mean to—"

Great, Muriel thought, as she brushed past him toward the front office. She knew Stowe had arranged this little show on purpose. *Asshole*. She began picking up files and moving them to the other side of the office for no reason at all when she felt a hand on her arm.

"Muriel," said Dr. Warnell, his eyes kind and soothing. "Go home. I'll lock up and take care of scheduling any follow-up appointments."

"I didn't . . ."

"I know," he said. "It's all right. Please."

Muriel nodded, feeling tears well up in her eyes. She picked up her coat from the back of her chair and reached for her purse. Without looking back, she hurried out the front door, which closed behind her with a jingle.

3

Detective Betty Munson pulled her car into a parking spot beside a vacant metal bike rack, a few yards from the corner of Lake Shore Avenue and Mercer Road. It was quiet despite the growing crowd of people, perhaps awakened by the sirens, who gathered around the police barricades in their bathrobes and flip-flops. She looked at her watch: 3:00 a.m.

All across Lake Shore, firefighters were returning ladders and hoses back to their engines, their boots dragging broken glass fragments across the ground. Behind them, the building façade looked wet and tarnished; fire stains appeared like black fingers along the perimeter of a second-story window. A small white placard, marred by the fire, had fallen off one of its hinges and hung crookedly against the building. Betty didn't know how many times she had passed this intersection going to and from the precinct, but it had been enough times to have memorized the phone number, which was listed below a line of cursive type that read simply: *Kirk M. Stryker, Certified Public Accountant.*

She made her way toward the intersection, where the smell of smoke was more pronounced. A uniformed officer nodded when she showed him her badge and opened the barricade to let her pass. The Ladies Auxiliary had set up alongside the fire department vehicles and looked as though they were wrapping things up as well, handing out the last cups of coffee to the EMTs who chatted up some of the women, most of them Betty's age—middle to late fifties, she'd guess. Betty recognized Cora, her neighbor, in the crowd and waved hello.

Behind the sidewalk's row of yellow forsythia bushes, which appeared gray at this time of night, Detective Pete Girardi was standing near the building's entrance, an unassuming glass door flanked by a Ralph's Italian Ices and a bagel shop. Standing next to him was a woman who wore a blanket draped around her.

"Detective Munson," Detective Girardi said when Betty approached, "this is Mrs. Francine Walker, the one who called in the fire."

"How do you do, Mrs. Walker?" Betty asked.

"It was *awful,*" Mrs. Walker said, emphasizing the familiar *aw* of the Long Island accent, although her voice seemed hoarse and tired. "I never seen anything like it. The room was like an inferno."

"Mrs. Walker, where were you when you saw the fire?"

"It happened so fast," she said. "I was driving my car on Lake Shore, coming back from the gym." She stuck out her right leg so that Betty could see her purple velour jumpsuit beneath the blanket.

"Which gym was this?"

"Long Island Fitness. In Mineola."

"At what time?"

"Probably around eleven. I had stopped off at Starbucks after my Zumba class, which ended at ten, but then got to talking with a friend of mine. I was just driving, listening to music, and actually got pissed off when I got caught at the light." She motioned to the intersection. "That one takes *forever*. But that's when I saw it. The fire. The curtains, they were flaming. I immediately called 9-1-1 on my cell phone and then pulled over to make sure that the fire trucks came. They were here within ten minutes." She said that last part with obvious pride.

"And you gave your statement to the police officers?"

"Yes, pretty much what I told you," she said. "Was anyone inside? I saw a bunch of emergency technicians run in and out, but no one else." She shook her head. "Kirk Stryker has been doing our taxes for years. Was it an electrical fire?"

"Well, I just got here myself, so I'm not really sure," Betty said, dodging the question. "It takes time, as you can imagine, to sort these things out."

"Yes, of course," Mrs. Walker said.

"But one thing I do know, Mrs. Walker. Your taking the time to call 9-1-1 probably saved this entire row of buildings from burning down. Because the firefighters were able to get here so quickly, they were able to contain the fire to the few rooms at the corner of the second story. So thank you for that."

Mrs. Walker smiled.

"Now, you should go home. I'm sure you're exhausted. We'll contact you if we need anything further."

Mrs. Walker glanced at Detective Girardi, who nodded.

"Okay, good night then," she said and headed off toward the Ladies Auxiliary with the blanket dragging behind her.

"She seems pretty believable," Betty said, watching her go.

"I thought so too," Detective Girardi said.

"Check out her story in the morning, though. Call the gym." Betty unbuttoned her jacket and looked at the building façade. This side didn't appear to have any damage. "How is it in there?"

"Not pretty." Detective Girardi shook his head. "I'll bet you didn't expect something like this just before your retirement, huh?"

"In Gardenia? I never expected it at all," Betty said and entered the office building.

The front door led to a narrow stairwell that went only one way—up. At the top level, which was the second floor, the hallway split into three directions—right, toward a suite of offices comprising Griffin Media, a small advertising firm; straight, to a set of bathrooms; and left, to the accounting offices of Kirk M. Stryker. The smell of burned wood permeated the air, but otherwise there was no noticeable damage to these rooms.

The door to the CPA firm's offices was open, and Betty stepped into a large room containing five desks, and an area with about twenty chairs, which, she assumed, was where customers sat waiting for one of the accounting professionals. She was surprised the electricity was still working; the overhead light was on and a few computer terminals hummed in the corner. Again, other than the smell and the soot, the room looked pretty much undisturbed. She crossed to a door that had the words *Kirk M. Stryker* etched onto a panel of frosted glass, like in an old private eye film; the doorway was cordoned off with one taut strand of police tape. At the back of the room, Detective Sergeant Tom Williamson stared pensively out Stryker's office window.

"Hi, Tom," Betty said, ducking under the police tape.

"Didn't think I'd see you here this morning," Williamson said, rubbing his chin. "Looks like retirement might have to wait."

The side of the office near Williamson showed the most fire damage—the walls and ceiling were marred black. It didn't take a fire scene investigator to figure out that that was probably where the fire had begun, near the window—perhaps from the curtains, as Mrs. Walker mentioned. The flames seemed to have gotten more than three-quarters of the way across the ceiling before the firefighters were able to extinguish them.

"Poor guy," Williamson said with a sigh, motioning toward the other side of the office where the body of Kirk Stryker lay on the floor, a khaki-colored raincoat folded over his body. Stryker's eyes were half-open, his jaw slackened, and his cheeks colored a deep red.

"What happened?" Betty asked.

"Not sure. The fire chief seems to think if the guys had gotten here just a few minutes sooner he might have lived."

"He died from asphyxiation?"

Williamson shook his head. "Gunshot wound."

"Gunshot?" Betty stepped closer to the body. A large pool of blood surrounded Stryker's upper body, which was caked red. "Where?"

"Looks like it's just below the clavicle."

Stryker appeared to have some kind of head wound, like he had fallen or been hit with something pointy, but then she saw it—a small hole the size of a button in his chest area. "Self-inflicted?"

"Don't know yet, but don't think so. No gun."

She nodded. "What's with the raincoat?"

"Firemen found him with the coat over him," Williamson said. "The guys picked him up at first. Thought they would bring him outside and try to revive him, per protocol, but noticed the blood and realized it was a possible crime scene and put him back down, since the fire had already been extinguished. CPR was administered on the scene, but the techs said there was no pulse when they got here." He shook his head. "Guy lost a lot of blood."

"Jesus, I just saw Gloria Stryker in town the other day," Betty said. "She was with the kids."

"Want to see something strange?" Williamson pointed to the melted smoke detector on the ceiling. "The smoke alarm appears to have been disarmed, which is why the fire department didn't get notified."

"That *is* strange," Betty said, looking up. She examined the rest of the room. There were charred, wet papers everywhere. She pointed at the open safe in the closet. "A robbery?"

Williamson shook his head. "Don't think so."

"Why not?"

"If you were a thief, would you leave fifteen thousand dollars behind?"

"Fifteen *thousand* dollars?"

"Give or take."

Betty bent down beside the closet, which had been cleaned out with the exception of a few empty hangers, a teddy bear toy, and the safe, which was no bigger than a small refrigerator. She examined the safe's exterior. "Doesn't look like a forced entry. What else is in there?"

"Some financial papers—you know, stocks, bonds— some kiddie Christmas cards made out of printer paper, crayon, and glitter."

"So," Betty stood up, "whatever happened here had nothing to do with money?"

"Hard to say," Williamson said. "Maybe there was more money in there, and the guy just took as much as he could carry. Want to see something else?"

"There's more?" Betty asked.

Williamson slipped a glove onto his right hand and slowly lifted the raincoat from Stryker's body.

"What the hell are those?" Betty asked, crouching down.

Across Stryker's abdomen was a series of raised circular red marks, like welts.

"I was thinking burn marks, from fire ash," Williamson said.

"Maybe." Betty got a little closer. "But they don't appear random. Could he have gotten these injuries elsewhere?"

"He could have gotten them anywhere, although they look fresh," Williamson said. "Maybe from the person who shot him?"

"Could be," Betty said, "but it would take a long time to make those marks. I'm no forensics person, but my guess is hours." She looked at Stryker's wrists and ankles. "It doesn't look like he was bound, so it doesn't make sense that the guy would stand for this."

"I think I know . . ." Williamson lifted the raincoat a

little higher, revealing two additional marks that Betty recognized.

"A Taser?" she asked.

"Looks like it. The teams found some dispensed tags and cartridges near the door."

"So he was incapacitated when these marks were made."

"Could be unrelated," he said. "Maybe it was . . . consensual?" Williamson's weathered face turned a slight pink.

"You mean, like a sex game?" Somehow the toughest-looking cops at the precinct turned out to be the most prudish. "Could be." She didn't know Stryker personally, but by most accounts he was a pretty reserved person, not that that meant anything. "Any witnesses?"

"Not that we can tell. No one was around, really. I'm assuming the employees had all gone home."

Betty walked around to the other side of the office where Williamson had been standing by the window. Stryker's desk, made of metal, had withstood the fire, although whatever had been made of paper around it hadn't fared so well. A lone glass, a tumbler, in a plastic sandwich baggie, sat squarely on what used to be an old-fashioned desk blotter before it melted. She put on a pair of gloves and opened the top drawer—pencils, pens, paperclips, boxes of staples, and, in the back, a pack of cigarettes and lighter. She pulled out the pack and looked inside; there were three left.

"I see why the smoke detector may have been disarmed," Betty said, holding up the pack.

"Perhaps, but my bet is that 70 percent of the desks on

this street have a lighter and cigarettes stuffed in them," Williamson said with a shrug.

She closed the drawer, opened the one next to it, and pulled out a daily planner, which was opened to today's date, April 2; at the top of the page it noted that Stryker had a meeting with Sebastian Colby at nine o'clock that morning. She flipped the page backward to the day before.

"There's a notation here of *BENNING*."

"Benning? Marty Benning?"

"Yeah, why?"

"I don't know," Williamson said. "I just had the impression that those two didn't get along."

Betty wished she had more of an immediate impression. It was strange how little she knew about Kirk Stryker. Although Sam had attended high school with Kirk, they had lost touch, other than occasional run-ins on Facebook, and Sam insisted on doing the taxes himself every year, for better or worse. Her only knowledge of the Strykers stemmed from idle chitchat at various community gatherings over the years, although she did know that the Strykers were almost universally well-liked.

"Well, you know what they say," Betty said, replacing the planner and closing the drawer. "Accounting makes for strange bedfellows." She snapped off her gloves as Detective Girardi stuck his head into the room.

"Team's done, Sarge," Girardi said.

"Well, I'll take a look at the report later this morning and talk to the coroner," Betty said. "I'll be in touch, Bill. Thanks."

"No problem," Williamson said. "And tell Sam I said hey."

"Will do." Betty took one last look around Stryker's office. The eyes of the sodden and befallen teddy bear, glowing from reflected light, stared blankly into the room. On the wall hung a collection of homemade cards, made from things like beads and raw macaroni. The pasta was slightly charred from the fire, and the paper curled, but the cards had otherwise escaped destruction. She thought of Stryker's young boys—safe and sound in their beds, just like her own children—who would wake up in a few hours to find that their father was gone. And now it was up to Betty to find out why.

4

John Parker's feet dangled off the twin-size bed. One of his socks was missing, and he was rubbing his bare foot against the edge of the flat sheet for warmth when there was a bang on his bedroom door.

"Johnny!"

Parker covered his head with the blanket.

"Johnny!"

"What, Ma!" he yelled. "I'm sleepin'." He looked at the clock on his nightstand. It was 5:30 a.m.

"Telephone!"

"Take a message!"

"It's Mr. Gardner!"

Parker stuck his head out from under the blanket. Why was Gardner calling his mother's house phone? He reached up onto the night table for his cell. The ringer was off, and he had four missed calls and four messages. All from Gardner. *Shit.*

"Johnny!" his mother yelled again.

"All right, all right." Parker kicked the covers off and sat up in bed. "Tell him I'll call him on my cell."

"All right, dear."

Parker picked at the crust in the corners of his eyes as

he listened to his mother's footsteps retreat on the creaky wood flooring of the upstairs landing. It was still dark out, the glow of his nightlight illuminating his college diploma, which leaned, frameless, against a shelf of dusty middle school basketball trophies.

Parker huffed. A degree in digital media production at SUNY New Paltz had been a veritable waste of time. Despite a 3.8 GPA, Parker had no decent-paying job, no apartment he could afford, and no prospects for either. It had been nearly a year since he had been forced to take the drive of shame back to his parents' house after graduation.

At least, he had *a* job. He was doing better than most of his college buddies, except for Stan who fell into an entry-level position at a casino in Atlantic City, but that was only because his uncle worked there. Although if Parker hadn't heard about the assistant editor position at the *Gardenia Gazette* from his mother, he wouldn't have a job at all. Fucking minimum wage. He would have been better off becoming a waiter at Friendly's. He dialed Gardner on his cell. *At least Friendly's didn't open until 8:00 a.m. . . .*

"Yeah, it's Parker," he said when Gardner picked up. "You called?"

"Parker, where you been?" Gardner's gruff voice powered through the tiny speaker.

"Sleeping."

"I need you to head into town to help Kramer cover a story."

"Now?"

"Yes, now. There's been a murder."

"A *what*?" Parker sprang out of bed. "Where?"

"At least, it *might* be a murder," Gardner said. "Details are still fuzzy. Kirk Stryker. Ever hear of him?

"No."

"Well, he's a longtime resident. Kramer got a few things from one of his police contacts, but no one's really talking. I think it might be arson *and* a mortal gunshot wound."

Shit, Parker thought, *Kramer was already on the scene.* Figures. The guy had been working the local beat for, like, ten years and strode around the newspaper office like he was William Randolph Hearst.

"The *Times* reporters are sniffing around, though, and I don't want to get scooped by those bastards again. I need a two-person team. This is your chance, Parker. Don't let me down. Get me something for the website so I can run it later this morning. Can you be there in ten minutes?"

"I'll be there in five."

"Good." Gardner hung up.

Parker stumbled around the room and found a semi-clean pair of jeans on the floor. He took off his T-shirt, flung it across the room, and was grabbing another from a pile of clean laundry on his desk chair when there was a knock on his door.

"What, Ma?" Parker grabbed a sock ball from his top dresser drawer.

"Johnny, is everything all right?"

"Yeah, Ma. I gotta go."

"Are you gonna have any breakfast? I'll make you something."

"No, Ma, that's all right. I don't have time. I'll grab something along the way."

"Are you sure?"

"Yes, Ma, yes." She was always asking if he was sure. It drove him crazy.

"All right then. Oh, and Daddy told me to remind you about your car inspection. It's due tomorrow."

"I know, I know," Parker said, searching his desk for his digital tape recorder.

"All right then. Have a good day at work, dear."

A fucking murder, Parker thought, pulling on his sneakers and lunging for a baseball cap from the top of his desk lamp. In Gardenia. And not some gang shit at the mall.

He looked at himself in his bedroom mirror. *This is your chance*, Parker thought, rubbing more sleep out of his eyes. He threw open his bedroom door and ran down the stairs like his career—and the rest of his adult life—depended on it.

5

Three and a half months earlier

Muriel crammed her minivan into the parking spot and checked the street signs three times to make sure she wouldn't get towed. She used to get mad at Doug for being too cheap to spring for garage parking on those rare occasions they had an outing in Manhattan, but these days her checkbook wasn't letting her be so decadent. She ran down Seventy-First Street toward Guinevere's.

The entrance to the restaurant was crowded, and Muriel was glad, at least, that she wouldn't have to wait for a table since there was a reservation. Inside, the mood was festive with holiday string lights wrapped around poles and across the ceiling like a clothesline. She wasn't used to eating in fancy restaurants anymore. The local fast food joints had become her home away from home.

She looked at her watch. It was just about seven. Stowe detested lateness more than sloppiness, and after the showdown with Mrs. Bernstein in his office the night before, Muriel figured she'd better forgo a quick stop to the bathroom if she wanted to keep her job—if she even still had one. She fluffed her hair with her hands and moved toward the maître d' who had finished triaging parties of two and three when she stepped up to his podium.

"Do you have a reservation?" he asked Muriel.

"Yes." Muriel tightened the belt on her coat. "Under Stowe. Party of twelve."

"Stowe, Stowe . . ." the maître d' said, shaking his head. "Ah, yes. Wait, did you say party of twelve?"

"Yes," Muriel said. "Seven o'clock."

The maître d' looked at her the way she often looked at her students when they answered a question incorrectly. "Hmmm . . . 'Stowe,' you said?"

"Yes, for 7:00 p.m."

"And your name is?"

"Muriel Adams," she said. He checked his listing and shook his head. "Is there a problem?"

"Well, I'm not quite sure. Can you step aside for a moment?" The maître d' waved his hand toward the bar. "Let me seat these gentlemen."

Embarrassed, Muriel took a step back and let a band of men make their way forward. Was it possible she was in the wrong restaurant? Had the wrong time? Day?

"Excuse me, did I hear you say your name is Muriel Adams?" asked a waitress, holding a round tray of drinks.

"Yes," Muriel said.

"Great. Your party is expecting you. Come this way."

Relieved, Muriel followed the young woman into the dimly lit restaurant.

Guinevere's was lovely. Although a King Arthur theme called to mind hokey castles and oversize turkey legs, the restaurant offered more of a contemporary and subtle take—red heraldic banners were tucked high and out of the way on the walls and draped over tables, which were, of course, round, and decorated with classic white tableware and linens on which the silver cutlery sparkled. It amazed Muriel how, for such a narrow Manhattan street façade, the restaurant could be so large and cavernous. The waitress wormed her way around a series of tables until they reached a back section that featured a large fireplace and a fountain bearing a woman made of stone, draped in robes, presumably Guinevere herself.

"Here you go," the waitress said, pulling out a chair with her free hand at a small, neatly set table for two, not twelve. At the far end sat a nicely dressed gentleman whom Muriel suddenly realized was Marty Benning. He stood up.

"Please don't leave," he said when he saw Muriel's face.

The waitress raised her eyebrows. "Is everything all right?" she asked.

"Fine," Benning said.

"I'm confused," Muriel said. "Where is everyone?"

"We're fine," Benning said again to the waitress who stood balancing the tray of drinks with one hand. She nodded skeptically and walked toward another table.

"Where is everyone?" Muriel asked again.

"Don't be mad," Benning said. "They're not coming." He was wearing a charcoal gray suit and red tie, and Muriel could tell he had gotten a haircut since she had seen him the day before.

"What do you mean they're not coming?"

"I mean, it's just us," Benning said.

"I don't understand."

"Are you ever going to sit down or do you plan on eating standing up?"

"I don't plan on eating at all," Muriel said, aware of eyes throughout the room beginning to focus on them.

Benning leaned toward her. "Just sit down for a minute, please."

Muriel hesitated. She wanted to leave, but it had taken two hours to make her way into the city, a city she rarely visited anymore. Plus, the kids were with Doug, the car was safely parked, and, unfortunately, she had nothing better to do.

"Listen, you have every right to walk out of here," Benning said. "I get it . . . but there's no harm in sitting down for a minute while I explain."

Slowly, as if gravity were taking hold, Muriel sat, followed by Benning. When they did, everyone around them went back to their conversations and meals.

"Thank you," Benning said.

"Why am I here?" Muriel asked.

Benning reached for a glass of red wine on the table and took a sip. "Because I didn't think you would come if I asked you to dinner."

"Asked me to dinner?"

"That's right."

Muriel crossed her arms. "So you thought manipulating me would endear you to me?"

"I just wanted you to come."

"Is Stowe in on this?" Muriel imagined the two of them having a good laugh about it right after Stowe fired her.

"No." Benning shook his head. "He doesn't know anything about this. Look, something came up at the practice, an emergency Botox injection or whatever, and Samantha called me this morning when Stowe had to reschedule. On a whim, I asked her if she had called anyone else in the office. She said no and that I was the first person she called."

I bet you were, Muriel thought.

"I told her that I would take care of it, you know, call everyone else, and that she didn't have to worry about it."

"How nice of you."

"So I called everyone."

"Except me."

"Except you. Then I changed the reservation to two, and here we are."

Muriel stood up again.

"Wait," Benning said, standing up as well. "Aren't you at all flattered that I did this for you, to have dinner with you?"

"Should I be?" Muriel asked. "Why? Why do you want to have dinner with me? Did one of those half-wits that I've seen you around the office with turn you down?"

"Who?"

"I don't know, that blonde twelve-year-old you had in the office the other day."

Benning smirked. "I didn't think you noticed."

"I didn't." She felt her face redden.

"Yeah, well, that didn't work out."

"What a shocker."

"Are you always this charming on a first date?"

"This is not a date," Muriel said.

"No?"

She put her hands in her coat pockets. "I don't know what this is. It's . . . just . . ."

"On Stowe's dime."

"*What?*" Muriel asked. It was the first time she ever felt her mood lighten at the sound of Stowe's name. "For real?"

Benning nodded. "He left his credit card in order to reserve the table."

"Oh, that's good." Muriel laughed. "That in itself is worth staying and ordering dessert." She thought back to the night before, the look on Stowe's face as she stood there facing Mrs. Bernstein. She had half a mind to order six bottles of wine to go.

"He was out of line, you know," Benning said. "For what it's worth, I thought you handled yourself—"

"It doesn't matter," Muriel said, sitting back down.

Benning sat down too. "So you'll stay?"

"I didn't say that."

"Well, while you decide . . ." He picked up the bottle of wine. "Would you like some?"

"No, thank you."

"Are you sure?"

"Yes."

Benning placed the bottle down. "You look very pretty tonight."

Her knees buckled so violently that had Muriel not been sitting down she would have fallen down. She reached for a dinner roll on the table.

Benning also reached for a roll. "But it's not a first date, right?" He sliced off a pat of butter and slathered it onto the bread.

"Nope."

"It kinda feels like a first date, though."

"I wouldn't know. I haven't had one in a very long time."

"Well, I have them all the time, so maybe I'd know."

"All first dates, and no second dates, huh?" Muriel asked, dabbing butter on her bread.

"Something like that."

"Why do you think that is?"

"Oh, I don't know. I'm usually not interested in much more."

"Hmmm . . . so it's you who ends it."

"Oh, yeah." Benning took another sip of wine. "Lots of times they even tell me they love me, just before I call it off."

"On the first date?"

"Yep. That they *feel it in their soul.*" He put his wine glass down and smiled. "Apparently, I'm irresistible."

That familiar feeling of disgust returned—the one Muriel felt whenever Benning showed up at the practice. She wiped her mouth with her napkin and sat back in her chair.

"Is something wrong?" he asked.

Muriel shook her head. "No."

Benning sighed. "Go ahead. Lay it on me."

Muriel broke off a piece from her bread, the crumbs falling onto her lap, and shoved it into her mouth. "So let me get this straight," she said, chewing in a way she knew was totally unbecoming. "These women tell you they love you—these *babies* who barely know what love is—pour out their feelings, and then you boot them out the door."

"You catch on fast," Benning said. "I take it you disapprove."

"Do you know how *hard* it is to say *I love you* to someone?" she asked.

"No," he said. "Actually, I don't."

"You've never been in love?"

Benning shook his head. "No. You?"

"Um, of course," Muriel faltered. She wanted to say yes, that she must have been in love at some time, with Doug, but she couldn't remember if that was true or what it felt like; all that was left was some vague suspicion of having been in it. She didn't want to say any more about it, but she didn't have to, because Benning changed the subject again.

"So where do you live?" he asked, opening the menu.

Muriel was quiet.

"I live a few blocks from here," he continued. "Wanna see?"

"No."

He smiled. "Now, it's your turn. You really don't have much practice at this, do you?"

Muriel rolled her eyes. "Massapequa Park."

"Ah, Massapequa . . ." Benning said, "the home of actors and comedians and kidnapped women."

"Cute. Not a fan, huh?"

"Not a fan of Long Island."

"Really? That's funny, considering your practice is there."

"Yeah, looking to move there too. Just looked at a place, a condo, in a new development in Gardenia. It's nice. Wanna see?"

"No." Muriel ripped off another piece of her bread.

"I find the people, though, on Long Island to be weird."

"Really. How so?"

"I don't know. All this wealth, the SUVs, the big homes, all this *stuff*, but the people are . . . well, empty."

"We're talking about Stowe now, right?" Muriel asked.

Benning smiled and took another sip of his wine. "Maybe I am."

"You realize that I live on Long Island," Muriel said. "Maybe I'm empty too."

"Yeah, but aren't you from somewhere else?"

Muriel studied him. He'd either done a little research on her or he was perceptive. "Did Stowe tell you that?"

"I don't talk to Stowe about you."

"Really? That's funny, because he talks lots about you."

"What does he say?"

"Oh, plenty. Like about the time the two of you in college had these contests to see who could sleep with more women in an afternoon."

"Did he tell you who won?"

"Yeah, he said you did."

Benning lifted his glass of wine. "What can I say? Women are stupid."

Muriel shook her head. "And men are jerks."

"Really? What if I were to say that those women knew exactly what they were getting into?"

"You mean, the women who said they loved you after the first date?"

"They don't love me."

"Oh, really?" Muriel reached for the bottle of wine, poured herself a glass, and took a long sip.

"They like the lifestyle. The *money*," Benning said. "That's all it is."

"So you don't believe in love at first sight?"

Benning closed his menu. "Listen, I've never been anything but honest with them."

"Whatever. You can be whatever you want to be. No skin off my nose." She picked up her menu. "And all this time, never married?"

"Nope. You?"

Muriel shifted her feet; she had the feeling he already knew the answer. "Yes. Separated. Two kids."

"Ugh, *kids*."

Despite herself, Muriel let out a laugh. There weren't many people she knew who would say something like that out loud, except maybe Roxanne. "You didn't know? Stowe didn't tell you I had kids?"

"I don't talk to Stowe about you, remember? Where are they now? The kids?"

"They're with their father."

"In *Mas-sa-pe-qua*?"

"Yes, that horrible place."

"Republican country."

"I see. Democrat?" Muriel asked.

"Card-carrying. Don't tell me . . . You're one of these Republicans who can't be seen having dinner with a Democrat."

"No, I'm one of those liberals who marries into a Republican family and spends twenty years of her life fighting a losing battle at holiday get-togethers."

"So you like a good debate?"

"I don't mind one, just not all the time."

Benning dipped his bread into the olive oil on his plate and rolled it around. "I take it that's why you took the job with Stowe."

"I'm still trying to figure out why that guy hired me."

"He saw something in you."

"I don't think so," Muriel said. "It was Warnell's idea to have me work there, I'm sure."

"I'm not so sure."

"Why? Did Stowe say something?"

Benning raised his eyebrows.

"Never mind. Let me guess. You don't talk to Stowe about me."

"You learn fast."

Muriel reached for another piece of bread from the basket and realized there wasn't any left. *How much had she eaten?*

"I'll ask for more," Benning said, signaling the waitress.

Muriel placed her hands in her lap. "I needed the money," she said. "After the separation. I mean, that's why I took the job with Stowe."

"Is that the only reason?" Benning asked. "You don't seem like the type to just take any job."

"You mean, I seem like a snob?"

"No, that's not what I mean."

"I know," Muriel said. "I'm just kidding."

"Is kidding allowed on a first date?"

"You tell me. You're the expert."

"I don't usually experience much kidding on a first date," he said.

"I don't see why. You're usually on a date with a kid."

Benning laughed so loud that he had to cover his mouth. The man and woman at the next table stared.

"Nice," he said, patting his lips with his napkin and placing it back on his lap. "So, separated, huh?"

"Yeah. As my mother likes to say, 'There's still turning back, you know . . .'"

"Ah, she likes him. Your ex-husband."

"Still husband. Technically."

"Whatever." Benning waved his hand. "So what do you do? You know, outside of Stowe's place."

"How do you know I do anything else?"

"It doesn't take a rocket scientist to figure out you need another source of income if you live on Long Island with two kids, no husband, and you only work part-time telling off cosmetic surgery patients." Benning poured another glass of wine for himself and went ahead and poured Muriel one as well. She didn't object.

She picked up the glass. "I'm an elementary school teacher."

"Jesus, *more* kids?"

"I'm a masochist," she said, taking a sip. The fire beside them suddenly seemed to roar, and Muriel took off her coat and hung it on her chair. "So what about you? No kids, but how about family? Brothers and sisters?"

"Nope."

"Your parents still around?"

"Not my mom. Just my father."

"Are you close?"

"No."

"Why not?"

"I don't want to talk about my father," Benning said abruptly. His features changed, and Muriel was surprised at the thought that she may have offended him. She changed the subject. "So what do *you* do? You're an accountant, right?"

"Stowe tell you that?"

"I don't talk to Stowe about you." She smiled.

"Good," Benning said. "I run a firm in downtown Gardenia. Not far from the cosmetic practice, actually. I opened it a couple of years ago. We mainly do tax prep. I even conduct tax prep courses online . . . This is fascinating, isn't it?"

"No, I'm really interested. You don't seem like the CPA type."

"You mean nebbish?"

"Well, I didn't . . ."

"Or maybe Jewish?"

"No, no . . . I don't mean religious affiliation . . ."

"I hope you don't mean boring."

"*Certainly*, not boring," Muriel said, but then she realized that Benning had tricked her into paying him a compliment. He chuckled.

The waitress returned and placed another order of bread onto the table. "So have we decided?" she asked, looking at Muriel. "Will you be staying?"

It was a question to which everyone in the room seemed eager to hear an answer, as the couples around them paused their conversations and glanced over at their table. Muriel gave a perfunctory look at the menu and at Benning. She hesitated, but she knew the decision had already been made.

❂

As they left the restaurant, the night air was crisp and electric, and Muriel was feeling more alive than she'd felt in years. She told herself it was the wine, or the fact that Benning insisted that they go all out and order the most expensive items on the menu to stick it to Stowe. Muriel couldn't resist. She had the filet mignon—a far cry from the soggy chicken nugget leftovers she usually ate right before bed.

"So what do you want to do now?" Benning asked.

"Now? Oh, no, I have to get going . . . Long day. I'm exhausted. It's at least a forty-minute drive back."

"You know, my apartment's not far from here."

"Funny. No, seriously, I should get back."

Muriel put on her gloves and cinched the belt on her coat. Snow had started to fall in large flurries that were sticking to the ground.

"I'll walk you to your car," Benning said.

"No, that's all right," Muriel said. "I'm just down the block." She was about to cross the street when a horse and buggy stopped in front of them to let off a family of tourists.

"Hey, want to go for a ride?" Benning asked. "It must be fate."

"On that thing? In the snow? No, really, I'd better—"

"C'mon, have you ever been on one of these before?"

"Yes, but I must have been in my twenties . . ."

"That's okay. Not much has changed. You climb in, the driver says 'Giddyap,' and that's it."

Benning had already handed the driver a fifty-dollar bill before she could answer and was standing with one foot on the carriage step. He reached his hand down. "C'mon . . ." he said.

"It's thirty degrees out here."

"Where?" he said, unbuttoning the top button of his overcoat. "Plus, these things have heated seats. They've gone hi-tech."

Before she realized what she was doing, she extended her hand to Benning, who took it and pulled her up. When she stepped into the carriage, her foot caught on the step, twisting her ankle, and she fell unceremoniously into its well.

"Shit," she said, landing on the metal of the carriage floor. She *definitely* had too much wine.

"Are you all right?" Benning lifted her up and sat her down as the oblivious driver had already lurched the carriage forward.

Embarrassed, Muriel brushed herself off. She was thankful her cheeks were already red from the cold—and the wine. "It's nothing. I'm fine."

Benning sat next to her. "Let me see it." He reached for her leg.

"No, no, that's okay," she said, pulling back. "It's fine."

"Let me look at it."

"No, really, I'm okay."

"Holy cow, look at that," Benning said, pointing across Fifth Avenue toward Central Park.

"What?" Muriel said, but as she looked away, Benning pulled her leg toward him. The feel of his cold hands on her skin almost made her scream. He gently held her foot and tilted it right and left, studying her reaction. Muriel held her breath.

"See, I'm fine," she said, although she was starting to sweat. She was about to pull her ankle from Benning's grip when he said, "My father was a drunk who did everything he could to make sure I'd end up a failure. That's why I don't like to talk about him."

He cradled Muriel's ankle in his hands.

"My mother died when I was fourteen. I left home when I was seventeen and never went back." Benning released her leg and gazed out at the city landscape, as if watching a movie. "All I took with me were the clothes on my back, some pocket money I earned working a newspaper route, and some mementos of my mom, which I piled in the trunk of my old, beat-up car. My father still lives somewhere upstate in the Hudson Valley. I haven't seen him in more than thirty years."

It took a few moments for Muriel to realize that Benning had stopped talking. His words were still floating in the air as the carriage passed the lights of Tavern on the Green, which were shining like stars, blurred by the light snowfall. When Muriel started to shiver, Benning placed on her lap a blanket that smelled like a cross between rain and horse.

Benning then told her how he had arrived in New York City and stayed in the apartment of a friend, sleeping on his couch, until he decided to enroll in school, how he had chosen accounting on a whim when he had to declare a major, how he worked three jobs to pay for college, and how he had met Stowe at the campus library when Benning had managed to get some coed to believe he worked there. His words appeared as white puffs of air that disappeared almost as quickly as they formed. His lips cracked with dryness. She didn't know how long they rode around for, but when the carriage stopped, she said, "That's it?"

The driver jumped out from his perch. "Are you kidding, lady? We've been driving for half an hour."

"We have?" Muriel asked. She stood up.

"Your ankle okay?" Benning asked. A young man and

woman were already standing near the buggy to take their places.

Muriel nodded. "It's fine," she said and stepped off the carriage.

The two of them walked down Fifth Avenue and turned left onto Seventy-First Street. Neither one spoke until Benning said, "So where's your car?"

Muriel thought of her filthy minivan, of the streaks left from the last winter snow, of the empty soda cans rolling from side to side as she drove, and she suddenly felt as if she had stepped off a chariot in a fairy tale and was heading toward a pumpkin. "It's not far."

"I'll walk you," Benning said.

"No, that's okay," Muriel said. "I'll be fine."

"There's that word again. *Fine*. I know you'll be fine." Benning stuck his gloved hands into his pockets. "I'm not worried about you, but can't I walk you anyway?"

"Oh," Muriel said. "Okay, I guess."

They walked mostly in silence, as if they had already said too much. As her minivan drew closer, Muriel thought about walking past it and standing in front of the blue Lexus that was parked two spots down, but she stopped in front of her Old Betsy anyway. "Well, this is me," she said.

"Minivan," Benning said.

"I know. The Rodney Dangerfield of the automotive industry."

He smiled.

Not sure of what to do, Muriel stuck out her hand. "Thanks for a surprisingly nice evening," she said.

Benning chuckled, as if amused, and took her hand and shook it. His gloved hand was large and warm and furry.

They stood there a few moments, and Muriel was about to turn away when Benning leaned forward and gently placed his hand at the back of her neck. Before Muriel could stop herself, she leaned toward him until their lips met. His lips were cold, but his breath was warm, and he kissed her in a way she had never been kissed before, the kind of kiss little girls daydream about, the kind of kiss that Muriel stopped believing was real.

When they parted, he stepped back, and Muriel felt herself wobble. She didn't know what to say, but she didn't have to say anything. Without another word, Benning turned on his heel and took off down the sidewalk. Muriel watched him go, the falling snow grazing her cheeks.

What just happened, she wondered.

She rummaged through her purse, took out her keys, and got into her minivan. The leather of the front seat felt cold through the wool of her coat as she watched the image of Marty Benning walk away through the clear areas of her windshield, her breath fogging up the glass, and she was overcome with a sudden urge to cry. She started the car and was about to take out her cell phone to call Roxanne when she was startled by a knock on the driver's-side window. She wiped the fog away with her hand. It was Benning.

She pushed a button, and the window rolled down, the snowflakes bunching at the bottom of the glass until they fell off. "Hi." Her voice was like a little girl's.

"Hi," he said. "What are you doing next weekend?"

"Next weekend?" Muriel couldn't remember what day it was. "Oh, um, I, um . . ."

"I thought maybe your ex had the kids again?"

"No. Actually, he's going on some firehouse ice fishing trip. He's a volunteer EMT. I have them next weekend."

"Oh." Benning took a step back. He looked as if he was about to walk away again.

"But I'm free tomorrow. Why don't you come over for dinner?" Muriel blurted before she remembered she couldn't cook.

"In Massapequa?" Benning shook his head.

"Yeah, I know, enemy territory."

"What is your address?"

"Oh . . ." She fumbled through her bag and grabbed a pen. "I can write it down. Or do you want to give me your phone number or email address, and I'll send it to you."

He hesitated.

"What's the matter?" she asked.

"I don't really do email."

"Don't you have your own firm?"

"What I mean is, for personal stuff. I try to keep that separate and off-grid. Just tell me your address. I'll remember it."

Muriel told him, and he nodded and put his gloved hands back in his pockets.

"Well . . . Bye." He took a few backward steps. "See you tomorrow night. 7:00 p.m.?"

Muriel nodded. "Bye," she said, mostly to herself, as he walked down the street and out of sight.

She closed the window, picked up her phone, and dialed, her hands shaking.

"So," Roxanne said as soon as she picked up on the

other end. "How did the dinner go? Did that fuck fire you for showing health pamphlets to a teenager who shouldn't be getting plastic surgery anyway? Did you tell Stowe to shove his dollar-an-hour raise up his ass? But you know, in a classy way, pinkies up?"

"Oh, Roxanne . . ." Muriel burst into tears.

"What's the matter? What happened? Oh, fuck, did he really fire you?"

"Worse," Muriel said. "I think I'm in love."

6

That same evening

Bobby dropped the plastic supermarket bags onto the short kitchen counter and walked straight into the bathroom. He spun the cold water faucet clockwise and stuck his right hand under the stream; the water circling the drain turned pink. It amazed him how much the small cuts on his knuckles stung, and he opened and closed his fist until the throbbing subsided. For such a tiny guy, Jumpin' Jim Perkins had a hard jaw and a surprising left hook. Bobby looked into the grimy vanity mirror at his right cheek where Perkins had landed a solid blow beneath his eye, just before the ref threw him out of the bout. Bobby was usually better about protecting his face, but he had no idea the little guy had it in him. He pumped a bit of hand soap onto his knuckles, opened the medicine cabinet, and poured a few drops of hydrogen peroxide, gritting his teeth.

He dried his hands on his jeans, went into the kitchen, and dumped the contents of the grocery bags onto the counter: two onions, a can of tomato sauce, a box of cornbread mix, four Bartlett pears, half a pound of tortellini salad that he was sure had been sitting in the deli counter all day, five pounds of potatoes, and a family pack of raisins. He opened the utensil drawer below the counter, fished out a fork, and slid it up his shirt to scratch the small of his back. Then he grabbed the tortellini salad and headed into the living room.

He plopped onto the sofa and searched for the remote control, which he found hidden between the cushions. When he pushed the power button and the television didn't respond, he checked the back of the remote—the batteries had popped out again, ignoring the piece of Scotch tape he had placed there that morning. He reached down between the cushions and moved his fingers around until he found the batteries, and he stuck them back into the remote and held them there while he pressed the power button.

The set turned on with a crinkle, and Bobby clicked around until he was in his DVR and a long list of cooking shows appeared. He resumed play on the oldest one, and when the sound of Paula Deen's boisterous Southern accent filled the room, he kicked off his shoes and put his socked feet on the coffee table. Paula had already begun putting together a Christmas shepherd's pie. Bobby scanned the ingredient list to make sure he had remembered to get everything and stopped when he came to *kosher salt*. Fuck. He glanced at his purchases on the counter and at his dusty spice rack hanging on the wall, wondering whether Kosher salt was different from table salt.

His cell phone vibrated. He pulled it out of his pocket and glanced at the screen, which read simply: *Benning.*

"Yeah," Bobby said into the phone, leaning his head back. He stretched the fingers of his right hand, the cuts appearing like tiny red mouths opening and closing on his knuckles. "No, no problem . . . Yeah . . . Wait, who? . . . What's the plate number? . . . A red . . . Did you say *minivan*? . . . Yeah, got it. When? . . . *Now?*" He looked at his watch. "All right." Bobby stuck his phone back into his pocket and reached for the remote. Paula Deen was stirring the tomato sauce and about to mix the vegetables. He stopped the playback and clicked off the TV.

Back to work, he thought, as he slipped on his sneakers. He grabbed his keys and dropped the remote control onto the floor, the batteries springing loose and rolling under the coffee table.

7

State Assemblyman Anthony Satriano dragged himself into his office, put his glasses onto his desk, and slumped back into his swivel chair. There was no doubt about it—he was hungover.

Last night's annual Women of Distinction awards dinner was one of his least favorite events of the year. All those accomplished women, after a drink or two, turned into giggling school girls pawing at him like he was some kind of Chippendales act. Although he drank only club soda at the event, he made the mistake of going home and drowning his cooties in a half bottle of vodka. He reached into his desk drawer, shook a bottle of aspirin, and threw two tablets into his mouth as his office door opened.

"Good morning, Ton," Mary said a bit too loudly. She put a cup of coffee on his desk and reached for the remote control behind him. She pointed it toward the far wall, bringing the flat-screen television to life. "Long night?"

"Yeah, yeah," he said, sipping his coffee. He was in no mood for a talking-to from his sister; he put his head on his desk.

"You've got an appointment at ten."

"Can't you cancel it?" he said into his hands.

"No, I can't. It's with Mommy, dumbass."

"Mar, first of all, Mommy stopping by isn't an *appointment*. And, secondly, enough with the names. I'm not in the mood."

Mary punched him in the arm. "What's your problem, huh?"

Satriano leaned back in his chair. "Nothing, forget it. What else is up for today?"

"Well, you're presenting citations this morning at eleven over at Eisenhower Park to the family and friends of wounded Marine Corporal Jason Canter, and then after that you've got the luncheon at the American Legion in East Meadow at one."

"Oh, is that all?" he groaned.

"And then an interview scheduled with *Newsday* at three."

"Jesus, I forgot. Where? Here?"

"It's a phoner."

"Oh, good. That's the last thing I need, for a news reporter to see me with these eyes." He booted up his laptop. "Anything else?"

Mary crossed the office toward the television screen.

"Mar? Hello?"

"Holy shit, Ton," she said, increasing the volume on the television. "Did you see this?"

"*. . . Police say Stryker was found dead early this morning in his office after a fire tore through the building.*"

"Who?" Satriano stumbled out of his chair and moved closer to the screen. "Kirk Stryker?"

"*. . . The cause of the fire is still under investigation, although Stryker's death may have come as a result of a gunshot wound* *to the chest. We are waiting on the coroner's report. As you can see*"—the reporter motioned behind her—"*not much structural damage was done to the building's exterior. A fire department spokesperson told us that the damage would have been much worse had it not been for a Gardenia resident who saw the flames while driving home last night and called 9-1-1. At this point, it appears that Kirk Stryker is the only casualty. No word yet on whether the fire is being flagged as arson . . .*"

"Did they say—?"

"Shhhh . . ." Mary said.

"*. . . Sources tell News 12 that there may have been a faulty smoke alarm in the office. We will have more on this story as it develops. Jill Sansone for News 12.*"

"I just saw Stryker the other day at the fruit market buying apples," Mary said.

Satriano also had seen him recently, in his office, to discuss reelection strategies. Kirk Stryker's Super PAC almost single-handedly financed his campaign for the state assembly two years before. "Mar, we need to write something up . . . you know, about this. I'm going to have to make a statement, I think."

Mary nodded, her eyes on the television screen.

"I mean, like, now," he said.

"Oh, right." Mary handed him the remote control and left the office.

News 12 was already running another segment on the death of Stryker. The burnt-out building being shown on the screen was located only about a half mile from his office and just several storefronts from his parents' fruit market. Had Satriano driven down Lake Shore this morning instead of coming around the back way, or if he had stopped at the store, as he had intended to, he would have driven smack dab into the pandemonium.

He logged into his computer and saw he had more than two hundred new emails, which, these days, was considered a light morning. He scrolled through them absentmindedly, his thoughts turning toward the awards dinner the night before—*Jesus*, Gloria Stryker had sat right next to him. He tried to remember what he had said to her. She was generally not all that talkative, so he figured it wasn't much beyond *hello*, *good-bye*, and *nice weather we're having*. She had no idea that her husband was dead . . .

"Anthony!" Satriano mother said, startling him.

"Ma . . ." He sat back in his chair. "You have to knock, remember? What if I was on the phone?"

His mother waved her hand dismissively and hurried around the desk.

"Did you hear what happened to the tax man?" She grabbed him in a big bear hug. "Such a tragedy."

"I know. Mary and I just saw it on TV. Is Daddy at the market?"

His mother's cheeks flushed. "This is terrible to say, but business has been very good all morning. All those young newspeople and police and firemen like to eat fruit. It does my heart good to see."

"Is Daddy alone?" Satriano knew how rattled his father could get when the market was busy.

"Yes, but I'll only be gone a few minutes. I wanted to make sure you were okay."

"I'm fine, Ma."

She handed him a bag of fruit and crossed the room,

stopping at the office door. "Where is your smoke detector?"

"It's right there, Ma." Satriano pointed to the ceiling near the doorway.

"Good. Did you change the batteries when the clocks moved?"

"It's hardwired, Ma. No batteries."

She looked concerned.

"Ma, it's fine. See the blinking light?"

"C'mon, Ma," Mary said, popping her head in. "Let's leave the assemblyman to his work." She winked.

"Oh, and, Mar . . ." Satriano said. "Find out when the funeral services are. You know, for Kirk Stryker." Mary nodded and closed the office door.

The television news was now doing a short bio on Stryker. The package looked like it had been thrown together by elementary school students, with random photos pulled from assorted social media profiles and newspaper clippings.

Satriano continued scrolling through his emails and found only two of what he was sure would be a bevy of interview requests in the next few days. The first, from *Newsday*, had the subject line *comment needed/Kirk Stryker* while another from the *Gardenia Gazette* was more casual: *Anthony, got a minute?* Satriano didn't have to open it to know what it was about.

He scrolled past them and waded through the usual fare—appearance requests, activist groups looking to get his ear. One by one, he deleted them or moved them into new folders. About thirty clicks in, an email stopped him cold. The sender's name was *Kirk Stryker, CPA*. No subject line.

Satriano looked over his shoulder as if he expected

someone to be there. The time stamp on the email was 8:22 p.m. and the subject line *Benning*. He clicked on it:

> *Tony, we need to talk. It's urgent. About Benning. Please call Eva in the morning to make an appointment. Thanks. And don't forget the Merchant Association carnival on the 13th and 14th. Perfect time to announce reelection plans. Bring Pina. She'll have a ball.*

Benning?

Rumor had it that Benning was planning to run against Satriano in the next assemblyman race once he established residency; Satriano wasn't sure if he had. He read the email again and wondered what he should do with it. Forward it to the police? Print it out? Get rid of it? His finger hovered over the delete button.

The television showed Stryker's building again. Police officers were carting things out the entranceway, including a computer, which made Satriano pull his finger away from his keyboard. If the email was in his in-box, then that meant it was in Stryker's sent box.

He looked again at the email's subject line: *Benning*.

What had Stryker wanted to discuss that was so urgent? Suddenly, a lingering hangover had become the least of Satriano's problems. It looked like he might have been virtually dragged into a possible homicide.

8

"Can I give you a ride, pretty lady?"

Sam rolled his wheelchair into the entryway as Betty walked in the door. She smiled.

"That's the best offer I've had all day," she said. She sat on her husband's lap and kissed him hello, tucking some stray hairs behind his ears. She remembered when those errant spikes had been long, smooth, and brown, rather than wiry and gray.

"Exciting day at the precinct, I bet," Sam said. He swiveled the wheelchair around and rolled through the kitchen to the dining room where a large bowl of chili and a bottle of wine stood in the middle of the table, next to a carefully arranged place setting for one.

"Chili?" Betty asked. Her favorite.

"I thought you'd need something a little special after today."

"I hope it's five-alarm," Betty said. She put her jacket on the back of the chair, sat down, and scooped some into her bowl.

"That bad?"

"It was pandemonium, Sam." She had a headache. The last time downtown Gardenia had been that noisy and crowded had been during the village's Memorial Day Parade.

"Does it look random?" he asked with concern.

Random crime was always scarier than targeted crime, particularly for a cozy village such as Gardenia, where people roamed around as if protected by an invisible barrier of wealth and privilege. Targeted crime was common, if not expected—spouses arrested for domestic abuse against philandering spouses, periodic stings rounding up doctors who doled out oxycodone prescriptions in parking lots, and assault charges just about every subway series against a Yankee fan or a Met fan, depending on how the season was going. Yet, the thought of individuals committing a crime—and a violent one—against someone they didn't know? That was concerning. Betty thought about the money left behind in Stryker's safe. It wasn't official, but her senses told her the person who shot Stryker knew him. Not that that made her feel any better. She thought of the marks on his belly and the mortal gunshot wound. There seemed to be real hatred there.

"We can't be sure yet," she said cautiously. "But I don't think so."

"Mommy!" Jesse came bouncing into the kitchen, his wispy bangs bouncing with him.

"Hey, Peanut Butter," she said.

Her son ran to a counter drawer, pulled out a Sharpie, and stepped onto the stool just under the hanging wall calendar; he scrawled a big X on the April 2 box. "Only one, two, three days to go," he said, "before you return!"

"Retire," Sam corrected.

"Yes, before you retire," Jesse said, "and you're home forever!"

Betty looked at Sam. The death of Kirk Stryker had the potential to delay her retirement indefinitely. She wanted to see the case through as much as she could but couldn't bear to dampen Jesse's excitement, so she decided to change the subject.

"Hmmm . . . Sam, I forgot to mention. I found something in my coat pocket again this morning."

Jesse giggled and ran behind Sam's wheelchair.

"Really?" Sam asked, as was the routine. "What did it say?"

Betty pulled out the Post-it note embossed with the fingerprint. She loved this little ritual she and Jesse conducted every evening. He had shown such an interest in fingerprinting after his school took part in a child identification program that she and Sam decided to surprise him with a stack of Post-it notes, each stamped with a different fingerprint, in his Christmas stocking. Each morning since, Jesse surreptitiously placed a new Post-it note into the pocket of her overcoat before he left for school.

She pretended to study the fingerprint on the note. "It says *I love you*."

Jesse frowned. "That's what it said yesterday."

"Oh, wait." Betty pretended to look again. "I misread it. It doesn't say *I love you*; it says *I like peanuts*."

"I do like peanuts," Jesse said, his face brightening. "Daddy, Mommy is a great detective!"

"That she is," Sam said with a wink. "Hop aboard, bud. Let's let Mommy eat."

Jesse climbed onto Sam's lap, and Sam escorted him back toward the bedrooms. Betty watched them go. When she had gotten pregnant in her midforties, it had been a big decision for them to have children. They had become a bit set in their ways, worrying that it was too late and they were too old. Some of their fears were warranted—she and Sam were two of the most senior parents milling around the bus stop and at class parties, and Betty lost her breath during even a short game of tag. But watching the love grow between Sam and the boys had been one of her greatest joys. Age was just a number, and she thanked her lucky stars every day that they had decided to roll the dice on theirs.

She put the Post-it note back into her pocket and scooped some more chili into her bowl. She was going to have to tell Jesse about the delay in her retirement eventually. It wouldn't go well.

When she sat down to eat, Sam rolled next to her and whispered in her ear: "I have another surprise for you later."

The last time Sam said that he had taught himself to pop a wheelie with his wheelchair. "Oh?" she asked.

"Yep." He wheeled over to the kitchen counter and grabbed a bag of Lay's Sour Cream & Onion potato chips. "For the Knicks game, later."

"You're too good to me," Betty said with a smile. She rested her head in her hands. "This is a violent one, Sammy. I've never seen anything like it."

"They're thinking it's arson, right? I saw the reports on News 12. It's been the top story all day. But he was shot too?"

Betty nodded. "And the body was a mess. Wait?

Did you say News 12?" She wiped her mouth with her paper napkin. "A Jill Sansone was hovering around the precinct all day, asking questions. I don't know why we bother holding press conferences. No one believes a word we say."

"Can you blame them?" Sam poured some chardonnay into Betty's wine glass. "This is the most news that's happened around here in a long time. I'm surprised a reporter didn't follow you home."

They looked at one another.

"I'll be right back," Sam said and rolled toward the front windows.

"Hi, Mom!"

Scott came into the kitchen and walked straight to the refrigerator, which was where her ten-year-old could be found most hours of the day. He took out the apple juice and poured himself a cupful.

"Hi, baby. How was your day?"

"Awesome!" he said into the cup as he drank, his voice an echo. "I totally knew all the answers on my social studies test. And, you were right, that question *was* on it, the one about the Three-Fifths Compromise."

"Great. I'm glad we studied that one extra hard. C'mere." Scott sat on Betty's lap. "Oooh, you're getting so big."

"You say that every day, Mom."

"I know, but it's true." Scott leaned back and rested his head on Betty's shoulder. She didn't know how much longer Scott would be willing to sit on her lap, so she tried to soak it in as much as she could. "Honey, did anyone at school talk about the fire that happened downtown this morning?"

"A fire?" Scott bolted upright. "I don't think so. Was anyone hurt?"

Betty nodded. "Yes, but I really can't discuss it with you, honey."

"Right. Police stuff. That's okay. I'll just google it," he said, standing up.

"Wait," Betty said, "I don't think that's such a good idea."

"Why? I thought you told me I should look things up when I don't know them."

Betty hated it when her own advice came back to bite her. "Well, sometimes the information you find online isn't correct," she said.

"Yeah, I know, but, Mommy, if you don't tell me, how am I going to get the right information?"

He was right, of course. Betty imagined that Jill Sansone of News 12 was probably wondering the same thing. "Okay, let me finish eating, and then I'll come by and I'll tell you about it."

"You mean, secret police stuff?"

"Yes, but you are *sworn* to secrecy, okay?" She'd have to give him the PG version of events. He smiled.

Sam rolled back into the room. "The coast is clear," he said. He looked at Betty's half eaten bowl of chili. "I see you didn't make much progress on your dinner."

Betty shrugged her shoulders. "It's okay, Sam." He was always looking out for her. Most days, Betty felt every day of her fifty-four years, but somehow Sam still managed to make her feel young and cared for.

"Yeah, we're talking secret police stuff." Scott put his cup on top of the pile of dishes in the sink. "Oh, wait,

Mom, I forgot to tell you. You got picked to be a chaperone for my planetarium trip."

Betty's heart sank. She was about to disappoint both of her sons within minutes. When she had signed up to be a parent chaperone she thought she would be a retired police detective without a care in the world, not one who had just been handed an apparent homicide. "That's great, but Scott . . ."

"Finally, you get to go on one of my trips!" he said, walking toward the bedrooms and disappearing down the hall.

Sam rolled up to the dining room table, picked up the bottle of wine, and poured himself a glass. "Let's see what happens," Sam said, reading Betty's face. "You may not have to tell him. This thing might be wrapped up by then."

"What are the odds?" Betty asked, chugging her glass of chardonnay. She preferred to be a little tipsy when she watched the Knicks play. "I have a feeling that this is just the beginning."

9

Three and a half months earlier

Muriel couldn't remember the last time she was this nervous about being with a man.

She uncovered, stirred, and recovered the baked ziti that was warming in the Crock-Pot and surveyed the dining room table, which was set for two using her "special plates," as Zack called them—the ones that rarely made it out of the china closet. Originally, she had put out the crystal candlesticks too, the ones her uncle had given her for her wedding nineteen years ago, but she stuck them back on the display shelf: they reminded her of Doug, and she thought they made the evening seem too important to her, like she was trying too hard.

And she most certainly wasn't, she had decided.

The euphoria of the night before had quickly morphed into something resembling disbelief and denial once she had gotten Roxanne off the phone and driven across the Queens/Nassau County border. Muriel could not be in love with Marty Benning. That was ridiculous. But as the time inched closer to seven o'clock, a kind of panic was setting in, and Muriel felt like she was going to pass out. She sat down on a stool in the kitchen, picked up the phone, and dialed.

"What happened?" Roxanne said breathlessly after the first ring. Muriel could hear Zack and Gordy giggling in the background.

"Nothing," Muriel said. "He's not here yet."

"Are you all right?"

"No."

"This is good, Mo. Good for you to be nervous."

"He's a dick, Roxanne. I know it in my head. A womanizing, self-centered, egotistical dick."

"So, okay, he's a *dick*," Roxanne whispered into the phone, presumably so that Gordy and Zack couldn't hear, "but you like him. And why can't you have some fun? Be wild, Mo, for once in your life."

"But let's be realistic . . . I haven't done this in a long time. What if . . . I just don't . . . Doesn't cooking dinner mean . . ."

"You don't have to do anything you don't want to do, dinner or no dinner," Roxanne said. "There are no rules. That's bullshit."

"Mom," Muriel heard Gordy caution in the background. "You cursed again."

"Sorry," Roxanne said, away from the phone. "I meant to say, That's *bananas*."

"Sure, you did," Gordy said, and Muriel heard him and Zack cackle.

"This is a good thing," Roxanne said into the telephone. "Be strong, Mo. Eye of the tiger."

"Strong? How about sensible? I mean, I'm forty-five years old. When I think about it, it seems so silly."

"Why? You're not dead."

"And I have children. I can't be running around with

men. I really shouldn't do this. I should cancel. I should be with Zack."

"Zack is fine. Gordy was thrilled that he decided to come over instead of spending another night with Doug. I mean, can you blame Zack? No offense . . ."

Muriel knew that Roxanne was trying to make her laugh. She had been trying to make her laugh since high school. She smiled.

"Do you hear those knuckleheads in the background?" Roxanne continued. "They're having a ball destroying my kitchen with Play-Doh. Just have dinner. What's the harm? You don't have to be Harlequin Romance Muriel. You can still be Level-Headed Muriel and have a good time. It's not one or the other."

"I guess."

"Be honest. Isn't this why you kicked Doug out?"

Muriel exhaled. Roxanne had a habit of blurting out things that Muriel couldn't bring herself to say aloud. "I don't know."

"Well, it is," Roxanne said. "Because you weren't happy, and you wondered if you could be happy. When you called me last night, Mo . . . You were happy. Really happy."

"I was crying."

"You know what I mean."

"Well, it faded overnight," she said.

"So what. Who cares. Whatever happens happens."

Muriel recalled her wedding day, moments before she was to walk down the aisle. She had gotten cold feet and suggested that she and Roxanne run out of the church and away with the limo drivers. "Oh, please, marry the shmuck. It doesn't have to be forever," Roxanne had said calmly with a smile, pulling down Muriel's veil and whispering, "although Lord knows a week with Doug *feels* like forever. Just in case, I'll get the limo drivers' phone numbers. Whatever happens happens."

"Okay," Muriel said. She was feeling a little better.

"Now, I've got some pink spaghetti I need to make."

"You're doing blue, Mom," Gordy said in the background.

"Oh, blue. Good. Blue's my color. Brings out my eyes. Mo, I love you. You're the best. You deserve to be happy. This is so great. I'm totally thrilled. Now, go and knock 'em dead, Mo!"

"Knock 'em dead, Mo!" Gordy and Zack mimicked on the other end of the line before Roxanne hung up.

Knock 'em dead, Muriel thought. *Sure, if I don't have a panic attack first.*

She looked at the clock. Six thirty. Benning was supposed to be there in a half hour.

Maybe he wouldn't show, she thought hopefully— maybe he would *ghost* her, or whatever it was Ellie and her friends called it. Something told her she wouldn't be that lucky.

She did some last-minute checks of the dining and living rooms; everything looked in order—well, neat, if not stunning. She glanced at herself in the living room mirror and resisted the temptation to give herself the same assessment: *neat, if not stunning.*

She examined the forest-green sweater dress she had bought on a whim that afternoon. Was she too dressed up? She felt a bit silly wearing anything but jeans in her own home.

She walked closer to the mirror and looked at her face, checking for falling mascara and sliding her finger along the thin lines around her eyes and mouth. She thought about the comment from Stowe on Thursday about her laugh lines and about the newspaper photo of him and Benning with the women half their age. Was she wearing too much makeup? Not enough?

This is crazy, she thought, as she leaned back against the wall. She looked at the phone in her hand. *I should call it off, say I'm sick, not feeling well.* Did she even have his number? The living room seemed so desolate without the kids. After six months of Doug being out of the house, Muriel still wasn't used to it.

She straightened the photograph of Ellie and Zack on the fireplace mantel, as if doing so would erase the guilt Muriel felt. What had she done? Taken away their daddy. Why? Because she was bored? Because she was unhappy? By most standards, her marriage was a good one—well, decent, at least. Now she slept in a king-size bed alone, unless Zack crept in at night after having a bad dream. Wasn't it wrong for a middle-aged woman to use the warm body of her five-year-old as a substitute for a man?

The doorbell rang, and Muriel jumped. *Holy shit, he was early.* She put the phone down on the hall table and took one last look in the mirror. She ran her fingers along the curves of her hips, took a deep breath, and opened the door.

Benning stood behind the glass of her storm door, looking confident but fidgety and out of place, like a wild animal at a zoo. Unfortunately, he was as handsome as Muriel had recently discovered—possibly even more so, surrounded by the emptiness of the suburban night. He was wearing a black turtleneck, blue jeans, and boots, with a red woolen scarf wrapped around his neck. Even though it was cold, he wasn't wearing a jacket, which reminded Muriel of the "cool kids" in her high school who, no matter the weather, always managed to get by in a T-shirt and jeans. If Muriel could dress a man any way she wanted, it would be exactly the way Marty Benning looked right now. She put on a smile and pushed open the storm door.

"Hi," she said as nonchalantly as she could.

"Hi," Benning said. Muriel braced herself for a kiss hello, but Benning stepped past her and into the house, and she felt both relieved and hurt as she closed the door behind him.

"Did you find the house okay?" Muriel asked and then worried that she had said *do* instead of *did*.

"Yeah. *Fine,*" he said with a smirk.

He looked almost too large standing there in the middle of her living room, glancing around like a tourist. His eyes rested on the photo of her children on the mantel.

"Those are my kids," Muriel said.

"I figured."

An awkwardness hung over them, and it lasted so long that Muriel almost cheered when the Crock-Pot timer beeped. She walked into the kitchen and clicked it off. When she turned around, Benning was right behind her, and for a moment she thought that perhaps being in the living room alone with the photo of her children may have been too much for him.

"Are you hungry?" she asked, filling the silence with words, any words. "I didn't know what you liked, so I made baked ziti, because I figured everyone likes baked ziti, right?"

Benning was looking around the kitchen, his eyes flitting from the small brown stain on the ceiling, where there had been a leak last winter, to the drying dishes in the sink rack.

"Listen," Muriel said, crossing her arms, "I guess we should get this out of the way. I don't know what you . . . I mean, I haven't done this in a long time. And I know what the expectations are about asking a man over for dinner, and I want you to know that as much as I'd like to consider myself a modern-day woman, that doesn't mean that I feel like I need to prove myself in any—"

"Do you feel this?" Benning asked, his eyes now on her.

Muriel's pulse quickened. "What?" she asked, her voice almost inaudible. "Do I feel . . . what?"

"*This*," he said, without gesturing, his hands in his jean pockets. "Do you feel it?"

There was a pounding in Muriel's chest now, and she leaned against the kitchen counter to steady herself. Images were flashing before her eyes—the kids, Doug, Stowe, rainbows, unicorns, the lights of Tavern on the Green—and she had the urge to burst into tears, and she wasn't sure why.

"Muriel?" Benning asked, almost in a whisper.

Suddenly, the air left the room, and Muriel's shoulders slumped. Her throat tightened, but she managed to eke out the words.

"Yes," she whispered with a swallow. "I do."

With that, Benning came toward her, and she reached up for him, her fingers combing through his hair, pulling his face down to hers. His lips were still cold from the outside air, and his kiss now familiar, powerful, yet gentle, and she wrapped her arms around his neck, pulling his red scarf onto the floor. She felt his hands on her arms, her hips, and then her butt until Benning lifted her into the air. She leaned down and kissed his neck and the cleft in his chin, as he pivoted and carried her up the short set of stairs that led to the master bedroom. There was no hesitation. He knew exactly where to go, as if he'd been there before, or perhaps because he'd been to many master bedrooms before. But Muriel shooed away all intrusive thoughts, and suddenly Level-Headed Muriel was gone. And all that Harlequin Romance Muriel could think was *good riddance*.

10

John Parker sat at his desk at the *Gardenia Gazette* and read over the article that was set to run in the print edition of the weekly, an updated, more detailed version of the story that had run on the *Gazette's* website the day before. He smiled at his name, which was written just below the italicized headline: *Prominent CPA Found Dead; Gunshot Wound to the Chest, Arson Suspected.*

"Hurry up, Parker. We gotta get that bio on Stryker laid out pronto," said Steve Kramer, leaning over him and pointing to the screen. "I changed the word *area* to *local*. I think it sounds better, don't you?"

Kramer had a habit of making changes to Parker's copy that were unnecessary. "Sure. Whatever," Parker said.

"And be careful with those typos," Kramer added, returning to his desk. "It's police *chief*, not *chef*. You can't rely on spell-check."

Parker took a bite of his donut and continued scrolling through his story. Gardner had insisted that he and Kramer pool their information and share a byline for the article on the investigation, which, as of that morning, was officially being called a homicide. Kramer's idea of sharing had been to spend the better part of the morning lecturing Parker about the finer points of the inverted pyramid and poking holes through most of the information Parker had collected. He was waiting for Kramer to wipe the powdered sugar from his chin with a napkin.

The sound of the front door opened and closed, and Gardner stormed into the editorial office. "It's a goddamn freak show downtown," he said. "National news. Cable news. Can't even walk down the street without bumping into a guy with a microphone." He hung up his suit jacket on the coatrack. "The *Post* come yet?"

Gardner spent most Wednesday mornings slamming drawers and cursing at his desk, yammering on and on about how the *Post* had managed to scoop the *Gazette* yet again. Lucky for Gardner, Stryker's body had been found early Tuesday morning, too late for the *Post* to have gotten anything solid, but perfect for the *Gazette,* which was published on Thursdays. Finally, they had a chance to make some editorial headway.

"I'll check out front," Kramer said and left the room.

"I still can't believe that son of a bitch Stryker is gone," Gardner said, shaking his head. "He was at the chamber meeting just the other day. Was in good spirits." He sat on the corner of Parker's desk. "Parker, did you finish the piece yet?"

"Got it up now. Just checking it over."

"Good. Let me know when it's final, and I'll take a look at it."

Kramer came back with the *Post* in hand. "They got nuthin'," he said, unfolding the front page. "Nothing but the fire and finding the body. No word on the homicide investigation. We're gonna kill 'em this week."

"Yeah, well, let's not get cocky," Gardner said. "I'm sure there'll be updates posted on the *Post's* website today, so we can't rest on our laurels. I need that story, guys." He took the paper from Kramer's hands and went into his office. "And I need you both out there gathering more info. *Pronto*."

"Right," Kramer called, putting on his jacket. "Parker, you finish up. I'll work some of my sources downtown and get a jump on things." He ran out the door.

Parker could feel his adrenaline pumping. Ordinarily, he'd spend his days typing in peewee soccer scores and press releases from the local library. He rarely left the office. There was never any reason to.

"Goddammit!" Gardner banged his fist on his desk.

"What's wrong?" Parker asked.

"How did the *Post* get this quote from Gottlieb? I thought you said Gottlieb wasn't talking to the press."

"She wasn't," Parker said.

"Then how do you explain *this*?" Gardner asked, holding up the *Post's* Page Two, which featured a large, italicized pull quote from the mayor of the Incorporated Village of Gardenia.

Parker knew how to explain it. And so, for that matter, did Gardner. The *Post* was the number one paper in town, had a downtown street-front office, and was part of a large chain of weeklies, which meant it had resources up the wazoo. Meanwhile, the *Gazette* was a struggling mom-and-pop operation with an editorial staff of two, not including Gardner, and was located in a suite of rooms behind an optometrist's office twenty blocks away from Lake Shore Avenue. They were so off the radar that even the mail carrier had problems finding them.

Parker said instead, "I'll get on it, boss," to which Gardner huffed and turned back to the *Post*, hunched over the tiny paper and devouring every sentence as if it were a cheeseburger.

The office phone rang; the caller ID read *Village Hall*.

"I got it," Gardner called. "About fucking time the mayor's office returns my call."

Parker looked up at the newspaper awards and citations decorating the editorial office as Gardner picked up the phone and fought for "his rightful time" with the mayor, using his "long history of public service" to get it. There was something unsettling about a sixty-three-year-old man working so hard after thirty years in the trenches. Parker didn't know whether he should feel sorry for Gardner or be awed by him.

Parker's cell phone vibrated. He looked at the screen. The message was from Kramer:

LET'S GO. WHERE ARE YOU?

Parker typed: I'M ON MY WAY, ASSHOLE. And then he deleted the word *ASSHOLE* and sent the text.

When he looked up, Gardner was putting a twenty-dollar bill on his desk.

"What's this for?" Parker asked.

"Grab yourself a sandwich for lunch. On me," Gardner said. "You've been working hard the last twenty-four hours, and I appreciate it."

Parker picked up the bill and handed it back to Gardner. "This really isn't necessary."

"Nah, take it, as long as you promise to buy something

healthy, maybe some fruit. Buy a little something for Kramer too. It'll be a nice change from his diet of Red Bull and Skittles."

Parker smiled and put the bill in his pocket. "Thanks."

"Did you get the times for the Stryker funeral?" Gardner asked.

"It's scheduled for tomorrow night," Parker said. "Seven to nine, barring any glitches."

Word on the street was that Gloria Stryker had refused an autopsy, but had been overruled by homicide, which needed to know the official cause of death. She agreed to a posthaste procedure, so that funeral services could be held after the coroner made his preliminary report, which was expected to be delivered that afternoon.

"Nothing tomorrow afternoon?" Gardner asked.

Parker shook his head.

"All right. We'll have to go, you know. All of us. You have a tie?"

"Um . . ."

"No matter, I'll give you one of mine. I'll need photos, close-ups of the grieving family, of any politicians—and there will be quite a few—who are there." He put his hand on Parker's shoulder. "I may have to admonish you in front of the family and the others to save face—make it look like I can't believe you would take photos at a man's funeral, *what a newbie, how disrespectful,* and all that—but, dammit, get me something good."

"Got it," Parker said.

"Same goes for Kramer." Gardner opened the small fridge near the window and took out a quart of milk, sniffed the top, and tossed it into the trash. "Pick up a quart of milk too. And don't forget to send me the story before you head out. You're doin' good, kid. I knew you would. I had a sense about you. Keep it up," he said, shuffling back to his office.

"Thanks, sir," Parker called. He sent the article file to Gardner and threw his SUNY New Paltz hoodie over his head. He opened his desk drawer and took out his iPad and camera, checking the battery level, and stuck them both, along with his cell phone and digital recorder, into his backpack.

He glanced at his boss who was again on the phone, no doubt working his sources, keeping the newspaper alive, if just barely. *Maybe I'll get lucky today and find a lead for the old guy*, Parker thought. He had picked up his tiny notebook and flipped to a clean page when he heard his cell phone buzz in his backpack. *Goddamn, Kramer.* He'd have to get that dude off his back. With a little elbow room, Parker knew he could do a lot more than manage a few good funeral photos. He could break this story wide open.

11

Roxanne boosted Gordy onto the bench seat and sat next to him. She hadn't been to the Queensborough Public Library in about thirty years, when smoking in the bathrooms and the Dewey Decimal System reigned supreme. From the looks of things, that was probably the last time the place had gotten a facelift. Between the ripped, stained fabric seating, the peeling paint on the walls, and the cracked linoleum floor, the children's reading lounge looked like an unfinished basement.

Gordy had a big smile on his face as he waited for LEGO Club to begin. The little guy had been asking to attend activities at the library for eons and had finally worn her down—she had nothing better to do anyway, since Muriel had been virtually MIA for months.

A door opened at the far end of the room and, as if on cue, all the kindergarteners in the room jumped down from their seats and made a beeline for it, like someone was giving out free candy.

"Well, well, we have a few eager beavers here I see," said the young man who, Roxanne assumed, was heading up this afternoon's meeting of the LEGO Club; with his red hair and freckles he looked like a kindergartener himself.

"I'll be taking attendance once we get started. If anyone has any questions, please let me know. I'm sure your children will have a wonderful time." And with that he was inside, leaving her with the other mommies and daddies, most of whom were holding smartphones, Kindles, toddlers or, in the case of the parents in the far corner, grudges.

She was surprised to see anyone at the library at all and thought she would be the only one waiting around. *Did people really still come here?* With the Internet, she couldn't imagine why anyone would take the time to get in a car and drive somewhere to get a book.

Her cell phone buzzed, and she looked at the screen. It was Muriel.

Well, well . . . Roxanne was tempted not to answer. She was still feeling upset—and abandoned. When she had encouraged Muriel to go out with Benning, she didn't realize that meant that she'd hardly ever see her anymore and wind up sitting in a moldy library on a weekday with a bunch of strangers. She let the phone ring and ring until she sighed and swiped the screen with her finger.

"Hi," Roxanne said, nonchalantly.

"Hey," Muriel said.

Silence.

"What's the matter?" Muriel asked. "Are you okay?"

"I'm fine."

"What's with the 'tude?"

More silence.

"Are you mad at me?" Muriel asked.

"Why would I be mad at you?"

"Why are you whispering?"

"I'm at the library."

"The *library*?"

"It's not *that* surprising," Roxanne huffed. "What's up?"

"Nothing's up. Just thought I'd say hi."

"Oh, is Marty in the shower or something? Let me guess, he's on a business call, and you had a few minutes to spare, so you thought you'd give your old friend Roxanne a call."

"Very funny," Muriel said.

"Oh, wait, maybe he's sitting next to you right now, and you had a few minutes between orgasms, so you figured you'd check in." A woman rocking a toddler in a stroller a few seats down glared at Roxanne.

"Don't you think you're exaggerating a little?" Muriel asked.

"*Exaggerating?*" Roxanne squealed, and now all the moms and dads were looking at her. She lowered her voice. "When was the last time I heard from you?"

"I don't know. Monday?"

"Try again."

"The weekend?"

"Uh uh."

"Well, I'm sure you have it etched into your memory, so why don't you tell me?"

"It'll be two weeks tomorrow."

"Two weeks?" Muriel said. "Is that possible?"

Roxanne nodded, as if Muriel could see her.

"I'm sorry, Rock. This is just . . . I don't know where my head is these days. I've been, like, totally blindsided by this. You really have to meet him."

"Whatever. I don't want to meet him."

"You know it was you, lady, who gave me that eye-of-the-tiger shit and told me I should have some fun and have him over for dinner and go out with him."

"Yeah, but I didn't think it meant I wasn't going to see you anymore."

Roxanne could hear Muriel sigh. "I know. It's not just you. I feel like I haven't been spending enough time with the kids, at my job. But Rock, this feels like nothing I've ever felt. Like storybook stuff."

"Well, he has you practically locked up in a castle."

"He doesn't have me locked up anywhere," Muriel said. "It's just that he doesn't really like to go out. He likes spending time with just the two of us."

"Yeah, yeah, amazing, romantic, whatever."

"I'm sorry if I've been a bonehead," Muriel said.

"Oh, forget it." Roxanne leaned back against the wall of peeling paint. "I'm just feeling sorry for myself."

"Which totally explains why you're sitting in a library."

"I know, right? How did I let Gordy talk me into this?"

"Because you're a good mom," Muriel said.

"When can I see you? Or do you have to approve it with what's-his-name?"

"Oh, please."

"What are you doing on Saturday? I can see if Gordy wants to spend the night with his friend next door."

"Saturday?" Muriel asked.

"Let me guess . . ."

"Saturday's the only day I can't do, Rock. Honest. Marty said to keep Saturday night open."

"For what?"

"I don't know. He said it was a surprise." Muriel sounded excited, and despite Roxanne's anger, she smiled.

"Do you need me to watch the kids?" Roxanne asked. *Do you need me at all?*

"No, Doug's got it."

"Okay, well, I guess I'll see you whenever."

"Don't be a baby," Muriel said.

"Well, I am younger than you, you know."

"Oh, sure, by five months."

"Well, that's a hundred and fifty days."

Muriel laughed. "I love you, lady," she said. "And I miss you. I promise I'll talk to you soon."

"Love you too," Roxanne murmured, clicking off the call. "Miss you too," she added quietly, as she put her cell phone into her purse.

"So you're the famous Gordy's mother." A woman rocking a stroller was looking over at Roxanne. She was young and had her hair in a ponytail and a toddler sitting beside her playing on a smart phone. "Sorry, but I overheard you talking."

"Yes," Roxanne said. "But I didn't realize he was so famous."

"Oh, he's famous, all right." The woman stuck out her hand, and Roxanne shook it. "I'm Janie's mom, Caitlyn. C. A. I. T. L. Y. N," she offered, as if Roxanne was going to write her a letter. "My Janie says that Gordy's very smart. He gets, like, a hundred on all his tests."

"He's a total sponge," Roxanne said with pride.

"Yes, it was a bit jarring at first. I mean, Janie wasn't used to not being the smartest in class. But having Gordy around has really been quite a good thing for her. It's made her work harder."

"Oh?" Roxanne said.

"And, now, well, you know, Janie's caught up. In fact, I think she got a point higher than he did on the last math test."

"Whew, finally," Roxanne said. "I'll be sure to tell Gord to stop letting Janie copy off his tests then. After all, it's every man for himself, you know, once they go into first grade."

"I'm sorry?" The woman's pale face seemed confused.

"I mean, I know Gordy is famous and all, but Janie will just have to start pulling her own weight. He can't carry her forever."

"Wait a second. Janie is quite—"

"But as you say," Roxanne picked up her backpack and put her arms through the straps, "it really was nice of Gordy to help her out. I'll have to give him an extra dollar in his allowance this week. Well, it was nice to meet you. I'm going to go browse some of those old paperbacks over there. Maybe pick up a nice trashy romance for Gord. Teach him some new words." Roxanne hurried away, sat down on the other side of the room, and hid behind an old Danielle Steel novel.

After an hour that felt like six, Gordy came running toward her.

"That was great, Mom," he said, holding up a perfectly striped square made with blocks.

"I'm glad." Roxanne put the book back. "They're letting you take that home?"

"Yeah, but we had to promise to bring it back next week."

"You mean we have to come back again?"

"Mom . . ." Gordy rolled his eyes.

"Just kidding. Of course, we'll come back."

"Did you make any friends?" Gordy asked, reaching for Roxanne's hand.

"Tons," Roxanne said. She watched Caitlyn scoop up little Janie, who seemed very preoccupied with the LEGO tower Gordy was holding. "C'mon, Gord, let's get out of here."

Outside, the day was winding down, which meant bumper to bumper traffic on Metropolitan Avenue. Roxanne beeped her car alarm and opened the rear door, pinching Gordy's butt as he hopped inside. Across the street, Caitlyn was helping Janie and her little sister into a brown minivan. Gordy watched the three of them climb aboard.

"Mom, do you ever think we'll get a minivan like all the other families?" he asked as Roxanne got into the driver's seat.

One of the hardest things about being a parent was not being able to give Gordy everything Roxanne thought he deserved. "What does Mommy say?" she asked, starting up the car.

"When hell freezes over," Gordy said, buckling himself in.

"No, the other thing Mommy says."

"Oh." Gordy thought for a moment. "If we spend our lives trying to be like everyone else, we'll never get to be ourselves."

"Right." She pushed on the glass of her driver's side window with her palm while holding the power button until it came down midway.

"But what if ourselves wants a minivan?" Gordy asked. "And it could have windows that aren't broken?"

"But then I wouldn't have these great-looking arms." She flexed her biceps.

Gordy frowned and looked out the window. "Mommy, what does *in the red* mean?"

"In the red?" Roxanne looked at Gordy in the rearview mirror. "Where did you hear that?"

"You said it. You were talking to Mo on the phone one time, and I heard you say, 'Well, that's what happens when you're in the red. You eat tuna fish for a week and drive a ten-year-old car.'"

"I did?" Roxanne generally tried to keep her money troubles from Gordy, since while she was growing up her mother made her very aware of every cent that was spent to feed, house, and clothe her. She would never do that to him. Unfortunately, Roxanne also rarely lied to Gordy, but she would have to make an exception.

"Oh, did you say *in the red*? she asked.

Gordy nodded.

"That means . . . that you're in love."

"It does?" Gordy asked. "The dictionary said it means *insolvent.*"

"Dictionary? What do those things know?"

"But why would you eat tuna fish for a week and drive an old car if you were in love?" Gordy asked.

"Why? Because you're so crazy in love that you forget to buy food and buy a new car. When they're *in the red*, some people even forget to . . . pay their credit cards or put money in the bank. "

"Really?" Gordy asked. "Oh, so it's *in the red* because, like, a heart's red?"

"Right. Red like a heart." Roxanne turned on the radio,

hoping to find something to distract Gordy and keep her from lying any further. She turned up the volume.

"So who's in the red? Is it Mo? Zack said Mo has a new friend who's a boy."

"Really?" Roxanne said. "I hadn't heard."

"And maybe that's why Mo is forgetting to call you. Because she's in the red."

"Alrighty then . . ." Roxanne put the car into drive. "How about some ice cream?" Clearly, the radio wasn't working.

"Ice cream? Yeah!" Gordy said, with a hearty fist pump. "Can I get chocolate *and* vanilla?"

"You can get whatever you want."

"Cool," Gordy said, settling back into his seat. "You're the best, Mom."

Roxanne let the comment coat her with contentment and pulled the car into traffic just as Janie's mom, across the street, was buckling her seat belt. *You hear that, C-A-I-T-L-Y-N with the big brown minivan*, Roxanne thought as she passed them. *Score one for famous Gordy's mother and her beat-up old Chevy.*

12

The Gardenia Funeral Home looked like a mini White House in the center of the village's downtown guarded by six-foot fencing and stadium-quality lighting. Over the years, the building had been expanded and renovated, leaving what was now only a small, oddly shaped parking lot that was no match for the grand two-level structure which, at its capacity, could house six memorials simultaneously. Even though Kirk Stryker's was the only wake being held this evening, the lot was filled with BMWs and Mercedes parked every which way, and Betty decided it was better to park her Honda three blocks away and walk rather than deal with the mayhem.

The line to get in the building was out the door, and Betty recognized several local dignitaries, including Assemblyman Anthony Satriano, with whom she had met briefly the day before; the two nodded their hellos. As probably the highest profile colleague of Stryker's, Satriano had been one of Betty's first stops in the investigation, a somewhat routine visit, so she was surprised when the assemblyman marched her straight to his computer to show her an email Stryker had sent him the night of his murder: The time stamp indicated that Stryker was apparently alive and well around 8:30 p.m. Monday night. Plus, Stryker's email mentioned the name Marty Benning, making it the second time Benning's name had come up since Stryker's death; the first being the meeting notation on Stryker's planner. Betty asked Satriano to forward her the email, and from there the meeting with the assemblyman had been uneventful. Betty got on the back of the receiving line as a pair of photographers lurked in front of her snapping photos of the mourners, who glared at them.

Inside, the funeral parlor was teeming with black suits and dresses along with police officers and firefighters in full regalia. If Betty remembered correctly, Stryker had been handling the taxes for many of the village's civil servants for years. She spotted Fire Chief Vincent Restonelli, whom she had met with that morning, at the far end of the room. That meeting wasn't all that informative either, since the chief was prepared with all the proper paperwork showing that the building's smoke alarms had been dutifully checked every three months for years. He seemed to have no idea why the alarm in Stryker's office would be disconnected, which meant that something must have happened sometime between the last inspection and Monday, the evening of Stryker's death, although Restonelli intimated that if there had been any foul play, that too would have been picked up by the department.

To accommodate all the mourners, the funeral parlor made use of both viewing areas on the main floor—a room divider had been opened—and long rows of chairs made the space resemble a large lecture hall. In the front, Stryker's casket, which was closed, sat atop a short altar. Before it, Gloria Stryker stood with her three boys: Craig, Steven, and the youngest, Mark, who was Scott's age and kept pulling at the collar of his dress shirt. Not surprisingly, Gloria looked even more tired than she had the day before when Betty stopped by her home. She had answered every question as Betty thought she would—Gloria couldn't fathom this ever happening to her husband, she couldn't think of anyone who would want to hurt him, and, yes, she would contact Betty if she remembered anything pertinent.

Betty watched as Mrs. Stryker limply extended her hand to each of the mourners at the funeral home, no doubt having to relive her husband's death and the details of the case as she spoke to every one; it must have felt like a recurring bad dream.

"I'm so sorry, Mrs. Stryker," Betty said when it was her turn at the front of the line.

"Thank you for coming," Gloria said, her words sounding as if they were on autopilot. She looked for her sons, who had wandered off and were seated lazily in the front row of chairs. "Boys, come here."

"That's all right, Mrs. Stryker. You can leave them."

"No, no, I'd like you to meet them, since you weren't able to yesterday." Mrs. Stryker extended her arm around her oldest, as the other two stood next to him. "This is Craig, Steven, and Mark."

"Hi, boys," Betty said. "I'm so, so sorry to hear about your dad."

"Thank you," they said in unison, their eyes finding the ground.

"Boys, this is Detective Munson," Gloria said, "the lady I told you who came by yesterday."

This seemed to make the boys perk up, and they looked Betty in the eye.

"Are you going to arrest the person who did this to my dad?" Steven asked from behind a pair of wispy bangs that he blew up and out of his eyes.

"I'm going to try my best," Betty said with a faint smile. "That's my job. To get the bad guys."

"All of them?" Mark asked in a tiny voice.

"As many as I can," Betty said.

"Okay, boys, you can sit down, if you like," Gloria told them, and they returned to their seats. Mark kept his eyes on Betty while his brothers took smartphones out of their jacket pockets.

"Has there been any progress?" Gloria asked.

"Not much, I'm afraid, Mrs. Stryker, but there's no need to discuss that now. I'll be in touch with any new developments. I promise." Betty was eager to disappear back into the crowd. "Again, I'm so very sorry."

Gloria Stryker nodded as Betty hurried to the other side of the room near a flat-screen television that was showing a digital photo collage of the Stryker family through the years. From there, she wandered up a side aisle, past Satriano who was seated with his parents—Betty recognized them from the fruit market—as well as his sister, whom she had met at his Gardenia office.

Despite the late hour, the room was still very crowded, and Betty searched for an open place to sit for a few minutes. She felt funny leaving right away. A group of women, all of them in dark blue suits, had rearranged some of the seating in the back and were chatting in a small, clandestine-like circle, while other mourners had pulled chairs in various directions, making for slim pickings. Betty found an available seat on a sofa next to an overweight woman who was sitting primly with her purse on her lap and appeared to be alone.

"Is this seat taken?" Betty asked.

"No, not at all," the woman said, brushing her skirt under her thighs and giving Betty room to sit.

"Thank you," Betty said.

The two women sat quietly, watching the receiving line inch forward.

"So many people here," Betty said.

"Yeah, I know," the woman replied. "He was very popular."

"I'm Betty. Detective Betty Munson."

"Eva Sansfield. I worked with Kirk."

"Oh, I'm sorry for your loss," Betty said. Now that Betty looked closely at the young woman, she recalled seeing Eva's face in a photo on the wall of Stryker's practice—a group photo in which the firm had been awarded a citation from a town councilman. So far, Betty had managed to speak with only one of Stryker's employees, a woman named Sandra, and had left messages for a few others. She hoped to get through the list in the next day or two. "Were the two of you close?"

"We worked very closely for two years," Eva said. She opened her purse and pulled out a tissue. "Did you know Kirk, or are you just here . . . you know?"

"Actually, I didn't really know him. My husband did, a long time ago. They went to school together."

"Are you, like, investigating here?"

Betty estimated Eva to be in her late twenties,

although her considerable size seemed to give her face a round, youthful appearance, so she may have been older. And, yet, her inquisitive expression made her seem like a little girl. "Not really," Betty said. "Just paying my respects, although I never really take off the badge, I guess."

"That's all right. You have to do your job." Eva shifted in her seat. Sweat was beginning to form on the sides of her face. Betty could feel it getting hot in the crowded room, and she imagined Eva's size only compounded the heat. The woman took a tissue from her purse and dotted her forehead. "I'm actually not staying long myself," Eva said. "I'm not very fond of funeral homes, but felt I owed it to . . . Kirk to be here."

"I'm sure he'd appreciate it," Betty said.

A tall fellow in a brown derby was scanning the room and when he saw Eva, he hurried toward her.

"Eva," said the man, distraught, "I was hoping to see you here."

"Hi, Mr. Colby."

"I hate to ask, but do you know, by any chance, if Kirk had gotten to . . . my return before he . . . well, before?"

Eva seemed uncomfortable, and Betty nearly reprimanded the man until a woman from the small group of dark blue suits called out Mr. Colby's name.

"Oh, never mind. I see Paulette," Mr. Colby said and hurried away as Eva blew her nose into her tissue.

"Are you all right?" Betty asked.

"I'm okay," Eva said and put her tissue in her purse.

"The question seemed a bit inappropriate," Betty said, "but I guess it shows how integral Mr. Stryker was to the community. I think he did returns for many of the people I see here tonight."

Eva nodded. "He did."

"Do you know if there's any talk about the accounting office reopening?"

"Without Kirk? I doubt it," Eva said. "He was the engine that drove that place. Most people think business will move to the practice across the street."

"You mean, Marty Benning's?" Betty asked.

Eva nodded. "There's also a rumor, though, that some of the employees are thinking about opening another firm in town."

"Really? Well, that's good news then. For Stryker's clientele. And also for you."

Eva shrugged her shoulders and looked toward the group of women talking to Mr. Colby. "I don't think so."

"What do you mean?"

"Did you ever find yourself in a place where as much as you tried you just didn't fit in?" Eva asked.

Being a female officer in a predominantly male police force, Betty knew exactly what Eva meant. Although she could never point to any actual discrimination or bad behavior, she could often feel it lurking under the surface, like a blood stain that is uncovered only when a black light is shone on it. She nodded.

"Well, that seems to be the story of my life."

"Don't let it get you down," Betty said. "I'm sure they need you. And even if they don't, my opinion is that good people always land on their feet." She stood up. "I'd better be heading off. Coincidentally, Ms. Sansfield—"

"Call me Eva."

"Eva, you probably would have heard from me either tomorrow or the next day. I'm doing preliminary interviews of Stryker's family, friends, and associates to try and see if we can determine anything about what happened. Just following procedure." Betty dug into her pants pocket and handed her business card to Eva. "You can leave a message at the main number, and they will get it to me, but I will be contacting you shortly for more of an official chat."

"Do you need my number?"

"I already have it," Betty said, a bit embarrassed, since she had been given a list of phone numbers for Stryker's entire staff. "But thank you."

The line of mourners had dwindled to about twenty, and Betty excused her way toward the funeral parlor front door when she spotted Marty Benning. Betty would have recognized Benning anywhere, since his mug seemed to be in the local paper once a month; the media loved him.

She had been trying to reach Benning since Tuesday afternoon and had left three messages with his assistant who said he was out of town. Betty thought that was odd considering Benning was supposed to have met with Kirk Stryker the afternoon of his death, according to Stryker's daily planner.

Dressed in a long overcoat, Benning bypassed what was left of the line and hurried over to Gloria Stryker who received him with, Betty thought, more energy than she had anyone else. Benning hugged Gloria and then shook hands with each of her three children. There seemed to be a familiarity between them that Betty found unexpected, and she wondered if perhaps she had misinterpreted Stryker's last email and whether he and Benning had somehow made amends. She turned to ask Eva Sansfield about the rapport between the two, but she was no longer sitting on the sofa. Betty scanned the room and found Eva by the guest book near the entrance, and, before Betty could get her attention, she disappeared out the front door.

Benning shook hands with Satriano, who had gotten up to greet him. Satriano seemed fidgety, aware that Betty was watching them. Several others also had wandered over to say hello, including a tall gentleman Betty recognized as a prominent cosmetic surgeon in town. Benning seemed friendly enough, Betty thought—he didn't appear nervous or agitated. He caught her eye for the briefest of moments, but showed neither concern nor interest or even recognition, and she wondered whether his assistant had given him any of her messages. She was reluctant to leave now that she had him in her sights, but a funeral home wasn't the place for a round of questioning, particularly with so many eyes around. She would have to take her chances and wait until morning.

Betty crossed the room toward the exit, passing a young couple who was signing the guest book.

"Who's that?" Betty heard the young woman ask.

"Who? Oh, that guy?" her companion answered. "That's Marty Benning. He owns that accounting practice. You know, the one in the old library."

"Oh," said the young woman. "That's right. He's that new awesome CPA in town."

Yes, Betty thought, stepping outside the funeral parlor, *and as of two days ago, he's the only one.*

13

Two months earlier

Bobby sat in his car watching a raccoon rummage through an overflowing garbage can. He hated the suburbs. He didn't know how people around here could stand the quiet. He was energized by the revved engines of the cars going by his apartment window in Queens, the honking of horns, the shouts of the hooligans gathering after dusk to drink beer on the corners. He tapped his fingers on the steering wheel and returned his eyes to the split-level house across the street.

On the passenger's seat next to him were the remains of a hastily ordered fast-food dinner, and Bobby poked around hoping to find a French fry or two. A light turned on in an upstairs-level room of the home, getting his attention, but it was off after a few moments, and Bobby settled back into his seat, grabbing his coffee cup from its holder. It amazed him that he could be only thirty minutes from home and find himself in a place like this, where raccoons ran free and the kids stayed inside.

Down the street, there was some movement, a figure in the darkness. A guy in a white T-shirt stepped under the glow of a streetlamp, trailed by his quick-legged puppy.

Bobby looked at his watch. Same time as last night. *It's like Groundhog Day,* he thought.

The sound of the footsteps grew louder, getting the attention of the raccoon who, disinterested, continued fumbling through the trash. Bobby crouched down in his seat, as the man came closer and passed him, as he had the night before, and the night before that, and Bobby listened to the fading muted rock music coming from the guy's earbuds. *Another typical day in Dullsville.* His phone vibrated, signaling a text, and he looked at the screen.

Anything?

Bobby typed.

Nope.

The phone pinged again:

All right, thanks. Have a good night.

Thank God, Bobby thought. He didn't know how many nights Benning was going to have him do this, but he hoped it wouldn't be many. He tossed his phone on the passenger's seat just as a sports car pulled up in front of the house across the street. The back door of the car opened and a young girl, dressed in a cheerleading outfit, got out and ran toward the house. She was giggling—a little too much, like she was trying to impress someone. The front door must have been open, because she got in quickly. The car drove away.

Bobby took out a small spiral notebook and made a notation of the license plate number with a pencil, but the point was so dull that it barely made a mark. It would be so much easier to have a tablet, he thought, since he could catch up on his cooking shows while he was sitting there like a lump on a log, but Benning liked to keep it old school, so he did the best he could.

The front door to the home opened again, and a woman came down the front steps carrying a large plastic bag. Bobby couldn't get a good look at her in the dark, but she was curvy with dark shoulder-length wavy hair. She disappeared around the side of the house, and Bobby got antsy, putting his hand on the door handle, but she reappeared dragging a garbage can, which she lifted onto the grassy area near the curb. She dusted off her hands, looking up and down the street, before returning inside and closing the front door. An entryway light was turned off.

Bobby noted the time in his notebook, which he put into his glove compartment, and started the engine. *I need a drink*, he thought, as he put the car into gear, turned the corner, and sped away from the home of Muriel Adams.

14

atriano walked into the fruit market. His father was wearing his red bow tie, a reminder that it was Friday. Ever since he was a little boy, Satriano could keep track of the days of the week by the color of his dad's neckwear.

"Hey, Pop!" he said as his father finished packing a grapefruit and a handful of oranges into a brown paper bag for a customer.

"There he is!" His father threw his hands in the air. The three customers in the market turned and smiled. Embarrassed, Satriano gave a quick wave. "My son, the assemblyman!" his father said, slapping Satriano on the back as he came behind the register.

"All right, all right, Pop. How's it going?"

"Going? You mean gone," he said, gesturing toward the store. "It's been a madhouse the last few days. We can't keep up."

Satriano looked around. The place had been cleaned out. He couldn't remember ever seeing the shelves so empty. "When's the next shipment?" he asked.

Satriano's father looked at his watch. "In about half an hour."

"Good, I'll stick around." Satriano rolled up his sleeves and grabbed a broom from the corner next to the register. "I've got some time before my first appointment."

"You hungry? I'll have Mommy fix you something."

"Nah, I ate."

"You sure? Here, have a banana," his father said, pulling one from the last bunch on the shelves.

Satriano knew it was no use to decline the offer. "Thank you, Pop," he said, taking it.

Satriano's mother came out from the back room with a boxful of plastic fruit bags. She hummed as she stopped to arrange what was left of the cantaloupes into a neat pyramid and to jiggle the basket of a nearby scale until the wand rested on zero. Not much had changed in the market over the years. The antiquated metal scales. The rolls of plastic, which drove his environmental constituents crazy. The sawdust on the floor in which he and Mary used to make tic-tac-toe boards with their fingers when the store was closed. That citrusy smell that followed him home every night, raising him to think that life would always smell as sweet.

"My baby!" she said when she spotted him. She ran over and squeezed his cheeks.

Satriano reached for the box of plastic bags in her hands. "I'll take this, Ma."

"Thank you, my boy." His mother frowned. "Why are you here?" She turned to Satriano's father. "Why is he here? What's wrong?"

"Nothing's wrong, Ma." Satriano placed the box on the floor behind the register. "My first appointment isn't for a while. Mary'll be at the office soon. Everything's fine."

"Anthony, I can tell something is wrong."

His father gave him a questioning look.

"I'm telling you both. Everything is fine," he said, sweeping some dirt behind the counter.

"Anthony, when you were a little boy, you used to come here when you wanted to hide," his mother said, raising her eyebrows. His father crossed his arms after handing a bag of groceries to a customer, who also looked at Satriano with concern.

"All right, enough, you two." Satriano put the broom back in its place. "Quit ganging up on me before I get the town supervisor to give you a summons for something."

"I think it was the memorial last night," his mother said to his father.

His father pursed his lips. "Could be."

"He does have a lot of pressure on him too," his mother added. "With the reelection coming up."

"I'm not listening!" Satriano said, walking toward the rear of the store. "If you need me, I'll be in the back room."

He ducked into the private space near the back entrance where all the deliveries were made. The table and chairs of his childhood stood in the same spot under what used to be a small television hanging from the ceiling but was now the flat-screen Satriano bought for his parents last Christmas. He opened the refrigerator on the counter, took out a bottle of water, and sat down on one of the folding chairs near the table, where he and his sister used to do their homework after school. It seemed like so long ago.

He picked up the *Gazette*, which was lying on the table; the entire issue was dedicated to the Stryker investigation—the cover image was a shot of the office building surrounded by police barricades with an inset photo of Kirk. Satriano skimmed the pages until he saw his press photo on page six. He read the caption: *Kirk Stryker was considered a fundamental player in Assemblyman Anthony Satriano's campaign for the state legislature. (Can Satriano make it without Stryker? Our own Monte Gardner weighs in on the junior assemblyman's political future and pending reelection bid on page 10.)*

Satriano sighed and closed the newspaper, turning his attention to the television, which was tuned to the local news station and broadcasting live from the front of Stryker's firm—only a half block away. He changed the channel with the remote control to one of the national morning talk shows instead, where a guest with bright orange hair was making bracelets out of toilet paper rolls.

Jesus, I really am hiding, he thought, taking a slug of water.

Detective Munson seemed to be watching him last night at the funeral parlor, particularly when he spoke to Marty Benning, who had come over to offer his condolences. Like most people, Benning associated Satriano and Stryker professionally, and the assumption was that the two were very close, although they were far from it. Before Stryker had become a major contributor to his campaign, they had traveled in different circles. Other than the occasional run-in in town, they rarely saw one another. He shoved the *Gazette* across the table. Those damn photographers seemed to follow him last night, documenting his every move, and Satriano could swear he saw someone sitting in a car down the block from his home that morning.

His mother came in with his banana, which he had left on the counter, and two Red Delicious apples. "For you, even though you're not hungry—and not hiding," she said, dropping them on the table and leaving the room.

Satriano rolled his eyes and reached for an apple. He rubbed it on his pant leg and took a bite, glancing at the TV, where the national morning talk show, too, had moved onto the Stryker investigation. It was big news. Satriano used the remote control to turn up the volume.

". . . Sources tell NBC that the police are talking to several persons of interest, but, as of yet, there are no suspects in the murder of Kirk Stryker . . ."

Murder.

Satriano still couldn't believe it. He tossed the apple core into the trashcan as his cell phone buzzed in his pocket. He looked at the screen. It was a text from Mary:

Detective Munson called. She told me to have you call her.

Satriano's heart thumped. He texted back.

What does she want?

His phone pinged.

Duh. I guess she wants to talk to you, dumbass.

"Anthony," his mother called, starling him.

"Yeah, Ma!" Satriano yelled. He put his cell phone back into his pocket.

"There's someone here to see you."

The skin prickled on the back of Satriano's neck. *How did anyone know he was there? Had the press seen him come in?* He peeked into the fruit market. At the front of the store stood a man in a baseball cap and sunglasses, a stocky fellow with a square chin and a serious look. Satriano didn't recognize him.

Suddenly, two bangs on the back door startled him again. *Jesus, he was surrounded.*

Two more knocks.

He picked up one of those doohickeys his dad used to get things from the top shelves of the store, the only weapon within reaching distance.

"Who is it?" he called, putting his ear onto the metal of the back door. "Hello?"

"Anthony, what are you doing?" his father asked, walking into the back room. He opened a cabinet drawer and slipped papers inside. "Your mother is calling you. A man is here to see you."

"I know. Who is it?"

His father shook his head. "I don't know. Why don't you go see?"

"But . . ."

"But what?" He came closer and peered into Satriano's eyes. "What is wrong with you? You look like you saw a ghost."

"Someone banged on the back door," Satriano said. He sounded like a little boy who thought there were monsters in his bedroom closet.

"What do you mean someone is banging on the back door? That's the deliveryman. He bangs every morning. You know that." His father pushed the heavy metal door open. "Hiya, Henry."

Henry walked in and dropped a crate of oranges on the floor, the twenty-something's well-honed muscles flexing beneath his long-sleeved T-shirt. "We got a lot of stuff today, Mr. Satriano. Hope you've got room."

"Oh, we've got room. Don't you worry."

"Terrific . . . Oh, hey, Tony," Henry said, before stepping back outside.

Satriano's father put on his eyeglasses. "Anthony, you don't look too good," he said, examining Satriano's face.

"I'm fine, I'm fine." Satriano picked up the crate of oranges from the floor. "I just need an aspirin or something," he said, walking toward the front of the store.

The market had become crowded. By the time Satriano placed the crate of oranges on the floor of the citrus section, half of the oranges were gone. He looked for the man in the baseball cap but he wasn't around. Near the front of the store, his mother was adjusting one of the signs for discounted fruit.

"Ma?" he called, walking toward her.

"Yes, dear," she said, smiling and making sure to point him out to a young woman in a business suit. She mouthed the words *He's an Assemblyman—and single.*

"Ma, who needed to see me?"

"Oh, it was . . ." She looked around. "Now where did he go? He was just here. Seemed like a nice fellow." His mother thought everyone seemed like a nice fellow. "Maybe he stepped outside?"

Satriano peeked out the front door. He was reluctant to go all the way out, lest one of those reporters down the block spotted him. Other than the lights of the television cameras on the north end, it seemed like a typical morning in Gardenia, although—he squinted his eyes—he thought he could see someone suspicious sitting in a parked car across the street in the municipal lot. Over the past few days, *everyone* seemed to look suspicious, and he wasn't sure why.

His mother planted a kiss on his cheek. "Don't worry,"

she said. "I guess the gentleman couldn't wait anymore, dear. He'll be back, I'm sure."

Satriano feigned a smile. "I'm sure you're right, Ma," he said as she walked back into the market. *That's what I'm afraid of.*

15

Roxanne pulled down the brim of her grandmother's old sunhat as she walked along Lake Shore Avenue toward the offices of Marty Benning. Her allergies were killing her from all the damn pollen from all the damn suburban trees, but she was determined to see for herself what a big deal this guy was. Across the street, the sidewalk was cordoned off with police tape, and a squad car sat in front of a building that had been ravaged by fire, and she recognized the scene from the news. Roxanne stood among the bystanders and after realizing there wasn't much to see, adjusted her sunglasses and pushed through the revolving door of the building marked *Marty Benning, Certified Public Accounting*.

The open-air office was swanky, filled with modern furnishings and gadgetry, which was deceiving for an office held in an old colonial-style brick building. It was bustling too, mostly with the very old and the very young, many of whom were holding paperwork and watching the news on one of several flat-screen televisions. Some were standing at kiosks that looked like ATMs and pushing buttons, and a video game console was set up in the corner where two teens were enjoying themselves.

For a waiting room, there wasn't one six-month-old, dog-eared magazine to be found.

"Hi, can I help you?" a young woman said, her smile wide and friendly.

"Yes, I'd like to see Marty Benning," Roxanne said.

"Is he expecting you?"

"Well, no . . . I just have some questions about a tax form."

"Well, Mr. Benning is in meetings all day, but I'm sure his associate, Tonya Hanson, can help you. Please take a seat."

"I'd prefer Marty."

"Oh, do you know Marty?"

"Yes," she lied, "we met last year at the Stratford luncheon."

"Oh," the receptionist said, her brows furrowed. "I see. Well, I'll let him know that you're here."

"Thank you," Roxanne said. The *Stratford luncheon*, her go-to lie, never failed.

She sat down on one of the plush velvet-covered metal chairs near the front of the practice. The large windows offered a view of the downtown area, a regular Small Town USA, and Roxanne imagined parades of red, white, and blue, and cotton candy.

How quaint, she thought, folding her arms. A small part of her still couldn't believe that Muriel left Queens and had been living out in Nassau County for more than seven years. Roxanne would die of boredom, or at least that's what she told herself, although she would love to be able to afford a house for Gordy; they were so cramped in the apartment. Every time Gordy asked to sleep over

Zack's "great big house," she wanted to lock herself in the bathroom and cry. She scratched under the dark brown wig, hoping her blonde hair wasn't showing, and took a tissue and the tax paperwork she had brought with her out of her purse.

Behind the receptionist, against the wall, two pairs of legs descended a spiral staircase—legs that, step by step, turned into two men who shook hands once they reached the bottom. Instantly, Roxanne identified Marty Benning, based not only on Muriel's brief description, but because he was quite a sight—in fact, seeing him was enough of an explanation as to why Muriel had been MIA.

A woman stepped in front of Roxanne's view. "Hi, can I help you? I'm Tonya Hanson."

"Oh, hi, Tonya, that's okay. I'm waiting for Marty Benning, but, actually, I think I might come back another day. I see he's busy."

"Oh?" Tonya said, confused.

"I forgot I had an appointment," Roxanne said, "and I really have to—"

"I got this, Tonya, thanks," Benning said, stepping in. Tonya smiled and retreated back to wherever it was she came from. "Hi, Ms. . . . ."

Roxanne smiled. "You mean, you don't remember me?" *He was even more handsome up close.*

Benning smiled. "Are you kidding? Even with those very large sunglasses, I'd know you anywhere. It's nice to see you again. Come on up to my office."

Ha, liar, Roxanne thought, following Benning up the spiral stairs.

Benning's office took up the entire second floor of

the building. More large glass windows revealed an even lovelier view of Lake Shore Avenue as well as of the police scene across the street. A massive black and oval desk was situated against the far wall across from a contemporary modular shelving system of books, all hardcover and rather boring-looking. Behind the desk, high on the wall, was a large deer head mounted atop a plaque of black onyx. Benning took a seat at his desk, just below the head, so that it looked as if it might eat him. He gestured for Roxanne to take one of the available chairs in front of him.

"So what can I do for you?" he asked.

"Great view," Roxanne said, sitting down.

"Yeah, it's okay. No midtown Manhattan, though."

"Did you know the guy across the street who got killed?"

"Yes, of course. Terrible tragedy. Did you know Kirk?"

"No. Never met him."

Benning studied her. "Where did we meet again?" he asked.

"Oh, at a Christmas party thingy last year."

"Stratford, you said?"

"I thought so, but, you know, I go to so many." She smiled.

"Well, what can I do for you?" Benning leaned back in his chair.

"I had a question about a tax form, and, you know, you said if I ever needed anything . . ."

"Yes, I do say that." He sat forward. "Can I see it?"

"See what?"

"The tax form you're holding in your hand."

"Oh." She handed it to him across the desk. "Sure."

Benning scanned it, looking confused. "It's blank."

"I know. I didn't want to fill anything out until I spoke with you."

"You know, you can do this online now, for the most part. There's something called the *Internet*." He smirked. "What exactly is your question?"

"Well"—she had practiced this—"I started an LLC last year."

"Congratulations."

"Thanks. But from what I understand, an LLC is treated like a partnership, as far as the IRS is concerned."

"That's correct."

"So I'm just not sure whether I should check the LLC box or Partnership box."

"Well, it would be the LLC box."

"That's what I thought. Silly me. Of course, it is." Roxanne stood up. "I told your receptionist this would be a quickie, so to speak. Well . . ." She adjusted her sunglasses. "I'm off to pick up my dry cleaning—I'll only go to the one here in town. Their pleats are one of a kind." She stuck out her hand. "Marty, always a pleasure. I'm sure you've got lots of appointments."

"Yeah." Benning stood and shook Roxanne's hand. "It's a busy time of year for us."

"Well, thank you. I'll see myself out," Roxanne said, before Benning could step out from behind his desk. "Errands, errands!"

Roxanne made her way to the spiral staircase, wiping her forehead with her tissue. The damn wig was making her scalp sweat. She waved again to Benning, who waved back, and as she looped around the staircase, the last thing she saw was Benning pick up his phone just before he, and that ridiculous deer head above him, disappeared completely.

16

Betty stared at the crime scene photographs spread across her bed, along with the pages of the preliminary coroner's report. She was in a foul mood. Benning had dodged her again. By the time she got to his office, he was gone for the day, or so she was told, and the receptionist cheerily agreed to give him Betty's message and to tell him it was urgent.

"You have to understand," the young woman said with a flip of her hair. "It's just such a busy time for him."

"Make sure you underline the words *homicide* and *investigation* on your little paper there," Betty had said through gritted teeth, "and also mention that if I don't hear from him very soon, next time I'll have a warrant for his arrest."

"Will do!" the young woman said with a smile.

That was ten hours ago.

She flipped through the coroner's report, which noted that the gunshot to Stryker's chest had caused his death and that he had not asphyxiated, despite the fire. A .38 special revolver was considered the official murder weapon, wherever it was. It certainly wasn't at the crime scene.

Betty picked up a photo of Stryker's bullet wound; the small hole just above his heart was barely noticeable amid the crusted blood stains. In fact, the photo of the fatal wound was the least compelling among all the images, particularly the ones showing the unusual marks across Stryker's abdomen. Those turned out to be, according to the coroner, welts caused by burns.

Betty fished around and picked up the photo of a short cigarette butt that had been found on the floor near the window of Stryker's office. The coroner detected small traces of Stryker's skin on the fringes of the ash side, which led him to believe it was the instrument used to create those burns.

She leaned back against her headboard. The report also noted that it was believed that the burns had been made *before* the time of death, which meant that Stryker had potentially suffered through each and every one— and, by the coroner's count, there were seven deep welts, or third-degree burns, as well as a few milder singes of the skin. What's more, the coroner suggested that as many as three hours had passed between the landing of the first cigarette burn and the last. *Three hours. Of enduring cigarette burns.*

The coroner claimed it was not out of the realm of possibility that some of the burn marks were self-inflicted. Betty thought about Detective Sergeant Williamson's suggestion of some sort of masochistic sex game. However, judging by the angle of the burns, it was likely that they had been inflicted by someone else. And, if that was true, it was believed that all of the marks, which were consistent in size and depth, were the work of one person, someone who was with Stryker in the hours leading up to his death and most likely the killer.

Betty heard the familiar roll of the wheelchair in the hallway. She quickly gathered the photos and stuck them in a manila folder.

"Hon, Jesse is asking for you," Sam said as he wheeled into the room. "I told him you were busy, but he wants you to wash his hair. He said, 'Mommy does it so much better than Daddy.'" He shrugged his shoulders.

Sam always felt slighted whenever the boys preferred that Betty do things for them. She didn't know why. The wheelchair hindered Sam in the bathroom, anyway— it was the one room in the house where he had trouble getting around, surrounded by unforgiving ceramic and hard edges. Betty put the folder on her nightstand and patted his shoulder. "It's no big deal, babe." She kissed his cheek. "And I could use the break."

The bathroom was filled with steam, and her son was making words on the tub wall with the foam letters she had bought for the boys when they were toddlers.

"Mommy!" Jesse exclaimed when Betty walked into the room.

"Hey, Peanut Butter." Betty unhinged the showerhead and wet Jesse's hair.

"Look, Mommy, I spelled *LUNCH*."

"I see that. That's terrific."

"I will spell your name next."

Betty looked around the water. "All you need is an *M*."

"No, Mommy, your real name. I want to spell your real name."

"Okay, let's look for a *B* . . ."

"I know how to spell it. Don't tell me." Jesse pushed her hand away. As he fished around the sudsy water for the rest of the letters, Betty reached for the shampoo, worked up a quick lather in Jesse's hair, and managed to rinse it all out by the time he had gotten to the Y.

"Ta-da!" he said, proudly.

"Very nice," she said, standing him up and then rinsing all the suds from his little body.

"Told you I could do it," Jesse said. He stepped out of the tub and onto the bath mat.

"You're a smartie, you know that." Betty toweled him off and helped him climb into his footed pajamas, which seemed a little too snug. Hadn't she bought him new pajamas just a few months ago? "Is it too tight?"

"No, it's fine, Mommy," Jesse said and skipped out of the bathroom before she could even comb his hair.

If only I had the same energy, she thought, draining the tub and giving the room a quick tidy-up. She padded back to her bedroom where Scott was sitting on her bed. He had the manila folder open on his lap.

"Scott, no!" she yelled.

Her ten-year-old jumped at the sound of his mother's voice and stood up. She could see he was about to cry.

"Hon, what happened?!" Sam yelled from the living room. "Is everything all right?"

"I'm sorry, Mom," Scott whispered, tears welling in his eyes.

"Everything's fine, Sam!" Betty called. She came around to the other side of the bed and closed the folder.

"Scottie, you know better than to look at Mommy's work." Scott buried his head into her shoulder. "I didn't mean to scare you, but there are things in there you shouldn't see."

"I didn't know what it was. I was waiting for you to finish with Jesse so you can see my math test." Betty noticed the wrinkled paper in Scott's hands.

"Let me see." She held out her hand. "Scott, a hundred, that's wonderful!"

Scott began to cry on Betty's shoulder.

"Oh, Scott." She rubbed his head. "It's okay. You didn't know. Everybody makes mistakes." She pulled him away so she could look at him. "Do you want to talk about what you saw in that folder?"

Sniffling, Scott shook his head.

"Did you see papers?" she asked. He may have only been a fourth grader, but he would have known a lot of the words on the coroner's report, and none of them were good.

"No," he said, shaking his head again. "I saw a picture."

Oh, Jesus, the photos. "How many did you see?" she asked, rubbing his head.

"The one on top."

"Just one?" She relaxed, but only a little. "Was it scary?"

Scott shook his head again.

"Are you sure?"

He nodded.

"What did you see in that picture?" She braced herself.

He rubbed his tears away with his knuckles and mumbled something she didn't understand.

"Did you say 'Ryan'?" she asked. "You saw Ryan?"

"No, Orion, the constellation."

"Orion?" Betty asked. "You mean, you saw stars?"

"Uh-huh."

Betty ran her hand through Scott's hair. "How did . . . I mean, how can you . . ."

"We're studying constellations in school. Getting ready for the trip next week," he explained. "Orion's one of my favorites, because I love belts."

"Belts?" Betty cringed again. She thought of the image of Stryker's pants down below his groin, his belt buckle hanging off the side of the exam table. "Did you see a belt?"

"Yes, well, kind of."

Betty picked up the crime scene folder and ran her fingers along its edges. Scott put his hands over his eyes. "I won't look this time," he said.

She opened the folder. The photo at the top of the stack was one of the left side of Stryker's abdomen. The image was zoomed in so close that it was difficult to see exactly what it was, thank God—the burn marks appeared only as black dots on a semi-white background. She looked down the hallway to see if Sam or Jesse were there, pulled out the photo, and held it up to her son.

"Is this the photo you saw?" she asked.

"You mean, open my eyes?"

"Yes."

Scott removed his hands and looked at the photo. "Yes," he said.

Betty looked at it again. "Where do you see Ryan?"

"O-rion, Mommy," he said.

"Orion," Betty repeated.

"Can I hold it?"

Betty checked the hallway once again and handed the photo to Scott, who turned it clockwise, his tongue sticking out of the corner of his mouth as it always did when he was concentrating, and then counterclockwise.

"Here," he said, placing the picture at a forty-five degree angle on the bedspread. "Here are the three stars. See? That's the belt, right there. It's called Orion's Belt. And here are the four stars that make up the body." He looked up at her. "Is that what it is, Mommy? Orion? Am I right?"

Betty stared at the image. "I don't know, honey," she said. "Maybe." She handed him back his math test. "Why don't you run off to bed, and I'll come in and read you a story."

"Can we read about the stars?" Scott said. "We always read the books Jesse likes."

"Sure, tonight's your night, kiddo. With a test grade like that, you'll get to pick for two nights in a row."

"Awesome!" Scott said, and although he was still sniffling, he ran out the bedroom door with a smile.

Betty picked up the photo and held it at the same angle that Scott did. She walked over to the small bookshelf in the corner of her bedroom where two dusty rows of outdated encyclopedias were shelved—a wedding gift from Sam's parents twelve years before, probably the last sale of encyclopedias ever made. Betty had nearly thrown them out several times, but found something about them reassuring, as a chef might find a batch of old cookbooks. She pulled out the volume labeled *O* and thumbed through the pages until she reached the entry for Orion:

Orion, often referred to as The Hunter, is one of the most beautiful of all constellations and one of the easiest to find. Resembling a large rectangle high in winter's south-southeastern sky, Orion features two of the evening sky's brightest stars lying at opposite corners of the rectangle—bright red Betelgeuse and Rigel. Near the center, there is a short diagonal line of three stars, which is known as Orion's Belt. Extending south from the belt is another, fainter line of stars that form Orion's Sword.

Flanking the definition was a diagram of the constellation, and Betty held up the crime scene photo next to it. Large rectangle. Three-starred belt. Betty looked closely. There was even a faint cigarette burn where the tip of Orion's sword was supposed to be.

Scott was right—it was a perfect match.

The Hunter, Betty thought, placing the encyclopedia on the bed. She didn't think it was possible, but this investigation had taken a turn for the worse.

17

John Parker burst through the front door carrying a stack of *Gardenia Gazettes*.

"Hello, Johnny," his mother said. She was crocheting in the living room while watching television. "Did you have a good day at work?"

"A good day? Ma, look!" He dropped the stack of newspapers and his backpack on the top of the sofa and showed her the front page.

"Dear, you're going to get newsprint on the sofa."

"Forget the sofa, Ma. Look!" He pointed to his byline on the cover.

"Wow," she said, holding the paper in her hands. "That's very nice, dear." She put it on the coffee table. "Did you have dinner? Would you like me to make you something?"

"Yeah, I had a slice."

"Are you sure?"

"Yeah, yeah ... But can you believe it? My name is on the front page!"

For the past twenty-four hours, his cell phone and Facebook page had been buzzing with congratulations. If Gardner hadn't made him wait a day before taking a bunch of issues home—the old guy was hoping the edition would sell out—he would have spent the day putting newspapers on the windshields of all the cars in the municipal lot at the railroad station.

"Is Dad home?" Parker couldn't wait to show his byline to his father, who hadn't been too happy about Parker having to move back home—even less happy than Parker had been about it.

"He's asleep, dear, but I promise to show it to him first thing in the morning." She smiled absently.

"Great, thank you. I might miss him, because"—he puffed up his chest—"I have to get to the office early again." He pointed to the front page of the newspaper. "Remember, it's right here. Top left."

"Yes, yes, I know," his mother said, putting her knitting down and turning off the television. "I left your clean laundry on the chair near your desk."

"Thanks, Mom!" Parker grabbed his backpack and the rest of the newspapers and took the stairs by twos.

He put the stack on his bedroom desk, brought one to his bed, and lay down with it held over his head. J-O-H-N P-A-R-K-E-R. There it was. For all to see. *Who knows,* he thought, fifty years from now, historians might look back on Long Island during these early years of the twenty-first century and find *his* story and remember *his* name—that intrepid young reporter who went on to do great things. Of course, beside Parker's byline was Kramer's, but he covered that with his thumb and took a photo to post on Instagram.

He reached for the remote control on his nightstand and flipped on the television, which warmed to show Scooby-Doo and Shaggy on the Cartoon Network. He switched the channel to the local news station, which was still reporting that the Nassau County police were talking with persons of interest regarding the Stryker investigation—nothing new there. Still no word, though, on whom those persons actually were. Stryker was well-known and well-connected, so it could be anyone.

He set the newspaper down on his nightstand and rummaged through his backpack until he found his notebook and digital camera. He started flipping through all the photos that he'd taken over the past few days, jotting down the names of faces he recognized or, if he didn't, their descriptions. As he went along, he realized there were a few folks who popped up numerous times, mostly police officers and a few detectives, who were recognizable by their long trench coats—how ironic that the coats were worn to conceal the detectives' firearms but always gave them away as detectives.

Parker noticed an older lady detective, probably midfifties, who had been to the crime scene quite a bit. He looked at his list; he had six photos of her from Lake Shore Avenue. Red hair. Kinda frizzy. Something about her sparked a memory, and he flipped back through a bunch of photos until he got to the batch taken at Stryker's funeral.

"There," he said to himself, looking at the same woman entering the funeral parlor. *Who was she?* The department had refused to divulge the names of any specific officers or detectives working the Stryker case—all press inquiries had to be funneled through the department spokesperson—but something told him that she was one of the detectives spearheading the investigation. Why else would she be there? He had to find out for sure.

Parker looked at the time on his nightstand alarm clock. It was almost ten thirty.

If he was ever going to get out from under the arm of Gardner or the shadow of Kramer, or have a name worth remembering by future generations, he was going to have to be proactive. He picked up his cell phone. The line rang three times before someone answered.

"Fourteenth precinct," said a young female voice.

"Hi, my name is John Parker. I was told this was the number to reach the detective in charge of the Stryker investigation."

"Are you with the press?"

Parker sat up in bed and played with the shutter of his camera. He wasn't sure if he should lie, if he could get into any trouble for misidentifying himself.

"If you are a member of the press," she said, "you'll need to be routed to the main line."

"No, no, you don't understand," Parker said, pausing to think. "I spoke with her yesterday morning, and she said I should contact her directly, but I lost her card. I actually feel kind of silly and embarrassed."

"Um . . ."

"Actually, this is one of the first cases I've ever worked, and I'm thinking that the detective kind of felt sorry for me and wanted to help me out a little. She was *so* nice."

"Well, our detectives have been told not to speak to the press."

"I realize that. And I don't think she was going to tell me anything, and I certainly don't want to get anyone in trouble." Parker looked again at the picture. "Especially her. She actually looks a lot like my grandmother, who also has red hair." He paused, but there was silence on the other end of the line. "I was just asking her about some basic police procedures—I was embarrassed to ask this guy I work with, because he thinks he knows everything."

The woman laughed.

Keep going, Parker. "And she offered to help me, which was really nice, because she didn't have to do that."

"Listen, I just—"

"She actually said I reminded her a little bit of her son," he said, taking a chance. "Between you and me, I think that's the reason she ever gave me the time of day in the first place."

Although the young woman didn't speak, Parker could hear voices in the background, so clearly, she hadn't hung up yet.

"Do you think there's any way you can put me in touch with her?" he asked finally.

"I'm sorry," the woman said, "but I'm afraid I can't give that information out."

"Oh, I see," Parker said, lying back down and kicking the pillow off his bed. "Well, it was worth a try."

"I'll tell you what, if you give me your name and phone number, I'll be sure Detective Munson gets it."

Parker bolted upright. "Oh, that would be so great." He gave the woman his name and cell phone number. "Thank you so much," he said and clicked off the call.

His heart was beating so fast that he got up from his bed and walked around his small bedroom, stopping to look at himself in the mirror over his dresser.

Detective Munson, Parker thought, watching his reflection smile. *Bingo.*

18

Practically every encyclopedia she owned was open on the floor, circling Betty like a giant whirlpool. And after hours of research, she felt like she had landed in the middle of one.

The International Astronomical Union recognized eighty-eight constellations covering the entire northern and southern sky. She had managed to check out every one of them, but none seemed to match the array of marks on Stryker's abdomen other than Orion.

What am I doing, she wondered, the sounds of Sam's snoring floating above her. She readjusted her legs, which had become stiff, and looked at the clock. It was nearly 3:00 a.m. She had to be up in three hours to get the boys to school.

She threw all the paperwork and photos into her folder and decided to leave the encyclopedias where they were for now. She got onto all fours, feeling the tension in her back, crawled on her hands and knees over to her bed, and rolled herself under the covers, placing the folder under her pillow—safe from Scott's prying eyes. She turned off the light on her night table, and, as she did, her detective's mind turned on: *Why would someone burn a constellation into*

Kirk Stryker, a Gardenia CPA, a philanthropic fellow who, by most accounts, was good-natured and friendly?

It didn't make any sense, and Betty was starting to feel foolish, having embarked on a flight of fancy egged on by a ten-year-old's imagination. She thought again of the constellation nickname: The Hunter. *Was there a connection?*

Betty reached across her nightstand and turned on the lamp.

"Again?" Sam groaned.

"Just for a minute, Sam." She sat up. "Go back to sleep."

"What time is it?"

"Too early. Go back to sleep."

She pulled the crime scene folder out from under her pillow and rummaged through the photos until she got to one that the photographer had taken at Stryker's window, the place where it was believed the fire had begun. It was a canted shot that caught the edges of the window as well as the view outside on Lake Shore Avenue. Across the street was the old library, the building Benning had refurbished for his accounting firm. She looked at the old stone façade and peered closely at the tall windows, the streetlights illuminating most of the second floor. A large shadow loomed high, and Betty brought the photograph closer to her eyes until the commanding antlers came into focus. A mounted deer head. Above his desk.

She leaned back onto her pillow once again.

Marty Benning, Betty thought, her pulse quickening. *The Hunter.*

19

"Hey, Bobby, want to play?"

A baseball came flying at Bobby's head as he walked down his stoop carrying a trash bag. He caught the ball with his free hand.

"Not today, Frankie," he said, putting the trash in the can and tossing the baseball back. "Don't you have school today?"

"It's Saturday," the boy called.

"Already?"

"You say that every Saturday," Frankie said, throwing the ball back. "Come on. Let's play."

"And what else do I say every Saturday?" Bobby threw the ball.

"That you have to work."

"That's right."

"C'mon, Bobby . . ." Frankie began drawing a chalk outline of home plate on the asphalt. "Call in sick. Don't be a pussy."

"Hey, watch your mouth, little man," Bobby said, zipping up his jacket. "I'll catch you later this afternoon."

Bobby strode down Sixtieth Place toward Metropolitan Avenue. The drone of a furniture delivery truck hummed down a side street, and a soft breeze kicked up an empty beer can, which rolled over the sewer grate. It did his heart good to see children come out of every nook and cranny of the two-family homes lining the street—unlike the ghost towns of suburbia. When he hit Metropolitan Avenue, he spotted the city bus on the corner as it was pulling away from the bus stop and into traffic. The driver looked at him.

"Hey, Ken!" Bobby waved.

Ken opened his tiny driver's side window. "Walking today, Bob?"

"Yeah, stretch my legs."

"All right, then. Have a good one," Ken said and drove off.

Bobby bought a cup of black coffee at Dunkin Donuts and walked west, passing his alma mater, Grover Cleveland High School, which he could see just beyond the new construction. It had been years since he had been caught smoking cigarettes in the schoolyard and feeling up Melissa Carpenelli after home economics. *I wonder whatever happened to her,* he thought. Most of the kids he had hung out with back then hadn't fared very well over the years— early pregnancies, drug addictions, misdemeanors, ugly divorces. Bobby very likely would have ended up among the casualties of the graduating class of 1987 if it hadn't been for Marty Benning.

After a few minutes, a small graffitied sign signaled the beginning of the decaying landscape of Brooklyn's North Industrial Business Zone. Bobby read somewhere that Oscar Wilde had once said, "There is no country in the world where machinery is so lovely as in America," and he thought of that quote every time he walked past the old brick factories, small shops, and fenced-in yards of this main thoroughfare. He stomped onto each metal cellar door he came upon, as if a child, listening for the change in his footsteps, and ran his fingers along the dirty glass of the storefronts. Although it wasn't much to look at, there was something homey about the place, with its crumbling walls and haphazard design, as if Bobby could imagine throngs of immigrants working the factories in the early twentieth century. He bent down to pick up a penny, stuck between two cement slabs, and put it into his pocket.

As he continued west, the New York City skyline rose in the distance, a view that always filled him with pride. Not many people could see the Empire State Building from their neighborhood. There was something comforting about growing up so close to one of the world's most recognizable monuments, as if it were a rail post at the end of a large backyard, or a watchdog forever on guard.

The subway station ahead was filling with a few Saturday commuters, and Bobby turned left and headed south, passing a few folks wearing backpacks and carrying briefcases. A flat row of industrial exteriors came into view, each building distinguished only by a different-colored brick face. Bobby walked until he got to a dull yellow building centered by a bright-purple door—inset just enough to keep it secret unless someone was looking for it. He opened it and went inside.

The cavernous warehouse echoed with loud squeals and squeaks, as a pack of men banged into one another on the flat circuit track.

"Hey, Bobby Flaygrant!"

Boyd Blue Balls skated over and slapped him on the back. "Skate Spade's been asking for you."

In the corner of the room, three women were taking off their helmets as the female roller derby team made its way off the track so that the local men's team could get in a quick practice before the afternoon bout. Skate Spade, who was looking extra sweaty today, her tight curly hair sticking outside her helmet, glared at Bobby as she untied her skates.

"Yeah, well, that ship has sailed," Bobby said. "Is King Cool here?"

He always felt a bit silly saying the nicknames out loud, but he didn't know the real name of Cool or any other of his teammates. So it went with roller derby.

"Not yet. You staying?"

"Nah, I can't today. I wanted to let Cool know. I gotta work."

"Awww, c'mon, that's the third bout you've missed this season. We need our best blocker."

"I know, and I'm sorry, but I've been working more hours these past few months." Bobby said. "You know the deal. Just can't say no to work these days."

"Yeah, I hear ya," Boyd said. "Can you squeeze in a quick practice, though? We're playing Hartford this afternoon."

"Sorry, mate. Don't have my skates today."

"I got an extra pair in my bag." Boyd pointed to the other side of the room where a bunch of the guys were sitting on a bench lacing up.

"Like I would put on your stink-ass skates." He pushed Boyd in the arm. "Balls, when Cool comes in, tell him I can't make the bout and to give me a call, would you?"

"You got it," Boyd said, skating backward onto the track. "Last chance. You know you want to."

"Sorry, mate, some of us have to work for a living."

"You'll be out of here in twenty minutes. Thirty max."

Bobby sighed and looked at his watch. "Okay, you're on."

He went to the back of the warehouse, where the guys greeted him with a rousing string of fist bumps, and pulled Boyd's skates out of a bag lying on the floor. He headed to his locker at the end of the long line of green metal lockers that had been set up for derby season and that, in the off-season, made their home in King Cool's basement.

Bobby spun the combination lock, opened the narrow door, and fished out his elbow and knee guards. From a high shelf, he pulled down his helmet, spilling a bunch of loose papers onto the concrete floor.

"Whoa . . ." Jam Janson opened the locker next to Bobby's and stuck a briefcase inside. "You got a lot of shit in there."

"You're telling me." Bobby bent down to pick up the paperwork. "Nice tie."

"Thanks, a birthday present from the wife." Jam removed his paisley tie and started unbuttoning his white shirt. "Haven't seen you in ages. Where ya been?"

"Been busy," Bobby said, shoving the papers back onto the locker shelf.

"Hey, you missed one," Jam said. He picked up a crumbled piece of paper from the floor. "Geez, you're like my daughter. You've got names and phone numbers scribbled everywhere. And you call that handwriting?"

"Thinking about getting an iPad," Bobby said, taking the paper from him.

"Best thing you'll ever buy. Give me a call, I'll hook you up."

"I'll do that," Bobby said. He looked down at the small piece of lined paper where Benning had written the name *Kirk* along with Stryker's license plate and cell phone number. Bobby folded it in half, stuck it back on the shelf, and slammed his locker door closed.

20

One month earlier

Muriel turned over in bed and faced Marty, who lay sleeping next to her, so that the tips of their noses nearly touched. He looked peaceful, which is how she felt. After months of wrestling with the whys and ifs of what they were doing, she had finally decided that she was tired of wrestling with the whys and ifs and would just admit it to herself: She had fallen for this guy who was probably no good for her.

Since December, she had been gliding through her days, feeling more alive than she had in years—making school lunches and kissing boo-boos with a flourish, administering state tests with nary a complaint, and ignoring the rolled eyes of Ellie and the sourpuss patients at the cosmetic surgery office. She was even smiling at Stowe.

The kids seemed to accept Marty—even Ellie, which was shocking. Zack considered him a playmate, dragging him here and there, and Marty always seemed to acquiesce, despite his insistence that *he didn't do kids*. Muriel smiled as she remembered the first time Zack crept into her bed and slipped under her arm in the middle of the night, unaware that Marty was sleeping behind her. Marty had whispered into her ear, "Is it always this crowded?" and playfully squeezed her side.

She thought of Doug and winced. She didn't know if the kids had said anything to him. Doug hadn't mentioned Marty, so neither had she. She looked at Marty's face, at the lines on his forehead which were as asleep as he was. Muriel told Ellie that she and Marty were "dating" back in January and that she liked him, but she never let on how much.

The morning sun passed behind a cloud, dimming the bedroom glow for an instant. She loved waking up here.

"What are you thinking about?" Marty asked, putting his arm around her. His eyes were sleepy and small.

"Fake relationships," Muriel said with a smile.

Marty pulled away. "I'm sorry?"

"Don't pull away, dopey." Muriel laughed. "My daughter. She was upset yesterday because a group of girls had decided that they were going to create something called Fake Relationship Week. Mind you, she didn't tell me this at first. I heard her telling Doug on the phone— God forbid she confides in *me*—but then I asked her about it. Apparently, five of them were going to pick a boy—Ellie said the more *revolting*, her word, the better—and pretend to date them for the week."

Marty rubbed his eyes. "Do the boys know?"

"She wasn't sure. She didn't even want to play. She was just upset that nobody had asked her to."

"Ah, to be a teenage girl," he said, replacing his arm around her. "What did you tell her?"

"I told her that I know what it feels like to be left out, and that it hurts. And that what those girls were doing was wrong. To be used like that. It reminded me of those college fraternity pranks where guys are asked to bring an ugly girl to a party, and the guy who brings the ugliest girl wins. Or those pig parties, where the guy who brings the fattest girl wins. It's gross."

Marty shifted under the blankets.

"It's tough to be thirteen years old," she continued. "I thought going through it myself was hard, but I think it's even harder watching your own daughter do it."

"I did that," Marty blurted.

"Did what?"

"Went to a party with an ugly girl in order to win a contest. In college." He looked at her and shrugged. "Long time ago. Does that bother you?"

Muriel thought for a moment, waiting for those feelings of disgust to emerge—the ones that seemed so at the ready last year whenever Marty walked into a room—but they didn't. "I don't know," she said. "I guess it should."

"It was one of those things. I didn't even think much about it at the time. Stowe was there."

"Of course, he was," Muriel said, wrinkling her nose. "Did you win? The contest?"

Marty nodded.

"Geez, did you win *every* contest?" she asked. "What happened to the girl?"

"I don't know. I never saw her again after that night. Or maybe I did, but didn't notice." He pushed the blanket down, revealing his muscular legs. "So you're not pissed? Where's the Muriel Adams who would have no qualms about ripping me a new one?"

Muriel shrugged her shoulders. "I don't know where

she is," she said. "Do you miss her?" She rumpled his hair. "You know, *that* Muriel?"

"Something tells me she'll be back."

She snuggled against her pillow. "What's the weather going to be like today?" she asked. "Maybe we could actually venture outside."

"Are you saying you don't like staying in bed all day?" He pinched her cheek before reaching for the television remote. He clicked on the set.

"What show is this?" Muriel asked, leaning her head on Marty's chest.

It looked like one of those home-building programs. A contractor with a Boston accent was stomping around an old Victorian and appeared to have found some love letters slipped under the floorboards. The camera zoomed in on the brittle, yellowed edges of the handwritten notes in his hand.

"Isn't that nice?" Marty nudged her. "C'mon, aren't you supposed to be some kind of romantic?"

The letters, the contractor said, had been written in the early nineteen hundreds, judging by the date in the right-hand corner, by an estranged lover who had been working as a shoemaker's apprentice in hopes of one day earning enough money to marry the object of his affection.

"I can't imagine ever finding something like that in *my* house," Muriel said. "The only thing we found when we moved in were old copies of *Playboy* magazine hidden in one of the upstairs bedrooms."

"*Playboy*? Now, we're talking," Marty said with a laugh, and Muriel poked him in the stomach. "Actually, you just reminded me. I have something for you."

"You do?" Muriel sat up. "What is it?"

"A surprise." He reached down under the bed and pulled out a small package wrapped in white tissue paper. She took it.

"Can I open it now?" she asked, her voice sounding like a little girl's.

"Sure."

She tore open the wrapping paper and uncovered a small box filled with even more tissue paper. She dug underneath and saw the blue feathers first, and then the beading. She reached in and picked up the object so that it dangled from her index finger.

"A dream catcher," she said.

"What a man has to do to keep children out of his bed," Marty said, pulling Muriel onto him and kissing her on the mouth. "It was either get a dream catcher or a deadbolt."

Muriel laughed and ran her finger along the cleft in Marty's chin. "I love it, and so will Zack," she said, resting her head again on Marty's chest. "Thank you." She lifted her hand in the air and swung the dream catcher like a pendulum. On the television screen, the Boston contractor's lips were mouthing the heartfelt words belonging to a long-ago lover, but Muriel could only hear the beating of Marty Benning's heart.

21

The doorman was signing for a package when Betty walked into the apartment building. When he was done, he gave her a cursory smile and asked, "Can I help you?"

"Marty Benning, please," she said.

"Is Mr. Benning expecting you?"

"No."

The doorman looked her up and down. "Who should I say is calling for him?"

"Detective Betty Munson, Nassau County PD." She showed him her badge.

The doorman smirked. "PD?"

"Yes, you know, police department," Betty said. She wasn't in the mood. She was missing Jesse's Saturday morning soccer game and had to schlep all the way into the city, all because Benning had been dodging her.

The doorman inspected it. "That's a pretty real-looking badge," he said.

"Thanks," Betty said. "That's because it's pretty real."

"Whatever you say, sweetie," the doorman snickered. "I'll bet the handcuffs you've got in your pocket are real too."

"They are," Betty said.

"Right." He leaned on the desk. "You know, you're a bit older than the usual."

"The usual what?" Betty asked when a couple came through the lobby, and the doorman ran to hold the door open for them. "Have a nice day, Mr. and Mrs. Wilson," he said with a smile before returning to his place behind the counter and picking up a phone. "Hold on a minute," he said.

Betty stepped into the small lobby, which resembled a contemporary-styled living room with leather couches, glass tables, limestone walls, and travertine floors. The doorman was dressed in business casual, a Navy blue blazer paired with a khaki pant. Betty somehow expected his uniform to consist of a red suit with gold trim, like something out of an old Hollywood movie.

The doorman hung up the phone. "Mr. Benning said you can go right up. Eleventh floor, 1102." He smiled and took his package into a back room.

On the eleventh floor, the elevator doors opened to reveal Marty Benning standing a few yards down a long, narrow hallway, leaning against an apartment doorframe with his arms crossed. He was barefoot and wearing a flannel shirt over a white tee and jeans.

The Hunter, Betty thought as she approached.

At forty-eight years of age, he had a youthful face with graying temples, a dimpled chin, and what Betty was sure was a practiced twinkle of the eye. He was muscular and athletic-looking, but not too thin, and he looked wet, as if he had just come out of the shower.

"Betty Munson, Nassau County police department,"

Benning said, shaking Betty's hand. "You're a long way from your jurisdiction, Detective?"

"I appreciate you seeing me without any notice, Mr. Benning."

"Call me Marty," Benning said. "Come in."

The apartment was far more furnished than Betty had expected for a man living alone. It seemed that Marty Benning had very good taste. The living room was dressed with a shabby chic vibe, which provided contrast to the wood strip floors and iron table lamps, coffee table, and other decorative accessories. It reminded Betty of a spread out of a home design magazine.

"Mr. Benning, this won't take long," she said. "I'm assuming you know why I'm here."

"The Kirk Stryker investigation?"

"Yes."

"I was wondering if I'd made the *persons of interest* list." Benning picked up a towel that was on the kitchen counter and threw it into the bathroom. "Do you often make house calls?"

There was a flippancy to Benning's demeanor that Betty found irritating, although somewhat expected, considering his playboy reputation. "I do when the person I'm trying to reach doesn't return my calls."

"I'm sorry, have you tried to reach me, Detective Munson?"

Betty nearly laughed. "Yes, several times. Your receptionist said she would give you the message and that . . . Oh, let me see, that you were out of town, and then you were out of the office, and then you were in and out, so very busy."

"They always say that," Benning said. "Sorry about that. I'm sure she didn't realize the severity of the situation."

"I would think showing my badge and mentioning a homicide investigation would show the severity enough," Betty said.

"Not always." Benning opened the refrigerator. "Would you like a drink, Detective?"

"No, thank you." The refrigerator was filled with several six-packs of soft drinks, beer, water, a stack of lunch meats, several bags of broccoli crowns, and a variety of yogurts. Benning noticed her eyeing the shelves and shrugged. "I like to eat in," he said.

"May I ask what you mean by *not always*?"

"I'm sorry?"

"You said that showing my badge and mentioning a murder might not get your staff's attention."

"Oh." Benning opened a bottle of iced tea and took a long sip. "I have a circle of jokester friends," he said, "always sending all kinds of freaks into the practice—women dressed as French maids, police officers, singing telegrams, that kind of thing. It's been going on for months. I think Veronica—she's my receptionist—has become immune to anyone strange coming in and asking for me. She basically just tells them I'm out of the office and that she'll take a message." He leaned against the kitchen counter. "Sorry about that."

"So that also explains why your doorman downstairs had trouble believing I was a real police officer?"

"Probably," Benning said with a smirk. "Would you like to sit down?"

"No, thank you, Mr. Benning, if I may—"

"I would assume you're here because you're questioning everyone who knew Kirk Stryker or worked on or around Lake Shore. Actually," he said, moving to the dining room table and taking a seat, "I wasn't anywhere near the office that evening. I think the girls closed up around six o'clock. I'm afraid I couldn't be of much help. I couldn't tell you anything about anyone who was around Lake Shore Avenue that night."

"This must be your busy season," Betty said. "I'm surprised you didn't have late hours."

"We do. I mean, we have. My Manhattan office is open late nights. I tried doing late nights last year in both locations, but it was a bit too crazy. Now, I work Saturday mornings out East and have the Manhattan office closed on the weekends."

"So you were in Manhattan the night of the murder?"

Benning was quiet. "I didn't say that," he said finally.

"You didn't have an appointment with Kirk Stryker around 3:30 in the afternoon after his death?" Betty asked.

"An appointment?" He sounded surprised. "Where did you hear that?"

"Please just answer the question, Mr. Benning."

"No, I didn't have an appointment." The levity had disappeared from his voice. "Why would you think that I did?"

"I'm afraid I can't comment on that, Mr. Benning." She took another step into the apartment, but when Benning pulled out a chair for her at the dining room table, she declined. "So you've known Stryker how long?"

"A couple of years, I guess. After I opened the shop in Gardenia, I met him at one of the merchants association meetings. Or maybe it was a chamber of commerce meeting, I don't remember." He took another sip of his iced tea. "I became president of the merchants association last year, and he's on the board."

"You're also on the board of the ASPCA here in the city, aren't you?"

"Yes," Benning said. "And of the New York State Society of CPAs. I'm also on the co-op board here in the building."

"Busy guy."

"I have a library card too." He smiled.

Betty ignored the remark. "What was your impression of him? Of Stryker?"

Benning shrugged. "Well, he was pissed at me for opening the practice there. That was for sure. He was the only big fish in a small pond, and I think he liked it that way."

"I guess you can't blame him. What made you decide to open the second location there?"

"I looked in a few places and found the old library building suitable for what I was looking for. I have colleagues in the area, and I wanted a two-story building this time—with Manhattan rents I could only get a small space. Plus, I think I liked the idea of setting up shop in a building with a little history, as opposed to a strip mall."

"But there was already an established accounting practice across the street. I'm not sure that makes a whole lot of business sense."

"Detective, walk downstairs, and within the span of one block, you'll see two banks, several delis, and three fast-food restaurants. In Manhattan, I compete with several

CPA firms within a three-block radius. Maybe I have a city mentality, but a little competition doesn't bother me."

"Fair enough," Betty said. "Speaking of your Manhattan location, wasn't there another CPA firm on that same block not too long ago?"

Benning put the bottle down on the table. "You've been doing some research. Yes, there was."

"What happened to them?"

"Why don't *you* tell *me*?" Benning said, the playfulness returning to his voice.

"It closed down about six months ago. It looks like one of the firm's partners had a heart attack after having lunch at the Greek restaurant down the street."

"Yeah, Jim. I knew him. Nice guy. It was a shame."

"Records show that he was doing quite well before his . . . sudden death."

"Surely, you're not pinning that one on me, Detective," Benning said with a laugh. "High cholesterol is high cholesterol."

"No one is accusing you of anything, Mr. Benning. What I mean is, on a business level, his death was a boon for you."

"We did get some runoff, sure, but that doesn't mean that his death wasn't a tragedy and that I wasn't sad to see the guy go. We were friendly. He was in excellent shape— or at least it seemed he was. Young guy, midforties. No family. No kids." Benning shook his head. "It hit a little too close to home. Jim Crosby was the life and soul of that business. The fact that the company couldn't be sustained without him is not all that surprising."

"Kirk Stryker was the life and soul of *his* business."

"That's debatable," Benning said.

"Really? That's not what I hear." Betty recalled what Eva had told her in the funeral parlor.

"Listen," Benning said. "I don't want to badmouth the poor guy. He's gone. What I'm saying is that I wouldn't be too sure that the accounting practice will die with him. He had some pretty good people."

"Like Paulette Krause."

"For sure."

His tone was even—unaffected and natural, as if rehearsed. "Is it true you tried to lure Ms. Krause to your practice?" Betty asked.

"Where did you hear that?"

Betty crossed her arms.

Benning smiled. "I'm always on the lookout for good people. That's not a crime."

"So you're thinking Ms. Krause might just take over where Stryker left off?"

"Why not? She's certainly capable, and, let's face it, she's out of a job."

"Well, this would be the perfect opportunity to snatch her up then."

Benning shook his head. "Paulette's not interested in working for me. Trust me. I've tried. She's too power hungry. She likes being number one. My guess is Paulette will take care of Kirk's clients in the next two weeks and then start up her own firm."

"How do you feel about that, Mr. Benning?"

"I told you. I don't mind competition. Bring it on." Smooth as silk.

"Ms. Krause won't manage to keep everyone. Where else

will clients go but to the only other accounting firm in town? Your office seemed to be quite busy when I was there."

Benning stood up and put his bottle in a recycling bin. "You know, this is beginning to sound a bit like an interrogation, rather than an interview. Should I be getting a lawyer?"

"Just asking questions, Mr. Benning."

"Of course, I got spillover. It's a week before the tax deadline. People are panicking."

"Tell me about Gloria Stryker," Betty asked, pivoting.

"What about her?"

"You seemed friendly at the funeral."

"Of course, we are. We've been to quite a few events together in Gardenia—charity benefits. Gloria tended to find herself alone at those things, always making an excuse for Kirk who was off doing who knows what. If you ask me, she was a very unhappy woman."

"Really? Most people would say that they had a strong marriage."

"Most people don't look closely enough," Benning said, running his fingers through his wet hair. "They also tend to spread gossip about things they know very little about."

"Speaking of gossip . . ." Betty took a step forward, closing the distance between them. "Rumor has it that you're considering a run for the assemblyman spot."

Benning laughed. "You see what I mean? That's an old rumor, Detective. I haven't even established residency in the district yet."

"You don't need to, Mr. Benning. I think we both know that. As long as you're a registered voter in the state that suffices."

"I think we also both know that I won't have a chance in hell of winning the support of a district where I don't live."

"People seem to like you, Mr. Benning. Enough for Kirk Stryker not to."

"So if he didn't like me, why—if the information you have is correct—would he want to meet with me?"

"Who knows? Maybe to call a truce? Maybe to pool your resources? Maybe to have it out? Perhaps he found out you were wooing his people?"

"Person."

"OK, person then. Or that you were considering a run against his boy Satriano?"

"Which is a total rumor."

"So you say."

"So let me get this straight," Benning said, crossing his arms. "Are you saying that because I'm supposedly considering a run for the assemblyman spot in Gardenia, and because a competing Manhattan CPA died of a heart attack while having lunch, and because I had a conversation with one of Stryker's employees that I shot Kirk Stryker and torched his office?"

"Where were you on the night of April first?"

"Unbelievable," Benning said, shaking his head. "Who told you I had a meeting with Kirk Stryker?"

"As I said before, I can't answer that. But I'd like you to tell me where you were the night of April first. I'd be happy to discuss it back in Nassau County if you don't want to tell me here and now."

She watched him carefully, expecting him to appear angry or riled, but instead he seemed somewhat vulnerable and—as he sat back down on the dining room chair—somewhat defeated.

"I have a feeling you know I was on Long Island. What was it? My E-ZPass?"

"Why don't you worry less about what you think I know and just tell me the truth," Betty said. "Makes things easier."

Benning hesitated. For the first time during the interview, he looked uncomfortable. "I was with a lady friend."

"A lady friend." Betty took out her notepad. "Can she corroborate that?"

"Does she have to?"

"I'm afraid she does."

"May I ask why you're asking? Does everyone who knew Kirk Stryker have to have an alibi for the night of April first?"

"Is that what your lady friend is, Mr. Benning? An alibi?"

Benning let out a laugh. "You're good. Nassau County PD, huh? You should have your own show." Betty could see he was getting a little unhinged.

"Can I have your lady friend's name?"

Benning hesitated again.

"Mr. Benning, I—"

"It's Muriel Adams," he said.

"Muriel Adams." Betty wrote down the name. "Can you provide me with her address?"

"Twelve fifty-two Pittsburgh in . . . Massapequa Park."

"Is there a problem?" Betty asked.

Benning shook his head. "It's just . . . Silly, I guess.

But you're the first person I've spoken her name to. Well, actually the second."

"How long have you known Muriel Adams?"

"I don't know, maybe a year or so, but we've only been . . . well, for about three months."

"All right, Mr. Benning, thank you. I'll be in touch if I need anything else."

Betty started toward the apartment door, but stopped when she saw a telescope sitting on a tripod in the corner of the living room, its narrow eyepiece peeking out from behind the drapes near one of the windows.

"I never would have taken you for a Peeping Tom, Mr. Benning," she said, motioning toward the telescope.

"That's funny," Benning said. "Most people would."

"Do you mind?" Betty asked.

"Be my guest."

Betty brushed the curtains aside, bent down, and looked through the eyepiece. From the telescope's position, all she could see was blue sky where she was sure, at night, an eyeful of muted constellations would have greeted her.

"Know anything about stars?" Benning asked.

"I've recently been brushing up on my astronomy," she said, standing up. "I can't imagine you see a lot of constellations from here with all the city lights."

"You'd be surprised what you can find if you know where to look," Benning said.

"I imagine so." She glanced at the floor-to-ceiling bookshelf with rows of hardcover texts—accounting, marketing, business law. Nothing unusual, such as astronomy. Or body mutilation. The only book that seemed out of place was the Bible.

"You have quite a selection here," she said.

"Not really," Benning said with a shrug. "What can I say? I'm a boring guy. Overworked and underwhelmed."

"No hobbies?"

"No, I guess, no official ones."

"Not even hunting?" Betty asked, watching his response.

"Hunting?" Benning said with surprise. "What makes you say that?"

"I don't know. Why else would a guy have a large deer head hanging in his office?"

"Oh, that old thing?" Benning shook his head. "It's . . . well, it's sort of a private joke. It was my father's."

"It's a strange keepsake for someone who doesn't hunt."

"Yeah, I guess you're right. I keep it . . . well, for a lot of reasons. But mostly as a reminder."

"Of what?" Betty asked, taking the bait.

Benning smirked. "Not to lose my head."

Betty put her notepad in her pocket and handed her card to Benning. "Well, here's my card. Thank you again for your time, Mr. Benning."

He took it and walked Betty to the apartment door, which he opened. "It's Marty," he said, leaning on the doorframe and assuming the pose he had when she had first arrived.

The doors to the elevator opened as soon as Betty pushed the button, and she stepped inside. She and Benning stared at one another as they waited for the doors to close.

"Feel free to contact me if anything should come to you," Betty called.

Benning held up her card. "I will. I've got nothing to hide," he said, and as the elevator doors clicked and began to close, added, "not many CPAs can say that."

22

Bobby stood outside Benning's apartment building. His arms were sore. He should have never stayed for derby practice. Bad decision. His body didn't recover the way it used to. Across the street, Detective Betty Munson was returning to her car, which had been parked by a fire hydrant. She pulled into traffic just as his phone rang.

"Yeah," he said. "She's gone. Got in her car and drove off. But believe it or not, we've got more company. I'll get back to you."

Bobby put his phone away and watched some guy in his early twenties run back to his car after seeing Munson take off. Bobby had noticed him right away—the kid wasn't that adept at staying out of sight. He had obviously been following the detective and had been pacing within a small doorway while she and Benning were talking, snapping about fifteen photos with his digital camera of the outside of Benning's building.

An SUV double-parked in front of the kid's car, and he couldn't get out. He was banging his fists on the hood like a lunatic. Bobby crossed the street.

"What's the problem, kid?" he asked, stepping onto the curb.

"What do you fucking think? I can't move my fucking car."

"Calm the fuck down," Bobby said, putting his hands up in front of him.

The kid caught himself. "Sorry, man. It's just that I'm running late." He looked toward the end of the street, where the traffic light had turned green and Munson's car turned right and out of sight. "Whose car is this, do you know?"

"Have no idea," Bobby said. "But it ain't gonna do much good to bang on it."

The kid opened his car door, reached inside, and pressed on his car horn, and a blaring sound ricocheted along the narrow street.

"What are you doing?" Bobby asked. "Do you want to get a ticket? There's a noise limit around here."

"There is?" the kid said, taking his hand off the horn. "That's hilarious. I can barely hear myself think." He kicked his tire. "Great. I'm stuck here."

"C'mon, it can't be that bad," Bobby said. "Listen"— he pointed to the pub two storefronts down—"why don't you join me for a drink? I was just heading in. It'll calm you down. And maybe after a few minutes whoever this car belongs to will be out here. He'll move it, and you'll be on your way."

"I don't know . . ." The kid shrugged.

"Name's Bobby," Bobby said, sticking out his hand.

"Parker. John Parker," the kid said, shaking Bobby's hand.

"C'mon, Parker, John Parker, the first round's on me."

Parker looked again down the block and then checked his phone and threw up his hands. "Why the fuck not," he said.

Mickey's Pub already had a few patrons, who were watching the local news. Bobby waved a quick hello at Skip, the bartender, before he and Parker sat at the bar.

"I see you're a regular," Parker said. "You always drink this early?"

"Only on weekdays," Bobby said. "On weekends, I start at ten o'clock."

"Nice." Parker put his phone into his pocket. "My senior year in college, I had a few regular haunts myself. Fell asleep on a barstool one night. Not my finest hour."

"Where did you go to school?"

"New Paltz. Graduated last year."

"Well, congratulations. What are you drinking? It'll be a graduation gift." Bobby waved Skip over.

"You don't have to do that," Parker said.

"Why not? You earned it."

"All right, I guess. Thanks. I'll have a Guinness."

"Two Guinnesses, please, Skip." Bobby grabbed a handful of pretzels and dropped them into his mouth.

"I take it you live around here, Bobby?" Parker asked, as the bartender put two bottles of beer in front of them.

"Not too far. You?"

"Long Island." Parker took a swig of his drink.

"So you work here in the city?"

"I guess you can say that. Working on a story."

"Oh, you're a reporter?" Bobby asked. The kid seemed a little wet behind the ears to be a journalist. *"New York Times?"*

"I wish." Parker downed more of his beer.

"For what paper then?"

Parker swallowed. "Trust me, you've never heard of it."

"Try me."

"*Gardenia Gazette*."

"Oh, sure, I know that one." Bobby smiled and shook his head. "Not really."

"I didn't think so."

"So what interest does the *Gardenia Gazette* have with the Upper West Side of Manhattan?"

"That's a good question," Parker said.

"Investigating a story?"

"Chasing my tail, I think." Parker chugged the rest of his beer as Bobby looked on with admiration. Gone were the days when he could throw back sixteen ounces of suds within seconds and still remain standing. There was nothing that reminded you that you were no longer twenty-two years old more than being with an actual twenty-two-year-old. He waved to the bartender. "Skip, another one, please, for me and my friend."

"Wait, I don't know. I should get going." Parker looked outside the pub window where the SUV was still blocking him. "Where's a cop when you need one? Can these guys just double-park like that?"

"No, but they do it anyway," Bobby said. He was hoping the guy whose car it was would be delayed further. He wanted to get a little bit more out of Parker, John Parker. He pushed the second beer toward the kid's seat.

"All right," Parker said, sitting back down. "Only one more, but this one's on me."

✹

"And, from what I hear, that guy Stryker had burn marks

all over him," Parker said, downing the last of his fourth beer. He put the empty bottle on its side and started rolling it with his fingers.

The kid had been spilling his guts since he finished his second beer—not only about the Kirk Stryker investigation, which was apparently why he was tailing the Gardenia detective, but about cheating on his SATs, some offshore bank account his father had, and an affair he had during spring break last year with someone in his mother's knitting circle. All that aside, the kid still didn't know that Detective Munson had come into Manhattan to see Marty Benning.

"So you just decided to follow this cop into the city?"

"Yep." Parker took out his notepad. "One thirty-seven West End Avenue, Manhattan. *What's at one thirty-seven West End Avenue?* Who the fuck knows? First, she went into some building in Midtown, some office building. Look,"—he showed Bobby his notes—"I jotted down all the names of the businesses on the doorbell. And then she came here. For all I know, it's where her goddamn sister lives, or her shrink, and I'm on some kind of wild-goose chase." He looked at his watch. "Christ, I have to go."

Parker stood up, holding onto the bar to steady himself.

"Whoa there, big guy. I don't think you're in any shape to drive. Maybe you should sleep it off."

"No, I'm fine. Really." Parker swayed on his feet, and Bobby threw his arm over his shoulder and walked him outside, both of them shielding their eyes from the bright sunshine.

The double-parked car was gone, and Parker was resting his head on Bobby's shoulder.

"Where are your keys, man?" Bobby asked.

Parker dug into his pockets and dropped them on the sidewalk. Bobby leaned him against a traffic sign, picked them up, and opened the back door to Parker's car.

"You should just lie down for a few minutes and rest," Bobby said, helping Parker slide across the backseat.

"Good idea. I just need to put my head down for a few minutes."

Bobby slid behind the steering wheel in the front seat. From the rearview mirror, he could see that Parker had his eyes closed, his head tilted back against the seat's headrest.

Bobby started the car and glanced again in the rearview mirror—no movement from John Parker, who looked dead to the world. Again, the kid had Bobby's admiration. If only Bobby could fall asleep that quickly.

Bobby threw the car into gear and drove into traffic. By the time he got to the Queensborough Bridge, he could no longer see Parker in the mirror. A quick turn of the head showed that the guy had passed out and was lying in a fetal position across the backseat. Bobby took the lower level of the bridge and drove along Queens Boulevard until he reached the Queens Center Mall and turned off into a parking lot. He slid the car into a space between two SUVs, took the keys out of the ignition, and reached back and stuck them into the kid's pocket. He pulled out Parker's notebook and ripped out the pages where he had scribbled the address of Benning's office building and residence. He crumpled them and stuck them into his own pocket, returning the notebook into Parker's jacket. Next, he took out Parker's digital camera, deleted all the images taken in Manhattan, and put it back where he found it. Then Bobby got out of the car, flicked the button to lock all the car doors, and eased the driver's side door shut.

"Thanks for the ride, kid," Bobby said before hurrying across Queens Boulevard, where a bus was picking up a line of passengers. He got on the back of the line, boarded, and then settled into a front seat, heading home.

23

The home of Muriel Adams was located on a pretty suburban block that smacked of middle class. Most of the modest homes were split-levels and ranches—several of which had been extended way too high for their tiny plot and looked like they were about to tip over.

Betty drove past the rows of neatly manicured lawns and around some helmet-less boys on bicycles who were watching utility workers mark up the street with chalk. She pulled in front of 1252 Pittsburgh Avenue.

The split-level was in need of some basic repairs—the paint on the upstairs awnings was cracking, the slats in the wooden fencing sagged, and a few bricks had come loose from the main walkway. A garbage can had fallen over, its duct-taped lid stuck behind the back wheels of the minivan parked in the driveway. The home reminded Betty a bit of her own; since the boys were born, she and Sam never seemed to have enough time for the upkeep—or to buy pajamas that actually fit.

Betty had been to this neighborhood and others like it on the south shore of Long Island many times in the months following 9/11. She would hazard a guess that as many as half the residents were either police officers or firefighters, professional or volunteer. Just a few blocks north, she drove past three streets that had been named for fallen first responders, and so many front yards were waving American flags it looked like a parade. She took out her notepad and skimmed the front page: According to her research, Douglas Adams, Muriel Adams's husband, served as a volunteer EMT, or so said his tax returns. Betty hadn't found that nearly as surprising as discovering that Muriel Adams *had* a husband.

And, apparently, a boyfriend.

Aside from that bit of news, Muriel Adams had come up with no record other than an unpaid parking ticket.

The boys who had been ogling the utility worker began tossing a baseball in the middle of the street. They watched her as she got out of the car and headed up Muriel Adams's walkway.

The storm door to the home was closed, but the front door was open, and Betty could see through the wire mesh a woman standing by the sink emptying the dishwasher. She was wearing a pair of jeans and a black sweater. She had a slim, but curvy figure, and there was a cheeriness to her demeanor. Betty rang the bell, and the woman turned toward the front door. Muriel Adams was pretty, that was for sure, but from what Betty had researched, about twenty years older than Benning's type.

"Muriel Adams?" Betty called.

The woman closed the dishwasher and headed in Betty's direction but was interrupted by a little boy who came shooting down a flight of stairs.

"Is it for me?" the boy asked excitedly, running toward the door. He stopped once he saw Betty.

"No, no, Zackie, come back. It's not for you. It's for Mommy," the woman said.

"Oh," the boy said sadly. "Is it another package from the ESP guy?"

"That's UPS, and, no, I don't think so."

"Okay, I'm packing my bag," Zack said. "Daddy's going to be so happy. I'm bringing my Frisbee."

The little boy returned up the stairs, and as Muriel Adams approached, Betty could see soft wrinkles around her eyes and mouth, which gave her face a kind appearance. "Hi, can I help you?" she said.

"Mrs. Adams?"

The woman nodded.

"My name is Detective Betty Munson. I'm with the Nassau County police department. I'm investigating the murder of Kirk Stryker."

The word *murder* seemed to cause Muriel to flinch. "In Gardenia?" she asked. "The CPA? I don't understand."

"I'd like to ask you a few questions about Marty Benning."

"Who is it, Mom?" A teenage girl came up behind Muriel and peered at the detective.

"Ellie, go inside, honey. I have it."

The girl crammed herself in the small space between Muriel and the wall. "Did she say Marty Benning?" she asked.

"Ellie, please, do me a favor and watch Zack before Daddy gets here. I'm going to step outside for a moment."

Betty detected a hint of tension between mother and

daughter, but the girl nodded as Muriel closed the front and storm doors and she and Betty walked down the porch steps.

"I'm sorry, Detective, it's just that we'll have more privacy out here. I hope you don't mind." Muriel looked at her bay window, where the curtains moved and her daughter's head popped through, watching them.

"That's fine. I understand," Betty said.

"What can I help you with? What about Marty?"

Betty looked at her notepad for no reason. "Well, I have a few questions. May I ask how you know Marty Benning?"

"Well, we're . . . um . . ." Already, the first question seemed to put her off-balance. "I guess we're . . ."

"Dating?" Betty offered.

"Yes, I guess so."

"For how long?"

"About three months. Why do you need to know this?"

"Mrs. Adams, I need to know if Marty Benning was with you on the evening of April first at around eleven p.m."

"April first? May I ask why?"

"Please, ma'am, it's very important that you remember."

"That's the night of the fire? The murder?" Muriel pulled her sweater down over the top of her jeans. "Do you think he knows something about this or is involved with this? That can't be."

"Why is that?"

"Well, because . . . he . . . I don't . . ." Muriel sat down on the top step of her stoop. "Let me think a minute . . . April first, that was last Monday. April Fool's Day . . . Yes, we had dinner that night, here, and he . . . he . . ."

"He . . . ?" Betty asked.

"Slept over, I guess." Muriel's cheeks reddened. "I'm sorry, this dating thing is so new to me. I feel a bit shaken up talking about it." She looked again toward the bay window. "I haven't really told anyone about Marty and me except a friend of mine and my kids, and they don't know much."

Muriel's behavior brought to mind Benning's when Betty had asked him about Muriel. For two people who had been dating for three months, or so they said, they seemed somewhat startled by the fact that they were dating at all. "Was anyone else in the house?"

"On April first? Yes, everyone. Well, no. Not that night. My kids went to their father's after dinner."

"Mr. Adams doesn't live here?"

Muriel shook her head. "No, he doesn't."

"This home is listed as his permanent address," Betty said.

"I know. Trust me, I've been trying to get him to change it for over a year, but he won't. He has an apartment . . . Well, he's staying in the basement apartment of a friend not far from here."

"So you're . . ."

"Separated, yes."

"I see," Betty said. "May I ask how you met?"

"My husband?"

"No, Mr. Benning."

"Sure," Muriel nodded. "I met him at work."

"Do you work at his CPA firm?" Betty already knew that Muriel was a third-grade teacher at Satmore Elementary School in North Massapequa.

"No, I work at a cosmetic surgery office part-time up in Gardenia, and he's friends with one of the owners."

"You work there off the books?"

Muriel hesitated.

"Mrs. Adams, I'm not looking to report you to anyone. It's just that that income is not listed on your tax return."

"You were looking at my tax return?"

"Mrs. Adams—"

"Yes, I've worked there part-time—off the books—for a few years," Muriel blurted.

"I see," Betty said. Her sense was that if Muriel Adams was feeling guilty about working off the books, she would probably tell the truth about whatever she knew about Marty Benning. "Getting back to April first, when did you and Benning arrive here, after dinner?"

"Maybe around six o'clock."

"So Mr. Benning was with you all night that night?"

Muriel brought her fingers to her lips and looked off toward the boys on the bicycles. Betty could tell she was thinking, which wasn't a good sign.

"Mrs. Adams?"

"I'm sorry. Yes, he was with me, Detective."

"At eleven p.m.?"

She paused again, but then said, "Yes, he was with me."

"Okay then," Betty said. "Well, if you think of anything else, please contact me." Betty handed Muriel her card and began walking down the path.

"Wait!" Muriel called and met her before she reached the sidewalk. "Listen, I know he was with me, but . . . I mean, I was sleeping. I fell asleep at seven o'clock, and he was right next to me. I woke up sometime in the morning, maybe around three o'clock or so—I didn't look at the clock—and he was right there. *Right there.* That means that he was next to me all night, doesn't it?"

"Then why do you look so doubtful?" Betty asked.

"I'm not. I mean..." She fumbled for words. "Detective, are you married?"

Betty's thumb instinctively rubbed her wedding band on her ring finger. "Yes, I am."

"If someone were to ask you if you were with your husband last night at midnight, and you were next to him when you fell asleep and also when you woke up, wouldn't you say yes?"

Betty was struck by how Muriel Adams was defending Benning, someone whom, by her own admission, she hadn't known for all that long and didn't seem comfortable telling many people about. She was also surprised that, after their chat that morning, Benning hadn't contacted Muriel to warn her that Betty might be coming around and asking questions. Or maybe he had.

"I guess I would," Betty said. "Did Benning ever mention the murder to you?"

"Yes, of course. It happened right across the street from his office. He said he was going to the funeral. He said he knew him, but not all that well."

"Did he mention anything about a meeting with Kirk Stryker the day of the murder?"

"A meeting?" Muriel shook her head. "He didn't. And we've spent a lot of time together. Practically every weekend, except last weekend."

"Oh?"

"I had a family party to go to with the kids. Marty said he had to go out of town anyway. A business trip."

"Do you remember where it was?"

"The trip? Yes, it was in New Jersey."

"Are you sure?" Betty asked.

"Yes. Newark. Why?"

Betty flipped a few pages back in her notepad. "According to Mr. Benning's EZ-Pass statement, he was on Long Island last Sunday—went through the Midtown Tunnel at around 10:30 a.m. and then back through around four in the afternoon."

"On March thirty-first?" Muriel asked. "But that can't be right."

Betty suddenly felt sorry for Muriel Adams, as if she had told a child that Santa Claus wasn't real. She seemed like a very nice woman, kind and smart, different from what Betty had expected, but at the same time she fit the stereotype of what could only be described as a patsy— someone in a vulnerable place in her life for whatever reason, bad marriage or money troubles, someone who could easily be taken advantage of by someone with despicable motivations, particularly when he had a cute little cleft in his chin. What was it Benning had said that morning? *Overworked and underwhelmed?*

"You have my card, Mrs. Adams. If you can think of anything that might help the investigation, please contact me."

Muriel nodded and placed the card into the pocket of her jeans. "I will."

As Betty returned to her car, she watched Muriel retreat to her home. That cheeriness from earlier had dissipated.

Muriel Adams straightened the black metal numerals of her street address outside her front door and slipped inside without turning back, but as the door closed behind her the numerals fell crookedly again.

24

"What did she want, Mom?" Ellie asked as soon as Muriel shut the door. Her daughter was holding the house phone to her ear. "What about Marty? Is he in trouble?"

"Never mind, Ellie. The detective just wanted to ask me some questions."

Ellie spoke into the phone she was cradling with her shoulder. "She said that the detective just wanted to ask her some questions . . . Uh huh . . . Okay." She held out the phone to Muriel.

"Who is it?" Muriel asked.

"It's Daddy. He wants to talk to you."

"You called Daddy?"

Ellie didn't answer. She handed Muriel the phone and ran upstairs.

"Ellie, I'm talking to you!" Muriel yelled when she heard Ellie's bedroom door slam. A few months back, Roxanne had suggested that Muriel remove the hinges from Ellie's bedroom door. A couple more slams, and Muriel was going to fish the screwdriver out of the junk drawer. She put the phone to her ear. "Doug . . . I can't talk, I have to get ready . . . Doug, listen to me, it's nothing . . . Just a few questions . . . Doug . . . I'm not listening, la la la . . . I'm hanging up . . . I mean it . . . See you in a little while . . . Good-bye."

Muriel clicked off the phone and tossed it onto the couch as Zack came running down the stairs, his suitcase bouncing behind him. "Did you finish packing for Daddy's?"

"I'm almost all done. How many nights are we staying?"

"Just tonight. I'll be home tomorrow."

"Are you going by Marty's house?"

Muriel nodded.

"What if he murders you?"

"What?" Muriel said. "Why would you say such a thing?"

"That's what Ellie said, that he's going to light our house on fire and murder you."

Muriel's cheeks became hot. She took a breath and ran her hand over Zack's hair. "That's not true, sweetie. You met Marty. He's a nice man, isn't he?" As she said the words, Muriel thought of Detective Munson. She was sure the police were questioning the whereabouts of a lot of people on April First, not just Marty. But that bit about Marty being on Long Island last weekend? Muriel was sure he had told her that he was going to Jersey.

Zack nodded. "He bought me a dream catcher!"

"That's right. He did." She bent down so that she could look into Zack's eyes. "You know that Mommy would never do anything to hurt our family."

"I know."

"And since when do you listen to Ellie anyway? Who's the smartest one in this house?"

"You are, Mommy."

Muriel smiled.

"Especially now that Daddy doesn't live here anymore."

"Gee, thanks," Muriel said, hugging him a little tighter. "Now go finish packing."

"Okay." Zack ran toward his bedroom, and Muriel charged up the stars behind him. She stopped at Ellie's closed bedroom door and knocked. She tried the doorknob; it wouldn't turn.

"Ellie, open this door right now."

Muriel waited what was probably only a few seconds but seemed like an eternity until she heard a soft click, and the door opened.

"Why did you call Daddy?" Muriel asked.

"I can't call my own father?" Ellie said, with sarcasm. She was wearing her hair different lately. Gone were the ponytails and barrettes. Instead, she was letting her hair fall to her shoulders straight, parting her hair on the side and sweeping her long bangs across her forehead, which made her look older.

"You can call him whenever you want, but why now? And watch your tone with me, young lady."

Ellie shrugged. She crossed her arms and sat on her bed, running her hand along the frill of the comforter.

"What's going on with you lately?" Muriel asked, sitting on her bed. She and Ellie had been so close before she and Doug separated. She reached for her hand.

"What's going on with *you* lately?" Ellie said, pulling away.

"What's *that* supposed to mean?"

"Nothing," Ellie said.

Her daughter's phone, which was between them on

the bed, beeped, and the screen lit up. It was a text from someone named Michael.

"Who's that?" Muriel asked.

"Nobody." Ellie pulled the phone toward her.

"It said Michael. Who is he? Someone in your class?" The kids rarely lied to her—at least they hadn't until now—and she had learned the best way to get information from them was to ask direct, pointed questions.

"Not really."

"Can I see the phone, please?" Muriel asked. She held out her hand.

"Mom, it's personal."

"I hate to pull rank here, El, but please give me the phone."

Ellie pouted but handed it over. Muriel entered Ellie's passcode, which didn't take. "Did you change the code? You know the rules, El. I need to know all phone codes and passwords for social media." She read what she could see of the text:

Loved seeing you last night.

"Last night?" Muriel said. "I thought you said you were with Cathy."

Ellie stared at the floor.

"I'm going to ask one more time, El. Who is Michael?"

"It's Ellie's boyfriend," Zack yelled from the next room.

"Shut up, *idiot*!" Ellie screamed.

"Boyfriend?" Muriel asked.

"He's just someone I know, Mom."

"Did you see him last night?"

Ellie was quiet again.

"El?"

"Yes, but Cathy was there too. I didn't lie."

"Is he your boyfriend?"

Ellie shrugged her shoulders. "I don't know," she finally said.

"What do you mean you don't know?" A wave of panic swept over Muriel. She hadn't really discussed what that meant, having a boyfriend, with Ellie. She was only thirteen. Muriel thought she had time. Plus, she wasn't even sure she knew what having a boyfriend meant herself anymore. "I mean, do you like him? Do you hold hands? Have you kissed—?"

"Mom . . ."

"Ellie, we agreed that there would be no boyfriends until you're sixteen."

"That's three years from now, Mom . . ."

Muriel leaned back on Ellie's pale purple wall. It had only been a year and a half since the two of them spent the day redecorating her bedroom, giggling and dabbing each other with paintbrushes. "I wish you would have come to me about this."

"When?" Ellie said, with a roll of her eyes. "You're never here."

"Eleanor Adams, that is not true, and you know it." Muriel stood up. The comment both hurt and infuriated her. "No boyfriends, El. That's the rule."

"Why not?" She crossed her arms. "*You* have one."

"Keep it up, El. We'll finish talking about this tomorrow. Daddy will be here soon, and you have to get ready." Muriel slipped the phone into her pocket.

"What are you doing with my phone?"

"You won't need this tonight. You'll be with Daddy.

Michael Whoever-He-Is can wait until tomorrow. And I'll need the new passcode too, by the way. Now, finish packing."

"That's not fair," Ellie said and buried her head into her pillow.

Muriel wanted to bend down and wrap her daughter in a tight hug, but she was too mad—or maybe she was tired of the rejection. Instead, she headed into her bedroom to grab her overnight bag when Ellie's door slammed again. Muriel dropped the bag onto the floor and marched downstairs, making a beeline for the junk drawer.

25

Bobby held the door open for an elderly gentleman with a walker before heading inside the assisted living facility.

"Hello, Mr. Chaucer," Roger said from behind the counter. "All dressed up today, aren't we?"

"Yep," Bobby said, pulling down on his suit jacket. He hated when Benning told him to wear a suit. To Bobby, it was like wearing a suit of armor. The last time he had worn it was for his mother's funeral eight years earlier, and it still smelled like a combination of formaldehyde and fresh flowers.

Roger buzzed Bobby through the automatic door that led to the facility's west corridor. Many of the residents were having dinner inside the cafeteria and were being helped along the buffet line by staff members. Bobby turned the corner, past the small theater, which was dark and empty, toward room 352.

"Hey, buddy," the old man said when Bobby entered. He was sitting in his wheelchair, with his usual plate of food in front of him—a bowl of oatmeal, a plastic container of applesauce, and a small cup of room-temperature tea. The old man slapped him on the back. "Good to see you."

"How are you doing today, Mr. Chaucer?" asked the nurse on duty who was fluffing up the pillows on the bed. "Don't you look handsome?"

Bobby felt his cheeks burn with embarrassment. The nurse motioned toward the old man. "Today was a good day," she mouthed. She winked and left the room.

Bobby took a seat near the wheelchair and checked his phone to see if Benning had texted him, but there were no new messages. "So, Dad, what did you do today?"

"What?" the old man asked, his happy face now a snarl. "Are you a comedian? What the fuck do you think I did?"

The mood changes seemed to be getting worse and worse as the dementia progressed. "I'm just asking," Bobby said. "Never mind. It doesn't matter."

"Damn right, it doesn't matter," his father said. He reached for the plastic spoon on his tray, poked at the applesauce, and glanced up at the television monitor, which was showing a Major League Baseball game. He clucked his tongue.

"Goddamn Yankees," he'd murmured and taken another sip of his applesauce when his face broke out into a smile again. "Hey, buddy, did I ever tell you about the time I was the starting pitcher in the game against Forest Hills High School?"

"A million times," Bobby said with a sigh.

"I batted clean-up that game. Coach said he'd never seen a ball get hit so far into the parking lot until I hit that home run. I was quite the baseball player back then."

"Right." Bobby checked his watch. He told Benning he'd be in Manhattan by seven o'clock, so that gave him about an hour or so before he had to leave.

"What's the rush?" his father said. "Got a train to catch?"

"No rush, I'm just checking the time."

"So, go, no one's keeping you here."

"I don't want to go. Why, do you want me to go?"

"No skin off my ass," the old man said, his eyes returning to the game.

The words stung, as they always did. Bobby sat back and unbuttoned his double-breasted suit jacket.

"You know what you need?" The old man scraped his spoon against the bottom of his oatmeal bowl.

"What's that?" Bobby asked.

"A woman. To keep you limber." He threw his spoon into the bowl and pushed away his tray. "In my day, I had plenty a women all over me, I'll tell ya. You got a girl?"

Bobby shook his head.

"No?" the old man said incredulously. "Why not?"

"Just unlucky, I guess."

"Take it from me. You need someone to come home to. Someone to take care of ya. You know, cook, clean, fuck. You gotta keep 'em in line, though. They say they don't like it rough, but, trust me, they do. They know they need it."

"Yeah," Bobby said. "I remember."

His father looked at him. "What the fuck does that mean? *You remember?*"

An image of his mother holding a cold compress to her bleeding forehead came to Bobby's mind, but he pushed it away. He was sure his father no longer remembered, so he figured why should he. "Never mind," he said.

"No, I fucking mind.

"It doesn't matter anymore, Dad."

"Stop calling me Dad. I'm not your dad."

"No?" Bobby asked. He could feel the pressure building in his temples. "You're not my dad? Who are you then?"

"Get the fuck out of here, you little shit." The old man slapped at the bowl of oatmeal, which fell onto the floor. "Goddammit, look what you made me do."

"Calm down. It's not a big deal, Dad." Bobby picked up the bowl, but he made the mistake of getting too close to his father's wheelchair and was rewarded for it with a swift punch in his right eye.

"Fuck," Bobby said, reeling backward.

"C'mere, you son of a bitch," his father screamed, pushing on the arms of his wheelchair to stand. "I'll kill you."

"Dad, sit down, you're going to hurt yourself."

Two attendants ran into the room as his father fell onto the floor, knocking over his tray table, the tea and applesauce spilling on the floor tiles. The attendants slid as they tried to restrain his father, but for a feeble old guy Pete Chaucer still showed impressive force.

"Get off me, you goddamn bastards."

"Dad, stop fighting," Bobby said. He touched the side of his eye, which felt tender and swollen. "They're trying to help you."

"What do you mean *dad*?" the old man said. "Who the fuck do you think you are? I don't know you. Get out of here."

"Dad, please, just—"

"I said get the fuck out," his father screamed as the attendants maneuvered him toward the bed so they could restrain him.

"Mr. Chaucer," one of the attendants said, "I think—"

"I'm going," Bobby said. He rushed out of the room. His father's screams echoed all the way down the corridor as Bobby slammed his fist onto the button that opened the automatic doors.

"Is everything all right, Mr. Chaucer?" Roger asked as Bobby stormed past the main desk toward the exit.

"Everything is fine," Bobby said, avoiding the man's gaze. "I'll see you tomorrow."

26

Betty watched the car air fresheners spin like tops near the small, narrow windows of the illegal basement apartment of Hugo Lurch in south Bellmore. Below them were dark flood water lines that resembled scribble marks parents make to measure their children's growth.

Lurch stood at the kitchen counter, one of those old-fashioned ironing boards that came out of the wall, over a cereal bowl and cup of tea. A cell phone lay a few feet away near the tip of the board. The apartment was hardly furnished—a futon, a television, a lamp. Benning's place put this one to shame. The concrete floor was bare, and the cold of the earth was coming in through the soles of Betty's shoes. The only other room in the place was the bathroom, which had exposed hinges on its doorframe—a dirty toilet stood naked and lidless.

Lurch appeared nervous. He glanced occasionally at a photo of two little girls that had been cut into a heart in such a way that only their heads were showing. It was tacked to the bottom of a cabinet and was the only photo on display.

"Thank you for seeing me, Mr. Lurch," Betty said.

The truth was, like Benning, Lurch seemed to be evading her for days. He hadn't been at Stryker's office building—apparently having taken the week off—and was not returning calls. Since she had been on a roll with both Benning and Muriel Adams that day, she decided to try Lurch's place after a quick pitstop home. She was three for three.

According to the owner of the building that housed Stryker's practice, Hugo Lurch had served as the building supervisor for more than twenty-five years. Nothing seemed out of the ordinary about him on paper—fifty-seven years old, divorced, high school education, clean work record—but now that Betty was there, she wasn't so sure. He looked tired and weathered, not much like a man who had spent all of the last week on vacation. She was waiting for him to say something, but he avoided making eye contact and seemed content to stand there, stirring his tea.

"Mr. Lurch, I'd like to ask you a few questions."

He didn't move, and Betty wasn't sure if he had heard her until he stopped stirring.

"Sir, do you work at the building in downtown Gardenia located at 523 Lake Shore?"

He looked at her for the first time since he answered the door; she thought she detected a scratch mark above his right eyebrow. "Yes."

"What is your position at the building?"

"I'm the building supervisor," he said, his creaky voice like a gear in need of oil.

"How long have you been the building supervisor?"

"Twenty-six years."

"As building supervisor, are you in charge of the smoke alarms in the building?"

Lurch lifted the teacup to his lips. It seemed to be too hot, as he recoiled, but he forced himself to drink it anyway. He placed the cup back on the ironing board. "Yes."

"Mr. Lurch, did you know Mr. Kirk Stryker."

"Yes."

"I'm assuming you've heard about what happened to Mr. Stryker."

The cell phone on the ironing board buzzed, but Lurch ignored it. He nodded.

"Sir, were you aware that the smoke alarm in Mr. Stryker's office had been disconnected?"

Lurch reached up to a cabinet, and Betty instinctively undid the safety on her gun, but his hand came down with a sugar packet, which he fumbled to rip open. She continued. "Mr. Lurch, I checked the fire inspector's log, and it seems that all the smoke detectors in the building had been looked at only two weeks ago, and all appeared to be in working order. Your name, sir, appears on that log. You approved it."

"I don't know nuthin' about no smoke detector," he said finally.

"So how do you think it got disconnected?"

"I don't know what Stryker does . . . *did* . . . when I'm not there," he said.

"Fair enough," Betty said. "But if he did anything, wouldn't it have set off the detector or alerted the local firehouse?"

"Don't know."

"But shouldn't you know? You're the building supervisor."

"I don't install the smoke alarms," Lurch said, resting

his teaspoon neatly beside his cereal bowl. "I just check that they're working."

Lurch picked up his cereal bowl and placed it in a dirty slop sink, his frail, crooked figure looking as if it were about ready to break. If Betty had been harboring any ideas about Lurch having murdered Kirk Stryker, they disappeared fast. She couldn't imagine this man overtaking anyone, although it didn't take much brute force to shoot a gun and light a match.

"So let me see if I understand correctly, Mr. Lurch. Are you telling me that as far as you know the smoke detector, which you checked only two weeks ago, was in working order and should have gone off at the first sign of smoke?"

"That's what I'm saying."

Betty sensed he was lying.

"Is that all you need, Miss?" Lurch asked.

"Well . . . actually, I do have another question for you."

She reached around in her pocket for Jesse's Post-it note with the embossed fingerprint. She had tried this trick before, with a teenager suspected of scribbling graffiti on the local Gardenia railroad station's waiting room. He confessed at the sight of it. Hugo Lurch was no teenager, but she took a chance and placed it on the ironing board.

"If you don't handle the smoke detectors, sir, why was your fingerprint found on the underside of the detector in Mr. Stryker's office?"

The smoke detector in Stryker's office had been so charbroiled that there was nothing left of it other than a clean paint mark on the ceiling to indicate where it had been.

"What is this?" Lurch asked, looking at the paper. "This don't look like no photo."

"It's a copy, sir. You don't think I'd bring the actual photo here, do you?"

Lurch dragged the square Post-it toward him and pressed his index finger over the imprint and then his middle finger. "It's too big," he said. "It ain't mine."

"It's been enlarged, sir, to show the detailing. I'm going to ask you again, Mr. Lurch," she pressed. "Did you know that the smoke detector in Mr. Stryker's office was disconnected?"

Lurch furrowed his brows and shifted his feet, before eliciting a short nod, his eyes still on the Post-it note.

"Is that a yes, Mr. Lurch?"

He nodded again. "Yes," he said, his voice barely a scratch.

Betty let out a breath she didn't know she was holding. "Sir, why then was the alarm disconnected?"

Lurch's gaze drifted again to the photograph of the two children hanging from the cabinet. He shook his head. "It isn't my fault."

"What isn't your fault?"

"The fire."

"Sir, I'm going to need you to come down to the station with me. We should continue the conversation there, for the record. Can you do that?"

Lurch placed his teacup into the sink and clicked off the light on the microwave oven, which hung precariously from a leaning shelf. "Now?" he asked.

"Yes, actually. Right now would be best."

He looked around his apartment, as if seeing it for the first time. "All right," he said. "I'll need to get my things."

She took a step forward and picked up Lurch's cell phone. "I can hold onto this for you," she said, placing it in her pocket.

He hesitated. "Fine. I need to use the restroom."

Betty eyed the unshielded toilet. Unless Lurch had intended to shinny his way through the tiny windows near the ceiling, the only way out of the apartment was through the front door. "I'll wait outside," she said. "Please hurry."

Betty left the apartment and climbed the cement steps back up to street level. She took a long breath of fresh air into her lungs and leaned against her car, which she had parked intentionally too close to Lurch's Toyota, blocking it in. She was surprised at how easily he had come clean about the smoke detector and felt somewhat guilty for tricking him. She had to remind herself that innocent people rarely confessed to crimes they didn't commit— even when confronted with false physical evidence of their involvement. She was certain Lurch knew more than he was letting on.

Betty took out her cell phone and was about to let the precinct know she'd be bringing him in for questioning when the phone rang in her hand. The caller ID read: *Detective Pamela Sanderson.*

"Got him," Pam said as soon as Betty answered.

"What?" Betty asked. "Got who?"

"You know that half print we found in Stryker's office? On the glass on his desk? The one we couldn't ID?"

"Yeah."

"Benning's."

"What?" Betty said, glancing at Lurch's door. "So we can place Benning at the scene of Kirk Stryker's murder?"

"Yep."

"But we have no murder weapon."

"Nope."

"But we have the print."

"Yep."

"Thanks, Pam. Talk to Girardi. Let's get the warrant. I'll be right there."

Betty clicked off the call and looked at her watch. It had been five minutes since she left Lurch. Even with his frail frame, it shouldn't be taking him that long to take care of business. She started walking toward the apartment when a *bang* cut through the air. The sound came from Lurch's small windows. She ripped her gun from its holster and ran down the stairs.

"Mr. Lurch?" she asked, pushing the ajar door all the way open and peering inside the apartment.

No answer.

She took out her cell phone again to request backup, giving Lurch's address. Then she readied her weapon and slowly eased inside.

The room was as quiet and bare as it was before. The square Post-it note was where she had left it on the ironing board, but behind it lay the lifeless body of Hugo Lurch slumped over the toilet in the bathroom, a self-inflicted bullet wound oozing from his forehead.

27

"What the fuck was *that?*"

John Parker was sitting in his car down the block from Munson's vehicle. He reached for the door handle but saw the detective barrel back down the steps of the high-ranch basement, gun in hand, and decided to stay put.

He popped another two aspirin into his mouth, hoping to ease his headache, which had been hammering him since he woke up in the Queens Center Mall parking lot—how he got there, he still didn't know. All he could remember was having drinks on the Upper West Side with some guy whose name he couldn't recall, in a bar whose name had slipped his mind. After checking his pockets and finding all his money and his car keys, he assumed he must have somehow driven himself into Queens before deciding to sleep it off.

His phone rang. He checked his caller ID and groaned.

"Yeah, Ma," he said, cradling the phone.

"Johnny, are you coming home for dinner? Aunt Peggy is here and wants to see you."

"No, Ma, I ate."

"Are you sure? I'm making pot roast."

"Yes, I'm sure," he groaned. "Ma, I can't talk. I'm working."

"Working? On a Saturday? Well, I hope you're getting overtime, dear."

Overtime? Parker would pay Gardner not to have to go home and see his Aunt Peggy. "Ma, I gotta go. News is happening."

Parker clicked off the call and searched the sidewalk and driveway of the high ranch. It was easier than he thought it would be to track down Detective Munson's private home. A Samuel Munson had been listed on whitepages.com, along with two other Munsons in the Gardenia area. He expected to spend most of the day locating each one but was astonished to see Betty Munson leaving the first home and getting into a car. A lucky break.

He checked his notes. Munson had stopped at a house in Massapequa Park that belonged to a Muriel Adams, age forty-five. Parker thought perhaps it was a personal visit until he saw Munson show her badge at the front door. A quick Google search hadn't turned up anything unusual other than a Facebook profile page for Adams, but several local newspaper articles mentioned she worked at the local elementary school as a third grade teacher. *What did journalists do before the Internet?*

He picked up his notepad where he had jotted down Muriel Adams's info. He wondered if there was any connection between Muriel Adams and the Manhattan building Munson stopped at that morning. He flipped a few pages back to check his notes from his stakeout—he smiled at the word *stakeout*—but couldn't find them. He flipped back and forth. *Where were they?*

Sirens filled the air, and three police cars zoomed past Parker's car, along with an ambulance, pulling up beside Munson's vehicle. A line of officers entered the basement as residents began filing out of their homes all along the street, blocking his view. Parker grabbed his digital camera, opened his car door, and darted outside.

By the time he walked down the block, three EMTs were rushing down the basement steps with a stretcher, as police officers fanned out to keep the onlookers at bay. Parker wormed his way through the crowd until someone tapped him on the shoulder. It was a young woman.

"What happened?" she whispered. She was holding a child with chocolate stains around his mouth.

"I don't know," Parker said. "Do you know the person who lives there?"

"I know the upstairs family," the woman said. "My oldest boy plays with their son. But they rent the downstairs to some guy. Some weird guy."

"How is he weird?" Parker asked.

"If you saw him, you'd know."

"What's going on?" a chubby man with a thin mustache asked the young woman.

"We don't know," she said, gesturing to Parker. "Charlie, what's the guy's name again who lives downstairs there? The weird one?"

"Lurch," the man said. "I'll never forget it. Lurch, like in that old TV show."

"Hugo Lurch?" Parker asked.

"Yeah, that's it," the man said. "You know him?"

Parker remembered seeing the name on some paperwork he had come across during his investigating.

Lurch was the supervisor of the building that housed Kirk Stryker's office. "I think so," he said. Why had Munson been there? Had Lurch been a person of interest? *A suspect?*

More police cars pulled up to the house, their sirens causing the residents to cover their ears. The entire street was now blocked off, and the sidewalk was filled on one side with uniforms and on the other with about twenty or thirty residents.

"Officer! What's going on?" yelled a dark-haired woman who was standing on one of the rungs of a chain-link fence, rising above the onlookers.

A young policeman shook his head. "I really can't say, ma'am," he said. "We're investigating."

"Was that a gunshot I heard?" the neighbor Charlie asked.

"I have young children," demanded another neighbor with streaked blonde hair. "If there is a murderer on the loose, I think it is our right to know."

"That's right," said the young woman next to Parker, holding her child closer.

"Settle down, settle down," said the young officer, who appeared to be inhaling this sudden moment of power. "There's nothing to worry about, folks."

"That's easy for you to say," the blonde sneered. "You're not in the dark."

"Was it a home invasion?" the young woman asked.

"My sister lives in Seaford, and there was a break-in a few days ago," yelled the dark-haired woman. "Could it be the same guys?"

The policeman looked behind him at the other officers and leaned closer to the group. "Suicide," he mouthed.

Suicide, Parker wondered. Munson had knocked on the door three times before she was let inside. Unless someone else had been in the apartment, Hugo Lurch must have been alive enough to open the door. And then she just walked out and let him commit suicide?

"At least it wasn't a burglary," said the dark-haired woman, getting down from the fence. "Suicide I can live with."

Detective Munson appeared at the top of the apartment steps, looking, Parker thought, a bit rattled. Another cop tapped the shoulder of the officer in front of Parker.

"That the one?" he asked. "Munson?"

The officer nodded. "Yeah, she found him."

"She found him *dead*?" Parker blurted.

The officers looked at him, and the young woman holding the child put her hand on Parker's shoulder. "I think he knew the guy," she told them.

"Sorry for your loss," the younger officer said with a grave nod.

"Excuse me," Parker said and filed back through the crowd until he got to open street, his mind racing. Munson was in that apartment *before* Lurch shot himself, he thought. *She was lying.* She didn't find him dead. What did that mean? He took out his smartphone and dialed Gardner's phone number.

"Yeah, kid, this better be good," Gardner said as soon as he answered. "I'm at my nephew's Communion."

"It is," Parker whispered, cupping his hand over the phone. "You know Hugo Lurch, the supervisor of Stryker's building?"

"Yeah."

"He just killed himself." Until Parker could prove otherwise or figure out what had *really* gone on, he had to go with what the police were claiming.

"What?! How do you know this, kid?"

"I'm here. At the scene."

"Holy shit, kid. This is big. Are there any other reporters there?"

Parker looked around. "No, none that I can see."

"Holy shit!" Gardner said again. "Take pictures. Verify your info. We gotta get something up on the website, you hear me?"

"Got it, boss. I'll have the story filed in a couple of hours."

"Quicker, Parker, quicker. Let's be the one to break this puppy. News moves at lightning speed nowadays. Get me something in thirty minutes. Send it to my home email, and I'll get it up."

"Will do," Parker said. He clicked off the call, his heart pounding. He turned on his digital camera and took three shots—a close-up of Lurch's apartment, a long shot of the street scene, and a tight close-up of Detective Munson—before sprinting back to his car with a smile.

28

Muriel put her purse on the empty seat next to her as the train spurted forward.

She hadn't planned on taking the Long Island Rail Road into Manhattan, but she also hadn't planned on her minivan not starting, or Doug arriving two hours earlier than when he said he'd pick up the kids.

"What do you know about this guy, Mur?" he had asked in that paternal voice she hated, following her from room to room as she tried to pack an overnight bag. She couldn't get out of the house fast enough. "Don't you think it's something to worry about when a detective shows up at your door asking about a guy you're dating?"

"You don't know him, Doug," she had said, grabbing random pieces of clothing. She could only imagine what her outfit was going to look like tomorrow.

"Have you ever considered that maybe you don't either?" he managed to call to her before she left the house and ran toward the train station.

Muriel leaned her head back against the worn leather seat. She hated to admit that Doug had a point. Did she really know Marty Benning? *After three months?* She dug her cell phone out of her bag and tried calling him but got his voice mail again. After a few minutes, she heard a beep and quickly reached for her phone, but there were no texts. She heard another beep: it was coming from her pocket where she had placed Ellie's phone. She took it out and looked at the locked screen:

Michael: Hey u there?

Michael: Can u talk?

Muriel replaced the phone into her pocket. A boyfriend would explain Ellie's mood lately—and the change in hairstyle. It would also explain why she was so hostile toward Muriel. Maybe she had questions and Muriel had been unavailable, distracted. *Mother of the Year* again. She looked out the window at the suburban neighborhoods passing by. It was going to be a long train ride. She took out her phone and did what she always did when she didn't know what else to do: She called Roxanne.

❂

By the time she got to Marty's block in uptown Manhattan, Muriel was determined to take Roxanne's advice: She would let Marty know what had happened with Detective Munson, and she would make him explain why he lied about being in New Jersey last weekend. As she approached Marty's building, the doorman came running out from behind his desk.

"Good evening, Ms. Adams," he said, holding the door open and handing her an envelope.

"What's this?" she asked.

"From Mr. Benning," he said with a smile. "He told me to give it to you when you arrived. Oh, and"—he added, before hurrying back toward his spot—"the car will be ready at nine o'clock, as requested."

"What car?" she asked, but the doorman answered a call on his phone.

Muriel opened the envelope and found Marty's apartment key inside. She glanced at the doorman before heading toward the elevators. It was the first time she hadn't been announced. When she got to Marty's apartment door, she brought the key to the lock, but decided to knock first. It suddenly seemed too forward to enter without being accompanied.

No answer.

She inserted the key and opened the door.

"Marty?" Muriel asked, stepping inside the apartment. She wheeled in her bag and stood it next to the front door.

The view of the Hudson River crackled through the windows, as the last remnants of the sun set amid the twinkling lights of the city skyline. Beyond that, the apartment was empty and dark, except for a lamp that had been turned on in the bedroom.

"Marty, are you here?" she asked, putting her purse and the key on the dining room table. "I need to talk to you."

The bedroom was empty, but on the bed, which was neatly made, a black sequined cocktail dress had been fanned out across the comforter. Beside it was a black chiffon wrap. On the floor were a pair of black strappy heels and a matching purse.

"Marty?" she asked, flicking the light on in the bathroom. On the vanity was a bouquet of flowers in a vase and a small Bloomingdale's brown bag. She peeked inside the bag and saw assorted cosmetic items—

foundation, blush, eye shadow, mascara, lipstick. She pulled out the tube of lipstick and examined it. It was her brand and favorite shade. Her belly fluttered. Doug never even noticed that she wore lipstick let alone knew what brand or shade to buy. She checked all the other makeup items, and they were her favorites as well.

Despite her best efforts, the doubts about Marty that had been floating around in her mind since that afternoon began to fade. *Was that all it took,* she wondered. A shade of lipstick? Was she that shallow? She reached out and touched the petal of one of the red roses, which was in full bloom, and thought about Ellie. *How could she not know her daughter was interested in a boy?* She looked in the bathroom mirror at her reflection, at her hastily tied ponytail. She should go home, her brain told her, and yet she didn't move. She thought of Doug, of Detective Munson. *Could Muriel really be this wrong about a person?* She sighed. There was only one way to find out. She yanked the scrunchie out of her hair, dropped her coat to the floor, pulled her T-shirt over her head, and turned on the shower.

✪

At nine o'clock on the dot, Muriel stepped off the elevator in the black dress and black heels, the smell of Marty's cologne following her from the apartment. A group of men and women who were in the lobby smiled at her, and the doorman ran out from behind his post and opened the front door. Outside, a limousine was parked in front of the building, as he had promised. A driver opened the back door.

"Have a good evening, Ms. Adams," the doorman said with a nod.

Muriel expected to see Marty inside, but the limousine was empty. The driver handed her a glass of champagne before closing the door, and soon they were easing into traffic. Muriel sipped the champagne as the limousine made a series of turns into the relative dark of Central Park before reappearing on Fifth Avenue, not far from where she and Marty had their carriage ride. Muriel's purse vibrated. She reached in for her phone, took a look at the caller ID, and swiped the screen.

"Hey, Rock," she said, the champagne giving her voice a relaxed timber.

"Well? Did you give him hell for lying to you?" Roxanne asked.

"Not exactly," Muriel said.

"Why? He was naked?"

"No," Muriel said with a laugh. "He wasn't there. I haven't seen him yet."

"You what? It's twenty after eight. Where are you?"

The limo driver made a turn and parked before the Guggenheim Museum, where a crowd of well-dressed men and women were congregating outside the front doors.

"I'm actually sitting in a limousine in front of the Guggenheim and wearing a beautiful black cocktail dress, dazzling strappy pumps, accompanied by a sexy purse and fresh makeup."

"Did you hit the lottery?"

"No," she giggled. "All this was waiting for me at Marty's place. All this, but not Marty." Muriel looked out the car window at the happy, chatty faces. "I don't know where he is." The limo driver opened Muriel's door. "Rock, I gotta go. The limo driver is helping me out."

"Oh, well, excuse *me*, let's not keep the limo driver waiting. Okay, Cinderella, have fun at the ball."

The Guggenheim Museum was aglow with light, its cylindrical design cutting a playful and sophisticated edge across the clear dark sky. As she approached, the chatter of the visitors standing along the sidewalk grew in volume, and Muriel searched their faces and found Marty standing a few feet from the front entrance talking to another gentleman. She caught her breath. He was wearing a long coat, which was open and showed his tuxedo underneath. She had never seen him look more handsome. As Marty spoke, his eyes were searching the sidewalk, and Muriel tingled inside at the thought that he was looking for her. When their eyes finally met, he excused himself and walked in Muriel's direction.

"You look beautiful," he said, leaning forward and kissing her cheek.

"You have wonderful taste," Muriel said, flattening the dress along her hip.

"I certainly do." Marty squeezed her side. "Let's go inside."

"Wait," Muriel said.

"What?"

"I tried calling you today."

"Sorry about that," Marty said. "I lost my phone. I can't find the damn thing anywhere. Is everything okay?"

"I really need to talk to you."

"Inside first. It's chilly out here," Marty said, locking elbows and walking with the crowd into the museum.

Muriel had been to the Guggenheim only once before, a school trip. Her students mainly found the contemporary exhibition boring—"it's just a black painting," one little boy had complained with a roll of his eyes—and instead wanted to run up and down the museum's coiled walkways. Tonight, those coils were tinted blue, and over the ceiling a tarp glistened like a Van Gogh starry night. A chamber orchestra played softly while waiters zigzagged with hors d'oeuvres and champagne. Marty grabbed two flutes from a passing tray and gave one to Muriel.

"A toast," he said, planting another kiss on Muriel's cheek. "To the most beautiful woman in the room."

"Marty—"

"I know," he said, sipping his drink. "You want to talk. Did Detective Munson come and see you?"

Muriel exhaled. *So he knew.* She nodded.

"She's investigating the murder of Kirk Stryker."

"I know," she said, "but why was she asking about you?"

"I don't know. She paid a visit to me this morning and was asking questions. I'm assuming she's asking a lot of people where they were that night, but I don't know." He smirked. "Luckily, I was with you that night."

"Hey, Benning!"

Muriel would have recognized that haughty voice anywhere. Stowe glided before them wearing a tux, smelling like a mix of cigarettes and hair spray, and slapped Marty on the back, nearly spilling his drink.

"Wasn't sure if you'd make it," Stowe said. "And who is this lovely . . . *Adams?*"

"Dr. Stowe," Muriel said with a nod and a smile.

"What the hell are you doing here?"

"She's with me," Marty said, his words wrapping Muriel in a warm blanket.

"With *you*? No, really, what is she doing here?"

"Ben, guess what?" Marty said. "She's off-duty. Now, if you'll excuse us . . . We're going to get another drink." He turned to Muriel. "Shall we?"

"Surely," she said and walked with him across the lobby.

The bar was crowded, but there was a sliver of space between two occupied barstools, and she and Marty squeezed through. "Boy, that felt good," Muriel said.

"I'll bet it did." Marty brushed a hair away from her cheek. "You really do look beautiful tonight."

Muriel smiled. "I feel beautiful," she said. She glanced at the men and women around them, who all seemed elegant and sophisticated. For them, this may have been an average weekend outing, one of the perks of living in upper Manhattan, but for someone like Muriel, Saturday nights had long since lost their specialness. There were also quite a few young people, who looked so grown up in their suits, ties, and dresses. On the other side of the bar, three young women huddled together in a way that reminded Muriel of Ellie and her friends when they were gossiping about a boy. She smiled at them when they looked her way, but they didn't return the gesture.

"Hey, is that all you wanted to talk about? Munson?" Marty asked.

"Well, there was something else too."

"What is it?"

"Last weekend . . . You said you were going into

New Jersey, but Detective Munson said you were on Long Island."

The words seemed to catch Marty off guard. "She did?"

"Yes," Muriel said, putting her empty glass down and glancing again at the three young women across the bar, all of whom were staring at her. "I think those women are staring at me," she whispered.

"Who?" Marty asked.

"*Those* women." Muriel pointed with her chin.

Marty glanced at them. "Just ignore them," he said.

"Do you know them?"

A gentleman with ruddy cheeks and a bulbous nose wrapped his arm around Marty's neck. "So what's this I hear about you abandoning Manhattan to become a Long Islander?"

Marty smiled, glancing at Muriel. "Nothing has been decided yet," he said.

"Well, that's not what I hear, Mister. I think you've been keeping some secrets."

"Dan, I'd like you to meet Muriel Adams," Marty said.

"Hi," Muriel said to the man who, despite being clearly drunk, had a kind face. "Nice to meet you."

"And you as well, my dear. Do you mind if I browbeat your date for a little while?"

"Not at all." Muriel said. "I'll be right back."

She followed the signs to the Guggenheim's restroom, which was as small as an airplane's, but as hip and geometric as the building itself. She checked her make-up in a trapezoidal-shaped mirror and then surprised herself by doing a twirl, letting her dress flip upward, like a dancer's. She smiled. When she opened the bathroom door, she was startled by several women standing there and realized they were the three young women from the bar. They stood together like a firing squad.

"Excuse me," Muriel said.

"Wow, you're old," the tall blonde one said.

"I'm sorry?" Muriel asked.

"Deborah, that was rude," said the short brunette with a bob. "What she meant was you're older than we expected."

"Do I know you?" Muriel brushed past them. "If you don't mind, I need to get back to the—"

"Listen, you need to stay clear of that guy," the blonde said. "He's no good."

"Who?"

The brunette rolled her eyes. "Benning. Duh." She cracked her gum. She couldn't have been older than twenty-five.

"How do you know Marty?" Muriel asked.

"Who doesn't know him? Right, Carrie?" the blonde one said, nudging the third girl, who looked at the floor.

"I'm sorry, if you'll excuse me . . ."

"Listen, we're trying to do you a favor, old timer," the blonde said. "If you don't want to listen, that's your right."

"Give her a week," the brunette said to the blonde. "She'll be in our Facebook group."

"Facebook group?" Muriel asked, before realizing the words had slipped out.

"Yeah," said the blonde. "The Many Women of Marty B. It's an open group, so everyone can join."

"And everyone has," said the brunette, putting her arm over the shoulder of the blonde.

Muriel wondered if any one of these girls had been the ones to say they loved Marty on the first date. If so, they weren't how she had pictured. They were harder—young, yes, but angry. She turned to go when the third woman, the quiet one, reached for her arm.

"We're just looking out for you," she said, her eyes huge puddles of brown. She really did remind Muriel of Ellie.

"I appreciate that, young lady." Muriel gently pulled her arm away. "But I can take care of myself," she said and hurried toward the main room.

"Trust me," the brunette called behind her. "When you least expect it, when you need him most, he'll be gone."

When Muriel returned to the bar, her heart was beating fast. She glanced back toward the bathroom, but the women weren't following.

The crowd seemed to have surged while she was gone— it looked as though a presentation was about to begin—and there was even less elbow room than before. She looked around for Marty but didn't see him. The man he had been talking to when she left for the bathroom was chatting with someone else. Muriel drifted toward the edges of the round room and spotted Stowe with a young redhead, who was sitting provocatively on a cushioned bench. She avoided him and took a seat on the other side of the room as the music stopped and a distinguished gentleman stood up on a small stage in the center of the room.

"Thank you, everyone, for coming this evening," he said. "I am delighted to see you all for tonight's special gala honoring contemporary artist Mika Razkel." A young woman, with pierced eyebrows, took a bow as the group applauded. "Ms. Razkel is . . ."

"Well, well, well," Stowe said, standing next to Muriel, "if it isn't Adams all dolled up."

"Hello, Stowe."

"It's *Dr.* Stowe," he whispered, his breath reeking of cigarettes. "You know, your *boss*?"

"Have you seen Marty?"

"Don't tell me Benning wisened up already?" Stowe said with a laugh. "I'd think he'd at least fuck you first, or has he done that already?"

"Good-bye, Dr. Stowe," Muriel said, standing up just as the crowd began to disperse, most of them following the gentleman and young artist toward the ramp that led to the upper floors. Muriel walked to the far side of the bar, where the bartender was pouring drinks for a young couple. She figured this was the first place Marty would look for her. In pairs, the crowd funneled onto the ramp, trailed by Stowe and the redhead who were the last ones to begin their ascent.

Within minutes, the room was largely empty, except for the bartender, waiters, and orchestra members, who began packing up their instruments. Muriel searched the empty space, walked to the center of the room, and gazed upward into the starry canopy. On the third level, a woman peeked over the side of the ledge, looking down at her, and Muriel realized it was one of the three young women who had confronted her at the bathroom—the quiet one, the one who looked like Ellie. The girl shook her head sadly at Muriel and disappeared among the bobbing heads as they traveled up and around the blue spirals, giving Muriel the sensation that she was at the center of a shimmering twister. She suddenly felt woozy—and alone.

29

Roxanne turned up the volume on *Saturday Night Live* with her remote control and took a sip of her hot cocoa—another thrilling night of fun, she thought, for the middle-aged mother of one. Smitty was wrapped around her feet, and she gave the cat a quick scratch behind the ears.

"Who needs a man when I've got you, Smit," she said. Her cell phone vibrated. It was Muriel.

"Hey, lady," she said. "How was the ball?"

There was noise on the other end, and Roxanne realized that Muriel was crying.

"Shit, what's the matter?" she asked. "I'll be right there."

"No, that's okay," Muriel said. "I'm already here."

"You're what?" Roxanne jumped off the couch, causing the cat to run for cover and slam his furry little head into the coffee table. She dashed toward the apartment door and found Muriel standing on her porch in a lovely black dress, black streams of makeup falling from her eyes.

"Oh my God, you look . . . beautiful," Roxanne said, which made Muriel cry even more. She ushered her inside, sat her on the couch, took off her shoes, and handed her a tissue from a box on the coffee table. "What happened? Why are you here and not at the Guggenheim?"

"I don't want to talk about it," Muriel said, wiping her eyes.

"Okay. How did you get here?"

"I took a cab."

"Why didn't you call me? I would have come to get you."

"I didn't want you to wake Gordy."

"Oh, please. Gordy has been woken up so many times, he can put on his shoes and coat and strap on his seat belt while he's half-asleep." Roxanne looked at Muriel's dress. "Wow, you weren't kidding. That dress is gorgeous."

"I know," Muriel said and started crying again.

Roxanne sat beside her. "What's the matter? What did that prick do?"

Muriel drew in a deep breath. "He just . . . left me there."

"What do you mean *left you there*?"

"I went to the bathroom, and when I came out, he was gone. At first I thought that maybe he was in the bathroom too, but I didn't want to wait near the bathrooms, for a variety of reasons, so I went back to the bar, and I stood there, but then the presentation was about to begin, so I found a seat in the back, and that's when Stowe, that ass, saw me again—"

"Stowe was there?" Roxanne asked.

"—and," Muriel nodded, "then everyone filed upstairs, and they were having such a good time, and I was all alone. He just left. I don't know where. I stood there waiting for more than an hour. Like an idiot." She blew her nose. "I knew this would happen."

"No, you didn't."

"Rock, no, really. I shouldn't have been there. I should have been home. With the kids. With Ellie. She needs me."

"Why the fuck shouldn't you be there? You're a beautiful, wonderful person who, for the last few months, has been blissfully happy for the first time in her life, and I've known you forever."

"*In the red*," Gordy whispered, peeking out from his bedroom door.

"You, mister, get back to bed," Roxanne scolded, and Gordy quickly shut the door.

"What did Gordy say?" Muriel asked.

"Never mind him . . . ." Roxanne squeezed Muriel's hand. "Don't tell me that it doesn't matter. You love him. Don't you?"

Muriel hid her face behind her tissue. "I do . . . *did*," she said, dotting her eyes.

"Did you talk at all about the detective?" Roxanne handed her another tissue.

"He brought it up, and I was so relieved. He didn't seem to be hiding anything. At least about that."

Then why the fuck did he pick up and scram, Roxanne wanted to say. "And what about the lying thing, about supposedly being in New Jersey?"

Muriel shook her head. "He didn't get to say, but I can tell that it was true, that he had lied. But then we got distracted and didn't get a chance to talk more . . . and then he was gone."

Roxanne put her arm around Muriel's shoulder, and the two leaned back against the couch cushions. "What a jerk. What did you do then? Did you have anything to eat?"

"No, I just stood there. Dumbfounded." She blew her nose. "I'm freakin' starving."

"Well, there you go." Roxanne went into the kitchen and grabbed a frying pan from the cabinet under the sink. "Sunnyside up or scrambled?" she asked and saw that Smitty had jumped into her spot on the couch and was nuzzling Muriel's arm.

"You don't have to go to any trouble, Rock . . ." Muriel scratched the cat behind his ears.

"Trouble? It takes two—"

The doorbell rang, and Roxanne and Muriel jumped at the sound.

"Who's that?" Muriel whispered. "At this hour?"

"I have no idea."

"Mom?" Gordy called from behind his bedroom door.

"Gordy, stay in there. It's okay. Go back to sleep, honey."

Roxanne crept toward the front door with the frying pan in her right hand. She peeked through the peephole and saw a burly man she didn't recognize. It definitely wasn't Benning, not that she expected it to be.

"Who is it?" Muriel whispered, standing behind her.

Roxanne shrugged her shoulders. The doorbell rang again.

"Who is it?" Roxanne called, mustering a deep, guttural voice. "How can I help you? Do you know what time it is?"

"I need to talk to Ms. Adams," the man said.

"What did he say?" Muriel whispered. "Did he say *me*?"

Roxanne held her finger to her lips. "There's no Adams here," she said into the door. "I think you've got the wrong apartment."

"I know she's there, Ms. Somers. I followed her from the Guggenheim."

"Holy shit," Roxanne whispered, grabbing her cell phone from the entryway table. "Listen, buddy, I don't know what kind of stalker you are, but if you don't leave I'm calling the police. I mean it."

"I'm a friend of Marty Benning's."

Muriel peered into the peephole. "What's your name?" she asked.

"Bobby Chaucer."

"Do you know this guy?" Roxanne whispered.

Muriel stared through the peephole. "Kind of," she answered and put her hand on the door's security chain, sliding it open until Roxanne stopped her.

"What are you doing?" Roxanne asked. "Are you crazy?"

"I think it's okay."

"Think? My son is in the other room. *Think* isn't good enough."

"Roxanne Somers," Muriel folded her arms, "you know I would never do anything to hurt Gordy."

"Yes, I know, but I don't think you're thinking clearly these days," Roxanne said, nudging Muriel away from the door.

"Ladies, it's cold out here," Bobby said.

"Who the fuck cares, buddy?" Roxanne called. "Why are you here?"

Bobby sighed. "I need to talk to her."

"Yeah, well, how do I know you aren't a mass murderer?" Roxanne asked. "This neighborhood isn't what it used to be."

"Because if I really wanted to come in there

unannounced instead of making a racket out here and being glared at by your neighbor upstairs, I would have used the unlocked window in your bedroom to get into the house instead of ringing the doorbell."

Roxanne's eyes opened wide. "Stay here," she said to Muriel and dashed into her bedroom. She pulled the curtain away from the window. *Dammit, she had forgotten to lock it again.* She turned the lock on the window pane.

"Well?" Muriel asked when Roxanne returned.

Roxanne nodded.

"I'm letting him in." Muriel pulled the latch off the security chain and opened the door. Bobby stepped inside.

"You really should keep that window locked," he said, closing the door behind him.

"Says the stalker." Roxanne sized him up—he was more muscular than he appeared in the peephole, which made him look fat. She gripped the handle of the frying pan tighter.

The three of them stood looking at one another in the apartment's small entryway until Bobby reached out to shake Roxanne's hand. "I'm Bobby Ch—"

"You better keep your distance, buddy." Roxanne held up the frying pan.

Bobby put his hands in the air. "I'm here as a friend."

"I have enough friends," Roxanne said.

"I'm Muriel," Muriel said, standing beside Roxanne.

"Bobby Chaucer."

"Nice to finally meet you," Muriel said. "Where's Marty?"

Bobby sighed. "Marty's been arrested."

Roxanne jumped in front of Muriel with the frying pan

held high. "For the murder?" she asked, backing away and pushing Muriel behind her.

"He didn't do it," Bobby said.

"Sure, that's what *you* say," Roxanne said. "That's what they all say."

"Listen . . . he had a feeling this might happen," Bobby said. He looked as if he was fumbling with where to put his big glovelike hands and finally shoved them into his suit pockets. "He told me this morning after Detective Munson paid a visit to his apartment that he had a bad feeling that he was the key suspect in this thing."

"I'll bet he did," Roxanne said.

"Listen, he didn't do it. And anyway that night he was with Ms. Adams," Bobby said. "Right, Ms. Adams?"

"Don't talk to her," Roxanne said.

"It's okay, Rock," Muriel said.

"Marty was with you that night, right?" Bobby asked.

"Yeah, as far as I can remember," Muriel said. "But I was sleeping."

"From what I understand you both were," Bobby said.

"How convenient," Roxanne said, tightening her grip on the frying pan's handle.

"Roxanne, please . . ." Muriel placed her hand on Roxanne's arm. "Why did you follow me here, Bobby?"

"Marty told me to make sure you got home safely," he said. "I waited until you came out of the museum and saw you get into a cab. I followed you here in another. The guy made me pay extra to drive into Queens. Ridiculous."

"If Benning was arrested, how come there was no buzz in the museum?" Roxanne asked. "Did it seem like anyone knew anything, Mur?"

"No," Muriel said and looked at Bobby.

"I saw Detective Munson and several officers pull up outside the museum," Bobby said. "I guess about a half hour to forty minutes after you and Marty went inside."

"How did you know it was Detective Munson?" Muriel asked. "Did she come speak to you too?"

"No, but I'd seen her before," Bobby said. "When I saw her car turn the corner, I phoned Marty, and he came outside, so there wouldn't be a scene. He texted me that you were in the bathroom and that I should make sure you get home okay and tell you what happened. And then they took him away."

"In handcuffs?" Muriel asked.

"Yes."

Roxanne thought she saw Muriel shudder. "And you followed me all the way here?" Muriel asked.

"Most of the way. I actually don't live too far from here . . ."

"And we care because . . . ?" Roxanne asked.

"Anyway, my cab lost you near the cemeteries. We got turned around in the Maspeth area, but I took a chance that you might be coming here to see Ms. Somers."

"What do you mean?" Roxanne asked. "How do you know where I live?" She raised the frying pan.

"Next time you decide to go on a snooping excursion to Marty's office in Gardenia you might want to check to see if you're being followed."

Muriel looked at Roxanne. "You're kidding me. . . . Your grandmother's wig?"

"What?" Roxanne asked, her cheeks warming. "I wanted to see him for myself, see what all the hubbub was about. And why are we talking about *me*?" She put her hands on her hips, the frying pan pressing into her side. "What's your story, bub? You're hired to follow people around?"

"Bobby works in security. He's like Marty's personal bodyguard—and friend," Muriel said, an explanation that made this Bobby person smile.

"Why the hell does a CPA have a bodyguard?" Roxanne asked. "And why didn't you tell me, Mo?"

"There isn't anything to tell," Bobby said. "You can put the frying pan down, you know."

Roxanne raised the pan higher. "I hate to break it to you both, but *my* tax guy doesn't have a bodyguard."

"Marty had gotten into some trouble a while back and had taken on a political client with some nebulous financial backers. He thought that was all behind him until recently."

"What do you mean?" Muriel asked.

"I really can't say. He doesn't want you involved, but suffice it to say that I've been busy lately."

"Mom?"

Gordy, the right side of his hair suffering from a severe case of bedhead, peeked into the room and ran to Roxanne's side.

"Gord," Roxanne said, wrapping her arm—and the frying pan—around him, "go back to bed, sweetie."

"I can't sleep. Hi," Gordy said to Bobby. "I'm Gordy."

"Gordy, you're not supposed to talk to strangers," Roxanne said.

"Hi there, young fella." Bobby stuck out his hand. "I'm Bob—"

"Okay, that's enough," Roxanne said. She opened the front door, tucking Gordy behind her. "It was nice of you to stop by, Mr. Chaucer . . ."

"Roxanne," Muriel said, "it's—"

"No, it's all right," Bobby said. "I should be going. I said everything I had to say." Bobby stepped outside. "Good-bye, Gordy. Nice to meet you. Good-bye, Ms. Adams."

"Call me Muriel," Muriel said. "And thanks."

"Muriel then." He smiled at Roxanne. "Good-bye, Roxanne."

"Call me Ms. Somers," Roxanne said, folding her arms.

"Good-bye, Bobby. Nice to meet you!" Gordy called with a wave.

Roxanne gently elbowed Gordy behind her, closed the door, and turned the deadbolt. He got so excited whenever there was a man around. The kid was starving for a father figure.

"He was nice, Mom," Gordy said, his big, innocent blue eyes blinking with hope.

"Okay, back to bed with you, mister," she said and shooed him into his bedroom.

When Roxanne returned to the kitchen, Muriel was humming and setting the table for two.

"What's with you?" Roxanne said. "You look like the happy homemaker."

Muriel shrugged her shoulders and folded two paper napkins. "I don't know," she said. "They arrested him."

"And that's *good news*?" Roxanne said. She put the frying pan on the stove and turned on the burner beneath it.

Muriel sat down. "I mean, he didn't *leave* me."

"Jesus, Muriel, are you kidding me? In what universe is getting arrested for a murder not worse than standing someone up?"

"I don't think he did it."

"Muriel, you—"

"You heard what Bobby said."

"C'mon, Mo. How long have you known this guy? And let's not forget that you hated him before three months ago. Let's think reasonably for a minute."

"I thought you said Level-Headed Muriel could take a backseat?"

"Yeah, but I didn't say to throw her out of the car," Roxanne said. "Obviously, the police have enough evidence to bring Benning in. That has to mean something. And whoever this Bobby person is isn't really on your side, or our side. He's on Benning's side. Do you understand that?"

"It's the same side." Muriel moved the salt and pepper shakers from the counter to the table. "Listen, I know how this sounds, but you don't know him."

Roxanne exhaled loudly. She had been so happy to see Muriel finally allow herself to fall head over heels for someone, and now that she had, reeling her back wouldn't be easy. She leaned against the refrigerator. "I know I don't. And I'm willing to give him the benefit of the doubt, if you're willing to see things from my end. Don't you think it's a little convenient that he was at your house the same night of the crime, but that you can't remember if he was there at the actual time the crime occurred?"

"What are you saying?" Roxanne could tell Muriel was getting angry, because the wrinkle between her eyebrows deepened. "Like he knew I would drink too much wine that night and pass out on the couch. The wine was *my* idea."

"It didn't have to be wine." Roxanne folded her arms. "It could have been anything."

"Are you saying that he *drugged* me?" Muriel said. "Roxanne Somers, do you think I'm naïve?"

"No," Roxanne said gently. "But I think you are in love, and that's just as bad."

"He didn't do it. I know it."

"Because he bought you a dress?"

"*No,*" Muriel snapped and stomped into the living room, nearly stepping on Smitty who became so disoriented that he backflipped and slid under a chair. "You're starting to sound like Doug. I thought you were on *my* side."

"I *am* on your side."

"If you are, then believe me. Marty was with me that night. Next to me on the couch. All night long. And that's exactly what I'm going to tell Detective Munson."

"*What?*"

"I'm going to call her first thing tomorrow and tell her—beyond any reasonable doubt—that Marty was at my house at the time of the murder. End of story. And then they'll have to let him go."

"Like hell you are," Roxanne said. "Don't lie for him. You can get into a lot of trouble."

"I'm *not* lying. It's the truth."

"You already told the detective the truth. You think so, but you don't remember. And that's that."

"He was *there.*" Muriel opened the refrigerator and reached for a stick of butter and carton of eggs. "I know it," she said. She sliced a pat of butter into the pan and then cracked two eggs.

Roxanne slumped onto one of the kitchen chairs, as two yolk-colored eyes began to sizzle in the iron skillet. She wanted desperately to believe her best friend was right, but Muriel was too woo-woo to even think clearly about the guy. Where was Level-Headed Muriel when Roxanne needed her?

30

The wind whipped across the Jones Beach parking field as Satriano jogged in place to keep warm. He had been worried that, considering the circumstances, fewer people would show up for this year's Agnes Stryker Walk for Cancer but there appeared to be even more participants than last year. Nothing like a murder to bring out the curiosity—and generosity—in people.

"They should have these things in the summertime," his sister groaned from behind him so that he could shield her from the wind. She was wearing a hat, gloves, and a scarf.

"What a sissy," he said.

"Shut up, Ton," Mary said, rubbing her gloved hands together.

Satriano's parents had set up their annual fruit stand, donating apples, oranges, bottles of water, and, new this year, organic hot chocolate to all registered walkers, who were lining up in huddles of twos and threes and presumably all chatting about the same thing: that morning's arrest of Marty Benning.

"Here, Anthony, have some hot cocoa. It will keep you warm," Satriano's mother said, handing him a paper cup.

"Where's mine?" Mary said.

"Oh, you can get it yourself. You have two legs."

"Typical . . ." Mary said, storming off.

Satriano's mother zipped up the front of his jacket.

"I'm fine, Mom."

"I'm worried about you, Anthony. You haven't been looking too good lately. Do you know this Martin Benning person?"

"Yeah, I know him. Not that well, but I've seen him around."

"Well, I don't like him."

"Ma, you don't even know him."

"I know enough," she said. "I see the way he looks at Mary when he's in the store. He's not a good boy, but . . . do you think he could do *this* to the tax man?"

He had been wondering about that all morning, and about the email he had gotten from Stryker on Monday night urging him to meet in order to talk about Benning. "I just don't know, Ma," he said.

A limousine entered the parking field, chased by members of the press, who had been boxed out of the event by a row of policemen stationed along the perimeter of the boardwalk.

"Looks like Gloria Stryker's here," his mother said, as Mary returned with her cocoa. "I'd better get back to your father."

"I wasn't sure she'd come," Mary said.

The limo parked behind two ambulances, its back door opened, and Gloria's three boys, dressed in dark basketball shorts and jerseys, emerged followed by Gloria Stryker who was wearing a black velour jogging suit. The reporters allowed the three boys to pass, but not Gloria, whom they descended upon with force:

"Gloria Stryker, have you heard the news that Marty Benning has been arrested?"

"Gloria, tell us how you're feeling!"

"Is it true, Gloria, that Marty Benning is a friend of yours?"

Satriano pushed through the crowd. "Please, everyone, enough," he said, but instead the reporters pivoted their microphones toward him:

"Assemblyman, can you give a statement on the arrest of Marty Benning?"

"Assemblyman Satriano, what do you think—"

"I'll answer all your questions later." He took Gloria Stryker's arm and guided her past the line of policemen and onto the boardwalk.

"Thank you, Tony," Gloria said. She pushed her large black sunglasses up the bridge of her nose.

"I wasn't sure you were going to make it today," Satriano said.

"I had to come. For Kirk." Gloria glanced at the ocean, where soapy waves were crashing in quick succession on the shore. "When he established this walk six years ago in memory of his mother, he told me it was one of his proudest accomplishments. He was always so excited to see all the young girls attending with their moms and other family members. I refuse to let this die with him." Gloria scanned the boardwalk and waved to several race participants. "Excuse me," she said. "Duty calls." She put on a smile and waded into the crowd.

A small stage had been set up by the flagpole at the Center Mall. About five hundred feet away was the old

Boardwalk Bandshell, which had seen better days, but was still a popular spot during Long Island summer nights. Gloria Stryker was helped up onto a platform, her boys beside her, as the crowd gathered round. She was holding a microphone.

"Good morning, everyone," she said, her voice sounding over-modulated and tinny from two portable speakers. "I want to thank you all for being here today on this very chilly morning. As you know, my husband, Kirk, usually speaks at the beginning of this event." Gloria paused for a moment to clear her throat. "It meant the world to him to be able to give back to the community in this way after losing his mother to cancer. In six years, the Agnes Stryker Walk for Cancer has been able to raise more than three hundred thousand dollars for charity." Hands went into the air as the crowd hooted and hollered. "And we've been able to do that because of you. Of your support. A big thank-you to Satriano's Fruit Market, which is kind enough every year to come here and donate to this cause." Gloria paused, giving the crowd the chance to applaud. "And"—she motioned to Satriano—"to Assemblyman Anthony Satriano, a man whom my husband was very proud to work with and support. I hope you know, Assemblyman, that you will continue to not only have my appreciation for all that you do for our family and our community but also my continued support for your campaign."

This was followed by another round of applause, and Mary squeezed Satriano's arm. He smiled appreciatively, catching a glimpse of his mother and father, who were beaming with so much pride they practically glowed.

"On a final note," Gloria continued, "I hope you

understand, but I will not comment on the police investigation and any news that has happened in the past few hours regarding the death of my husband." Gloria's youngest son looked up at her, and she put her arm around him. "Instead, I'd like to concentrate on this amazing community and all the good work it has done and for helping this event grow bigger and more successful every year. To all of you who are fighting this horrific disease, know someone who is, or someone who lost their battle to it, this walk is for you. If there's one thing I learned this week, it's that life is too short to focus on all that we can't do and don't have. Sometimes we are taken too early to get to do the things we've planned, so let us celebrate right now our community, our family, our friends, and continue to fight for the things and causes we believe in. Thank you. And have a good and safe walk."

As the crowd erupted in applause, Gloria Stryker stepped down, gathered her boys, and led the walk down the boardwalk, officially signaling the beginning of the event. The participants funneled behind her, including Satriano and Mary, who plugged her earbuds into her ears. They waved to their parents who had already begun packing up the produce.

Although it was cold, the sun was bright, and after ten minutes of walking, Satriano felt his internal heater kick in and unzipped his coat. The crowd had begun to disperse—the faster walkers took the lead, while the slower ones settled into a comfortable pace in the rear—and as Satriano reached into his pocket for his iPhone, he felt a tap on his shoulder. He turned to see Paulette Krause sidle up beside him, pumping her arms in rhythm with her long strides.

"Looks like your campaign financing is in the bag," she said in between puffs of breath. She checked the Fitbit on her wrist. "I know Gloria Stryker. And she wouldn't say it if she didn't mean it."

"How are you holding up?" Satriano asked, changing the subject, although by the looks of her, she seemed to be holding up fine. He didn't know Paulette well, but she had always seemed like a survivor.

"We're hanging in there . . ." Paulette motioned behind her where several of Stryker's employees were walking together. "Being busy helps. Crazy about Benning, huh?"

"Yeah," Satriano said.

"He was supposed to keynote a conference down in Atlantic City on Tuesday."

"During tax season?"

"I know, the timing's ridiculous, but they can't get enough people in the off-season when the muckety-mucks are on vacation. Looks like they'll have to find a last-minute replacement."

Satriano scanned the faces of the walkers. He hadn't seen any of Benning's team around. Despite Benning and Stryker's differences, Benning supported this charity event every year, and his team usually arrived en masse wearing matching red T-shirts.

"Kirk had a hard-on for that guy, I'll tell ya," Paulette continued, waving to a walker to her right. "I think it would be an understatement to say he was obsessed with Marty Benning from the moment he opened his practice. I always thought he was crazy, but after this morning's news, I guess there was something there, after all."

They came upon a large woman struggling to keep

pace with the group. Satriano recognized her to be Eva Sansfield, Kirk Stryker's administrative assistant.

"Hi, Paulette," Eva said as they passed her.

"Hey," Paulette said, dismissively.

"Hello," Satriano said with a smile.

When he and Paulette were a few yards ahead of Eva, Paulette leaned over and whispered, "We've been walking for just over ten minutes, and she's huffing and puffing already."

"That's a bit harsh," Satriano said. "Takes guts to be out here. She's got the right attitude."

"There's nothing right about that girl, I'll tell ya," Paulette said before picking up speed. "Nice to see you, Assemblyman." Paulette speed-walked ahead and the rest of Stryker's team, who had been hovering in her wake, raced to catch up with her as Eva Sansfield seemed to be falling farther and farther behind.

31

Muriel opened the dishwasher, the steam washing over her and fogging the air before her eyes. Across the tiny kitchen, Doug took off his fireman's jacket and plucked a green grape from the fruit bowl.

"Don't you have to be at the firehouse?" Muriel asked, hoping he'd leave now that he dropped off the kids.

"I have time." He looked around the kitchen as if he hadn't seen it in years. "I need to fix that," he said, pointing to the water mark on the ceiling. Muriel didn't know why Doug was always reminding himself he had to fix things. He never did.

"It's just a stain. Not a big deal," she said, dumping some water out from a Tupperware bowl. Muriel could hear voices from downstairs where the kids were watching TV. If Doug intended to stick around and annoy her about Marty, she was glad the volume was loud.

"You know, the kids aren't doing so great," he said, crossing his arms.

"The kids are managing, Doug."

"This separation thing is really affecting Ellie. Or haven't you noticed?"

The barb buried itself in Muriel's chest, where it

always did, joining a collection that was fifteen years in the making. "Ellie is all right."

"Oh, she's perfectly fine, which is why you removed the door to her bedroom . . ."

"Doug, it's fine. Don't worry about it." She gestured toward the divorce papers she had drawn up lying on the dining room table. "Since you're here, maybe you can finally take a look at the paperwork from my lawyer. I think you'll find it's fair."

Doug barely glanced at the table. He twisted his wedding band.

"You're still wearing that?" she asked.

"Why not? I'm still married, aren't I?" He put his hands to his sides. "You know, I really thought that you'd get over this separation idea sooner or later."

Muriel stuck two tablespoons into the flatware drawer. "That's just it, Doug." She slammed the drawer closed without meaning to. "That's what you always think. That *I'll get over* things. And I have. For *years*. You act like a jerk. I get mad, and then I get over it. You use part of our savings to buy a pair of hockey tickets—"

"They were *first row*, Muriel."

"That's irrelevant, Doug. And what happened? I got mad, and then I got over it."

"Yeah, well," Doug shrugged, "I thought that's just what we did. That's how we got through things."

"No, it's how *I* got through things. To survive. To get through the day. To get through the *years*. I don't want to live my life being in a perpetual bad mood, so I get over things." She placed a mug and a cereal bowl into the cabinet above the stove. "It's not a fun way to live—for either one of us. C'mon, Doug, be honest. You can't have been that happy the last few years we were together . . ."

"Please," he said, with his disgusted face, "don't try to make it seem like you're doing *me* a favor, Muriel, with this separation. This is *on you. For you.* Some quest for a happily ever after that doesn't exist."

"You think this is easy for me, Doug? Trust me, it would be far *easier* to stay married."

"So why didn't you?"

Muriel laughed. "Wow, with a proposal like that, how could I say no?"

The landline rang, and Muriel was inclined to ignore it since the vast majority of the calls were from telemarketers, but she was happy for the distraction. She looked at the caller ID and didn't recognize the phone number but picked up the handset anyway.

"Maybe it's your boyfriend's one phone call from jail," Doug said snidely.

"Funny," Muriel said and pressed the *Talk* button on the receiver. "Hello?"

There was a pause, then a beep, and Muriel knew that it was an automated call before the robotic voice even spoke. She had half a mind to stay on the line just so Doug would leave the room but ended the call as Zack came up the stairs. He threw a banana peel into the garbage and reached for a chocolate chip cookie. "Who was that?" he asked.

"Nobody," Muriel said, taking the cookie out of Zack's hand and putting it back in the nearly empty box. "It's a little early for cookies."

"Daddy lets me have cookies in the morning."

Doug smiled with satisfaction. "What does it matter, Mur? It's just a cookie." He eyed Muriel's wall calendar. "Why do you have Atlantic City written in tomorrow's box? Are you going to Atlantic City? Don't you have to work?"

Shit, Atlantic City . . . With everything that had happened over the weekend, Muriel had forgotten all about it.

Before Muriel could explain, Zack said, "Aunt Jo is in Atlantic City."

"What else is new?" Doug said.

"And Marty has a conference or something there on Tuesday," Ellie said, coming up the stairs.

"Geez, Mur," Doug crossed his arms, "can't you do *anything* without that guy?"

"I forgot all about it," Muriel said, ignoring Doug. "Maybe I'll just cancel and stay home."

"Won't Aunt Jo miss you?" Zack asked.

She would. It had been months since they had spent time together. "I'll see her another time."

"Who was supposed to watch Ellie and Zack?" Doug asked.

"My mother offered to—"

"I'll take the kids," Doug said, wrapping his arms around them. "They'll be safe with me."

"What is that supposed to mean?"

"It means exactly what it sounds like," Doug said with a familiar finality. He took three cookies out of the open box, stuck one in his mouth, and handed one to both Zack and Ellie. Her children smiled at her conspiratorially. Before Muriel could complain, Doug said, "What are you guys watching?" and walked downstairs, the kids following behind him like ducklings.

Muriel was about to say something she was going to regret when the landline rang in her hand, startling her, but this time she recognized the number. "Hi, Rock," she said. "Why are you calling this phone?"

"You're not picking up your cell," Roxanne said. "How are you?"

"All right. Doug's here."

"Ugh, then you're definitely not all right." Muriel smiled. "Doesn't he have a stray cat to save from a tree?"

"He's busy saving his children from their delusional mother," Muriel whispered, wiping the cookie crumbs from the counter.

"Forget him," Roxanne said. "Did you call the detective yet?"

Muriel sighed. "No." Roxanne had been trying to talk her out of calling Detective Munson most of the night. Apparently, she still was. "I was just about to."

"You can change your mind, you know."

"Marty's innocent, Rock."

"You don't know that."

Muriel didn't want to argue again, so she changed the subject. "You know, I completely forgot I was supposed to go to Atlantic City tomorrow after work."

"Atlantic City? You got Wednesday off?"

"No, it's Superintendent's Day."

"Whatever *that* is. I mean, do suburban kids *ever* go to school?" She laughed at her own joke. "What's in Atlantic City?"

Muriel hesitated. She didn't want to lie to Roxanne, so she decided to leave out the part about Marty's conference and tell her only about Aunt Jo. It dawned on her that she was behaving just like Ellie—lying by omission. Maybe someone should take Muriel's bedroom door off its hinges.

"My aunt's down there," she said. "I thought we could spend some time, but after all that's happened I think I'm going to call her and—"

"That's wonderful! You should go. Clear your head. Get out of dodge for a while."

Muriel smiled. "You think going will make me change my mind about calling Detective Munson, don't you?"

"I didn't say that," Roxanne said.

"You didn't have to."

"Just take some time for yourself, Mo. Away from Doug, the kids, from . . . well, all of it. Get some perspective."

Muriel shrugged. "I guess. It's really been a long time since I've seen Aunt Jo."

"Then it's settled. Go to A.C. tomorrow and kick Doug out of the house now so you can spend time with your kids. *Alone.* Especially El. Having a boyfriend is a big deal, Mo. Of all people, *you* should know that."

"I know. I will. I'll talk to you later."

Muriel clicked off the call and placed the phone on the counter. She went into the living room and rummaged through a small bowl on the bookcase that held buttons, paper clips, and scraps of paper. She picked out Detective Munson's card with her phone number.

Marty is innocent. No trip to Atlantic City would make her change her mind about that. She knew it. She *felt* it. She listened to see if anyone was coming up the stairs and then dialed the detective's phone number. *Who knows,* she thought, as the line rang on the other end. With Muriel vouching for him, maybe Marty would be out of jail in time to attend his conference on Tuesday in Atlantic City—he could meet her there. She smiled. Happily ever after, indeed.

32

John Parker strode into the police precinct with the air of the commissioner himself. Since his Hugo Lurch story hit the *Gazette's* website, he had become a celebrity in local journalism circles—reporters from *Newsday*, News 12, and several of the network television affiliates followed him on Twitter and had commended his investigative work. Gardner was so excited that he decided to open the office that day, even though it was Sunday, to bask in the glow of the scoop. Kramer had mysteriously called in sick, much to Parker's delight.

Still, the arrest of Marty Benning that morning had caught Parker by surprise. He wasn't sure why they brought Benning in or how Benning and Lurch were connected. He couldn't remember whether Detective Munson had paid a visit to Benning during her recent trip to Manhattan. He knew the guy had an office there, but wasn't sure if the address she had gone to was his. His notes had somehow disappeared, and he couldn't remember a damn thing.

The police department was scheduling a press briefing for three o'clock, which would probably answer some questions, but Parker was feeling empowered and wanted to sniff out new leads on his own. He tucked his press badge under his jacket and approached the front desk, where there was a line five people long.

As he waited, officers crisscrossed the room with a renewed swagger, obviously excited by all the attention. One of them put down a telephone receiver and hurried over to the female officer manning the front desk, saying, "This is for Detective Munson." The woman at the desk nodded, tucked the note under her desk calendar with several others, and barked at the next person in line to step forward.

"Can I help you?" she said to Parker when it was his turn.

"Busy today, huh?" Parker said, stalling.

"Yeah, very." She looked at him expectantly.

"Yes, um, I need to report a . . . theft."

"What was stolen?" the woman said, reaching into a drawer.

"My car," Parker lied.

"All right, fill out this form."

Parker reached over the counter so she could hand it to him, but the paper slipped out of his hand and floated to the ground.

"I'm so sorry," Parker said. "It's not my day today, I guess."

"Tell me about it." The young woman exhaled loudly, and he wondered if it was the girl he had spoken to on the phone the other day. She bent down to get the paperwork. As she did, Parker reached toward her as if to help and slipped the note for Detective Munson into his left palm.

"Here you go," the woman said, placing the sheet of paper into Parker's hand. "Fill that out and bring it back to me. What kind was it?"

"What kind was what?" Parker asked.

"The car."

"Oh, a Mustang. Ford Mustang."

"Oh. Nice. Well, I'm very sorry," she said, before yelling "Next!" to the person behind Parker in line.

Parker strode away as quickly and nonchalantly as he could until he reached the lobby. His adrenaline was pumping. He looked at the crumpled note in his hand. It was one of those old-fashioned *While You Were Out* pink notes, and written on the top line was *Muriel Adams* and a phone number.

Muriel Adams. Parker remembered the name from yesterday's stakeout. He still didn't know how she was connected to any of this.

He put the note away and lingered, wondering what his next move should be, but he had gotten the attention of a guard who was eyeing him suspiciously. He wandered toward a counter and pretended to read the paperwork the officer had given him when Detective Munson walked through the front door of the precinct.

She looked older close up and, not surprisingly, like she had a lot on her mind. When the woman at the front desk spotted her, she called her over and shuffled a few papers on her desk, looking confused.

"That's okay, Mickey," Betty said. "When you find it, give me a holla. I'll be in my office."

"Detective Munson," Parker called as she walked by him.

"Yes?" she said, turning around. She seemed to be sizing Parker up. He pulled down on his New Paltz hoodie and walked over. "Can I help you?" she asked.

He pulled out his press badge. "John Parker, *Gardenia Gazette*."

He extended his hand, but Munson didn't shake it. "I'm sorry, this isn't a good time," she said.

"But—"

"I'm sorry, Mr. Parker. I have no comment. You'll have to wait outside with the rest of the press."

"I know about Hugo Lurch," he whispered.

"So does everyone, thanks to you." Munson walked toward the guard who had been watching Parker. She gave him a fist bump. "Hey, Jose," she said.

"Wait," Parker called, running toward her, causing Jose to stand at attention. "I mean. I *know* about Hugo Lurch."

"You know this guy, Detective Munson?" Jose asked.

Munson gave a resigned sigh. "It's all right," she said. "All right, Parker, you got five minutes. Come with me."

Parker smiled and raised his hand to give Jose a fist bump, but the guard wasn't amused. Parker put down his hand and passed through a metal detector, following Munson to a side door. She opened it and gestured for him to step inside.

The small room looked less like an interrogation room, which is what Parker hoped it might be, and more like an office. It had a conference-room-type table, several chairs, and a metallic smell.

"So," Betty said, closing the door behind them. "What exactly do you know?"

"I think you know," Parker said.

"Listen, kid, I'm not in the mood to play games."

"I know that Hugo Lurch was killed by a gunshot wound."

"Well, that's what I read in your article, Mr. Parker, isn't it?"

"I know that you were the officer who found Mr. Lurch."

"I'm afraid that information isn't being made public."

"And I know you found him *alive*."

This caught Detective Munson off guard, but the old gal recovered pretty quickly. "Really? I don't remember reading that bit of info in your article."

"I can't prove it," he said.

"Well, then how do you know that it's true?"

"I was there," Parker said. "I *saw* you." He took out his notepad and a pen. "What did you say to Lurch? Was it anything that might want to make him off himself?"

He thought he caught a tiny wince on Munson's part before she opened the office door. "Our briefing is in less than an hour, Mr. Parker. You can ask your questions then. Now, if you'll—"

"Detective Munson, do you really want me to stand in front of all the other reporters and ask the police commissioner why one of his detectives waited outside the home of Hugo Lurch after being inside for," he flipped a few pages of his notepad, "nineteen minutes, and only ran back inside once she heard a shot fired? I don't think you'd like that made public, considering that's not what's on the police report."

Munson crossed her arms, her red hair accentuating the wrinkles around her eyes, which were tightening. "Listen, kid, if you think you know something, and if you think the Nassau County police department is hiding something, then by all means go ahead."

"I don't think the department is hiding something,"

Parker said. "I think *you* are." Adrenaline was pumping through Parker's body. He had never spoken this way to a cop, and he hoped the goosebumps on his arms weren't visible through his cotton shirt. This journalism stuff was intoxicating. "Your police report details that Lurch was found dead at the scene. Now why would that be?"

Betty opened the door wider. "I would tread lightly if I were you, Mr. Parker," she said.

"What do you have on Benning?"

Betty stepped outside and nodded to someone, and within moments Jose appeared in the doorframe.

"Good-bye, Mr. Parker," Munson said, walking out of sight.

"All right, kid, let's go," Jose said, escorting Parker out of the building.

Outside, the sunny sky had turned gray as the reporters and news cameras gathered for the upcoming press conference. Parker smiled as several journalists whispered among themselves: "That's John Parker," he heard one say with admiration.

He strode toward them with confidence and then past them, in the direction of his car. He had no intention of staying for the press conference with the herd. *I've got something better*, he thought and squeezed his fist around the crumpled piece of pink paper that contained the phone number of Muriel Adams.

33

"**U**ncle Anthony, can you push me?"

Satriano stuck his car keys into his pocket and stepped around the tire swing. He pulled up on the bottom link of the suspension chain until his goddaughter's back was directly in front of his eyes.

"Is this good, Pina?" he asked.

"Higher, Uncle Anthony, higher!" the little girl squealed, her legs kicking with excitement under her white Communion dress.

"All right, if you think you're big enough!" He lifted the tire over his head and let it go with a *whoosh*.

"*Whee!*" Pina shouted, and each time the swing reached the pinnacle of its sweeping forward arc, she called over the white backyard fence, "Mommy, Mommy, look at me!"

"Now, don't forget to pump," Satriano said, giving her a few more pushes before heading toward the backyard, where Mary was standing by the gate.

"It's about time you got here, Ton." She was scraping macaroni salad into her mouth from a floppy paper plate. "You missed the church. Mommy was ready to send out a search party."

"I couldn't get away from them." Satriano plucked a

noodle from Mary's plate and dropped it into his mouth. "The reporters were outside my house. *Benning, Benning, Benning . . .* Just when one reporter finished, another one started up. I must have come up with fifteen ways to say *no comment.*"

"Ah, there he is!" his father called from the rear of the backyard. He was sitting at a picnic table, wearing his plaid bow tie, which was reserved for special occasions, with a bunch of uncles and cousins. There must have been at least fifty Satrianos of varying ages crammed into the small backyard, and not all of them, unfortunately, shining examples of good citizenry. At a glance, Satriano counted two cousins who had been incarcerated for grand theft auto, another for murder in the second degree, and still another who was on trial in Brooklyn for drug possession. Not the greatest commercial for a politician. Still, family was family.

"My son, the assemblyman!" his father said, standing, as all his relatives—well, *most* of them—clapped. Satriano gave a quick wave.

"Here's a tip," Mary whispered. She grabbed his arm before he could enter the yard. "Stay clear of Cousin Marco. He's on his second bottle of wine."

"Got it," he said, but when he walked in, Marco was standing right there, leaning against the back of the house, a cigarette dangling out of his mouth. He looked thinner than Satriano remembered, almost gaunt. The last time Satriano had seen him had been right around the time Marco was being investigated by NYPD for torching his father's pizza place for the insurance money. Nothing ever came of it, although he had almost gotten caught since Marco had a habit of standing around to watch his handiwork. Idiot. But the police could never seem to get enough evidence to make a charge stick. Marco had a way of getting himself out of even the most harrowing of jams, although, clearly, the guy had been eating less pizza.

"Well, well, well, look what the cat dragged in," Marco said. He was alone, at the edge of the yard, where people were exiled to smoke. His white button-down shirt was open, revealing a white wifebeater T-shirt. "Too busy to come to your godddaughter's Communion, I see. And don't try and blame it on the traffic on the Belt Parkway."

"Hey, Marco," Satriano said, ignoring the comment. He shook hands with his cousin and pulled a card out of his jacket pocket. "This is for Pina. God bless."

"Thanks." Marco shook the envelope. "Feels a bit light," he said with a smile before slipping it into the back pocket of his suit pants.

"Sorry I'm late. A lot of shit is going down in the district."

Marco snickered. "Move out to the suburbs for all that fresh air and grass, and look, more shit's going down in your neck of the woods than around here." He took a drag of his cigarette. "I'm surprised you even want to be seen in this neighborhood anymore. Might lose you a few votes."

"Gimme a break, Marc."

"I'm just sayin'." He rubbed the cigarette's filtered end with the pad of his thumb. "So I see they arrested some guy, the one who killed your boy Stryker."

"Seems that way."

"Lucky that gym bitch saw the flames or else that guy would have been responsible for the whole building going down and who knows how many more people." Marco took one more drag before stubbing out his cigarette on the brick wall. "You would have lost a few more votes." He laughed. "Oh well. Shit happens. Maybe without the old guy pumping a shitload of money into your campaign you'll have to do some real work for a living."

"What are you two chaps talking about?" Mary said, coming up beside Satriano. Leave it to his sister to step in and defuse the tension. Politics was rubbing off on her.

"Looking good, Mar," Marco said. "You turned into quite a beautiful woman. Looks like you got all the good looks in the family."

Mary pinched Satriano's back to keep him from saying something he wouldn't regret. "Thanks, Marc," she said.

"Mary!" Satriano's mother called, as the back door slid open. She was carrying a large white frosted cake in the shape of an open bible. "Can you call Pina? The cake's out. We want to take some pictures."

"Sure, why not?" Mary said with sarcasm. "There's only a thousand other people here who can do it." She turned to go.

"Stay, Mar. I'll get her," Satriano said.

"Awww, the public servant strikes again," Marco said as Satriano walked toward the front yard. He hoped Marco wouldn't keep this up for the rest of the afternoon; his patience was wearing thin.

Outside, he looked for Pina on the tire swing, but she wasn't there. "Peen!" he yelled, stepping onto the driveway.

"I'm here, Uncle Anthony!" Pina called from somewhere next door.

She was probably petting the neighbor's dog again—

she had been asking Marco for a dog for years. Little did she know she had a dog for a father.

Satriano circled around the front fence and froze. Pina wasn't petting the dog. She was talking to a person he didn't recognize, a tall man who was wearing a baseball cap and sunglasses.

"Pina!" Satriano called harshly, and the little girl came running. He bent down and put his hands on her shoulders. "Do you know that man?"

"No, Uncle Anthony."

"You know you're not allowed to talk to strangers."

"He's not a stranger," Pina explained, her brown eyes sincere. "He says he knows you. He told me to ask you to come outside, but you're already here." She smiled.

Satriano looked again at the guy. He was sure he didn't recognize him, although it was hard to tell with the cap and sunglasses. Suddenly, he remembered the man who had asked for him at the fruit market. He had been wearing a baseball cap too. If it was the same guy, whoever he was had followed him there. To his cousin's house. And who knew where else.

"Listen, Pina, unless *you* know who he is, then he's a stranger and you shouldn't go near him, got it?"

The little girl nodded. "I'm sorry, Uncle Anthony."

"It's all right. Go into the backyard. It's time for pictures and cake."

As Pina ran toward the gate, Satriano stood up, his thighs still sore from the cancer walk. "Can I help you?" he asked warily.

"I hope you can," the man said. "I'm looking for my money." He pulled on his jacket and revealed a pistol tucked inside the waistband of his pants.

"Whoa . . ." Satriano took a step back and put up his hands. "I'm sorry, but I don't know what you're talking about."

"Really?" the man said. "Well, then, that's going to be a problem."

"I've got a couple hundred in the car."

"A couple hundred?" He let out a small laugh. "I'll need more than fifty times that. And I'll need it this week."

Italian music began playing in Marco's backyard, and there was a chant of *Pina, Pina, Pina*. "I don't know what you're talking about," Satriano said. "I don't owe you any money."

"No, your boy Stryker did."

Stryker. Why did everyone keep calling Stryker his *boy*? "What does that have to do with me?"

"Everything, *Assemblyman*," the man said, placing his hand on the gun. "Let's just say your friend Stryker had a little goldmine of a thing going until Benning moved in. And let's just say that Stryker wasn't too happy with him. The best thing to happen to Marty Benning was when something happened to Kirk Stryker. And the best thing to happen to you was when Benning was arrested for murder."

"I'm not following," Satriano said.

"You don't need to. All you need to do is get me the fifteen thousand dollars that Kirk owes me by Thursday."

"Fifteen thousand dollars? I don't have that kind of money lying around."

"Yes, you do, Assemblyman. You just need to find it. Kirk knew how to."

"Uncle Anthony, Uncle Anthony!"

Pina was running toward him, her white veil trailing behind her and scraping along the concrete.

"Pina, stay back," Satriano warned. Gun or no gun, he couldn't risk Pina getting anywhere near this guy again. He ran toward her, scooping her up just before she reached the tire swing.

"We need to take a picture of you and me," she said, fidgeting in his arms. "Mommy says we need a godfather picture."

"I know, but I can't right now."

"Why?"

Satriano glanced back at the man in the baseball cap, but the neighbor's yard was empty. He was gone.

"Where's your friend?" Pina asked.

"He's not my friend." Satriano put Pina down and looked up and down the block, but the guy had vanished. He clasped her hand. "And from now on, I don't want you swinging in the front of the house alone."

They walked toward the gate, where Marco had appeared, smoking another cigarette.

"Peen, run ahead," Marco said. "I want to talk to Uncle Anthony."

"But we have to take a godfather picture," Pina whined.

"Take a few cousin pictures first," Marco said. "Tell your mother I said to. Now go."

Pina released Satriano's hand and stomped her way back into the yard, yelling for her mother. When she was gone, Marco took another drag of his cigarette and held his breath.

"Who was that?" he finally asked on the exhale.

"Who was who?"

Marco smirked. "Seriously? You must think I'm stupider than I look."

"You really want me to respond to that?"

"You getting my daughter mixed up in your shit?"

"My shit?" Satriano crossed his arms. "How interesting that you never seemed to care about exposing her to *your* shit."

"What is he, your fucking lover or something?"

"Give me a break, Marc. I don't know who he was. He just came out of nowhere."

"What did he want?" Marco asked as Satriano's father appeared holding a plate of baked ziti.

"Anthony, come, you need to eat something." He smiled and handed him the plate, along with a napkin and plastic fork, but his smile disappeared once he searched Satriano's face. "You've got that look again, like something's wrong. What's the matter?"

"Nothing's the matter. I'm just talking to Marco." He forced himself to take a forkful of ziti.

"Marco? Why?"

Why, indeed, Satriano thought. "Because I—"

"He's offering me a job," Marco said with a smile.

"A job?" his father asked, surprised. "Doing what?"

"Oh, you know," Marco said. "This and that."

"I thought Mary took care of this and that for you, Anthony," his father said.

"She does." Satriano glared at Marco. "It's not really a job, per se, it's just, you know, I need—"

"Protection," Marco said.

"Protection? From what?" his father asked, looking concerned again.

"From no one, Pop. Everything is—"

"What about the guy who was just here?" Marco said with a look of innocence. *Asshole.*

"What guy?" Satriano's father asked.

"It's nobody, Pop. Nothing to worry about."

"Does it have to do with that terrible business back home?" his father asked. "With that Marty Benning person?"

"I think so," Marco said.

"Marc, please ... " Satriano said. "It's none of your concern, Pop."

"They say he has a bodyguard, that Benning fellow," his father said.

"Hey, I can be *your* bodyguard," Marco said to Satriano.

"I don't need a bodyguard."

"That's what they all say, but politics is a dirty business," Marco said. "Look what happened to your boy, Stryker."

Satriano was busy looking at his father, who was absently tugging at his plaid bow tie. The last thing his father needed was to think that his only son was involved in one of Marco's schemes or in danger. The man had moved his wife and children to Nassau County to get away from all the lunacy in the boroughs, and Satriano wasn't about to pull him back in. If the guy in the hat and sunglasses was a problem, he would be Satriano's problem. "Pop, please," he put his hand on his father's shoulder, "I'm not in any danger."

"You don't think that this person—Benning's bodyguard person—will be coming after you, Anthony, do you?"

"Of course not. Why would he?" Satriano said as the memory of Stryker's email resurfaced in his mind: *Tony, we need to talk. It's urgent. About Benning.* He willed it away. "There's no reason to think—"

"You never know these days," Marco said. "That guy Benning won't be in jail forever. Will probably post bail in a few days." He puffed up his scrawny chest. "I can keep an eye on him for you, if you like. Follow him around, see what he's up to. Do some—you know—*investigating.*"

"Marc," Satriano said, "I appreciate the offer, but—"

"My Anthony is a good boy," his father said. He patted Satriano's cheek. "He fights the good fight. He doesn't want to get involved in any of your funny business."

"Unfortunately, the good fight doesn't always work, Uncle Frankie," Marco said. "People like *him*"—he pointed to Satriano—"need people like *me*. It's a fact of life. That's why Benning has a goon. He gets it."

"Uncle *Anthonyyyyyyy!*" Pina screamed from the backyard.

"We'd better go back there," Satriano said and hoped that would be the end of it. He took his father's arm and led him through the gate, Marco following behind, but as they reached the crowd of relatives hovering around Pina, Marco leaned toward him and whispered, "I can make all of your problems go away."

34

Paulette Krause reached her bare hands into the dirt and dug around the long roots of a rose of Sharon plant. When she pulled it out, a few earthworms fell onto the dry paving stones of the path, squiggling in confusion, but she dove in again for another root clump without noticing them. "These goddamn plants get everywhere," she muttered.

Betty watched her methodical movements, how her toned arms gleamed in the low afternoon sun and dug, dug, dug as if having performed the task hundreds of times. She thought of John Parker who, it seemed, had been doing a little digging of his own.

There had been such pandemonium at Hugo Lurch's apartment after the police backup and EMS teams arrived. Hours had passed before Betty even realized that the officers were operating under the impression that she had heard the gunshot on arrival and then found Lurch dead. She wasn't sure why she hadn't told them the truth. Had she been in shock?

She had had a lot on her mind, for sure—finding out that Benning's fingerprint had been at the crime scene; Lurch admitting that he knew about Stryker's disconnected smoke alarm, even though Betty wasn't exactly sure what that meant; the thought that Lurch's gun had been the weapon that murdered Stryker, although it turned out not to be a match. Then at some point it just seemed like a moot point to alter the narrative; she told herself the police report was simply a tiny reinterpretation of events that didn't really change the outcome.

But now Parker thought she had something to hide. She wasn't sure how he had followed her to Lurch's address, or even if he had—perhaps he was bluffing. The kid was definitely wrong about one thing: Betty hadn't been the cause of Lurch's death, no matter what she had said to him. Whatever demons had been lurking inside Lurch had done him in. Just like innocent men didn't cop to crimes because of fake fingerprints, they also didn't commit suicide.

"To be honest with you, I still can't believe it," Paulette said, grabbing the stems of the plants and tossing them into a nearby garbage can. "I had seen Kirk just before the police say it happened. I had said good night and asked him if he wanted Chinese food."

"That was around seven o'clock, correct?" Betty asked.

"Yeah," Paulette nodded, "around there, right before Sandra and I went to the bar across the street."

"And at eleven that night? Were you still at the bar?"

"I wish," Paulette said. "I ain't the gal I used to be. One beer and I'm ready for bed. . . . You know, I realized that if I had gone back to the office after Stevie's I would have stumbled onto whatever was going on there." She shook her head. "It's weird how such a small decision can have big consequences."

After the mix-up with the police report, Betty had to agree. "Stryker ever go with you? To the bar?"

"Never in a million years. Stryker was a total teetotaler. His only vice, as far as I could tell, was smoking, which he did on the sly in his office." Paulette rolled her eyes. "Like no one could tell."

"Do you smoke, Ms. Krause?" Betty had a feeling she knew the answer. Paulette's lifestyle seemed to be a model of efficiency, from the solar panels on her roof to the Fitbit on her wrist.

"Nope, was never even tempted to. Never appealed to me. My only vice is work."

"Did you ever see Hugo Lurch come around the office?"

Paulette shook her head. "Nah, not as far as I could tell, unless there was some kind of problem. After the last hurricane, there was a leak in our main room, near the front windows, so Lurch was around a lot then, but we've rarely seen him since."

"Did Lurch get along with Stryker?"

"Lurch wasn't what you could call *a people person*. I mean, he and Stryker got along, but they weren't best buddies, if that's what you mean." She shrugged her shoulders. "If there was something going on between them, I wasn't aware of it. Lurch was just . . . you know, there. Personally, I tried to avoid him."

"Why was that?"

"He was creepy. You know, pedophile creepy. I hate to say it. The poor guy's gone, but that's how I felt."

Betty thought of the photo of the two young children that had been hanging from Lurch's cabinet and had been taken into evidence. She had no IDs on either of the girls.

"Were you happy working with Stryker?"

"Happy?" Paulette wiped her dirty hands on her apron. "What was there to be unhappy about? I did my work—and did it well—came and went as I pleased. Got paid good money."

"Please don't take this the wrong way, Ms. Krause, but you don't seem all that shaken up about his murder."

Paulette thought before she answered. "Stryker was great and all, but he and I weren't what you would call *friends*. It was a business relationship based on money." She said the word *money* without apology. "I practically ran that office. Stryker knew it. I knew it. Everyone knew it. The place probably would have imploded if it weren't for me and the clients I brought in. I don't mean to brag, but it's the truth. The practice would not have survived if I hadn't been able to drudge up new business the way I did."

"Were there a lot of walk-ins?"

"Not so much. Benning got a lot, though. He outspent us in local advertising, that's for sure." Paulette pulled out a few more weeds. "Stryker had been saying for years that he wanted to do more of the common-man thing, but I persuaded him otherwise. Just too small potatoes, and then we'd be going head-to-head with Benning."

"You had a lot of influence on him then? Stryker, I mean."

"He respected my opinion. When Benning moved in, I suggested we target a completely different customer base, small business, that sort of thing, rather than relying on personal returns."

"Was it working?"

"It was starting to, but Stryker didn't want to spend

the money to really make it work. He could be a bit of a tightwad." She dug another hole, using a hoe to help get past a hard spot in the soil, and placed the last tulip plant into the ground.

"Did it bother you that you weren't made partner?"

Paulette patted the dirt around the plant. "It was only a matter of time," she said. "I think he would have sooner, but his wife didn't want to go for it."

"Gloria?"

"Nope. At least, that's what Stryker said. The guy was totally p-whipped."

A low plane flew overhead, dropping a shadow across the backyard that moved over the lawn like a windshield wiper blade. Paulette shielded the sunlight with her hands to watch it pass before picking up her toolbox and placing it into a nearby shed.

"There's talk that you might open up your own firm," Betty said.

"Yeah, the building landlord wants me to stay where I am now, but I want street level," Paulette called from inside the shed, and somehow Betty didn't have any doubts that she would get it. "Even if we don't go after the walk-in business, it would be nice to not have to go up and down stairs every time I wanted to buy a newspaper."

Paulette came back out and wiped the sweat from her forehead, leaving a smudge of dirt across her brow. "Detective Munson, I'm assuming that you already know that Benning offered me a job—several times," she said.

"I do. You must have been flattered."

"I was, at first."

"What do you mean?"

"It's weird." Paulette sat down on the back step of her home, the muscles of her lean calves shifting under her skin. "When Benning first asked to speak with me, I thought it was smart—you know, go after the top earner of your direct competitor and then drive him out of business."

"He didn't want that?"

"I don't think so. I felt like he wanted me for the opposite reason, actually. It wasn't so he could double up his efforts, but so he could spend *less* time at the office. He kinda looked disinterested in the whole thing, actually. I thought, Here was this guy, a Manhattan guy, a smart, attractive guy, who was going to get something going and create this chain of accounting offices and be the next H&R Block, but better. But, in reality, Benning seemed far less driven than Kirk, who, on the other hand, spent his days obsessing about Benning."

"Did you know anything about a meeting between Stryker and Benning?"

"A meeting? Between those two?" Paulette shook her head. "Unlikely."

"Did you ever tell Stryker that Benning had approached you?"

"Not really, but he knew. Word gets out, you know? We have a small office and do business in a small town. Plus, any time Benning's name came up, he didn't want to talk about him—unless *he* brought Benning's name up. Stryker's position seemed to be not to trust anything Benning said or did."

"What's *your* position?"

"My position?" Paulette stood up again. "Who the fuck knows. Can you ever really know someone? I mean, *really* know them? I just met the guy. He seemed nice enough, but if you've arrested him, well . . . I guess you know something I don't." Paulette waited for Betty to say something, and when she didn't, she took out the garden hose and began washing away all the dirt from the path before snapping off her gardening gloves. She seemed to have trouble sitting still.

"So if there's nothing further, Detective, I hope you'll excuse me." Paulette folded the gloves under her arm. "There's no resting on Sundays during tax season. I've got to get back to work. After all, I have an accounting business to save." She headed up the stairs and through her back door before Betty could answer—or ask any more questions.

35

Bobby measured three teaspoons of cayenne pepper and poured it into the bowl of the slow cooker. So many of the chili recipes out there were either too mild or too acidic, and he was ready to go a little rogue. It was the first time he hadn't followed a recipe to a T, and his finger trembled slightly as it drifted to the next line of text on the screen of his new iPad, as if the recipe teacher would catch him cheating. He reached for a can of drained kidney beans and poured them in.

His cell phone buzzed on the countertop. He checked his caller ID and swiped. "Hey. This your one phone call? I'm honored."

"You should be," Benning said. "She all right?"

"Yeah, she's fine. How about you?"

"I've been better. We good for tonight?"

"Yeah," Bobby said. "I'm leaving in a little while."

"Good."

Bobby reached for the bowl of chopped onions and poured them in with the rest of the ingredients.

"What did you find out about Munson?"

"Not much," Bobby said using a wooden spoon to mix the chili. He put the lid on the slow cooker and turned the knob to *low*. "Old broad's about to retire, from what I hear. Got two young boys. Husband's in a wheelchair. Car accident four years ago. Nearly died."

"She seems like a tough cookie. Was playing it cool. Took an interest in my telescope."

"Telescope?"

"Beats me. Probably thinks I'm spying on my neighbors."

"She's probably right." Bobby smiled.

"Listen, keep me posted on tonight. Take down this number."

Bobby grabbed a pen and wrote the telephone number on his palm. "Whose number is this?"

"Did the taxes for one of the guards in here last year. Says I saved him a shitload of money. He's getting more pussy from his wife. Asked if he could do anything for me to make my stay more comfortable. He's making his cell phone available."

"Got it." Bobby heard Benning say something, but the call was dropping. "What did you say? I missed that."

"I said this whole thing is bullshit. Gone are the days when a woman's alibi was enough."

"Muriel wants to believe," Bobby said. "I could tell. I'm not so sure about her friend."

"Who? The one in the wig and the hat?"

Bobby smiled. "Yeah, you thought *I* was tough. She's a viper, that one."

"She gonna be a problem?"

"Nah." Bobby licked the wooden spoon and tossed it into the sink. "Leave her to me."

36

Betty's car crunched along the pebbled grounds of the Stryker property. The wide circular drive led to a detached barn, which looked as though it did double duty as a garage and workshop, judging by the power tools, dirt, and wood littered beside it. Betty had never been to this second residence, the childhood home of Gloria Stryker, located about nine miles north of Gardenia. From the top of the drive, which was on a small hill overlooking Long Island Sound, Betty could see the shores of Connecticut, which were only a bridge away, if they ever managed to build one, and on a clear day she could probably see as far as Rhode Island. Not bad.

Gloria Stryker was sitting on the front porch when Betty walked up the path, a box of tissues and a glass of what looked like iced tea beside her.

"Hi, Mrs. Stryker. I hope I'm not disturbing you."

"Not at all, Detective. Just resting my legs." There were dirt marks on the knees of Gloria's pants, which were rolled up to mid-calf.

"Working in the garage today?" Betty said.

"Garage? Oh, no," she gestured dismissively, "Kirk had

been working on something in there for eons. Didn't really get around to cleaning that up yet." She gave a tiny shrug.

"I understand your walk yesterday morning at Jones Beach went very well," Betty said. "I'm happy for you."

"Yes, a bit of good news, I guess, in all of this. How truly lovely and supportive people can be."

There was an awkward silence, Gloria sitting somewhat rigidly in her wicker chair. Between Paulette Krause and Gloria Stryker, Betty was getting the strange sense that the late Kirk Stryker, whom, by most accounts, was well-liked, didn't seem much liked by those closest to him. "You have a beautiful home," Betty said.

"Could never sell the place when my parents died. So peaceful. This past week with all the television cameras and news trucks . . . the well-wishers coming in and out, it's been so busy and chaotic. The boys and I have been here for a few days. Since the funeral." Gloria stood up slowly and pushed down on her cotton pants, flattening the creases. "Please come inside. I'll get you something to drink. . . . And please forgive the mess."

The front entrance opened into a living room that was so pristine it looked like a museum and not a home that belonged to a family with three boys. Betty searched for a mess, but all she could find was a stack of boxes in the corner behind the door.

"I understand you're retiring, Detective," Gloria said.

"Well, that had been the plan. Friday was supposed to be my last day."

"Funny how things change when we least expect them to."

There was a detachedness about her. She was sad, yes,

but it was a managed sadness. Betty knew that Gloria Stryker had had a very wealthy upbringing on the Gold Coast of Long Island and had learned long ago how to wear a tightly fastened mask, whatever the circumstances. Betty was about to inquire about Marty Benning—who had been professing his innocence since his arrest—when she saw Mark Stryker peering down at them from an upstairs landing.

"Mommy?" he said, wedging himself behind a slatted wooden banister.

"Mark, it's all right, you can come down. You remember Detective Munson, don't you?"

The little boy tiptoed down the steps. He reminded Betty of Jesse and was probably around the same age; he, too, had dirt marks on his knees.

"Nice to see you again, Mark," Betty said when he reached the bottom.

"What can I get you, Detective?" Gloria asked, heading toward a large kitchen.

"Water's fine," Betty called and then turned to Mark. "How are you?"

He shrugged his shoulders and looked down at his hands. "Sorry, my hands are so dirty." Mark wiggled his fingers as he showed Betty his palms. "I was working in the garden with my mom. Wanna see my garden?"

He led Betty into the living room, which had large bay windows overlooking the Sound on the north and a side yard arboretum on the south.

"My garden's over there." Mark pressed his pointer finger against the glass, before pulling it back and wiping the small fingerprint smudge with his sleeve. "The one with the orange flowers. Orange is my favorite color."

"It's very pretty." Beside the flowers was what looked like a small grave, with white stones carefully placed in a square and a small plaque with writing in the center. "Oh, what a lovely memorial. Was one of your pets buried there?" she asked.

"No, that's my sister," he said as Gloria returned with a tall glass of water. She handed it to Betty.

"Why don't you run along, Mark, so I can talk to the detective?" She tapped the head of the little boy, who ran off toward the back of the house.

"He's lovely," Betty said, taking a sip of water.

"You were asking about the grave . . ."

"I'm sorry, I didn't mean to pry."

"Not at all." Gloria took a step toward the window and looked out. "Before I had Mark, I had gotten pregnant and lost the baby. It was a girl. I was pretty far along, four or five months. We were excited, knowing that it would be a girl—you know, after having two boys." She paused, seeming uncomfortable. "It was a difficult pregnancy. Afterward, I created the little memorial. Kirk thought it was creepy, but I like having it here. Having *her* here. I find it comforting. In the end, I believe these things all work out for the best."

She absently put her hand on her belly, and Betty realized that Gloria was sporting a small baby bump under her flared tank top. "I guess I can't quite hide it anymore," she said with a smile. "They call it a change of life baby."

"Congratulations," Betty said. "I had no idea. You can't even tell."

"A woman my age learns how to dress to hide a few pounds here and there." She shrugged. "I hadn't even told Kirk yet. Only one other person knew—Eva, from the office. I accidentally left an ultrasound photo at the practice. She found it and kindly gave it back to me and promised not to tell. Nice girl." She smiled wanly. "Forty-two and pregnant. Can you imagine? I guess with Kirk gone, she will be a change of life baby in more ways than one."

"She?"

Gloria nodded. "It's a girl." She caressed her belly with her hand. "So, what can I do for you, Detective? I'm assuming you're here regarding the arrest of Marty Benning."

"In part," Betty said. "Did the arrest surprise you?"

"It's hard to say. The way Kirk went on and on about him, I'm inclined to say no, but every time I saw him, he had been nothing if not extremely helpful and courteous."

"Did you know Hugo Lurch?"

"Barely. He was not what you would call a sociable fellow."

"So I've heard," Betty said. "Mrs. Stryker, I'm not quite sure how to ask this, so I'll just come right out and say it, okay?"

Gloria nodded. "Of course."

"Were you and Marty Benning having an affair?"

"An *affair*?" Gloria covered her mouth as if embarrassed by the question. "I'm flattered, Detective, but I think I'm a bit too old for Mr. Benning."

"I believe he's five or six years older than you are, ma'am," Betty said.

"What I mean is, I don't really think I'm his type. I've been to quite a few events with Marty—Mr. Benning—

over the years, mostly without Kirk who was off doing this and that, and most of the time he has attended with a much younger woman."

"Do you know his current girlfriend?" Betty asked.

The question seemed to pique Gloria's interest. "Current girlfriend?" she asked. "I can't recall seeing him with anyone these past few months. What's her name?"

"Muriel Adams."

"Muriel Adams, Muriel Adams . . ." Gloria's brows furrowed. "No, I can't say I do. Why do you ask?"

"No reason," Betty said. "Just trying to put the puzzle pieces together."

"I guess my having some sort of an affair with Marty would give you a motive. Is that right, Detective Munson?"

"I guess you could say that."

"Well, I'm afraid I can only give you the opposite."

"What do you mean?"

"I don't think Marty had anything at all to do with Kirk's death."

"And why is that, Mrs. Stryker?" Betty asked. "Please don't tell me it's his dashing smile. Mr. Benning, it seems, has an uncanny ability to enchant the women of Gardenia."

"Not all of them, apparently," Gloria said, nodding at Betty. "Call it a gut feeling, I guess."

"Noted," Betty said. "Well, I don't want to take up any more of your time, Mrs. Stryker."

"Call me Gloria."

Betty walked toward the door, eyeing the boxes stacked in the corner of the room.

"Just getting rid of some things," Gloria said. "Donating them to Big Brothers/Big Sisters. Kirk was a bit of a pack rat and also liked to shop garage sales on the weekends—I dread to find out what's in that garage."

"Do you mind if I take a look?" Betty asked, stepping onto the front porch.

"Be my guest. Just lots of clothing donations from the cancer walk and other fund drives Kirk organized. He was devoted to women's causes. Feel free to take whatever you like."

Betty crunched her way across the pebbled driveway toward the garage and peered inside. It looked as if Kirk Stryker had been preparing to have a garage sale himself. Clothing—mostly women's and girls'—was stacked in boxes with various labels. She poked through them, not really knowing what she was looking for. The murder weapon, perhaps? She picked up a little girl's dress that still had the price tag on it and then refolded it and placed it back in the box atop a pile of dresses. Next to the box were assorted pieces of jewelry, some with price tags, others looking as if they had been worn.

She returned to her car, taking one last look at beautiful Long Island Sound. She imagined the weapon that killed Kirk Stryker was probably somewhere out there floating away, taking its secrets with it. With any luck, she'd be able to solve this mystery without it.

37

Roxanne looked around her filthy apartment with dread. She had no desire to clean, despite the cobwebs that had taken up residence in the corners of the rooms and the cat litter smell that never seemed to go away. After depositing Gordy at a birthday party next door, she had been sitting around in a daze most of the afternoon. She couldn't concentrate. Muriel was off the deep end. She wasn't listening to reason. Roxanne had to do something.

She thought of that clever Bobby Chaucer and checked her bedroom window to make sure it was locked. It was. *Who is this fucking guy,* she thought. *What CPA needs a bodyguard?* She booted up her laptop and searched Benning's company website for any mention of Bobby Chaucer, but there wasn't any. She googled *Bobby Chaucer Queens New York* and got a hit for a *Helen Chaucer* on whitepages.com. She clicked through and was brought to a Ridgewood address that was only about fifteen minutes from where she lived. *Shit, that's probably him.* And he had a wife. Or a mother. Or something. She copied down the address.

Ignoring the vacuum cleaner standing in the corner

of her bedroom, she quickly got dressed and drove to the Ridgewood address, circling around the block a few times until parking a few houses away, not far from several teenage boys who were playing punchball in the street. Roxanne reached into the glove compartment for her wig and grandmother's hat, but changed her mind; Bobby had already seen her disguise. Instead, she leaned her seat back until she was nearly horizontal, keeping her eye on the two-level home's front door.

Now what, genius, she asked herself, twisting her hair around her finger. She considered walking to the house and checking the name on the doorbell but didn't want to attract the attention of the boys, when suddenly Bobby appeared at the front door. He glanced up and down the street and walked down the front steps, turning right toward Metropolitan Avenue. Roxanne put her car into drive and followed behind, keeping a half-block distance. *Let's see how YOU like being followed, asshole*, she thought.

Bobby walked about ten blocks down Metropolitan and entered a building: a seedy-looking joint called the Acrylic that was located between a hardware store and a deli. Roxanne parked across the street. On the place's neon marquee, the *A* and *lic* were broken, making the name of the place look like *cry*. That seemed about right. People congregated outside the front door dressed casually in jeans and T-shirts. Roxanne reached into the backseat, grabbed her New York Yankees baseball cap from the floor, and walked toward the front door.

The inside of the place, as expected, was a dump, but it was pretty crowded for a Sunday evening. Roxanne pulled the brim of her cap down and found a seat near the back of the bar where she would have a good vantage point. She checked the time and texted her neighbor to see if Gordy could hang out with her a bit longer. Just as she got a text back saying it was no problem, someone tapped her arm.

"Hello," Bobby said with a smile.

Roxanne feigned surprise. "Hey, what are you doing here?" she asked.

"I was just going to ask you the same thing," he said. "It's like maybe you *knew* I would be here."

"Don't flatter yourself," Roxanne said.

"Then what are you doing here?"

"I asked you first."

"What are we in third grade?" Bobby nudged into the open space next to Roxanne at the bar. "Can I buy you a drink?"

"I can buy my own drink, thank you." Roxanne flagged the bartender, a tubby guy in a Captain America T-shirt, and settled onto her barstool. "Jack and coke, please."

"Make that two," Bobby said. He leaned his elbow on the edge of the bar. "I barely recognized you without your frying pan."

"Hardy har har . . ." Roxanne rolled her eyes.

When the bartender brought their drinks, Bobby held up his glass. "To chance encounters," he said and took a long slug. His knuckles, wrapped around the beer, were red with cuts.

"You're bleeding," she said. "What happened? And it looks like someone punched you in the eye."

"It's nothing," Bobby said.

"Let me guess. Some weasel forgot to sign his tax form?"

"Hardy har har," Bobby said and took another gulp,

the outside of his neck rippling as the liquid went down his throat. Unfortunately, up close like this, or maybe it was because of the gloominess of the bar, Bobby Chaucer seemed ruggedly handsome—stocky yet muscular, with a rascally grin. *Fuck,* just what she needed.

"So let's talk," Bobby said.

"Sure, why not?" Roxanne said. "So what makes you so sure your friend Marty didn't kill that guy?"

"So much for small talk." Bobby put his glass on the bar. "Because I know my friend. What makes you think he did?"

"I don't. I'm just worried about *my* friend."

Bobby nodded. "He is too."

"What does *that* mean?"

"It means just what you think it means. He's worried."

"But, I mean, does he have a reason to be?"

Bobby's pocket buzzed. He pulled out his phone and looked at the screen. "I gotta take this." He pushed his way to the front of the room, high-fiving a guy seated near the jukebox who was wearing a sports jersey that read *Blue Balls* on the back.

It was pretty crowded now, and a hipster-looking type with a banjo jumped onto a short stage in the far corner as a few people clapped and left their seats to move closer. Live music had a way of bringing even the most faithful homebody out of the house.

Roxanne finished her drink and ordered another. "I'll be right back," she told the bartender. She picked up her purse and made her way to the back of the bar.

A narrow door, decorated with the outline of a big-breasted woman, denoted what she hoped was the ladies' room. She turned the knob and found herself in a small, rundown two-stall space that smelled of liquor and urine. One of the stalls was occupied, and Roxanne took the other. By the time she got out, a large woman was washing her hands at the room's sole sink so Roxanne stood aside and waited. The woman's long blouse had tiny wet spots on the shoulders.

"It's raining already?" Roxanne asked. "Wasn't supposed to start until later tonight."

"It began coming down when I was down the block," the woman said. "I'm lucky I made it."

"Here to see the guy with the banjo?" Roxanne said.

"No, I'm meeting someone here," the woman said, pulling down the paper towel from the dispenser. She checked her makeup and carefully fingered her curls, which had begun to frizz because of the rain. Her eye makeup was running, and she ran her finger underneath her eyelids.

"You look fine," Roxanne said with a smile.

"You think?" The woman looked at her through the mirror. "I want to make a good impression. It's kind of, you know, a first date. In a very long time. I almost didn't come."

"Just be yourself. That's all that really matters. I'm Roxanne, by the way."

"Eva," the woman said. She took in a deep breath and let it out slowly. "Well," she pulled down her blouse, "have a good night."

"Thanks. You too."

As the woman left, Roxanne washed her hands and looked at herself in the mirror. It had been a long time since *she* had a date. She reapplied some of her lipstick, although she wasn't sure why. This *wasn't* a date. A muffled round of applause came through the closed bathroom door, and she realized the musician had started playing. She left the bathroom and returned to the bar.

She took a slug of her drink, which was waiting for her, and looked around for Bobby. She found him near the stage talking to two other beefy-looking guys. Their eyes met, and then he was on the move, but instead of hooking left and coming toward her, Bobby opened the exit door and escorted Eva, the woman from the bathroom, out and into the drizzling rain.

Mother fucker, Roxanne thought, watching them go. That son of a bitch was leaving—and leaving her with the damn bar tab.

38

The school bus stopped outside the Mayfair Planetarium, which was housed in one of the few remaining Gold Coast mansions on Long Island. It had been at least forty years since Betty had been there, and her only memory of the place was making out with Trevor Seaman in the tenth row of the observatory; his mouth tasted like Juicy Fruit gum.

The ride from Gardenia had been filled with at least five sing-a-longs, which consisted mostly of forty nine- and ten-year-old students screaming at the top of their lungs. She was glad she had decided to take a few hours off from the Stryker investigation and come along; as Sam reminded her, the primary suspect was already behind bars. Plus, she hated to disappoint Scott, especially after already disappointing Jesse, who had been pouting all weekend since she hadn't officially retired last Friday. Today was the first day he hadn't put a Post-it note into her pocket.

Betty looked through the window at the cars and trucks in the lanes beside them and realized she was looking for John Parker; the guy was like a hat that was too tight, weighing on her. Scott had his nose pressed to the bus window on the other side of the aisle. She couldn't wait to tell him and Jesse the good news: She had decided to file the revised paperwork that morning—her last day as a police detective would be Friday, the day of Marty Benning's arraignment. Only a week behind schedule.

"All right, children," said Scott's teacher, Mr. Tucker, as he stood up at the front of the bus. Mr. Tucker was an imposing figure, about six foot three, with a large head and rotund body to match. "When we get into the planetarium—this goes for Mrs. Botwin's class as well as mine—I want you to behave like young ladies and gentleman. If you do not, you will be taken away from the group and asked to sit in the lobby for the duration of the visit. Does everyone understand?"

All the little heads nodded.

"All right then. Does everyone know who their chaperone is?"

Another round of nods.

"Good. If you do not, please see me at the front of the planetarium."

With that, the school bus door opened and the teachers filed down the steps, with the children tripping over themselves to follow along. Betty mussed up Scott's hair as he passed, and he smiled.

Outside the planetarium, the children were gathering around a large bronze statue of one of the first telescopes from the early seventeenth century, and Betty immediately thought of Benning's telescope sitting on a tripod partially hidden behind the curtains of his living room—apparently, a ride on a school bus wasn't going to be enough to get her mind off work. She still couldn't explain the strange markings on Stryker's body, but she was pretty sure she had let the imagination of a ten-year-old impede her judgment. After all, a Rorschach-like series of dots can be made to look like anything with the right mood or influence.

As the parents filed out of the bus, Betty checked to make sure no one was left behind before following the last person out. Scott and his two friends, Glen and Avi, were eagerly waiting for her outside.

"Ready, guys?" she said.

"Maybe we'll see a supernova!" Avi whispered to Scott. One of those brightly colored plastic tubes hung around Avi's neck, the kind that people usually wore when they went swimming so they could keep their money and driver's license dry; Betty assumed Avi's spending money was rolled up in there.

"Nah, these telescopes don't have the magnitude for something like that," said Glen, the most serious of the trio. Betty had known Glen for nearly five years, and she couldn't recall ever seeing him laugh.

Scott put his arm around Avi's shoulder. "You never know, Avi, we might," he said. Scott functioned as the leader of this little crew—the peacemaker, the negotiator, the facilitator, the protector. The apple didn't fall far from the police detective.

Inside the planetarium, the groups went off into different directions since the chaperones had been instructed that they had free rein for the first hour and a half until they had to report to the food court for lunch.

"Where should we go first?" Betty asked the boys.

"The observatory!" they said in unison.

Betty consulted the large bulletin board that loomed over the series of cash registers in the lobby. A show titled

"Starry Eyed: What We Know About the Constellations" was beginning at 9:30. She checked her watch. They had ten minutes.

"Sounds good to me," she said. "Let's get on line."

The observatory hadn't changed much in forty years, other than the seating having gone from wooden to plush. A large hulk of metal looked fast asleep in the center of the room as the boys quickly grabbed seats in the front row. Betty told them that if they sat farther back they might have a better view of the ceiling, but there was no explaining that to excited ten-year-old boys. She took a seat behind them.

"Mommy, now you'll see Orion," Scott said. "Like on that picture you had."

"Oh, yes, that's right," Betty said, cringing. She had hoped that Scott had forgotten about the photo.

As the lights dimmed, many of the students catcalled and whooped when the image of a large cigarette appeared on the ceiling. "Welcome to the Mayfair Planetarium," said a deep baritone voice. "There is no smoking on the planetarium premises."

"Hey, look!" Betty heard Avi's little voice call in the dark. "It's the constellation of Marlboro!" The students around them giggled.

"Imagine you are but a tiny grain of sand," the voice continued, as a large image of the Earth appeared overhead, replacing the cigarette and tinting the dark room blue, "on a beach that is endlessly long."

The sleeping metal monstrosity at the center of the room came to life, revealing a state-of-the-art digital projection system. *They didn't have* that *forty years ago,* Betty thought; she remembered something more along the lines of an overhead projector.

An explosion of tiny twinkling dots appeared on the aluminum dome, triggering flashes of Kirk Stryker's grisly murder—the wet skin across his abdomen, the redness of the welts dotting his body.

"Look, Mom, there it is," Scott whispered. "Orion's Belt."

"Yes, I see it," Betty whispered back as the dotted image of the Hunter appeared at the top left of the domed ceiling. She thought of Benning's deer head jutting into his office.

After the twenty-minute presentation, the boys blasted out of the observatory toward a row of large scales that allowed them to see how much they weighed on the sun, the moon, Mars, and the rest of the planets. Betty stood nearby beside another chaperone, a dad she recognized from the soccer field.

"What did you think of the show?" she asked.

"I think I slept through most of it," he said with a grin.

"Yeah, I missed a lot of it too. Daydreaming, I guess."

"Is not," Betty heard Avi say to Glen. They were arguing near the Saturn scale.

"Is too," Glen said back.

"Boys, boys," Betty called. "Excuse me," she said and hurried over to them. "What's going on?"

Avi spoke first. "Glen said that the discovery of dark matter was the greatest discovery of the twentieth century. But it's not. It's *definitely* the discovery that the universe was expanding."

"That is the most ridiculous thing I've ever heard," Glen said.

"Is not."

"Is too."

"Boys, please," Betty said. She looked around for Scott, her facilitator, and saw him near a statue of a man across the room. "Come on, boys. Let's get Scott and check out the rest of the planetarium."

Scott was reaching out to touch the statue's hands, which were made to look as if they were holding a small celestial object.

"Hey, Scottie," Betty said as Avi and Glen *ooh*ed and *ahhh*ed at the statue, having already forgotten about their disagreement. "Remember, don't go too far from the group. Who's this?" she asked, gesturing toward the bespectacled man in bronze.

"This is Dr. Henry Sansfield," Scott said.

"He used to work here at the planetarium a long, long, long time ago," Avi added. "Way back in the 1990s."

"Weren't you listening during the show?" Glen asked.

"Of course, I was," Betty lied. "I guess I just didn't recognize him with a tan." She smiled.

Glen sighed. "Dr. Henry Sansfield was the most famous astronomer to come out of Long Island. Everyone knows that."

"He's got that comet named after him," Avi said, helpfully.

"Comet?" Betty asked.

"The Sansfield Comet?" Glen said. When Betty didn't recognize it, he shook his head sadly.

"Come on, guys, let's check out the Black Hole room," Scott said, and the three boys put their arms around each other's shoulders and strode away, united by Betty's ignorance.

Betty read the plaque on the statue's large square base: *Dr. Henry Sansfield, a curator of the Mayfair Planetarium from 1980 until 1996, is best known for his discovery of the comet officially designated 13P/Sansfield and better known as Sansfield's Comet, a short-period comet with an orbital duration of one hundred sixteen years.*

The dad from the soccer field stood next to her and gazed up at Dr. Sansfield. "Looks like a big geek," he whispered.

"Have you ever heard of him?" Betty asked.

"Yeah, sure, but not about his science stuff. Don't you remember this guy? He was found dead in his bathtub like twenty years ago. Committed suicide, I think."

"Oh, yes, that's right. I remember that. That's why his name sounds familiar."

"It was really sad. His wife had died not long before he did, if I remember correctly. Left two kids, I think."

"Mom, come on!" Scott stuck his head out from behind a wall. "The black hole is so cool! You have to see it!"

"I'll be right there," Betty called.

"Here we go," the dad said. He had taken out his smartphone. "Let me click on Wikipedia . . . ."

"You really don't need to. I should be—"

"Early life . . . career . . . exploration years . . . personal life . . . ah, here it is." He enlarged the text with his fingers. "Sansfield, whose wife Irma succumbed two years earlier to cervical cancer, was survived by his two children—"

"I should be getting to my boys," Betty said.

"—Lily and Eva Sansfield."

"Wait? Who did you say?" Betty asked, tilting the

screen toward her, but the words were too tiny for her middle-aged eyes. "Did you say Eva Sansfield?"

"Yes," he said, pointing to the small screen. "And her twin sister, Lily. Oh, crap, I had forgotten that they were only eleven years old at the time." He shook his head. "How old would they be now? Early thirties? So sad. I wonder whatever became of them."

Betty's eyes gazed up at Dr. Sansfield, astronomer. She thought of the welts on Kirk Stryker's body, the celestial design. She knew exactly what had become of at least one of the twins. Eva Sansfield had grown up to become the administrative assistant of accountant Kirk M. Stryker. And, as of that moment, she had also grown up to become a person of interest in his murder.

39

S trolling along the boardwalk in Atlantic City, New Jersey, always reminded Muriel of her childhood and summers spent eating taffy and being strapped into old, clanky amusement park rides. The bright morning sunlight made both the sand of the empty beaches and the exteriors of the tall, sleeping casinos glow. Bicycles wheeled past her, the wooden boards beneath them bending and groaning in rhythm, as if someone were running their fingers along muted piano keys.

The area was surprisingly crowded for a Tuesday. Among the bikers, walkers, and gamblers, who were stumbling back to their hotels in rumpled suits, were gaggles of senior citizens, probably dropped off by a nearby coach bus. Up ahead, an old woman in tattered clothing was singing a church hymn and feeding the seagulls, which were swooping up and down as if attached by rubber bands.

She checked her phone, but there was no activity. Detective Munson hadn't called her back, and it had been three days. She thought about trying her again, but didn't want to push it or seem desperate—it was clear, though, that Marty wouldn't be joining her in Atlantic City.

She let out a yawn. Aunt Jo had kept Muriel up later than she would have liked—the woman had more energy at sixty-three than her five-year-old—but Muriel figured it would be better than spending the time in her hotel room watching the news coverage of Marty. Maybe she'd get a late checkout and take a nap before she attempted the three-hour drive home.

A large banner waved across the entrance of the Caesars Hotel & Casino: *32nd Annual Conference of Certified Public Accountants*. It was the event that Marty was supposed to attend—and probably could have attended if she had been able to get a hold of Detective Munson.

She thought of him sitting alone in a jail cell. The morning news reported that his arraignment had been scheduled for Friday. She would be there, if it came to that, even if it meant taking a day off from work. She checked her phone again. No missed calls or texts.

Muriel buttoned the top of her sweater as the wind kicked up. She stuffed her hands into her pockets and found something crumpled in the right pocket. She pulled it out. It was a hundred-dollar bill, with a tiny note clipped to it:

Spend some money. Live a little. Love, Aunt Jo.

She smiled. These last three months had felt like just that: *living*. Feeling. Being. After so many years of waking up in the morning only to look forward to going to sleep at night, Muriel had felt reawakened. Marty Benning had reignited something inside her that she was reluctant to let go. She knew that everyone thought she was crazy. Her mother. Doug. Even Roxanne, although she wouldn't say. But how could she explain something that she herself didn't truly understand. Muriel checked her phone one last time and headed toward the Caesar's entrance.

After her eyes adjusted to the dark of the casino, she walked toward a line of jingling slot machines near the Temple Lobby, an opulent four-story atrium made to resemble the glory of Ancient Rome, and stopped at a Joker Poker machine. She curled her fingers around Aunt Jo's money and was about to insert the bill, but thought about the phone bill and the mortgage payments and how practically every sweater she owned had a button missing, including the one she was wearing. She dropped the bill back into her pocket. What Aunt Jo didn't know wouldn't hurt her.

Across the atrium, another banner hung above a series of doors that read: *Welcome, Certified Public Accountants*. Men and women were gathering before a long table presumably to register. In the corner, to Muriel's surprise, was a large easel with a photograph of Marty. She moved closer to it and saw a red line through his name, with the word *Canceled* above it. Next to his name was a handwritten sign that read: *Paulette Krause, keynote*. Muriel gazed at the photo. He hadn't told her that he was supposed to keynote. She reached out to touch his two-dimensional cheek.

"Can I help you?" asked a young woman who was seated at the long table. "Name, please?"

"Um, I . . ." Muriel looked around at the others entering the conference.

"What's the name of your company?" The woman looked at the billboard and back at Muriel. "Are you with Benning & Associates?"

"Um, yes," Muriel said. There was a lump in her throat.

"Oh." The woman seemed shaken up. "I'm sorry to hear, you know. Well, innocent until proven guilty and all that . . ." She fumbled through her name badges. "Benning, Benning . . . oh, here it is." She checked off a box, and a printer jerked to action, revealing two black-and-white ID cards. She pulled two lanyards out of a box and a conference schedule out of another and handed everything to Muriel, pointing her toward a pair of double doors. "The keynote and all the panel discussions are right that way."

"Thank you," Muriel said.

"Is Jonathan with you?"

"Who?"

"We have two registered for today. I'm assuming you're Tonya."

"Oh, yeah, right," Muriel said, clipping the badge to her shirt under her sweater. "I forgot it was Jonathan who was coming. I kept thinking Kevin, but Kevin's got that thing in Manhattan . . ." *What was she saying?*

The young woman was already bored, but continued to nod her head politely.

"He'll be coming soon," Muriel said finally. She placed Jonathan's ID badge back down on the table and headed toward the double doors.

A long corridor led to a series of rooms, but most people were walking toward an ornate ballroom, where the keynote was to take place. Muriel walked along the perimeter of the room before taking a seat in the back. She checked her phone. It was nearly 10:30. And still no messages.

"Hi," said a man who sat next to her.

Muriel tensed. "Hi," she said.

"Can you tell me where the tax law seminar is being held at eleven?"

"Ummm . . ." Muriel scanned the conference schedule the young woman had given her. She found the seminar location on a loose sheet that had been stuck inside the book. "It looks like they changed the room to the Augustus pavilion," she said.

"Oh, thanks, no wonder I couldn't find it." He smiled. "Big crowd today, huh?"

"Yeah," Muriel said.

"To be honest, I think most people are here to see if maybe Benning might actually show up. I mean, the guy can do almost anything."

"What do you mean?"

"Let's just say that Houdini could learn a lot from Marty Benning," he whispered as a distinguished gentleman walked to the podium at the front of the room and tilted the microphone up. The chatter in the room hushed.

"Ladies and gentleman," the speaker said, "as many of you already know, Mr. Benning will not be able to give today's keynote address." There were a few groans from the audience, and several people stood up to leave. "But we are honored to have Ms. Paulette Krause speak in his place. Paulette is the manager of Kirk Stryker & Associates located in Gardenia on Long Island . . ." Muriel glanced at the statuesque woman on the stage who was straightening the front of her blue suit.

"It's no surprise they got Krause to replace Benning," the guy next to her whispered. "Probably trying to capitalize on Stryker's name recognition."

". . . We are honored she could be here," the speaker

continued. "Paulette, let me say that we are very sorry for the loss of Kirk Stryker this week. It was a terrible . . ."

"That Paulette Krause is a pistol," the man next to Muriel whispered.

"I don't know her," Muriel said.

"I do. Pretty well. The name's Jon, by the way," he said, extending his hand.

She shook it. "Muriel," she said out of habit before realizing she was supposed to be someone else, but couldn't remember who. Luckily, her nametag was covered by her sweater. "Wait, did you say *Jon*?" she asked.

"Yes, Jonathan Hawkes, Marty Benning & Associates. I understand my colleague Tonya is here too, but I can't seem to find her. Have you seen her? Long blonde hair. Tight face. Looks like she's giving birth—all the time." He smiled.

"No, I haven't." Muriel played with her necklace.

"And you're from . . ." Jon looked for her badge, but only the corner was sticking out.

"Dallas," she blurted, tugging the badge under her sweater. "Dallas, Texas."

"Really? You don't have much of an accent."

"Well, I'm originally from Long Island," she said and braced herself for the inevitable question.

"Really? What town?"

On the other side of the ballroom, just behind Jon, a door opened, and a tall, blonde, unhappy-looking woman walked in escorted by a security guard.

"Can you excuse me?" Muriel said, standing up. "I just realized I was late for a meeting."

"Oh." Jonathon stood up as well. "Well, it was nice to meet you, Muriel."

"Likewise," she said and slipped out a side exit just as Paulette Krause took the podium.

Muriel hurried past the conference check-in and slot machines and opened the heavy glass doors that led to the boardwalk. She breathed a sigh of relief as she dropped her name badge into a trashcan and quickly started walking back toward her hotel.

She had never met anyone in Marty's office: Jon, Tonya, or any of the staff, whose names, before today, she didn't even know. Jon seemed nice enough, although she wondered what he meant by the Houdini comment. She checked her phone again. Only a missed text from her aunt, who was expecting her for an early lunch—free, of course, courtesy of her slot host. Muriel hoped it wasn't a liquid lunch, but with Aunt Jo she could never be sure. She picked up the pace and let out a yawn. After another few hours of carousing with her aunt, she was *really* going to need that nap.

40

Paulette was sitting on the floor unpacking a large cardboard box when Satriano walked into the office space, located two storefronts down from Stryker's. The room was bare, except for stacks of boxes across the wall and two desks and chairs that Satriano recognized from Stryker's front office. A coat of dust covered most of the floor.

"Assemblyman," Paulette said, standing up. "What a surprise."

"Congratulations on the new office," Satriano said.

"Well," Paulette shrugged her shoulders, "I've got a long way to go until it's ready. The landlord has been trying to rent this room ever since the *Gazette* moved out of downtown. Didn't want to go too far. Clients tend to be pretty habitual—mess up their routine too much and they'll go someplace else, you know."

"I see you left the name, *Kirk M. Stryker & Associates,*" Satriano said, pointing toward a handwritten sign hung above the outside entrance.

"For now." Paulette nodded. "I was even thinking about keeping the name permanently once I get set up, but I'd have to ask Gloria, and I'm not so sure how she'd feel about it."

"It might be a nice gesture."

"You never know with that woman." Paulette sat down in a swivel chair and wiped her brow with the back of her hand.

"You look exhausted."

"Just got back from Atlantic City a little while ago. Traffic was dreadful. Part of me wanted to stay overnight, but Kirk's death left a lot of people in a lurch. And with Benning in prison, you wouldn't believe the number of his clients who are jumping ship and ringing my phone. I had to get here."

"Benning's not quite in prison yet," Satriano said.

"Yes, of course, but you know what I mean." Paulette reached for a cup and placed it under the spout of a Dunkin Donuts Box of Joe that was on a file cabinet behind her. "Would you like a cup?"

"No, thanks."

She took a long sip of coffee and put the paper cup on the desk. "So, Assemblyman, what can I do for you?" She rolled out a chair for him, and he sat down.

"Well, something happened over the weekend that I'm not sure what to make of."

"At the cancer walk?"

"No, it happened at a family event. In Brooklyn, actually. I was approached by a man for a large sum of money."

"What do you mean *approached*?" Paulette asked, intrigued. "Was it a campaign contributor?"

"No, I don't know who it was. I've never seen him before. Seemed . . . *shady*." Satriano had debated for the last few days whether or not he should go straight to the police about his visit from the guy in the baseball cap, and he probably would have if it hadn't happened at his cousin Marco's house. The last thing Satriano needed was a police officer poking around there; at that very moment, there were probably several bags of drugs or stolen electronics hidden in the attic and various closets. He didn't know Paulette Krause well, but she had worked closely with Stryker, and she might know something. "Said Kirk owed him money, and somehow he's under the impression that since Kirk is not here that I owe him the money. Do you know anything about this?"

"What did he look like?"

"Tall guy. Baseball cap. Looked kinda European, I guess. I don't know." Satriano stood up again and began to pace. "In my mind, there was no doubt that he was sending me some kind of message, you know, showing up at my cousin's house like that."

"He followed you?"

"I guess so, but I don't know for sure."

Paulette leaned back in her swivel chair. "I really don't know," she said. "I authorize practically every transaction that's done through this office—I mean, Kirk's office. I run a tight ship, unless it was a personal debt or . . ."

"Or what?" Satriano asked.

"Kirk insisted on handling your campaign separately. Actually, there were two things that were out of my jurisdiction. Your campaign and the breast cancer walk."

"Kirk handled that exclusively?"

"Yes, until recently. Since the end of March, he's had Eva Sansfield work on those accounts. Kirk threw the wacko a bone. Fine by me. I have enough to do."

"So who has the books for those?"

Paulette gestured toward the stacks of cardboard boxes in the room. "They could be here, but I'm not sure. Kirk kept those in his office. Or at least I think he did. That's probably a question for Detective Munson, but you're welcome to rummage through things if you like."

"I wouldn't want to go through your client files."

"I trust you," Paulette said with a smile.

"Frankly, I'm more concerned about the money."

"For that, you'd probably have to talk with Gloria. Or Sansfield."

Satriano hadn't wanted to bother Gloria, but it looked as if he had no choice. "I was trying to avoid that. She has enough on her mind."

"What makes you think this guy is for real?"

"Trust me, he's real." Satriano knew *real*. Half of his relatives were gangsters.

"No," Paulette said, "what I mean is how do we know that Kirk really owes him this money?"

"We don't," Satriano said, "but does it matter? Listen, I'm sorry to bother you with this. I'll let you get back to your work. I appreciate the help."

"Wait . . ." Paulette scribbled something on a piece of paper and handed it to him. "Here's my cell phone number. Call me if you hit a wall. We'll figure something out."

"This has nothing to do with you."

"Maybe not, but it doesn't mean I can't help." She smiled but then seemed to have a thought, and her smile disappeared. "This guy is scary?"

"Very," Satriano said.

"Do you think he had anything to do with Kirk's death?"

Satriano took the piece of paper from her. He hadn't considered that. "I don't know. They arrested Benning."

"That doesn't mean that this guy and Benning aren't working together."

Satriano thought about the email that Kirk had sent him; he didn't seem concerned about anyone else besides Benning. "I don't want to start throwing around accusations . . . I got the impression from this guy that he knew something, but I don't know what, and right now I just want to keep my family safe."

"What about Detective Munson? Does she know?"

"Not yet," Satriano said. "I appreciate the offer to help, but I'll figure this out." He headed for the door.

"Wait, I'll walk you out." Paulette picked up a bag of trash and followed him out the front door.

❂

Betty pulled into the parking spot and spotted Assemblyman Satriano walking toward his parents' fruit market. He was waving good-bye to Paulette Krause, who was hauling a bag into a trash can.

"You've got to be kidding me," Paulette said when Betty approached. "Assemblyman Satriano and I were just talking about you. He was just here."

"Is that so? What about?"

"I'm sure he'll tell you. Not my place. But, wow, apparently, I'm popular today. Come in." Betty followed Paulette into the building and looked around the new office. She remembered when the *Gazette* had operated there until the rents became too high and Gardner had to move to another part of town. "What can I do for you, Detective? I pretty much told you everything I know over the weekend."

"Actually, two things. First, I'm wondering if you've seen Eva Sansfield."

"You're kidding, right?" Paulette rolled her eyes as she dragged a box from a side pile to the desk. "Sansfield isn't here, and I'm not planning on her being here."

"I know the two of you don't get along, but I thought—"

"No offense, Detective, but that woman is fifty shades of fucked up. I'll be damned if I'm gonna let her drag her rain cloud into *my* office. If you ask me, Kirk should have booted her fat ass out of here long ago."

"That's a little harsh, no?"

Paulette gave a small smile. "Satriano told me the same thing. No, it's not harsh. Why? Because I can't think of one damn thing she's contributed to this company since the day she was hired. I can get a monkey to turn on the coffee pot in the morning."

"Surely, Kirk Stryker had his reasons."

"Well, if he did, he kept them to himself." Paulette crossed her arms. "Trust me, we had the conversation *many* times."

"And what did he say?"

"He told me to butt out, basically. Whatever. It's his money. He could waste it if he wants to." Paulette squatted down and picked up another big box and placed it on the desk. "But now it's my money, and she's out."

"Which leads me to the second reason I'm here," Betty said. "I received a call today from Gloria Stryker. She seemed a bit upset. She had some interesting news."

"Oh?" Paulette pulled open the top of a box. She reached in and took out a computer monitor and placed it on the desk.

"She was going through some paperwork that her lawyer dropped off this morning. Seems Benning wasn't the only one with something financial to gain with Stryker dead."

"What do you mean?" Paulette tossed the empty cardboard box onto the floor and picked up another.

"Well, it seems you received quite a large sum of money in Stryker's will."

Paulette ran an Exacto knife across the top of the box. "I'm a good worker," she said. "Pure and simple."

"You must have been a *really* good worker to be remembered in your boss' will," Betty said.

Paulette ripped open the top of the box and pulled out a computer keyboard. "You know, it's surprising to me that a woman still has to defend herself when it comes to financial compensation."

"I don't think this is quite the same as equal pay for equal work."

"Like hell it isn't. I consider this the bonus that I never got. Or do you think I had some *other duties* to garner this kind of devotion."

"Let's just say his wife seemed surprised."

"Frankly, his wife is a dolt, Detective Munson. Gloria Stryker had nothing to do with the business. All she cared about was what the business brought her—the chance to keep her luxury lifestyle. Not all of us were born with a silver spoon in our mouths, you know."

"So your relationship with Kirk Stryker was strictly business?"

"Listen, I'm no dummy . . ." Paulette pulled a clump of wires from the box. "Kirk and I got out of each other exactly what we needed. If he saw fit to leave me some money, I'll take it. I *earned* this money. And I have no qualms about using it and rebuilding Stryker's business. That's what he would have wanted."

"He probably also would have wanted you to hire everyone back. Especially Ms. Sansfield."

"He would have wanted me to run this business the way I thought it should be run. And that will be *without* Eva Sansfield." Paulette wiped the sweat from her brow. "Now, if there's nothing else, Detective Munson . . ."

Betty stood there a moment while Paulette lifted another box to the desk and opened it. Then she took the hint and left the office. She stood in front of the building, scanning Lake Shore Avenue, which had died down considerably since the murder. Things were getting back to normal, it seemed. She thought about stopping to see Satriano at his parents' market but changed her mind and walked back to her car. She started the engine, giving a quick check for John Parker or any other reporters, and then pulled out of her spot and onto her next destination. To find Eva Sansfield.

41

Roxanne opened her apartment door to get the mail but stopped when she saw Bobby Chaucer standing on her front porch.

"Well, well, well," she said, leaning against the doorjamb and crossing her arms, "if it isn't the flat-leaver. How was your date?"

"First of all," Bobby shoved his sausage hands in his pockets, "I didn't expect you to come snooping around behind me."

"Who says I was snoo—"

"And, secondly, that wasn't a date. That was work. Why?" Bobby said with a smile. "Jealous?"

"Fuck you. And that *was* a date. At least, it was for her."

"If you let me in, I can explain."

"You mean, let you in the *door*? You don't want to use the window?"

"I can't, you've been keeping it locked," he said, satisfied with himself. He was wearing baggy jeans cinched with a belt, as if he had grabbed any ol' size off the store shelves, a V-neck T-shirt, a pair of boots, and a leather jacket. He looked like a biker. He had a band-aid over the knuckles of his right hand that had been bleeding the other night, and the bruise around his eye had turned purple. In general, he was a mess. She sighed, opened the door wider so he could step in, and closed it behind him. "So," she said, "go ahead. Explain."

"That woman, the one I was with . . ." Bobby started. "Well, it was work."

"So that's your explanation. That was work? For Benning?"

"Yes."

"You already said that outside."

"Trust me, the less you know, the better."

"Let me guess. So basically your plan was to pretend to like her and go out with her. Why? Because it has something to do with Benning who is in jail. Is that about right? So you worked your way into her bed for what? Information? Creepy photos of her sleeping in a thong?"

"I knew you were jealous," he said.

"Go fuck yourself." Roxanne reopened the front door. "Why are you here? Was it to tell me this?"

"No, actually, I thought maybe Muriel was here. I didn't see her car at the house."

"Jesus, do you stalk *everyone*?"

"Look who's talking." Bobby folded his arms. "That's like the pot calling . . ." He stopped, his eyes glancing inside the apartment. "What's that smell?"

"What smell? Oh, shit." Roxanne ran toward the kitchen.

Gray smoke was coming from the stovetop, and she turned over the chicken cutlets that were sizzling in the frying pan.

"You really need to keep the flame a little lower on those," Bobby said, reaching out to turn the knob.

"Do you mind?" Roxanne said, turning it back to its original setting. "Maybe I like my flame a little higher."

"Well, then you must like your cutlets a little *burnt-er.*"

"Hi, Bobby!" Gordy looked up from where he was sitting on the floor of the living room. "Are you going to eat with us?"

"Hi, Gordon," Bobby waved. "And I'm not sure I'm invited."

"What a baby," Roxanne huffed. "You might as well stay. We have plenty of food."

"Not if you cook like that," Bobby said.

Roxanne scraped some black off a cutlet with the edge of a knife. "It builds character. And don't forget to wash your hands. Who knows how dirty they are?"

"Cute," Bobby said, stepping into the living room. When he wasn't looking, Roxanne lowered the flame on the stove.

Bobby laid his jacket on the arm of the recliner and sat down on the edge of the cushion like he was afraid to leave an imprint. "What are you doing?" he asked Gordy.

"I'm making a secret book club," Gordy said. He grabbed a stapler from the coffee table, fastened together sheets of construction paper, and placed the stack neatly at the center of the table.

"Is this for school?" Bobby asked.

"No, I'm just doing it for fun."

"Oh," Bobby said. He was eyeing the papers and pencils as if they were foreign objects. "So who's in your book club? Some of your"—Bobby looked around the room—"friends?"

Oh, brother, Roxanne thought.

Gordy stapled another batch. "There's nobody here but you and me, silly. I'm not *that* weird."

"Oh, I didn't mean . . ."

Gordy waved him off, and Roxanne recognized her own gesture when it came to conversations she didn't want to have. "So how do you know my mom?"

Bobby glanced at Roxanne who started pouring olive oil into the frying pan. It was clear he thought that she was pouring too much so she kept going until he looked away.

"Oh, we're, you know, friends, I guess," he said.

"She has a lot of friends."

"Really?"

"Yep, and most of them are boys."

"That sounds about right."

"Oh, please, Gord," she said. "Don't be dramatic."

"She says boys are easier to talk to than girls," Gordy said. "Except for Mo. Mo's her best friend."

"Mo?"

"Muriel Adams," Gordy said. "You met her the other night. Remember?"

"Yeah, don't you remember her?" Roxanne asked with sarcasm.

Gordy opened the top of a crayon box. "I actually find girls are easier to talk to, except for you, of course."

"Of course," Bobby said. "I like talking to girls too."

"Maybe it's just a guy-girl thing. You know, like, *in the red* stuff," Gordy said.

"In the—?"

"Here, this is for you." Gordy handed Bobby a construction-paper booklet.

"What do I do with it?"

"You read it."

"Right. Sorry if I'm not like those other guys. This book stuff is all new to me."

"What other guys?" Gordy asked.

"You know, the guys you said your mom hangs out with."

"Oh, but she never lets them come here. You're the first."

Shit, Roxanne thought and flipped the last cutlet onto the serving plate. "Dinner is ready," she called. She draped a plastic tablecloth over the small dinette table and then set it for three with her grandmother's ceramic plates, which— along with the wig—were the only things she had managed to pry from her cousins' greedy hands after her grandmother died. She set out forks and knives and the food.

"Great, I'm starving!" Gordy said, sitting at his place. He held up his plate and examined it. "Wow, Mom, you're using the good stuff too." He looked at Bobby. "She must really like you."

"Not really," Roxanne said, feeling her cheeks redden. She sat down at the table between Gordy and Bobby and started doling out mashed potatoes.

"So what do you do?" Bobby asked, reaching for a cutlet.

"I'm a speech therapist," Roxanne said.

"Really?" he asked, surprised.

"Yeah, why?" she said defensively.

"No reason. . . . Although I have to say, you certainly do have a way with words." He chuckled but then pointed to the kitchen counter where Smitty was sprawled out across the toaster oven. "What on earth is that?"

"Oh, that's Smitty Kitty, our cat," Gordy said. He plopped a chicken cutlet piece into his mouth followed by a heaping spoonful of mashed potatoes.

"You're not allergic, are you?" Roxanne asked. She scooped Smitty from the counter before he fell down.

"No." Bobby shook his head. "That's the fattest cat I've ever seen."

"Have you taken a look in the mirror?" Roxanne asked, sitting back down with Smitty on her lap.

"Is she always this funny?" Bobby asked Gordy, who nodded, his mouth full of chicken cutlet.

"How many chicken cutlets you feed that thing?" Bobby asked, eating a forkful of potatoes.

Roxanne ran her hand across Smitty's head as she ate with the other hand. The cat was pawing at Roxanne's fork but missing it.

"What's wrong with him?" Bobby asked.

"Nothing. What's wrong with *you*?" Roxanne said. She dropped the cat in front of his food bowl. Smitty bent down his head to eat but banged it on the metal of the bowl.

"He's got depth perception issues," Gordy said, reaching for another cutlet.

"He's got what?" Bobby asked.

"He can't see that well," Roxanne offered.

"Was he a stray?"

Roxanne shook her head. "He was my next-door neighbor's cat. Her husband would get really drunk sometimes—actually, lots of times—and he would take things out on the cat. The wife would come to me when her husband wasn't home and beg me to take Cooper—

they called him Cooper then—but I told her that I wasn't really into pets." Roxanne made tiny tracks in her mashed potatoes with her fork. "Then one day I heard a big racket going on next door, so I ran over and saw the poor thing hiding under the coffee table—that asshole was trying to get at it with a pair of scissors. That was it. I told him to stay the fuck away from that cat before I call the fucking cops or PETA or whoever I could think of, and I scooped the cat up, marched over here, changed his name, and we never looked back. Fucking jerk." She got up from the table and reached up into the cabinet to get three glasses. "Do you want something to drink?"

"She curses when she's angry," Gordy whispered to Bobby.

"I noticed," Bobby whispered back.

There was a tiny knock at the door, and before Roxanne could yell "C'mon in, Aaron!" little Aaron Benson appeared at the kitchen entryway.

"You really should keep your door locked, you know?" Bobby said.

"Gord, wanna play Xbox?" Aaron said.

"Gordy has to finish eating dinner first, Aaron. Would you like something?" But in a flash, Gordy speared four pieces of cutlet with his fork, stuck them into his mouth, and jumped off his chair, slipping on his sneakers. He ran toward Aaron, stopped, and then came back to the table. He stuck out his hand to Bobby. "I gotta go, but I hope to see you again, Bobby."

Bobby shook his hand back. "Bye, Gordon."

Gordy kissed Roxanne on the cheek, and then he and Aaron ran toward the front door.

"Come back in two hours, Gord," Roxanne called as the two boys disappeared. "I mean it. You have school tomorrow." The door slammed behind them.

"You've got a great kid there," Bobby said.

"I know." She took another cutlet. "So?" she asked.

"So?"

"So you're really not going to tell me what's going on with that woman? Eva?" Roxanne piled a lump of mashed potatoes on Bobby's plate and then on her own.

"How do you know her name?" he asked, surprised.

"I know a lot of things."

He shrugged. "There's nothing to know."

"You're a bad liar." Roxanne bit into her cutlet. "You gonna see her again?"

"I don't know," Bobby said. "She's not my type." He stabbed six pieces of cutlet with his fork and stuck the stack into his mouth. "I didn't sleep with her, if that's what you're wondering," he mumbled, grease pooling on his bottom lip. Roxanne had seen more couth on a pot-bellied pig.

"I wasn't . . . You want more?" she asked.

"No thanks. I'm stuffed. I haven't had a homecooked meal in . . . Well, since my grandmother passed away."

"Helen?"

Bobby chuckled. "Been doing your homework, I see."

They eyed one another until Roxanne threw up her hands. "All right then . . ." She pushed her plate toward the middle of the table. "We're gonna do this, right?"

"Do you want to do this?"

"Do you?"

"Are we in third grade again?" he asked. "Why do you think I came?"

"To find Muriel," Roxanne said.

"Who?" Bobby reached over and gently tugged on Roxanne's hand. When she let him, he stood up and planted a soft kiss tasting of olive oil and salt on her lips. She reached around his shoulders as he picked her up and carried her down the hallway. He opened the bedroom door.

"Next door, Swifty," Roxanne said into his ear. "This is Gordy's room."

Bobby pivoted and carried Roxanne into the next room, closed the bedroom door, and turned on the light.

"Don't worry, you can leave it open. There's no one home, and the window is locked." Roxanne slipped off her T-shirt and turned off the light.

"I like the door closed," Bobby said. "And the light on." He flicked the switch.

"Afraid of the dark?" Roxanne asked, teasingly.

"Depth perception issues," Bobby said and laid Roxanne down on the bed.

✿

"How much time do we have?" Roxanne asked, slipping on her shirt.

"Half an hour." Bobby rubbed the side of Roxanne's waist. "He's really great, you know. Gordy."

"I know. I'm very lucky."

"Is it rude of me to ask where his father is?"

"Is it rude of me to ask where *your* father is?" Roxanne said.

"This game again? He's at an assisted living facility. Your turn."

Roxanne bit her lip. "I generally hate telling this story, because I look like a whore in it . . ."

"I don't mind." He pinched her butt cheek.

Roxanne shrugged. "I actually don't even know his father's name." She looked for a reaction from Bobby, but he just nodded. "He was beautiful, though. Tall. Blonde. The strong, muscular type. Kind of like you, but not quite so chubby. Or hairy."

"Chubby?"

"He swept me right off my feet one night, and then continued to sweep me right out the door the next morning. Not that I would have stayed, mind you—I was out on the West Coast visiting a friend—but it would have been nice to take a shower. Apparently, his girlfriend was a nurse and was coming home from her shift, and he needed to make her breakfast or whatever. I barely made it to the car and out of the driveway before I saw her white Hyundai pull in."

"What do you mean *chubby*?"

"Oh, please. Stocky. Is that better?"

"When did you find out you were pregnant?"

"This is going to sound ridiculous, but I felt like I knew the moment it happened. I felt different." She touched her stomach. "I felt a heaviness in my belly, a grounding feeling, and I remember looking up into whatever-his-name-is's eyes and thinking, *This is amazing*."

"Did you ever tell the father?"

"About Gordy?" Roxanne shook her head.

"Don't you think he'd want to know?"

"By the time I was showing, I was back home in New York. Listen . . . I knew what I was getting into. It was a one-night thing. He had his life. I had mine. Haven't been back to Los Angeles since. And don't plan on it."

Smitty tried jumping up on the bed a few times, but kept missing the bed frame and slipping back down to the floor. Roxanne scooped him up and placed him on her pillow. "You don't strike me as the type to throw a woman out of the house in the morning before she can take a shower."

"That's true," Bobby said. "I throw her out the night before."

Roxanne smiled. "He saved my life. That kid. I was going nowhere fast until he came along. It's funny . . . I named him Gordon, because his biological father reminded me of Flash Gordon. You know, the guy who played him in that movie? And in the end, Gordy became my hero."

"That's kind of how I feel about Benning, *in a way*. Don't get the wrong idea." Bobby leaned back on his pillow, his head in his cupped hands, a bush of graying armpit hair matted against his skin. "He gave me a job when I really needed one. Pays me really well."

"To be his bodyguard."

"To protect him. You'd be surprised at the shit that goes on. Dirty games going on everywhere. That Stryker guy was not who he appeared to be."

"Listen, to be honest with you, I don't give a shit about your friend. All I care about is Muriel. Is she safe?"

"Marty would never hurt her."

"She's in love with him. Really bad. She's not listening to reason. Insists it can't be true, what they're saying about him. She barely knows him."

"It *isn't* true," Bobby said. "Trust me."

"I barely know *you*."

"You barely knew Flash Gordon, and something really great came out of that." Bobby got out of bed and slipped into his underwear and jeans. "I'd better get going. You know, before Gordy comes home."

"Okay." Roxanne stood up, and Smitty tried to follow her, but lost his nerve and lay back down on the pillow. "Are you sure you don't want to take a shower?"

"No, that's okay," Bobby said, "and I won't hold it against you." He pulled on his T-shirt. "Do you think she's home yet?"

"Who? Mo? She's in Atlantic City. I think she's coming home late tonight."

"Atlantic City? What is she doing there?"

"Probably being smothered by her aunt. Why, what's it matter?"

"I don't know. Just seems weird," Bobby said. "Marty was supposed to be there."

Benning? Damn you, Muriel. "Where?" Roxanne asked.

Bobby shook his head. "Never mind." He planted a kiss on Roxanne's mouth and disappeared into the kitchen. When he came back, he was holding his leather jacket and Gordy's construction-paper booklet. "Tell the kid I'll get my homework done right away."

"I will." She walked him to the front door and opened it.

"This was nice," Bobby said.

"It was *okay*." Roxanne gave him a playful punch in his arm.

"Can I see you again?" he asked.

"If you're lucky."

Roxanne watched Bobby descend the porch steps. There was something cowboy about his walk, as if he had just gotten off a horse. It had been a long time since she'd seen a man walk down the path of her home who hadn't just handed her a stack of mail. She closed the front door and, to her great horror, began wondering when she'd get the chance to see Bobby Chaucer again.

42

The *bonging* of the incoming Skype call sounded like an alien spaceship landing. Muriel peeked out from under the blankets wondering where she was until she saw the heavy window drapes of the dark Atlantic City hotel room. *What time is it?* she wondered.

The call rang and rang until Skype had had enough and terminated the unanswered call. She flipped to her other side and looked at the clock on the nightstand: 5:30 p.m.

Her eyes hadn't even closed when the bonging started up again, and Muriel sat up in bed, planting her feet on the floor. She checked her phone. There were a few missed calls from a number she didn't recognize. She stumbled over to the desk, which was in the far corner of the room, and tried to focus her sleepy eyes on her laptop screen. It was facing toward the window, which seemed odd, and she pulled it back toward her chair, the fluorescent glow burning her eyes. The two shots of bourbon her aunt had fed her during lunch were coming back to haunt her.

She squinted at the screen—a call was coming from someone out of her network. She pressed *ignore*, closed out of the document she had been drafting for a parent of one of her students, and tumbled back into bed. The bonging resumed almost immediately.

"Oh, come on," she grumbled.

She was about to turn off her computer when she had a thought: Ellie had contacted her once before through Skype, when she didn't have her phone. Maybe it was her. Before the call could terminate again, Muriel leapt across the room and clicked the green *answer* button. It took a few moments for the caller's screen to clear, but when it did she saw Marty's unshaven face appear.

"Marty!" she said, rubbing her eyes.

It felt like weeks since she had seen him at the Guggenheim. Had it been only Saturday? He looked tired and haggard, the fluorescent lights of the room he was in accentuating the deep grooves on his forehead and bags under his eyes.

"Hi," he said. "I tried your phone a few times, but there was no answer. I took a chance and tried finding you on Skype." He was looking down at whatever screen he was using, and Muriel could see an overhead light behind him. "Are you okay?"

"Am *I* okay?" she asked, but then surprised herself and shook her head. "Not really."

"What's the matter?" he asked.

"I don't know. I feel like this is my fault."

"*Your* fault?"

"When Detective Munson came to see me, she asked if you were with me the whole night, and I said yes, but then I said I was sleeping, so I couldn't really know for sure . . ." She couldn't stop the words from spilling out. "But I know for sure, and you were with me, and now you're there, and I tried calling her and she hasn't called me back . . ."

"It's not your fault, Muriel. But I just need you to know that I had nothing to do with this. Stryker and I . . . Well, we weren't the best of friends, but *this*? You believe that, don't you?"

Muriel nodded. "I do. That's why I'm trying to get in touch with Detective Munson."

"Where are you?" He was gazing into the screen, moving it around his face. "In Atlantic City?"

Muriel nodded. "I wanted to cancel the reservation, but everyone kept telling me that it was a good idea for me to get away."

The corners of Benning's mouth curved upward into a tired smile. "You look so . . . pretty," he said.

"Don't be silly. I was just sleeping."

"No, really, Muriel. You do."

Muriel's pulse quickened. *This* was happy, wasn't it? Doug was wrong. There was such a thing as happiness. "I'll speak to Detective Munson first thing after class tomorrow."

"I know you will."

"If I can't reach her by phone, I will track her down at the station."

"Let's go, Benning. Time's up," said a voice off-screen. "You owe me a big one for this."

"Just give me a minute," he said, his eyes momentarily looking away from the camera. "I gotta go, Muriel." He looked like he was about to say something else, but then added, "See you soon."

She smiled. "See you soon."

Marty stood up, the front of his jeans the only thing visible on Muriel's screen until he disappeared and all she could see was the light fixture in the center of the ceiling, which was causing the screen to pixelate, until the call clicked off.

Muriel glanced around the dark hotel room. She knew she should start packing for home but didn't want to get caught in rush-hour traffic. She got back into bed, stuck her feet under the blankets, and pulled them up to her chin, staring at the laptop screen.

You look so pretty . . .

People from all around the world came to Atlantic City to test their luck. Some people came again and again, like her Aunt Jo, never winning, but always hopeful. Muriel didn't really believe in luck or in pinning her hopes on a number or a color, but she couldn't help but feel that for the last three months she had managed to hit the jackpot.

She closed her eyes, and the hotel room air-conditioner kicked on not long after her breathing fell into a natural rhythm. The cold air billowed the long, heavy drapes, revealing a pair of sneakers that was artfully wedged into the corner of the room. The pair silently tiptoed toward the window, masked by the drone of the air-conditioning unit, which groaned with age and overuse, and as the curtains parted, a hand reached out toward the laptop computer, closing it and plunging Muriel's hotel room into total darkness.

43

etty pulled into the Roosevelt Field mall parking lot and drove to the upper level of the garage nearest Bloomingdale's, which was usually empty. She walked across the short footbridge to the main building.

She had never been to All Yoga before, but she had seen the local advertisements on News 12 and in *Newsday* and spotted the familiar *namaste* logo. The clothing shop was located in one of the many alcoves of the mall, away from the main shopping areas, across from a store that sold only socks. It appeared tiny, a sliver of a storefront, serving only as an addendum to the yoga studio next door, the chain's main business.

Although Betty had no idea what Lily Sansfield looked like, she recognized her immediately. She was standing near All Yoga's cash register, her face almost identical to Eva's, although much thinner. She appeared fit in her white T-shirt and charcoal gray yoga pants, which cinched at the waist with a draw cord and flared at the bottom; Betty noticed the same ensemble on the clothing racks at the far end of the retail floor. Lily was chatting with a customer, pointing out a blue yoga mat. When she saw Betty come in, she excused herself and walked over. "Hi, can I help you?" she asked cheerily.

Betty smiled politely and pulled out her badge. "Hi, my name is Detective Betty Munson, Nassau County PD. Lily Sansfield?"

Lily's smile disappeared.

"I was just wondering if I could talk to you for a moment."

"Me?" Lily asked. "Is there something wrong?"

"Well, it's about your sister."

"Eva? Is she okay?"

"Yes, yes, she's fine, but—

"Oh, wait. Is this about the Kirk Stryker murder?" Lily took a step away from the customer behind her and lowered her voice. "I read about that in the newspaper. I've been trying to get a hold of Eva, but she's not returning my phone calls."

"Do you mind if I talk with you for a few minutes?" Betty asked.

"Sure, I guess. I'm not sure what I can tell you. Like I said, I can't get a hold of my sister, but, frankly, that's not unusual. Do you want to step outside?"

"Would that be all right?"

"I think so." Lily called over to a woman who was bending over a box of multicolored headbands. "Donna, I'm gonna go on my break, okay?" Donna did a quick survey of the store, nodded, and returned to her box.

"Let's go upstairs," Lily said.

The upper-level food court was packed with shoppers, but a family of four got up from a table as Lily and Betty arrived, and Lily made a beeline for it.

"Gotta move fast around here," Lily said, gathering up the paper straw covers and napkins that the family left behind and tossing them into a nearby garbage can. "Do you want something to drink?"

"No, no, thank you."

"Do you mind if I get one? I don't leave until seven, and they don't let you drink on the sales floor."

"Sure, go ahead."

Betty sat down at the table and looked around at all the young mothers with their children. She wondered if she'd be spending a lot of time in the mall after she retired; it seemed like the thing to do.

Lily returned with a fruit smoothie and brought Betty a latte. "I know you said you weren't thirsty, but I thought I'd get you something anyway," she said, setting it down in front of Betty. "I wasn't sure what you liked, so I figured I'd get what I like. Just in case."

Betty smiled. "Whatever it is, is fine. Thank you." She reached into her pocket for some money.

"No, that's okay, it's on me," Lily said.

"That is sweet, but I can't let you do that." Betty put a five-dollar bill on the table. "Does that cover it?"

"It's more than enough." Lily stuck the bill under her T-shirt, into her bra, and sat down. "Now, what can I do for you? Is Eva okay?" Lily took a sip of her smoothie, bending her head down to the straw rather than raising her plastic cup. She looked like a little girl.

"Yes, Eva's fine."

"I really wish she would return my calls," Lily said, shaking her head. "I guess you can see, we're not exactly, you know . . . *close*. I did try stopping by her apartment right after I heard about her boss. I figured, well, there wouldn't be a better time to touch base, but she didn't answer when I rang her bell. I thought I heard her shuffling around in there, but I didn't see her car parked anywhere, so maybe I'm just being paranoid."

"Why aren't the two of you close?"

"We were once, when we were little girls, but that was a long time ago. Do you know how she's doing?"

Betty was amazed at the similarities between the sisters. Despite the difference in size, the physical likeness was uncanny—the facial features, the fair skin, the long blonde hair—and there was a naiveté and innocence that they seemed to share.

"She's all right, I guess, but upset about the loss of Kirk Stryker," Betty said. "I saw her briefly at the funeral parlor for the wake. She and Mr. Stryker seemed to be very close. However, she didn't seem all that attached to any of her coworkers."

"That doesn't surprise me," Lily said. "Eva never really had many friends. Only me." She took another slurp of her smoothie. "People think it was her weight, but it wasn't. She was actually very skinny as a girl. I could show you pictures. She just, I don't know, liked to spend a lot of time in the house."

"You were the outdoorsy one, I take it?" Betty lifted the cover from her cup and sipped her latte.

"Oh, yeah," Lily said. "Softball, swimming, basketball, running. I did it all. Anything to get away from him."

"Get away from whom?"

"My father."

"Why? Did you not get along?"

Lily shrugged. "Something like that." The way the young woman said the words made the hair on Betty's neck stand up. "You've heard of him, right? The great Dr. Sansfield?"

Betty nodded. "The Sansfield Comet."

"Let's just say that comet wasn't the only thing to make a pass every now and then." Lily took a long slurp of her smoothie, her cheeks caving, making her face appear hollow.

"You mean . . . wait . . . your father . . . he . . ."

"Yep, that's him," Lily said, sitting back in her chair. "World-renowned astronomer, closet child molester."

Betty tried to speak, but the words wouldn't come.

"Detective Munson, it's all right. I know he was an ass and a fucking loser, excuse my language. I really don't think about it much anymore. It was a long time ago. He's dead now, so whatever. I'm fine." She shrugged. "But Eva never was. She could never really talk about it. Between you and me, I think that's why she can't lose the weight— all that ugliness is bottled up inside."

"Did you ever tell anyone?" Betty asked.

Lily shook her head. "We never told, or at least I didn't . . . Listen, I'm over it," she said, with a wave of her hand. "Wasn't my fault. Yadda, yadda. I know it all."

"But, your sister . . ." Betty thought of Eva sitting in the corner of the funeral home, ostracized, and she suddenly felt a bereavement pang of a different kind. "She must have hated your father."

Lily laughed, tilting her head back, her long blond hair swishing like a horse's tail. "On the contrary, she *loved* him. He called her the brightest star in his sky. He would walk into the room, and she would light up like a bulb: *'Oh, Poppa, you're the best.'* She used to make these cards for our father every birthday, holiday, Christmas. With cutouts and hearts. Letters from magazines. If it wasn't so damn cute, it'd be scary, like a ransom note from a serial killer."

"Where was your mother?" Betty realized the conversation had veered far from police procedure.

"Oh, she was there. What can I say? It was a different time. My guess is that she told herself that my father really wasn't *hurting* us, you know—whatever it took to get her through the day. Or maybe she was just embarrassed that he wanted us and not her. She got sick, though, after a while. And then she was gone." Lily leaned forward. "Listen, I'm okay. Despite what people think, this kind of stuff doesn't mess up everybody. Some of us deal and persevere and make it to the other side."

"Is it true that your father died in a bathtub?"

"Yep, fell asleep in our bathtub and died at age forty-two. I can give you the exact date, if you'd like."

"No, that's all right. What happened then? To you and Eva?"

"We were sent to live with our uncle in Gardenia. My uncle and aunt were decent people, thank god, but Eva wasn't ever the same. My father's death affected her greatly. I mean, why wouldn't it? She was the one who found him."

"Eva?"

Lily nodded. "It was after school. He had just come back from some business trip. Had been on the red eye and traveled all night. He got in and took a bath that afternoon, or so the police said. I had stayed after school for Girl Scouts with my friend Dana. He fell asleep in the tub. When Eva got home from school, she found him."

"That's terrible . . ."

"By that point, he hadn't been bothering much with me. I had started to develop—you know, these things." Lily pointed to her boobs. "Maybe that was a turnoff. I don't know about Eva, but he seemed to be leaving me alone. In the end, though, the bastard got what he deserved, if you ask me. Karma, right?" Lily took out her phone. "I should go. Donna freaks out if there's more than one customer in the store." She got up. "Not sure I helped you that much."

"Oh, you have, Lily, thank you."

Lily smiled and bowed slightly. "Namaste. And if you think of anything else you want to ask me, you can come visit anytime. Do you have a pen? I'll give you my number." Betty handed her a business card and a pen, and Lily jotted down her phone number. "And if you talk to Eva again . . . well, tell her I said hi," she said with a shrug before floating away and disappearing into the lunch crowd.

All Betty could do was sit there and watch her go.

44

"Where ya been, Parker?" Gardner thundered as John Parker slipped behind his desk at the *Gazette* office.

"Investigating, sir." Parker ripped open his backpack and dumped its contents onto the desk.

"Well, that doesn't mean you don't answer your phone when I call, got that?" Gardner pulled up on his trousers and sat on the corner of Parker's desk. The old editor was wearing a clean button-down that looked like it had just been unfolded from the package. He examined the items splayed across Parker's desk. "You better have something good in there by the time we go to press tomorrow. We have 50 percent more advertising in this issue than any issue we've had for the past three years, and we need to deliver."

"Yeah," Kramer said snidely from across the room, "or else people might start to think that big scoop of yours was a total fluke."

"Don't worry," he said. "I got somethin'."

"Yeah?" Gardner said. "Do tell."

"It'll all be in my story. Give me a couple of hours."

Gardner bent down. "You look like shit, kid."

"I'm all right," Parker said, although he hadn't slept much or showered in days. He was hoping to catch Detective Munson at her home that morning, but he slept through his alarm and his mother had forgotten to wake him. By the time Parker got to her home, she was already gone for the day.

"Gotta take care of yourself, kid," Gardner said. "You're no good to me passed out on the floor with a fever." He took an orange from a bowl near the office coffee station and put it on Parker's desk. "Eat it. You need your vitamin C. And get me that story. By two o'clock."

"Got it," Parker said as Gardner shuffled off. He stuck his earbuds in, hit *Play* on his iPhone playlist, and opened a new document on his computer screen.

"So where ya been?" Parker heard Kramer ask over the bassline of a Macseal song. "I haven't seen you around the past few days."

Parker had decided to keep his investigating to himself. "I've been around."

"Chasing down leads, eh?"

"Something like that."

"Well, you got a call this morning."

"Oh, yeah?" Parker kept typing. "I get lots of calls."

"Well, this one," Kramer unfolded a piece of paper, "was from a Detective Munson."

Parker stopped typing and yanked out his earbuds. He reached for the note, but Kramer pulled it out of reach.

"Not so fast," Kramer said. "Detective Munson. What? She your Deep Throat?"

"Give it to me, Kramer. Don't be a jerk."

Kramer handed him the note, which had a phone

number written across the top. "What did she say?" Parker asked, sticking the paper in his pocket.

"How much do you want to know?"

"Go fuck yourself, Kramer." Parker wished the guy had called in sick again. Maybe he would give him a reason to.

"Easy there, newbie. I'm just joking around. She didn't say shit. She asked for you, I told her you weren't here, and she gave me her number and told me to tell you to call her."

"Well, you did, thanks," Parker said and resumed his typing.

"You know, you're letting this scoop really go to your head," Kramer sneered.

Parker threw his earbuds onto his keyboard. "All I know is that for a year you've been giving me shit, strutting around this office like you were Woodward and Bernstein. Undangling my participles like a fucking asshole," he hissed, glancing into Gardner's office, where the old editor had his back turned, on the phone. "The minute I get any fucking attention, you glare at me like an older brother whose mother didn't give him enough ice cream. Do me a favor and just leave me the fuck alone." Before Kramer could respond, Parker stormed out of the office and down the four flights of stairs until he was outside. *Asshole.*

He took a deep breath, but the bright sun only made him feel warmer. He walked toward the small parking lot where several of the building's tenants were smoking. Sy Reedus, the optometrist who owned the practice on the first floor, saw him coming and motioned toward a blue Mazda.

"Can you believe this guy?" Reedus asked. His face,

dotted with broken capillaries, was twisted into a scowl. "Parks in a handicapped spot . . . No handicap sticker." He slammed the banana peel he was holding into a nearby garbage can. The guy had developed a nasty banana habit ever since his doctor warned him that he'd be dead in a few years if he didn't quit smoking. "Probably some stupid entitled kid who got a car from daddy for his sixteenth birthday. No offense."

"None taken," Parker said.

Reedus looked Parker up and down. "Well, don't you look like somebody died. Why the long face?"

"Just one of those days." Parker kicked a rock into the parking lot.

"Perk up, kid. I mean, how bad could it be? I think you've got employee of the month all wrapped up." He nudged him with his elbow.

"Yeah, well, not everyone thinks so." Parker leaned against the blue Mazda. "My co-worker thinks I'm a fraud. My parents don't take me seriously. I'm busting my ass out here."

"Gardner seems appreciative," Reedus said. "I saw him pull into the lot at the crack of dawn and practically skip his way to the front door. I haven't seen the old coot this happy in . . . I don't know how long. It's nice to see for a change." Reedus pulled up on the belt of his pants. "Since Clara died, all he's had is this newspaper, and, well, as you know, newspapers aren't doing all that well these days. I got the feeling that maybe Gardner was thinking about throwing in the towel." He shook his head. "I can't imagine it. That guy lives and breathes news. Without it, I think he might shrivel up. But the last few days? He's a new man.

And you know what, kid? You're the one to thank for that." He put his hand on Parker's shoulder. "Listen, you can't expect everyone to give you a pat on the back every time you do a good job. The world doesn't work that way, but the good news is that you only really need one person to believe in you."

"I hear what you're saying. I've got Gardner."

"I wasn't talking about him, kid. I was talking about *you*." Reedus smiled. "Sometimes we're the only ones who can see a dream. No one expected me to survive when they started selling prescription eyeglasses in Walmart and all the rest of those big chain stores, but I believed, and I've had my practice running for more than thirty years. Did all right. This news business, kid. Is this your dream?"

Parker shrugged. He hadn't thought about it before. He had taken the job because he needed the money, but something had definitely changed. He hadn't been killing himself all week for minimum wage. He *liked* chasing down leads. He *liked* trying to put the pieces of the puzzle together. He *liked* the attention. He even liked riling up Munson. Somewhere along the line working at the *Gazette* had become the beginning of something resembling a career. "I guess it is," he said with a smile.

"That's more like it. Keep smiling, kid." Reedus pulled a banana out of his back pocket and began peeling it. "Now, I don't know what happened up there that drove you down here with us cancerous bastards, but do us all a favor, and get back up there, do this community proud, and find the fucker who killed my friend Kirk."

45

Satriano picked up his office phone, dialed the first three digits of Gloria Stryker's phone number, and then hung up. He couldn't come up with a good way to ask if she had any of her husband's fundraising or political ledgers. It seemed self-serving and impolite. But Thursday was coming, and he still didn't have the fifteen thousand dollars the man in the baseball cap wanted. If that's *all* he wanted. Satriano had a feeling it wouldn't be.

He reached for the remote control and turned on the television. The screen warmed to News 12, which, not surprisingly, was discussing Benning's arrest. As it had with Stryker, the station had put together a hastily assembled bio—of Benning's upbringing in upstate New York, his practice in Manhattan, his office on Long Island, his reputation as a womanizer. Satriano raised the volume. Footage from a Gardenia chamber of commerce event showed Benning holding a drink with a young, attractive woman beside him. Footage from the holiday tree lighting showed Benning with the Gardenia mayor—Satriano thought he could see Stryker in the background talking to the fire chief. Next was footage from Benning's ribbon cutting two years before. Satriano scanned the faces when suddenly his breath hitched.

He rewound a bit and paused the image. Benning was holding an oversized pair of scissors and was talking to a tall man in a gray business suit. Satriano got out of his chair and walked toward the television screen until he was eye to eye with the man, whose face he recognized instantly— even without his baseball cap and sunglasses.

46

"I don't understand . . . Weren't we just *at* Daddy's?" Ellie said, staring out the car window.

"Yes, we're not staying long," Muriel said. She was determined to drop off the divorce papers once and for all, since Doug was determined to conveniently ignore them, like he did most things he didn't want to be bothered with. "Okay, we're here," she said, pulling into the driveway.

As usual, the house where Doug was renting was perfectly manicured and decorated for spring with flags and banners in pastel colors, the kinds of seasonal adornments that Muriel never had the time—or money or inclination—to care about. She opened her door and quickly scouted the area. She didn't want to run into any of Doug's volunteer firefighter friends—six of them lived on this block alone, which is how he managed to score his apartment on the cheap. They hadn't forgiven her for kicking Doug out, and Muriel figured they probably never would.

"It's only for a little while, honey," Muriel said, as the kids opened their car doors. "I promise. And I brought stuff for you to eat while I talk to Daddy."

Doug's apartment door opened, and he appeared, surprised. "Hey, guys, what are you doing here?"

"Ask Mommy," Ellie said, passing him and walking inside, with Zack trailing behind her.

"Muriel, I wasn't expecting you," he said. "I've got a fund drive."

"This won't take long." She handed Doug a grocery bag when he didn't offer to carry one, and they followed the kids into the apartment.

Muriel was always surprised at how spacious the place was considering it was only half of the bottom floor of a dormered cape. As the kids settled in the living room, she put the grocery bag on the kitchen counter and took out the boxes of macaroni and cheese and cookies that were inside. Doug came up behind her and put his bag next to hers. She took out the bread and cold cuts.

"What's going on?" he asked.

She reached into her purse and pulled out the divorce papers. "You forgot these," she said, holding them out. "You forgot them when you picked up the kids. And you forgot them when you dropped them off. I figured I'd save you a trip and bring them myself."

Doug glanced at the paperwork but didn't take it. "Put it over there," he said, motioning to somewhere unspecified. "I'll look at it later."

"I'd rather you look at it now."

Zack ran in and reached for the box of cookies before Muriel could stop him. "Hey, mister, sandwich first," she said.

"I just want to hold them," he lied, running back into the living room with the box.

"How was Atlantic City?" Doug asked snidely.

"I don't want to talk about Atlantic City," Muriel said. "We need to talk about this. It's not working. This 'separation thing,' as you called it, isn't going to go away."

"You know what, Mur? For once, I agree." He reached into a cabinet drawer and pulled out a set of papers and handed it to her.

"What's this?"

"I've been doing a little legal consulting of my own," he said. "And I've decided that I want custody of the kids."

"*What?*"

"Can you blame me?" he asked. "You're not yourself, Muriel. Not lately. And you're making bad judgment calls."

"Oh, that's rich, coming from you."

"What's that supposed to mean?"

"How many times have I had to pick up Zackie because you and your firefighter friends got too drunk to drive him home?"

"He was never in danger, Mur. At least, *I* would never expose my kids to murderers."

"That's ridiculous, Doug. Marty is innocent."

"You know what Zackie was telling me when you were in Atlantic City?"

"What he *told* you?" she asked, crossing her arms. "Or what you *extracted* from him?"

"He told me all about how Mommy was having a sleepover playdate with Marty, the guy that was on television. A *sleepover,* Mur? With the kids in the house?"

Muriel scrunched the plastic supermarket bag in her hand and tossed it in the recycling can. "Doug, I'm not going to talk about this."

"And Ellie mentioned some guy—*a friend of Marty's,* she said—offered to teach her how to cook. Who is this guy?"

"It was just an offer, Doug, relax. From his friend, Bobby."

"Oh, a friend of a murderer. This guy has you all out of whack, Muriel."

"Oh, isn't that just—"

"You're yelling again," Ellie called from the living room.

Muriel lowered her voice. "Doug, I've been out of whack for a long time. You just didn't notice, and how ironic that you—"

"Mom!"

"Ellie, I'm not yelling," Muriel shouted, but her daughter came running into the kitchen, her face pale.

"Something's wrong with Zack!" she said. Behind her, Zack came running into the room, pointing to his throat. He looked scared to death.

"What the hell?" Doug asked, running ahead of Muriel and lifting Zack's little face toward him.

"I don't feel good," he moaned.

"Oh, my god, what is it?" Muriel cupped his cheeks. "What hurts, baby?"

"Mommy, make it stop." Zack pointed to his chest. "It feels like it's tight."

Muriel felt his head.

"Does he have a fever?" Doug asked, picking him up.

"No, he's sweating," Muriel said when suddenly Zack's little body heaved, and he threw up all over the kitchen counter and floor.

"Jesus," Doug said, taking a step back.

Zack began to cry and reached for Muriel, who took him from Doug and wrapped her arms around him. "It's okay. It's okay." She bounced him up and down. "You just threw up, that's all." She looked at Doug. "Maybe he's coming down with a virus."

"Great, and now we all will . . . " He grabbed a sponge and started sopping up the vomit. "Ugh. It smells like . . . *peanut butter*?" He glared at Muriel and charged into the living room, returning with the package of cookies. He held them in front of her. "You bought *peanut butter* cookies, Muriel. Are you crazy? Have you forgotten that our son has a peanut allergy?"

"Those aren't peanut butter cookies," Muriel said. "They can't be." She began reading the packaging's allergy information but Doug stuck his hand in front of the type to point out the word *Peanut* that was written in big orange letters across the top of the box.

Zack lifted his head from Muriel's shoulder. "Mommy, did you?"

Muriel's heart thumped against her chest. "I . . . I . . ." She peered into his bloodshot baby blue eyes. "I must have picked up the wrong carton in my rush. Oh, god, I'm so sorry, sweetie." She gently pushed Zack's head back down on her shoulder and told him to rest, but she really wanted to avoid the crushed looked on his face.

"Did you at least bring the EpiPen?" Doug asked.

"Of course, I did." Muriel opened her bag and took it out. "He seems okay, though."

"Yeah, well, we'll see." He grabbed it and plucked Zack from Muriel's arms, carrying him away like he always did when a medical issue arose—the proud EMT to the rescue.

"Way to go, Mom," Ellie said, rolling her eyes and following her father into the living room.

Muriel watched them go. How could she have made such a mistake? She pulled at her shirt, which was wet with vomit. It had gotten all over everything—the groceries, her purse, her car keys, the divorce paperwork, hers and Doug's. She tossed the box of cookies into the garbage, grabbed a handful of paper towels, and ran them under cold water.

"Muriel, I got it, just leave it," Doug called. "You've done enough."

"All right, Doug, I feel bad enough as it is." Typical Doug. He could make every mistake in the book, but her one mishap would be held against her for years. She leaned over, sopped up as much vomit as she could from the counter, and dropped the soiled paper towels into the garbage pail. "Is he all right?"

"I'm fine, Mommy," Zack called. "Even though you almost killed me."

Muriel sighed. She ripped another paper towel from the dispenser and lifted her car keys, which were coated completely with brown goo. She scraped off as much as she could from each key and a charm—*No. 1 Mom*—that Zack had gotten her last year for Mother's Day. The *1* had broken off, making what was left look like *No Mom*.

Great, she thought. She glanced into the living room, where Zack was sitting upright and watching TV. He seemed all right, but she had a feeling that if Doug had his way, that's exactly what Muriel would be. No mom.

47

As the fluorescent lights of the precinct's evidence room blinked on, Betty couldn't help but feel a bit of pride. The room was the most organized it had been in years, perhaps ever—the result of a weeks-long cleanup she had spearheaded in preparation for a massive review by the State Attorney's Office. That was before the Stryker investigation came along and sucked up all of her time.

She searched the aisles of neatly stacked floor-to-ceiling shelves until she found Stryker's case number and slid one of the boxes out of its sleeve and onto a nearby examination table. Even though the evidence was sealed inside plastic, Betty could still smell the charred contents. She pulled out a series of bags containing rug samples, fibers from Stryker's clothing, dispensed Taser tags and cartridges, and money that had been found in Stryker's safe—fifteen thousand dollars in hundred-dollar bills.

"*Here* you are," Pam said, walking into the room. She was carrying a cardboard box. "I was wondering where you were. This just came for you." She handed it to Betty. "So are you going to tell me why you wanted to see the evidence from this old case, or do I have to force it out of you?" She smiled.

"Long shot," Betty said.

Pam slid a seat out from the table and sat down. "I noticed the name. Sansfield. The same name as the gal from Stryker's office. Is there a correlation?"

Betty ran the blade of a pair of scissors across the taped top of the cardboard box. "Yeah, Eva was Henry Sansfield's daughter. He had two. Twins. He died in 1996 in his bathtub, and after that the two girls were alone. They were eleven years old."

"Suicide?"

"It was ruled a suicide, I believe." She pulled on a pair of plastic gloves and looked inside the box for the crime report.

"Where was the mom?"

"She had died of cancer two years before."

"Wow," Pam put on gloves as well, "seems like people keep dying around Eva Sansfield."

The Sansfield crime scene photos were clipped to the police report. Betty flipped through them and instantly noted the resemblance between Henry Sansfield and his daughters, particularly Lily. The first photos were close-ups of Sansfield's deceased face, his eyes shut and mouth open. Betty imagined a young Eva coming home from school and finding her father this way. How could that not impact a prepubescent girl? There was a shot of a bottle of pills lying on its side on the floor. Another showed a shelf at the top of the tub and an empty bottle of vodka.

She flipped to the next image—a close-up of Henry Sansfield's face taken from straight above. He looked almost peaceful, as if he were sleeping. The next photo showed the rest of his body, including toys—an orange rowboat and a couple of figurines—floating in the water near Sansfield's feet. She thought of Scott and Jesse's bagful of toys in her own bathroom.

"Anything?" Pam asked, flipping through pages of the report.

Betty shook her head. "No, not yet."

"Says here Sansfield drowned. An accidental drowning. No suicide."

"Drowned?" Betty said. "Not an OD?"

Pam pointed to the line that detailed the cause of death. "I'm sure the vodka didn't help. Are those toys?" she asked, glancing at the photo in Betty's hands. "Was Sansfield playing with them? That's kinda weird."

Betty put the first set of photographs down, picked up another, and started flipping through them. For this series, the body of Henry Sansfield had been taken out of the bathtub and laid onto a body bag. She stopped at a close-up of Sansfield's bloated midsection.

"What is it?" Pam asked, looking over Betty's shoulder.

"It's Orion," she said, stunned. She dropped the Sansfield photos onto the desk and quickly rummaged through the Stryker box. The photo of Stryker's abdomen, the one Scott had seen, was still at the top of the pile. She unclipped it and put it on the table next to the image of Sansfield's abdomen.

"Now that's strange," Pam said, bending down to look at the photos more closely.

The marks on Sansfield's abdomen appeared to be incisions, rather than burns, but were in the same pattern, the constellation of the Hunter. Betty pointed to the marks on Stryker's body.

"These are marks that we believe were made by Stryker's killer with a cigarette," Betty said. She moved her finger to the Sansfield photo. "Don't these look like they're the same pattern of marks?"

Pam eyed the two photos. "They do. But Sansfield's marks are smaller. More delicate."

"Yes, definitely not made with the butt of a cigarette, but they do look fresh."

"Some Satanic cult maybe?" Pam asked. "Does Benning have them?"

"Benning?" Betty asked, surprised. "I don't know."

"Do you think the marks were made by the same person?"

"I find that difficult to believe, considering the marks were made decades apart," Betty said. "But it's possible."

"There's only one person, you know, who is connected to these two photos."

"I know. Eva Sansfield."

"Have you spoken to her?" Pam asked.

"Not lately. I can't seem to get a hold of her. I did manage to find her sister, who, unfortunately, told me some disturbing things about the nature of the relationship between Henry Sansfield and his daughters."

Pam sat down on the chair, her eyes wide. "No . . ."

Betty nodded. "At least, according to Lily."

"Why, you don't believe her?"

"I didn't say that. Right now, I'm just gathering the facts and taking everything into consideration." She reclipped the photos to their respective reports. "Quite honestly, I'm not sure what I believe anymore."

"Does that mean you're having doubts about

Benning?" Pam asked. She lifted a plastic bag from the Stryker box. It contained the glass found at the crime scene with Benning's fingerprint.

"Not sure," Betty said. "Arguably, he has motive . . . But I'd feel a heck of a lot better if I had a murder weapon." She reached into Stryker's box and pulled out two ziplock bags containing homemade cards and placed them on the desk. Underneath them was the desk daily planner that showed Stryker's appointments. The page was still open to April First, the day Stryker had been killed.

Betty opened the plastic bag and pulled out the planner. She glanced at the crossed-out notation of *BENNING* before flipping back a few pages and then forward again.

"What are you looking at?" Pam asked.

"The handwriting," Betty said. "Besides the word *BENNING*, it looks like the rest of the notations were written in the same handwriting, no?"

Pam flipped a page back and forth. "It seems so. Is it sexist of me to think this handwriting, with its flamboyant flourishes, looks more like a woman's?"

"Probably," Betty said with a smile. "But I'd have to agree."

Betty put the planner back in the plastic bag and placed it in the box. She picked up the bag holding the homemade birthday cards—some of the raw elbow macaroni had fallen off and was at the bottom of the bag. She remembered seeing the cards taped onto the wall near Stryker's office door when she had first visited the crime scene. She read one of the inscriptions:

Happy birthday, Poppa. I love you so, so much.

Betty reached into the bag and pulled out another card.

This one featured magazine cut-outs of a little person and big person holding hands. A heart had been drawn at the center. Betty thought of Stryker's son, Mark, his tiny face squinting up at her when she visited Gloria Stryker's home.

"Such a shame," Pam said. "It's so hard for a child to lose a parent, whatever the reason." She took one of the cards from Betty and fingered the heart made of pasta. "Homemade cards are really the best. So much love created out of macaroni, glitter, and glue. Costs pennies, but is priceless, you know?" She handed the card back to Betty, who frowned. "What's the matter?"

"I don't think these cards were made by Stryker's children," she said.

"What do you mean?"

Something Lily had said was niggling at the back of Betty's mind, how Eva had adored her father despite all that had happened. *On the contrary, she loved him. He would walk in the room, and she would light up like a bulb: 'Oh, Poppa, you're the best.'*

Betty looked at Stryker's card:
Happy birthday, Poppa.

Poppa. It wasn't a term of endearment as common as *Dad* or *Daddy*, for sure, but it still could have been a coincidence. She looked at the card made from magazine photos as Lily's words floated to her: *She used to make these cards for our father every birthday, holiday, Christmas. With cutouts and hearts. Letters from magazines. If it wasn't so damn cute, it'd be scary, like a ransom note from a serial killer.*

Betty reached back into the Stryker box and pulled out the desk planner, taking it out of the plastic bag. She looked at the handwriting: The curlicue of the *b* in *Colby* was identical to the *b* in *birthday* on the card. She nudged at a piece of glued macaroni, wiggling it carefully until it fell into the bottom of the plastic bag and left a tiny spot of glue behind.

"What are you doing?" Pam asked.

One by one, Betty flicked off the noodles until they were all gathered at the bottom of the evidence bag, revealing a line of lettering that had been hidden at the top of the card:

From the desk of Eva Sansfield.

"Looks like there may be a reason why people are dying around Eva Sansfield," Betty said. "And I have a feeling there's at least one person who knows what it is."

48

Satriano pushed his sister ahead of him into the revolving entrance door of the News 12 offices.

"I'm going, I'm going," Mary said, swatting at him until the rubber flap of the glass wall sealed her inside the compartment in front of him. When they reached the lobby, Mary crossed her arms. "I still don't understand why we need to do this."

"Just trust me, okay?"

News 12 Networks comprised seven regional cable news television channels in the New York metropolitan area, all housed in one building. Satriano had been to the station several times since he ran for office, once to take part in a public service announcement and twice as a participant in a televised debate and public forum. The lobby was as cavernous as he remembered, like a bat cave. As he and Mary approached the receptionist who was seated behind a long black desk, Satriano's hands began to feel clammy. This wouldn't be easy. Despite his life in politics, he had a horrible poker face. His dad was right: he *was* a good boy.

"I think I should wait in the car," he whispered to Mary.

"No, Ton," Mary said, latching onto his arm. "You need to stay."

"Why? You remember what to say, right?"

"Duh. But this was *your* idea," she said, pushing her brother toward the front desk.

"Hi," the receptionist said when she saw them. She had a happy, but tired face. "Can I help you?"

Satriano gave Mary a soft shove, and she took a step forward, putting her hands on the smooth stone of the desktop.

"Yes, I'd like to speak with Jill Sansone, please. She's expecting us," Mary said.

"Certainly, and you are?"

"Mary Satriano."

"And you, sir?" the receptionist asked, peeking behind Mary where Satriano was hiding.

"Anthony Satriano," he said, trying not to stutter.

"Anthony Satri—" The receptionist studied his face. "Oh, Assemblyman, I'm so sorry. I didn't recognize you." The young woman scurried out from behind her post to shake Satriano's hand. "You're not my district, but if you were, I would certainly have voted for you. Big fan."

"Thank you," Satriano said, glancing at Mary, who rolled her eyes.

"I'll get Jill now," the receptionist said.

As the young woman spoke into her phone, Mary patted Satriano on the back. "Ask her if she's single, Ton. Mommy needs some grandbabies."

"Shut up, Mar."

"You better be nice to me. I'll walk out now, and then you'll have to be a big boy and ask the nice reporter for that name all on your own."

In a few moments, Jill Sansone strolled into the lobby

from the elevator bank. She was a waif of a woman, barely five feet tall, although her high heels added a good three inches.

"Well, well, well, Assemblyman Satriano. Imagine seeing you here in the lion's den." Sansone smiled and stuck out her hand. "I was beginning to think you had run away to join the circus."

"Ms. Sansone," Satriano said, shaking her hand. "I believe you know my sister, Mary."

"Yes, yes," Jill said. "Mary and I go way back. She's the one who keeps dodging my calls."

Mary smiled politely. "I appreciate you seeing us, Ms. Sansone," she said.

"Well, what is it I can do for you?" Jill asked. "You mentioned on the phone you had a request. As I said to you, I like to have any requests of me made in person."

"Right." Mary cleared her throat and glanced at Satriano. "Well, it actually has to do with my parents. A gentleman left his briefcase at the fruit market a few weeks ago, and they've been waiting for him to return and get it, but he never did . . . "

Satriano always marveled at how his sister could lie so easily. He couldn't remember how many times she had broken something or had done something wrong when they were growing up and then had stood, innocently, in front of their parents to accuse him of the crime. Maybe *she* was the one who should have gone into politics.

" . . . And this was such a fluke thing," Mary continued, "but they saw him on the report you did today on Marty Benning—you know, that this-is-your-life retrospective.

You guys do such a great job with those—and they couldn't believe it was him. What a coincidence, right, Ton?"

Jill looked at Satriano.

"Yes," he stuttered. "Such a coincidence. I actually didn't even know about this until Mary told me this afternoon. People are always leaving things at the market." He cleared his throat, trying to appear relaxed. "There's this law they passed recently in France—"

"Anyway, my parents," Mary said, cutting him off, "asked me if I could find out who it was—God forbid they ask Anthony to do anything." She rolled her eyes; she was laying it on pretty thick. "I spoke to Anthony about it, and he said I should call you, that you're terrific." She smiled.

"Really?" Jill said, glancing at Satriano.

Satriano nodded. "Any help you can provide would be greatly appreciated," he said. "My parents are very concerned."

"Well, we don't normally honor these kinds of requests," Jill said, "but since, well, it's you, Assemblyman, and considering that package was just recently pieced together, our interns should have that information handy. It shouldn't be a problem to get it for you."

"Great," Satriano said, relieved. "How long do you think it will take?"

"Oh, they should have it by the time we're done."

"Done?" Satriano asked. "Done with what?"

"Our exclusive interview," the reporter said. "You know, about your relationship with Kirk Stryker, your reelection campaign. Mary said that shouldn't be a problem."

"Problem?" Satriano glanced at his sister, who smiled

sheepishly. "No, of course not. That's right. I had forgotten that Mary mentioned that."

"Great. Well, right this way, Assemblyman," Sansone said, heading back toward the elevators. "The studio's ready for us. It should only take about thirty minutes to get through everything."

"Thirty minutes? Is that all?" Satriano reached for Mary's hand and squeezed it a little too hard as they walked behind Sansone, who was holding open the door to the first elevator.

❂

Satriano emerged from the tiny studio, and the technical director threw him a thumbs-up.

"You were great, Ton," Mary said. "Very natural."

"You could have mentioned that you had agreed to an interview, Mar."

"I'm doing you a favor, Ton," Mary whispered, pretending to straighten his tie. "You gotta stop hiding. You didn't do anything wrong, but for some reason since the Stryker thing started you've been skulking around the office like a criminal. This interview is the best thing for your PR. You were terrific. Sansone totally threw you softballs."

She was right. Sansone didn't seem to know anything about the Stryker investigation beyond what had already been reported in the press. He had tried to keep his answers as vague as possible.

"You answered Sansone's questions easily and breezily, like you always do," Mary said. "And you look as handsome as ever. Mommy's gonna freak when she sees you."

"But you should have—"

"If I would have told you about it, you never would have agreed to it—you know that's true. And even if you had, you just would have been a nervous wreck the whole time, like when you had to tell Daddy you had that car accident after the prom."

"Mar, I was eighteen . . ."

"Whatever, you avoided him for a week. You know how you get. This was the perfect opportunity to get your name out there in a positive way."

"Fine, fine, I get it," he said, wondering when Mary managed to go from a sister who needed a job to a bonafide press secretary. "Just don't do that again."

"Yes, Assemblyman," Mary said, nudging him.

Sansone came out of the small studio looking even thinner than she was going in. She spoke to a young man in a Queensryche T-shirt who handed her a folder.

"Looks like the interview came out great, guys," she said, hobbling over in her heels. "Thanks again for the exclusive, Assemblyman Satriano. I hope that we can maintain this relationship in the future."

"Anytime," Satriano said, hoping he never had to do this again.

"I'm going to take you up on that," Jill said with a smile. "And, as promised," she handed the folder in her hands to Mary, "here is the name of that guy in the montage. Looks like he worked for Benning. He was listed as one of the employees of the firm when the videotape was first shot."

Mary opened the folder, and Satriano immediately

recognized the man in the still photograph as the guy at his cousin's house. The name *Tom Cranston* was scribbled under it.

"Hopefully, he's listed," Sansone said, "so you can return his briefcase."

"Yeah, hope so," Satriano said, shaking the reporter's hand, although something told him that finding out Tom Cranston's name would be much easier than finding Tom Cranston.

49

"**M**s. Sansfield?"

Betty rang Eva's doorbell once more. She had been standing on the front doorstep of the apartment for five minutes now.

She peered through the vertical blinds of the front bay window, but it looked as though the room was dark and no one was home. Across the street, landscaping crews were mowing the development's lawn, and the noise made it difficult to hear if anyone was moving around inside the apartment.

A door opened across the way, and an old man walked out gingerly with a cane.

"Good evening," he said with a smile when he saw Betty standing there.

"Good evening." Betty reached in to pull out her badge but then thought better of it. "I'm looking for Eva Sansfield. She's your neighbor. Do you know her?"

"Eva? Yes. Lovely woman. She always brings out my garbage cans for me . . . And my recycling. She brings that out for me too." The old man pulled on his door, leaving it slightly ajar, and shuffled toward a white wooden bench that was located in between his and Eva's apartment.

"Do you happen to know if she's around? Have you seen her?"

The old man looked at his wrist and appeared confused when there wasn't a watch wrapped around it. "What time is it?" he asked.

Betty checked her phone. "Around seven."

"And the day?" the old man asked. He smiled. "Sorry, I lose track of time."

"Wednesday."

"Ah, almost time for *Jeopardy!*" The old man chuckled. "Ms. Sansfield usually goes to the library on Wednesday evenings. There's a poetry group that meets there. I see her come home with books all the time. Sometimes she likes to sit right here and smoke a cigarette"—the old man sat down on the bench and grunted—"sometimes for hours. She gave me a poem once. Would you like to read it?"

He reached into his pants pocket before Betty could answer and pulled out a tiny stack of cards, along with several used tissues. "I keep it with me. So very sweet." He fumbled through the stack, which consisted of health insurance cards and worn plastic-coated photos of children. "Dagnabit, where did I put the darn thing. Oh, here it is." He pulled out a folded square of lined notebook paper and handed it to Betty. She opened it:

Starry-Eyed
People ooh and ahh over starry skies,
Their twinkling eyes, glitter for the soul
But—

There it was: Eva's curlicued *B*.

My favorite nights are when the moon hides
And there is nothing to seek or find,
A darkness befitting neither princess, nor beau.

"It's lovely," Betty said, handing it back to him. "Eva gave this to you?"

"Isn't it?" The old man slipped it back into his pocket. "Yes, she gave it to me. . . . Let's see . . . Gotta be about a week or so ago."

"A week ago?"

The old man thought about this. "Yes, I think so. She seemed to have been crying at the time. I could tell, because her cheeks were puffy, and she looked sad—had never really seen her like that. And she said that she lost someone very dear to her."

"A friend?"

"No," the old man said. "Her father."

Her father? Betty thought of the homemade card in the evidence room written to *Poppa*. Had the death of Kirk Stryker triggered some sort of reaction to her own father's passing? Or had Eva always seen Kirk as a father figure? "I'm very sorry to hear that," Betty said. "Had you ever met him? Her father?"

"No, no. She doesn't seem to get many visitors, Eva. Such a shame, really. A sweet girl." He adjusted himself on the bench. "Shall I tell Ms. Sansfield you were here looking for her?"

"Yes, if you can, that would be great. My name is Betty. But I'll take a ride over to the library. Maybe I'll catch her there."

"That'll do," the old man said with a crooked smile.

He leaned his head on the curved back of the wooden bench and closed his eyes as Betty walked toward her car. She searched for John Parker, which had become a habit, before getting into the driver's seat and heading toward the Gardenia Public Library, her thoughts filled with starry skies on flesh abdomens and princesses who commit murder.

50

Parker, Kramer, and Gardner watched News 12's exclusive interview with Assemblyman Anthony Satriano on the small television Gardner kept in his office.

"I thought you said he wasn't doing interviews, Parker," said Gardner, who was leaning against the edge of his desk, arms folded. Sansone was winding down the interview with talk of Satriano's forthcoming reelection bid.

"He hasn't been," Parker said, more defensively than he intended. "He hasn't even been answering any press inquiries. As far as I can tell, reporters haven't been able to get further than Mary, his press secretary."

"Well, looks like Jill Sansone managed to," Kramer said, handing a cup of coffee to Gardner with a grin.

"Even so, boss," Parker said. "There's nothing here. Blah blah . . . Stryker financed him. Blah blah . . . hadn't seen him since March. Satriano had nothing to say."

"But I'd be a whole lot happier if he had nothing to say within the pages of the *Gardenia Gazette*." Gardner took a sip of his coffee, made a face, and placed the cup on his desk. "I shouldn't be drinking this. I'll be up all night, as if

I'm not up all night already." The old editor slumped into his chair. "That story you handed me this afternoon?"

"Yeah?" Parker said.

"It's crap, kid. Total crap."

"What do you mean?" Parker could feel his cheeks warming and avoided Kramer's eyes.

"It's just a rehash of what we already know. Nothing new. That doesn't sell papers." Gardner put his head in his hands, the strands of his comb-over falling onto his fingers. "Are we asking the right questions? Talking to the right people?" He pointed to the television screen. "Is Satriano going to Benning's arraignment? That's what I want to know," Gardner said, clicking off the set.

"Why would he?" Kramer asked.

"Exactly," Gardner said. "But I need to know. If he goes, that's a story. If he doesn't go, that's a story too. And I need a story, Parker."

"What? Like, *now*?" Parker asked.

"You got something better to do?" Gardner asked. "The print edition goes to press tonight. I can hold the printer off until tomorrow morning, but anything after that would be pushing it. I've got advertisers counting on this issue to be a Pulitzer Prize winner."

"I know," Parker said, "but—"

"Peewee soccer scores aren't going to cut it. Get me something. Something that"—he pointed to the dark screen—"Jill Sansone or nobody else has. And start with Satriano. Apparently, he's talking."

"But I—"

"Enough with the buts, Parker, *go*."

Parker hurried to his desk to gather his gear. Across the office, Kramer was doing the same.

"Where are *you* going?" Parker asked, putting on his backpack.

"I'm coming with you," Kramer said.

"Like hell you are. I work alone."

"Are you kidding me?" Kramer came up next to him and lowered his voice. "Listen, you little prick, until the Hugo Lurch thing, which was a total fluke, you were a glorified editor's assistant. As far as I'm concerned, you still are."

"Fuck off, asshole," Parker whispered so Gardner wouldn't hear him. He brushed past Kramer, shoving his notebook and digital camera into his backpack.

"From what I've heard, you would be working at Friendly's washing dishes if Gardner hadn't took pity on you and given you a job," Kramer said, following behind him.

"Be careful, Kramer, your jealousy is showing." Parker lifted his calendar from his desk and pushed around pencils, pens, and a calculator. He picked up a stack of newspapers and placed it back down, crossing his arms. "Okay, where is it?"

"Where's what, asshat?" Kramer asked.

"My digital recorder." Parker couldn't remember the last time he had it.

"I don't know."

"Bullshit." He reached across Kramer's desk and picked up a pen. "See?" Parker said.

"See what?"

"This is *my* pen."

"Yeah, so?"

"My pens. My Post-its. My batteries. My newspapers. Somehow they all land around your side of the room."

"You've gotta be kidding me," Kramer said.

"So where is it?"

"You're the star investigative reporter. *You* figure it out. The way you dump that backpack out, it's amazing that you can keep track of anything in there." Kramer pulled his jacket from the coatrack.

Parker checked underneath his chair and under his desk. He looked again in his backpack. "Pretty pathetic, Kramer," he said, checking behind his computer terminal and on the floor in front of his desk, "having to resort to stealing my notes, because you can't do your job."

"Fuck you, Parker. I don't need your lousy recorder."

"Boys! Boys!" Gardner screamed from his office. "All this pent-up energy should be used out there, not in here. Now go and get me something. Work together."

"*Together?* But," Parker said, "I—"

"That's an order!" Gardner said. "Go. Now."

Parker zipped his backpack and put his arms through the straps as Kramer lifted Parker's college hoodie from the coatrack. He handed it to him with a smirk.

"Looks like you're stuck with me, after all," Kramer said.

51

The Gardenia Public Library was one of the larger and more state-of-the-art libraries along the north shore of Long Island, a fact that district residents recited with pride. A large, historic oak tree—planted there by the founder of the community in the 1850s—stood proudly amid a grass field of miniature American flags, welcoming visitors to the stone and glass structure.

Eva's Hyundai was parked near the front of the lot, and Betty moved her car to the spot directly behind it, watching several teenagers ascend the steps of the library's grand entrance. This was the first time she would ever enter the library on official business; the gun on her hip pressed into her side.

As the automatic doors of the library slid open, Betty walked into the lounge, half expecting patrons to turn and stare, but all of them—and there were quite a few, despite the late hour—seemed engrossed in whatever they were reading. She quickly scanned the area around the main desk as well as the children's library, where, for some reason, she thought she might find Eva, but she wasn't there. According to the posted daily event calendar, the poetry reading group had already disbanded for the evening. Betty walked toward the back of the building, past the reference desk and aisles of computer terminals, into the adult section of the library stacks and checked each row one by one:

Empty.

Empty.

Two teenagers holding hands.

Empty.

A man sitting on a stepstool and reading.

Empty.

In the last aisle, at the far end, Eva was reaching up for a book on the top shelf. Betty looked at the shelving category: it was the self-help section. As she squeezed within the narrow aisle, Eva looked up.

"Detective Munson?" she said, surprised. "What are you doing here?"

"Hello, Eva." Eva was holding two books to her chest and wearing a long T-shirt and jeans that had been rolled up to her knees, revealing pasty and freckled chubby legs. "Actually, I'm looking for you."

"Oh?" Eva placed a third book she had chosen back onto the shelf and stepped into the main aisle.

"I was wondering if we could talk," Betty said.

"Sure. Is this about Kirk?"

"Yes, it is," Betty said. "I've been trying to reach you. I've left several phone messages. I actually just came from your apartment. I spoke to a lovely man who lives next door."

"Oh, that's Mr. Torres."

"I even spoke to your sister, Lily."

Eva stiffened. "Why did you speak to my sister?"

"I was looking for you. May we go outside or even down to the station to talk? Would that be all right?" A woman reading a trashy novel at a desk eyed them curiously.

"Sure," Eva said, although her facial expression seemed to say otherwise.

They began walking toward the exit. Eva stopped at the circulation desk and dropped the two books she was holding onto the counter. She fished into her purse and handed the librarian—a bored-looking young man with a goatee—her library card. As the librarian checked out the first item, a nonfiction book about overcoming shyness, Betty spotted the title of the book underneath: *Shooting Star*. It was a biography of Henry Sansfield.

"Are you reading a book about your father?" Betty asked, which gained the attention of the librarian.

"You've heard of my father?" Eva asked.

"Everyone has," the librarian said with sudden enthusiasm as he handed Eva both books. "He's the one Long Islander we can actually be *proud* of."

Eva gave a small smile. She retrieved the books and began walking toward the library's front entrance, still appearing relatively calm and at ease. "How is . . . my sister?" she asked when she and Betty were outside.

"Lily seems fine," Betty said. "She also seems like she misses you."

"Did you talk about my father?"

"Yes, we did."

Eva was watching two little girls playing with the entrance's automatic sliding doors, jumping in and out. "You know, don't you, Detective Munson?" They walked down the stairs toward the field of American flags, which were waving in the slight breeze. Eva pressed the books she was carrying against her bosom, and Betty had a vision of a school girl Eva coming home and finding her father dead in the bathtub. "About my father, I mean," Eva said.

"Well, your sister did tell me a few things, yes. But I would certainly like to hear your version of events."

Eva started thumbing through the biography in her hands, bending back the pages. "Since my father's death, four biographies have been written about him." She held up the book. "This one is the latest. I've read them all. Several times. Each time I think I'm going to learn something new, find some clue to tell me why he was the way he was. But I never do." She shrugged. "What's in here is really only part of my father's story. There's a whole other part that happened before nine and after five."

"Was that true of Kirk Stryker too?" Betty asked, carefully.

Eva watched a man and a little girl exit the library holding hands. "I loved my father," she said. "Despite . . . or maybe because of . . ." She shook her head. "When you're introduced to love in that way, it becomes this distorted . . . I didn't mean for any of this to happen, but . . . after I found out . . . after I *saw* . . ."

"Saw what?" Betty asked, but Eva grew quiet. Betty felt the hard edges of her pistol under her overcoat and tightened her belt. "It's getting chilly out. Perhaps we should discuss more together inside, down at the station."

"Am I being arrested?"

"Let's talk at the station."

"I can follow you in my car," Eva offered.

Images of Hugo Lurch swam through Betty's mind. She was reluctant to let Eva Sansfield out of her sight. "Actually, if it's all right, I'd prefer if we drive together," Betty said. "I can always drive you back afterward, if you need a ride." She pointed toward her car. "I'm parked right there. Behind you."

They walked toward the car in silence. *What had Eva seen*, Betty wondered. She wasn't sure if Eva had been talking about Kirk Stryker or her own father. As she chirped her car alarm, a voice called Betty's name.

"Betty Munson, is that you?"

Across the parking lot, Cora from the Ladies Auxiliary was waving at her.

"I thought that was you," Cora said with a smile when Betty heard a car door slam and the engine of Eva's car turn over. She ran toward the Hyundai and knocked on the driver's-side window.

"Eva, open the door . . ."

Eva's sad eyes looked up at her through the dirty car window. "I'm sorry," she mouthed.

"What's going on?" Cora asked as Eva put her car into gear and slowly pulled out of the parking spot.

"This isn't the way, Eva," Betty called. She turned to Cora. "Cora, please go inside the library and take anyone you see out here with you." She radioed for backup and reached for her pistol, but didn't want to alarm Cora or anyone else nearby more than she needed to, so she left it by her side—for now. She hoped she didn't have to use it.

"Eva!" Betty shouted, running after the car. "Don't do this!"

Eva made a turn at the back of the parking lot and was

heading for the next aisle, which—Betty scanned the lot—would take Eva straight to the exit.

Betty ran to her car, put her flashing light on the dashboard, and sounded her police siren. She threw the car into reverse, pulled out of her spot, and hit the gas hard.

Near the entrance, there was a bottleneck of cars waiting to enter a traffic circle that allowed patrons to return books and DVDs. Betty swerved left, blocking the cars from entering the parking lot as Eva slammed on her brakes, unable to leave. Eva put her car into reverse and accelerated toward the rear of the parking lot. Betty got out of her car.

"What's going on?" asked a dad driving a minivan.

"Everyone, out of your vehicles and get inside the library!" Betty shouted. Men and women began pulling children from car seats and strollers and hurrying toward the building entrance, where, despite Cora's attempts, a large crowd was gathering.

Eva was at the far end of the lot and racing around the back, tires screeching as police sirens sounded in the distance. She made a sharp turn and began driving toward the front of the parking lot again, picking up speed. This time, she was heading straight for Betty's roadblock and didn't look like she was going to change her mind.

Betty stood beside her vehicle and put up her hands. "Eva, stop!" she shouted, but the car kept coming at her.

She had no choice. She reached for her gun when Eva made a hard right turn and drove onto the grass field of miniature American flags, her tires knocking them down one by one. She was bypassing the roadblock and heading for the street.

"Dammit," Betty said, running after the car. She held up her gun and was about to take aim at one of Eva's tires when the Hyundai made another hard turn, accelerated, and crashed head-on into the Gardenia Public Library's historic oak tree.

52

atriano was sitting at his bedroom desk, his socked feet crossed underneath him. He had run online searches in every browser he could think of for *Tom Cranston*, but nothing came up in the Long Island area. He tried *Thomas Cranston*, *Tommy Cranston*, and *T Cranston*, but none of the relating images seemed to match the man in the manila folder Jill Sansone had given him. There were no Facebook, Twitter, or any other social media listings. No arrests or civil suits. It seemed somehow, in this tech-riddled world, Tom Cranston was managing to live off-grid.

Satriano's cell phone rang. Sansone had already called him twice since he and Mary left the News 12 offices, but he hadn't returned her calls. As far as he was concerned, he had spoken to her enough—*too much*, from what he saw on the televised interview on the evening news. He looked at the caller ID and exhaled. "Hi, Ma," he said, swiping the screen.

"Hello, Anthony"—his mother cupped her hand over the phone and murmured something, presumably to his father—"How are you? I hope I'm not disturbing you."

"No, you're not, Ma. What's up?" He looked at the

time in the corner of his computer screen. "Is everything all right? It's late."

"Yes, yes, everything is fine. We saw you on the news tonight. They replayed your interview. So handsome . . ."

"Thanks, Ma." He typed *Cranston Benning* into Google and hit *Enter*.

"So . . ." His mother hesitated. "So what are you doing?"

"Not much of anything, really." He tried *Cranston Long Island* and surveyed the results.

"You mean, you're alone?"

"Yep, alone, Ma," Satriano said. He hoped this wasn't about her neighbor's niece. He had told her more than once that she wasn't his type. "Just me, myself, and I."

"Anthony Satriano, Jr., this is not a time for jokes. Your father and I are worried about you."

"Ma, I told Pop I'm fine. Please don't worry."

"Do you have a good lock on your door?"

"Please, Ma, I'm safe. I'm in my house."

"You really should get a dog. And it would look good for your campaign. You know, a rescue dog."

"A dog? With my hours and travel schedule? The poor thing would be cooped up in the house all day."

"I could walk it for you," his mother offered. "Or you could bring it to the office. You could even leave it here, at our house, when you travel to Albany."

"Ma, I'm not getting a dog. Listen, I have to go. I'll talk to you tomorrow, okay? I'll stop by the store in the morning. Love you." He placed the phone on his desk. It was going to be hard to keep the Tom Cranston situation from his parents, but he had to try. They had enough to worry about. He typed *Tom Cranston*

Manhattan and then *Tom Cranston New York* into the search engine. Nothing.

He stared at his computer screen. The guy had no identifiable digital footprint. What next? His thoughts turned to his cousin Marco, but he quickly pushed them out of his mind. That was a can of worms Satriano didn't want to open, whatever predicament he was in. He placed his cursor in the Google search box and was about to try *Cranston accounting* when a voice behind him said:

"Why don't you try typing in *Thomas Joseph Cranston*?"

Startled, Satriano pushed himself from his chair, but his socked feet slipped on the wood floor. He landed on his back as Tom Cranston and his red baseball cap hovered over him.

"Easy there, Assemblyman," Cranston said with a laugh. "You're going to give yourself a heart attack."

"How did you get in here?" Satriano looked for his cell phone, but he remembered it was on his desk and out of reach.

"Don't worry. It wasn't that easy. You're safe from the general public."

"Do you make it a habit of breaking into people's homes at night?"

"I make a habit of breaking into all kinds of places," Cranston said with a snicker. "Listen, Assemblyman, I'm here to—"

"Is your name even Tom Cranston? Are you working for Benning? What did you mean Kirk Stryker knew how to find money?"

"Man, aren't *you* full of questions?" Cranston sat in Satriano's desk chair and pulled up on the brim of his cap.

He appeared older than when Satriano first saw him in Brooklyn. Deep forehead wrinkles made his skin look like leather, and the light from the computer screen gave him a ghostly pallor, as if he were an illusion.

"You said Thursday," Satriano said, standing up.

"Did I?" Cranston said, taking a gun out from his pocket. He pointed it at Satriano and then let out a deep, guttural laugh. "Just kidding," he said, putting it back. "Just a friendly reminder—you know, in case you forgot."

It was clear that Cranston was sending a message: *I can get to you. And your family. Anytime. Anywhere.*

"Well, unless there is any new business, I guess our meeting is adjourned." Cranston stood up, pulled down on the lid of his baseball cap, and moved toward the front of the house. Satriano immediately reached for his cell phone.

"I wouldn't do that if I were you," Cranston said, walking toward the door. He stopped at the home alarm box on the wall and pushed several buttons until the box beeped.

"How do you know my passcode?" Satriano asked.

"I know a lot of things." Cranston turned the doorknob of the front door. "By the way, nice place you got here. Your mother's right. You might want to get a dog."

"Stay away from my parents," Satriano said. "And stay away from my cousin's house."

"You mean, Pina?" Cranston let out a laugh. "Trust me, I'm no Stryker. I'm just a distributor."

"What's that supposed to mean?"

"You really have no clue, do you? Stryker ever ask you to bring your goddaughter Pina by, you know, for a visit? I'm sure he has. Watch out for her. Stryker may be gone, but there are others." With that, Cranston eased out of the house, closing the door behind him, the alarm box resetting with a beep.

53

Betty followed the medical technicians carrying Eva Sansfield's body into the hospital emergency room, where a trauma team was waiting. The techs handed Eva off to them, the gurney groaning under her weight as a triage nurse guided them through a crowd of beds, techs, and people to a room marked 7A. Inside, a family was surrounding a teenage boy in a sling. Betty looked around. There seemed to be teenage boys everywhere.

"What's going on?" she asked.

"High school track team was heading home from a meet in Rhode Island," said the nurse, looking tired. "Collided with an SUV on the expressway, and the bus overturned." She motioned to Eva. "But we'll get her in as soon as possible. We're discharging the kid in 7A now."

At the nurses' station, Betty spotted the Massapequa Fire District jacket of the tech who had ridden in the back of the ambulance with her. It had seemed strange that EMTs from Massapequa were covering a Gardenia call, but after taking a look around the room, Betty could see why. All the ambulances from Gardenia and the neighboring towns had been pretty busy.

On the gurney, Eva was still unconscious; she had

been listed in critical condition. Despite the deployment of her airbag, her face and chest had borne the brunt of the car crash. Her weight had made things difficult and time-consuming for the techs; it had taken three of them to extricate her from the automobile. And yet as damaged as Eva was on the outside, Betty knew her emotional injuries were just as severe. *What had Stryker done*, Betty wondered, *to set off Eva's latent fury?* Had there been abuse? She thought of the homemade cards. Why had Eva turned on him now?

Betty's cell phone rang. She looked at the caller ID and stepped outside of the noisy emergency room and into the back parking lot, where the motors of several ambulances were running, making it just as difficult to hear. "Go ahead, Pete," Betty said, but when Detective Girardi spoke, his voice was barely audible.

"Got the warrant," he said. "Judge Caruso wasn't too happy."

"Did you tell him I owe him one?"

"He said he just wanted you to remember him fondly when you're basking in the glow of retirement."

"When do you expect to get to Sansfield's apartment?"

"We're here now. Been here about ten minutes. Did a quick preliminary search, but so far no gun."

"Keep looking."

"We did find something, though," Girardi said. "A Taser."

Betty exhaled deeply. It wasn't the murder weapon, but it was probably close enough. "Do we know if it was used on Stryker?"

"Not yet," Girardi said. "The tags and cartridge

forensics found at the scene are in the evidence room. We'll see if they match up. And sometimes these things have a computer system that records every use."

"Good. Get it done tonight if you can. Personally. And keep looking. If the gun that murdered Stryker is there, I want it," she said and clicked off the line. She dug into her pocket for the business card with Lily Sansfield's phone number. She dialed.

❂

By the time Betty made it back inside the emergency room, Eva had been moved into 7A, where a doctor was examining her injuries. He was consulting with a nurse, who was adjusting the medication Eva was receiving intravenously. By his expression alone, Betty knew the situation was grave. The doctor saw her and waved her in.

"I wish I had better news, Detective," he said. "Ms. Sansfield's size is putting unnecessary strain on her body, which sustained a range of head, neck, and back injuries. And I'm afraid she's too far gone for surgery. I'm not even sure she'd make it if we tried to move her to the operating room floor." He shook his head. "I don't think there's much more we can do. Were you able to contact her family?"

"Yes, her sister is on her way," Betty said. "She's driving down from Schenectady. She had been out of town for a meditation retreat."

"Have the nurse page me if there is any change," he said solemnly. He nodded and left the room with the nurse, closing the door behind them.

It was quiet, and the faint beeping of Eva's heart

monitor punctuated the silence. Betty moved closer to the gurney; they hadn't even moved her onto a proper hospital bed. Her face was barely recognizable, her eyes two slits within a mass of blood, skin, bandages, and tubes. The door to the room opened again. It was the Massapequa EMT.

"We're heading out, Detective Munson. Another call, unfortunately," the man said. He had a kind face, and Betty could tell by the way he moved within the ambulance that he took his work seriously. "But I wanted to see if you needed a ride back to the library. I know your car is in the parking lot."

"No, that's all right. I'm going to stay. I appreciate it."

The tech nodded and was about to leave but hesitated. "One of the nurses told me that Ms. Sansfield"—he motioned to Eva—"worked with that accountant guy, Kirk Stryker, the one who was killed."

"I'm afraid I can't comment on that," Betty said.

"I understand. . . . I think you interviewed my wife, though. I recognized your name. Her name is Muriel Adams. . . . Well, soon-to-be ex-wife . . ." He twisted his wedding band absently.

Douglas Adams. He looked nothing like Betty thought he would, although she wasn't sure what she had been expecting. A Marty Benning lookalike perhaps? They were probably around the same age, he and Benning, but that was where the similarity ended. While Benning was urban and polished, Douglas Adams had a folksy way about him. It was like comparing the city mouse with the country mouse. Yet, Adams seemed like a good man who, for whatever reason, had been in a not-so-good marriage.

"I know you can't comment," Adams continued, "but I just want to make sure that . . . well, that my family is safe. I'm sure you know that my wife . . . ex-wife . . . had been spending time with the guy you arrested, Benning. And . . . "

Betty's cell phone rang. She looked at the caller ID.

"I'm sorry, I should let you get to it," Adams said, opening the door.

"Mr. Adams . . . " Betty wanted to say something comforting, but there was probably nothing she could say about Benning, or even Muriel Adams, that would make Douglas Adams feel any better about what was happening in his world. Police officers could do many things, but guaranteeing safety, unfortunately, wasn't one of them, so she settled for something simple. "Thank you for all you've done tonight."

He gave a small smile and left the room as Betty swiped her telephone screen. "What do you have, Pete?"

"We have a match," Girardi said. "Sansfield's Taser matches the paraphernalia left behind by the Taser that shot Kirk Stryker the night of the murder."

Betty let out a long exhale and looked down at the closed eyes of Eva Sansfield. "Prints?" she asked.

"Yep, hers. All over everything. That should do it, no?"

"What about Benning's fingerprint on the glass?"

Betty could hear voices and shuffling, as if Girardi was on the move, but then it got quiet, like he had found a good place to talk. "The truth is . . . well, anyone could have put that glass there, don't you think?" he said. "Seemed strange that it was there in a bag like that."

Betty thought of Benning's telescope. And of Stryker's

email to Satriano. Of the notation in Stryker's planner. Of the vitriol between Stryker and Benning. It had seemed so clean. She remembered how buoyant Benning had been when she visited him at his Manhattan apartment, a jokey lightness that seemed smug, like he was playing with her as a cat plays with a mouse. Perhaps he was just being innocent. Perhaps he *was* the mouse.

"And there's another thing," Girardi said. "I just spoke with Muriel Adams, who told me—'with conviction,' she wanted to make sure I said that to you—that Marty Benning was with her the night of the murder. *All night.*"

Apparently, Muriel Adams believed in Benning's innocence enough to lie for him.

Eva began to stir slightly on the gurney.

"All right," Betty said, "Let him go." She ended the call and hurried to the door.

"I think she's waking up," she called to the nurses' station, and several nurses and residents hurried with her into the room. "Eva, can you hear me?" Betty asked, standing beside the gurney.

She thought she saw Eva's eyes open, but with her injuries it was difficult to tell. She bent down toward the young woman's swollen face. "You're at the hospital. Your sister is on her way to see you. *Wants* to see you. Do you understand?"

A sound came from Eva's mouth. She was pursing her lips, trying to say something.

"Eva, what did you say?" Betty asked, but her light breathing was becoming agitated. Behind them, the door opened, and the doctor who had been examining Eva stepped into the room and stood beside Betty.

"She's conscious," he said, as if surprised. Eva stirred again.

"You're safe," Betty said softly near Eva's ear. "You're at the hospital."

Eva's mouth opened, her voice a raspy whisper. "*Safe . . .*"

"Yes, that's right." Betty had a sudden image of Eva Sansfield undergoing numerous surgeries and years of therapy only to, if she survived, be placed in prison or a psychiatric hospital. She was far from safe.

"Safe . . ." Eva said again, her breathing growing more and more strained. "All of them . . . are safe . . ." she whispered as her body heaved itself upward, and the machinery around her let out a stream of screaming beeps until the heart rate monitor registered a flat piercing tone.

"Detective, you need to go," the doctor said, brushing her aside as the medical team surrounded Eva's lifeless body.

Eva's torn and wet clothing was peeled from her skin so the doctors and nurses could work to restore her absent heartbeat. As they began cardiopulmonary resuscitation on Eva's chest, Betty's eyes were drawn to the skin of Eva's bulging abdomen, and the series of familiar marks that, although faded, she recognized instantly as the constellation of Orion.

54

"We're going to get into trouble . . ."

"Just drive, Kramer," Parker said.

He knew he should have staked out Satriano's place on his own, regardless of what Gardner had ordered. Kramer had been whimpering to go home ever since they got there. It finally dawned on him why Kramer had been at the *Gazette* for so many years instead of moving on to bigger and better papers. He was a complete pussy.

"Come on, you gotta keep up with him," Parker said. "But don't get too close." They had been tailing a man in a red baseball cap for fifteen minutes, and if Kramer kept driving like his grandmother they were going to get made.

"How do we even know this guy is worth following?" Kramer asked. "Shouldn't we stick to Satriano?"

"I just have a feeling." Normal people didn't loiter around someone's house before picking the lock on the front door and slipping inside. Parker looked out the window. Baseball-cap guy was taking them toward the canal, an exclusive section of Gardenia. Parker hadn't been to this side of town since he broke up with Brenda. He shuddered; homecoming queens were the worst.

"He's turning into that driveway," Parker said and instructed Kramer to ease behind a flatbed truck.

The guy got out of his car and was heading toward a dormered Cape Cod cottage at the end of a cul-de-sac. They watched him walk up the front steps and go inside.

"Stay here," Parker said, opening his car door.

"Where are you going?" Kramer asked. "We don't even know who this guy is."

"Exactly. I want to get a closer look."

"Wait, how close?"

"Real close." He stepped out of the car, but Kramer grabbed his arm.

"This isn't a joke, Parker. Press or no press, this is trespassing. If you get caught—"

"I won't," Parker said. "Keep your shirt on. And your phone too, in case I need to reach you."

Parker crept along the sidewalk until he got to the man's property line and ducked behind a row of short screening trees to keep from tripping any nearby motion security lights—a helpful tip he had learned from sneaking out of Brenda's house at night. All of the landscaping looked new, and he was careful not to step in any loose mud.

The backyard of the cottage, like many homes on the water, was narrow, and he was about to make his way across when the back door of the guy's house opened, and a big dog came galloping outside, triggering a motion sensor light. Parker hid behind a small shed in the neighboring yard, his heart thumping as the dog began to bark and run in his direction. He was ready to make a run for it when the dog was yanked back by a leash just as the man in the baseball cap emerged from the back door.

"Easy, Duke. Let's go. In the front. No more shitting back here, remember?" When the dog wouldn't let up, the man yelled, "No water tonight. I'm tired." Parker could hear the man pull hard on the leash, and the dog retreated reluctantly toward the front yard, the two disappearing down the sidewalk.

Parker's phone vibrated. He glanced at it:

WHAT THE FUCK??? GET BACK HERE

Parker texted Kramer back:

WAIT.

He didn't want to retrigger the motion sensor, so while the backyard light was still on, he sprinted in a crouched position toward the back door of the man's house. *All I need is a name*, he thought. He pressed himself against the wood, listening for any noise, and tried the doorknob. When it turned, he took a deep breath and slipped inside, easing the door closed behind him.

The smell of dog and cigarettes was overwhelming as he stood in a small kitchen—a television was on, and an open box of cereal and dog food was sitting on the counter next to a stack of mail. On the floor near a pantry were two suitcases.

Parker picked up a piece of junk mail from a local realtor on top of the stack; it was addressed to a *Tom Cranston*.

Bingo.

He put it back and reached for the doorknob of the back door when he heard barking again. It sounded like it was coming from the side of the house. He tiptoed across the room and, through the grid of a picture window, could see that Duke was off his leash and sniffing the area where he had crept along the property line. Cranston was standing right there smoking a cigarette. *Dammit.*

Parker hurried into a short hallway toward the front door. If he couldn't leave through the back, he'd have to try the front. He looked out a window and scanned the sidewalk, which was empty. He reached for the doorknob when Duke pounced onto the front porch, startling him, and he darted halfway up a staircase.

"What do you smell, boy?" Parker heard Cranston say just outside the door.

The streetlights made Duke's shadow appear three times larger than the dog's actual size, and Parker carefully began walking up the stairs, fearful Cranston would open the door and let the dog inside. He kept his feet at the corners of each stair to minimize creaking—another little tip he picked up from his time with Brenda.

He reached the top floor and crept toward the front window to take another peek outside. Cranston was gone, and so was the dog. Parker looked down the block for Kramer's car. It was gone too. *Fuck, he left me here.*

He was about to run downstairs and out the front door, but he had to be sure where Cranston was. The upstairs level was dark, making it hard to see, but to his left, there was a bedroom, and then a room that smelled completely like dog—it had a large pet bed and a cage. Cozy.

Next was a bathroom and what looked like a home office, with a corner desk beside a safe and two large file cabinets. On a whim, Parker reached in and pulled on the handles of the cabinets. Locked. Duke's howling bark came from the backyard, and Parker tiptoed into the dog's room to peer out the back window, which offered a bit of light. The dog was still off the leash, sniffing around where Parker had been hiding. The man in the baseball cap was sitting on top of a picnic table, finishing his cigarette and gazing out at the water. *Now was his chance.*

Parker made a dash for the staircase but slammed into the dog cage in the middle of the room, toppling onto the floor.

Shit, he thought, lying still, wondering if either Cranston or Duke had heard him. He pulled himself up to the window, pain shooting up his leg, and peeked outside. The man was still sitting on the picnic table, but the dog was barking near the back door, wanting to go inside.

Parker pulled on the dog cage to put it back, but the bottom got caught on a small pebble on the floor. He tried to kick it out of the way, but it wouldn't budge, and he realized it wasn't a pebble at all, but a hinge. He ran his finger along the metal and found a split in the floorboards that ran about one foot out and across, forming a square.

A secret compartment.

He quickly dug his fingernails into the groove, pulling the floorboard until it flipped up. Then he reached inside the large hole, feeling around, hoping there wasn't a mousetrap in there or, worse, dog shit. His hand touched something flat and smooth. He pulled it out. It was a manila folder.

The cover had a business card stapled to it that read: *Orion Project.* Parker peeked outside. The man in the cap was still on the picnic table. Parker flipped open the folder, and his eyes grew wide.

Images of naked little girls. Pages upon pages of them, all different sizes and skin types, all of them underdeveloped with strange branding marks on their abdomens and posing awkwardly in a variety of sexual positions. Taped to the inside of the folder was a thumb drive and a short handwritten note:

Tom –

Here's the new batch. Prices are the same.

– Kirk

"All right, already," Parker heard the man in the baseball cap say. "Let's go inside."

Quickly, Parker stuck the folder under his shirt and moved everything back to the way it was. Downstairs, a door creaked open, and the nails of the dog scratched frantically across the floorboards. Parker ran toward the door of the bedroom to close it, but realized that would alert Cranston that someone had been in the house. Instead, he pulled open the back window and stepped onto the adjoining garage roof, shutting the window just as the barking entered the room.

Carefully, he walked down the canted roof tiles, balancing himself with his arms, as Duke's barks intensified, his nails scratching at the window. He peered down the side of the garage—nothing to land on except grass, but he had nowhere else to go. He crouched down, grabbed onto the gutter, and lowered himself. It was about a six foot drop.

The bedroom window above him opened, and he let go, setting off the motion sensor lighting. He crawled behind a rosebush and checked to make sure the folder was still inside his shirt. It was.

"Who's there?" Cranston yelled, the dog barking fiercely next to him.

Parker made a mad dash for the property line and crept among the trees of the neighboring yard until Cranston disappeared from the window. Then he went barreling onto the sidewalk and down the dark suburban street.

55

Muriel sped north toward Gardenia, replaying Marty's phone message over and over in her mind: *Hey, I'm out. They finally let me go. I'm guessing you're sleeping . . . I'm at the practice. Took an Uber. Couldn't get a hold of Bobby. I'm going to try and get some sleep. Can't wait to see you. Call me when you get this message.*

"Mommy, slow down!" Zack called from the backseat.

"Yeah, you're going a little fast there, Mo," Roxanne said from the passenger seat. "I'm glad that you asked me to join you, but I'd like to live to see another day." She held onto her seat belt.

"You sure you don't know where Bobby is?" Muriel asked, easing up on the gas pedal.

"I don't keep tabs on the guy, Mo." Muriel shot Roxanne a look. "I mean, not *all the time.*"

"Are we going to school, Mommy?" Zack asked.

"I don't know," Muriel said. She hadn't been sure if she wanted to take the kids with her, but she also didn't want to leave them behind. Not anymore. *No Mom* was going to turn into *New Mom,* she had decided. She was grateful Roxanne agreed to come along. "Maybe I'll bring you in just a little bit late."

"Awww," Zack said. "Why does Gordy get to take the whole day?"

"Because his mother doesn't care about his education the way your mom does," Roxanne said with a smile.

"Lucky us," Ellie said, rolling her eyes.

Muriel glanced in the rearview mirror at her daughter, who was sitting in the middle seat between Zack and Gordy. Ellie hated the middle seat, but she hadn't protested. She had even been a bit nicer to her brother since the episode at Doug's. Baby steps.

"Ellie, do me a favor, can you try calling Marty again?"

"I can do it, Mo," Roxanne said.

"No, Ellie's got it." Muriel had also decided that if she wanted Ellie to be open about her life, particularly her love life, she had to do the same.

Ellie reached for the phone and dialed. "Still not picking up, Mom. Should I leave a message?"

Muriel sighed. That was the seventh message that Muriel would be leaving. "Sure."

"What do I say? That we'll be there soon."

"You can say whatever you like."

Ellie waited with the phone by her ear. "Hi . . ." she finally said. "This is Ellie . . . My mom wanted me to . . . Um, let you know that we're coming. All of us. *Surprise.*" Her daughter smiled, which made Muriel smile. "We should be there soon. I guess that's it. Oh, and I'm glad you're not in jail anymore."

"Me too!" Zack cheered.

"Me three!" shouted Gordy.

"Shouldn't you say 'Me four'?" Muriel asked Roxanne.

"I'm still deciding," Roxanne said.

"Okay, well, good-bye," Ellie said and put the phone back on the console. "Where do you think he is, Mom?"

"I don't know. Sleeping, maybe?"

She turned left when she reached Gardenia, passing the Plastic Surgery & Laser Center, where Stowe's BMW was in the parking lot, which wasn't surprising. The guy used the practice like it was a hotel—or maybe a brothel. She turned right onto Lake Shore Avenue but then came to a dead stop. In front of her was a line of cars that looked like it went on for blocks.

"What's this?" she asked, looking at the time on the dashboard.

"Rush hour?" Roxanne asked.

"Too early, I think." She tapped her fingers on the steering wheel and then honked her horn. "Jesus, what's taking so long?"

"Mo, that's not going to help. No one can go anywhere."

"Maybe they're all going to see Marty because he's not in jail anymore," Zack suggested.

Muriel stuck her head out the window to see if she could see anything down the road, but there was nothing but cars.

"I have an idea," Roxanne said. She unbuckled her seat belt. "Marty's office is only a few blocks from here, right? Why don't you walk?" She opened her door and ran around the car to the driver's side. "You go. I'll stay with the kids. The way it's looking, you'll probably get there before us on foot. I'll park the car—eventually. And meet you. Or maybe I'll take the kids out for breakfast."

"Yay!" Gordy and Zack cheered.

"This way, you've got some time alone." Roxanne smiled.

Muriel opened her car door. "You're the best, Rock." She wrapped her in a hug. "What would I do without you?"

"You'd be lonely and bored. Now, go, go, go," Roxanne shooed. "True love is waiting."

Muriel waved good-bye to the kids before hurrying down Lake Shore Avenue, which was becoming crowded as people left their cars parked in the middle of the street and began milling around and complaining. Shops were opening for the day; proprietors were lifting up metal gates and putting out signage, tables, and chairs. A few commuters and students were hurrying toward the local Long Island Rail Road Station, but most people seemed to be heading in the same direction as Muriel, probably wanting to see what was causing the traffic jam.

She crossed the street. A News 12 van had parked on a side road. Cameramen were spilling out of the back door, equipment in their hands and strapped to their backs, and she stopped walking.

"Do you smell that?" she asked an elderly gentleman who was standing in front of a fruit market and surveying the crowd.

The man sniffed at the air and nodded. "It smells like something is burning."

Muriel picked up the pace and hurried down Lake Shore Avenue when sirens sounded. They seemed to be coming from every direction.

"Out of the way," shouted a man in a fire department vehicle. He had his hand pressed on the horn and was driving on the sidewalk to bypass the gridlock. The man from the fruit market gently put his hand on Muriel's arm to pull her back as he passed.

More and more people appeared on the street, coming from stores and neighboring blocks, all walking in the same direction. Muriel pushed her way through the crowd until she saw Marty's building and gasped. Black smoke was coming from its windows, a wall of flames behind the glass.

"Oh, my god!" she screamed, running toward the firefighters, who were scattered throughout the intersection, calling to one another and assembling nozzles to hoses.

When she reached a barricade, a man wearing a badge held up his arm. "Ma'am, you need to step back," he said. "I can't let you come any closer.

"Take the window!" a fireman shouted behind him, followed by the sound of breaking glass.

"There's somebody in there!" Muriel screamed. "His name is Marty Benning." She felt a hand on her arm. It was the man from the fruit market.

"Are you all right?" he asked tenderly.

She was having trouble breathing and knelt down, wrapping her arms around the wooden leg of the barricade. The flames were reaching out of a broken second-story window, licking the side of the building and crawling along a string of pennant flags toward a street lamp. A woman placed a blanket over Muriel's shoulders.

"My name is Cora," she said, her voice gentle. "Are you okay?"

Muriel shook her head, unable to catch her breath. She prayed that Marty wasn't there, that he had decided to go home, that he was anywhere else, but she had a horrible feeling that that wasn't the case.

"Please, hurry," she whispered as firefighters began entering the building through the collapsed revolving door. "Please."

56

Satriano raced along the crowded sidewalk of Lake Shore Avenue toward the fruit market. Inside, he searched the store, which was filled with customers, and found his mother ringing up a young man in a business suit.

"Anthony!" she called. "The fire, did you see it?"

Satriano nodded. Benning's place, the village's former library, had been the oldest in Gardenia, and he wasn't sure how much of it the firefighters had been able to save. Between that flame-scarred building and Stryker's, the intersection looked like something out of a dystopian movie. Luckily, the fire had occurred late at night, like Stryker's, and Satriano hoped there were no injuries. "Where's Daddy?" he asked, coming behind the register.

"In the back room. Where's Mary?"

"At the office. She'll be here soon. Here, let me help." He finished ringing up the customer, putting the carton of eggs and a pair of plums into a paper bag. He handed the package to the young man, who was staring at his phone.

"Is everything all right?" Satriano asked, placing the purchase on the counter.

"Just got a CNN alert. That guy Benning, the accountant from down the block who got arrested? They let him go."

"They did?" Satriano said. "Jesus, he's coming home to a building that I'm not sure is habitable."

"He's not coming home at all." The young man's eyes turned sad. "He's dead."

"Dead?" Satriano glanced at his mother, who covered her mouth with her hands. "What do you mean *dead*?"

"Smoke inhalation. He was *inside* the building. Here, look . . ." The young man showed him the screen: *CNN reports that New York accountant Marty Benning, who had been arrested and released in the murder of Kirk Stryker, was killed in a fire at his accounting practice on Lake Shore Avenue in Gardenia this morning. Reported cause of death is smoke inhalation. Arson is suspected. A man is in custody, although his name is not yet being released. More details to come.*

"Arson?" Satriano asked. He thought of Tom Cranston.

"I told you . . . " His mother pointed to the smoke alarms on the ceiling.

The young man put his phone away and picked up his purchase. "Marty Benning did my mom's taxes last year when my dad left. He didn't charge her." He shook his head. "My mom never believed that he had anything to do with Stryker. She swore that they had the wrong guy. I hope she's hasn't seen this yet," he said before hurrying toward the store exit.

In the back room, Satriano's father was placing a broom into a closet. His shirt was wet and streaked with dirt, his bow tie undone. "Where's your sister?" he asked when he saw Satriano.

"Mary's fine. She's coming later. What happened?"

"I don't know." His father rubbed his eyes. "I was standing outside, and the cars stopped, and a lady was running, and then everyone was running. And then I saw the fire." He ran his hand through his unkempt hair. "Another fire? What does this mean, Anthony?"

"I don't know, Pop. . . . What's this?" Satriano asked, pointing to a stack of posters leaning against the wall. He thumbed through them. Each had his official headshot with the words *Reelect Assemblyman Anthony Satriano* in large red, white, and blue lettering.

"Oh," his father said with a shrug. "It was a surprise. For the new election. A present from your mother and me."

"You didn't have to do that, Pop. We use our campaign funds for that stuff."

"I wanted to get the ball rolling. You know how proud of you I am. It was going to be a happy surprise, but it didn't turn out to be a happy morning." His father reached toward him and cupped his cheek with his hand. "I love you, son. I need to tell you more."

"You tell me all the time, Pop."

"Well, we just never know when we won't get the chance again." He sighed. "Now . . . I'd better go help your mother."

"I'll be right there," Satriano said, watching his father go. He reached for the remote control and turned on the television, which blinked to News 12. Jill Sansone was reporting from outside Benning's building. He turned up the volume.

"*. . . No word yet on motive, or whether the killing of Marty Benning is in any way connected to the arrest of a Tom Cranston this morning, who is accused—along with a whopping two hundred prominent Long Islanders—of being part of a child pornography ring. The ring was allegedly being run from the accounting firm of*

Kirk Stryker & Associates and dates all the way back to famed astronomer Dr. Henry Sansfield in the 1990s . . . ."

Pornography? Satriano walked toward the screen.

". . . Sources tell News 12 that the money raised for Stryker's annual breast cancer walk established for his mother, Agnes Stryker, is being called into question, as is the campaign financing for Assemblyman Anthony Satriano. . . ."

Satriano's legs almost gave out underneath him. He pulled a chair toward him and sat down.

". . . This morning, officers searched one of Stryker's homes and found clothing and personal effects that they believe belong to some of the victimized girls, who have not yet been identified—or located. We'll have more on these stories as they develop. This is Jill Sansone reporting from Gardenia, News 12."

Satriano's heart was thumping inside his chest. What had Kirk Stryker gotten him into? He put his head in his hands when his cell phone rang, startling him. The caller ID read *Jill Sansone, News 12.* He dropped the vibrating phone on the table as if it were an insect. What was he supposed to say? Should he answer at all? Was it better to say nothing? He took a deep breath and swiped the screen. "Hello?"

"Assemblyman, it's Jill Sansone. News 12."

"I was just watching you," he said, trying to keep his voice light, but Sansone was all business.

"I'm going live again in about twenty minutes," she said. "Can you give me a statement?"

"A statement?" *Stay calm.* "About what?"

There was a pause. "Well, can you tell me what you know?" she said.

"I don't know anything."

"Assemblyman, Kirk Stryker practically funded your entire campaign singlehandedly. Surely, you knew where the money was coming from."

"What? You can't honestly believe that . . ."

"What about Tom Cranston leaving his briefcase in your parents' fruit market?"

Sweat was beginning to bead across Satriano's forehead. He wiped it with the back of his hand. "Jill, I have a confession to make. There never was a briefcase. I needed to know the man's name. . . . This is what happened . . . I was—"

"Are you saying that you don't know Tom Cranston?"

"I'm saying that when I contacted you—"

"You don't socialize with him?" she asked.

"Socialize? I had never even heard of him until—"

"I'm wondering why, then, the *Gardenia Gazette* has photos of Tom Cranston leaving your private home in Gardenia last evening."

It was as if the air left the room and Satriano had forgotten how to breathe. "Wait . . . This is all a big mistake," he said, forcing the words out. "Listen, this is what happened . . . I was at my cousin Marco's house when—"

"Marco Satriano?"

"Yes, he—"

"The same Marco Satriano who was arrested for the murder of Marty Benning fifteen minutes ago?"

A chill spread across Satriano's body. He leaned back in his chair. "That's impossible," he said.

"I'm afraid not, Assemblyman. Apparently, someone…" There was a pause, as if she was consulting her notes.

". . . A Paulette Krause saw him lurking suspiciously around the building just before it went up in flames. Apparently, the guy torched the place and then stayed around to watch. Not too bright. When they picked him up, the first thing he says is that he's working for you and that he's your cousin. So that's true?"

Satriano stood up and began to pace in the small room. "Yes, he's my cousin, but—"

"Second thing he says is that he didn't know Benning was in the building . . . He was probably right about that. No one knew Benning was out until hours later. Apparently, Marco Satriano was just looking to commit arson, not murder. Lovely."

Sansone's words were fading in and out; Satriano was having trouble concentrating.

"The way I see it," she continued, "what better way to get what you want than to rid yourself of your biggest competitor? You've got a probable reelection bid coming up, right, Assemblyman?"

"You're connecting dots that don't go together," Satriano said when his phone beeped, signaling a text. He checked the screen. It was from Mary.

"Assemblyman, I'm planning to go on air with the information I just gave you. Do you have anything to say?"

"Yes," he said. "I gotta go." He clicked off the call and swiped Mary's text:

TON, YOU BETTER GET BACK HERE. THE PHONES ARE RINGING OFF THE HOOK.

Before he could text her back, his mother appeared in the doorway.

"Anthony?" She looked pale, and a heaviness pressed

on Satriano's chest. "Two policemen are here to see you," she said. "I don't understand. What do they want?"

Satriano wanted nothing more than to tell his mother that everything was going to be okay, like he always had, to bring back that smile that appeared whenever he walked into a room, but all he could manage to say was, "All right, Ma. Let's go see."

He put his arm around his mother, and as he led her out of the back room, he swung the door closed, knocking over the stack of *Reelect Anthony Satriano* posters, which fell flat on the floor.

57

"Hot off the presses!" Gardner cheered, slapping the freshly printed stack of newspapers onto his desk.

The crowd in the small newspaper office raised their champagne glasses in a toast as hands began grabbing at the issues. When his phone rang, the old editor reached for the handset. "*Gardenia Gazette*," he cooed. "Local news at its best."

"Congratulations, kid," said Sy Reedus, who was on his third glass of champagne and his second banana. "You know, when I told you that you perked up the old guy, I didn't mean excite him so much he might have a heart attack." He laughed, slapping Parker on the back, and continued to mingle through the room.

The front door opened, and six more people strolled in, half of whom Parker didn't recognize. Since his child pornography ring story broke, the office had been inundated with everyone from chamber of commerce members to local dignitaries to neighborhood residents, all of them wanting to shake the hand of the *Gazette*'s new wunderkind. Even Parker's parents had come down to see what all the fuss was about.

Parker's cell phone beeped. He looked at the incoming text; it was from the *Washington Post*. He had already done interviews with two major networks, *Newsday*, and *The New York Times* and had been offered six-figure jobs from two New York City-based news outlets. It was hard to believe that just last week he had trouble paying for his car's inspection.

"This is what local news coverage is about," Parker overheard Gardner say loudly to someone he didn't know. "We may not have the resources of some of the bigger players, but we are the ones who know the neighborhoods. People trust *us* to get the story right." And everyone in the small office cheered.

Kramer appeared at the front door. For leaving Parker high and dry the night before, Gardner punished him by sending him to the precinct to wait around and get a shot of Tom Cranston, who had been arrested after trying to board a Malaysia Airlines flight to Berlin. Kramer held up his digital camera.

"Did you get it, Kramer?" Gardner asked. When Kramer nodded, he added, "Give the photo to Parker. He'll upload it. I need you to go down to the deli and get more milk for the coffee."

Kramer's shoulders did a detectable slump as he placed the flash drive on Parker's desk and then left the office again. Some people just weren't cut out for the news game.

"Everyone, everyone, your attention, please!" Gardner shouted and, to Parker's astonishment, climbed on the top of his desk to address the crowd, steadying himself by holding on to a file cabinet. "I have an announcement to make. Friends, there is much to celebrate here today.

First, another toast to John Parker for his exceptional investigative skills. I knew I saw something in you, kid, the day you walked in here."

Parker smiled, and the crowd cheered again.

"And now for more news," Gardner said. "As of this August, the *Gardenia Gazette* will be moving to a new location. No more of this outskirts crap. We're going back to where we belong, in the thick of things, on Lake Shore Avenue. We are in talks to take over the Griffin Media offices as, it seems, that tenant is breaking its lease and has decided to move to another location."

More hoots and hollers from the crowd.

"What about Benning's place at the old library?" someone yelled.

Gardner shook his head. "Not sure what will happen there yet. Historical society is talking about moving in." Gardner picked up his glass of champagne. "In fact, I would like to have a moment of silence for Marty Benning. He may have been relatively new to our community, but he was one of us, and he brought an excitement back to this town that we will always remember him for."

As the men and women in the room raised their glasses in a toast, the front door opened again. Parker wasn't sure how many more people the small editorial office could hold, but there was only one person standing in the doorway this time—Detective Munson, who was surveying the gathering.

Fuck. In all the excitement, he had never called her back. She met Parker's eyes and began walking in his direction. He brushed off the paper plates that were scattered on his desk.

"Detective Munson, what a pleasant surprise," Parker said. He gestured toward the room. "Pretty exciting, huh?"

"If you say so, Parker."

"What do you mean? This is the biggest story to hit Gardenia in forever." He took an issue from the stack of *Gazette*s on Gardner's desk and handed it to Munson. "The Orion Project's roster had about two hundred people on it—*two hundred*. Vincent Restonelli, the fire chief; Benjamin Stowe, some plastic surgeon in Gardenia; Jake Colby, the president of the board of ed., Hugo Lurch. . . . The list goes on and on. It's insane."

Munson put the issue down and looked at the paperwork stacked near his computer.

"You see all this? It's a theory I've got going," he said excitedly. "Want to hear it?" He didn't wait for an answer and grabbed a piece of paper, drew a stick figure in the middle of it, and labeled it *Eva Sansfield*. "I'm thinking Eva Sansfield was the first girl of the Orion Project, right?" He tapped his pen on the paper. "She's got the marks, right? On her stomach? I got a source at the hospital," he said proudly, but Detective Munson didn't seem all that impressed. "It looks like this thing has been going on for decades. I'm thinking Kirk Stryker took it over when Sansfield died in his tub, like a protégé."

"And your evidence is . . ."

"I'm working on that . . ." Parker made another stick figure, labeled it *Stryker*, and drew an arrow and dollar signs between the figures. "I'm also thinking that Sansfield didn't know what her father had been up to, probably thought the abuse was just her—and maybe her sister. She has a twin, you know." Munson remained quiet. "Sansfield must have cracked when she found out about the Orion Project. A Paulette Krause told me—" he reached for his notebook and flipped a few pages "—that Sansfield had taken over the books for the cancer walk in late March. Maybe that's when she figured out something was up, that money was unaccounted for. Maybe she found out about the pornography ring, and it triggered her, you know?"

Munson's poker face was beginning to irritate him. He was practically doing her job for her. This was good stuff. "Maybe she wanted to save those girls," he said. "Maybe she wasn't thinking at all and just did Stryker in . . . What do you think?"

"You're asking me?"

"Why not? Between your investigative skills and mine, we make a great team. Who knows? Together, we can find the gun that killed Stryker. The missing piece."

"There is no you and me, Parker."

"And we haven't even gotten to the whole Satriano thing," he said, his pulse quickening. "There's lots to unpack there."

She leaned toward him. "Parker, I came down here to do two things. The first was to tell you that my days as a detective are numbered—I'm retiring, paperwork's filed. I know you think we're a *team*"—she said the word with air quotes—"and that you know something about me, and about Hugo Lurch's suicide, and that you have these wonderful ideas about all the ways I can help you in your emerging career, but it's not happening. In fact, that leads me to the second reason why I came here . . . To return something to you."

She dug into the pocket of her overcoat and pulled out Parker's digital recorder, placing it on his desk.

"I was looking all over for this," Parker said. "I would have given money that that prick Kramer had it. How did you get it?"

"It was found in a guest room at the Bally's hotel in Atlantic City."

There was a slight hitch in Parker's breathing. "That's strange," he said.

"Isn't it? Benning called me a few nights ago from the lock-up—how he managed to do that, I'll never know—to tell me he had a feeling his girlfriend was in trouble, thought he saw something on some Skype conversation he wasn't supposed to be having in the first place. I didn't know what he was up to, but I sent someone down there to check her room after she checked out. Imagine my surprise when one of my officers found *that*"—she motioned to the recorder—"underneath the air-conditioning unit. Some interesting stuff on there, Parker. Private conversations Muriel Adams had with her boyfriend in the privacy of her hotel room. . . . Seems you've been making a habit of being where you're not supposed to be."

Parker glanced at his parents, who waved to him from the other side of the room. "Detective Munson, I don't know what—"

"Save it, Parker. I did a little digging, and it looks like there's a Bally's worker, a recent hire, who went to the same college as you. New Paltz. Same graduating class. Stanley Field. You know him?"

"Stanley Field?" Parker furrowed his brows, pretending to think. "I'm not sure I know who—"

"And we checked the hotel security cameras." She reached behind Parker's head and pulled on the back of his hoodie. "I have a hunch not many criminals wear a SUNY New Paltz hoodie when they're illegally trespassing." She glanced behind her, at the happy faces. "I'd hate to tell old Gardner that his star reporter is being arrested. That would certainly put a damper on the mood in here, don't you think?" She paused for what Parker thought was dramatic effect. "But I don't think there'll be any need for that, right, Parker?"

He didn't answer.

"Good. Now you go and have your big celebration or whatever it is you're calling it. I'm going back to my family and my life. *Alone.* I don't expect to see your car in any of my rearview mirrors anytime soon."

"Parker! Parker!" Gardner called. He was still standing on the desk. Parker wasn't sure if the old man liked it up there or if he couldn't get down. "Get over here, son," he said, "your public awaits."

"Speech! Speech! Speech!" the crowd began to chant.

"They're playing your song, Mr. Parker," Munson said.

Parker stood up from his chair and stepped toward the center of the room. Someone handed him a glass of champagne, and he was ushered to the top of Gardner's desk like a rock star on a concert stage. The editor wrapped his bony arm around him and lifted his glass.

"Go ahead, son," Gardner said.

Parker looked out into the crowd. As he began to speak, Detective Munson turned away and left through the front door, without looking back. With any luck, he would never see her again.

58

Bobby replayed the voice message on his smartphone:

Hey, Bob, it's me. They're springing me. Finally. You around? I need a ride. Next beer's on me.

"Would you quit it? I'm trying to figure out who the murderer is here," grumbled his father, who was sitting on the bed and watching an episode of *Matlock*. "It's never who you think it is."

"Sometimes it is," Bobby said and flopped into a chair. He pressed the tiny *Play* triangle on his phone screen again and again:

Hey, Bob, it's me. They're springing me. Finally. You around? I need a ride. Next beer's on me.

Hey, Bob, it's me. They're springing me. Finally. You around? I need a ride. Next beer's on me.

"What's with you?" the old man said. "I thought I was supposed to be the one with the memory problem."

"Nothing's with me. Eat your oatmeal before it gets cold."

Bobby pressed his thumbs into the corners of his eyes. He felt heavy and empty. The healing cuts on his knuckles began to sting for no particular reason, and he picked at the scabs until he had ripped them all off and they filled with fresh blood.

"Well, hello, pretty woman," Bobby heard his father say. He looked up and was startled to see Roxanne standing in the doorway of his father's room.

"Don't just sit there, dummy. Invite the lady in," his father said, fluffing up the pillow behind his back. He straightened the sheet over his knobby knees so that just the tips of his ribbed red socks were peeking out.

"That's a nasty habit you have, you know." Bobby stood up. "Following people around."

"I didn't follow you," Roxanne said. "I tried calling, but you haven't answered your phone all morning. I thought you might be here, since, you know, you mentioned your father was at a place like this." She smiled. "Only took me two tries to find the right assisted living facility."

"Your father's here?" the old man asked Bobby. "No wonder you're always around."

Bobby ignored the comment. "They just let you in? So much for security in this place."

"I said I was your sister." She shrugged. "Your stepsister."

"That worked?"

"Not really. I slipped in after an old woman fell down with her walker in the cafeteria. Caused a bit of a ruckus."

Roxanne looked pretty. She was wearing tight skinny jeans, a long red sweater, and cowboy boots that had seen better days. He hated to admit it, but it was good to see her. "Where's Gordy?" he asked.

Roxanne pointed down the hall. "We found a movie theater on the way to the room, so I told him he could wait in there while I tried to find you. They're playing *Forrest Gump*. It's one of his favorites."

"Pete, I'll be back," Bobby said to his father. "Want anything while I'm gone?"

"Yeah, I want you to take a long walk off a short pier," the old man said and cackled, his toothless smile a big hole in his sagging face.

Bobby grabbed the old man's empty coffee mug, brushed past Roxanne, and walked toward a small kitchen down the side corridor. Roxanne followed behind.

"Are you all right?" she asked. She was leaning against the doorframe as Bobby poured what was left in the coffeepot into his father's mug.

"I'm fine," Bobby said, replacing the pot.

"You don't seem fine."

"You don't know me well enough to know, do you?"

"Maybe not," Roxanne said. "But I'm a pretty good judge of *fine*—it's Muriel's favorite word—and you don't look it. Neither did she when I left this morning."

"Why'd you leave?"

"To find you."

Bobby added milk and sugar to his father's coffee and stirred it with a plastic spoon. He tossed the spoon in the trash, pulled out his phone, and showed the screen to Roxanne. "Three missed calls from Marty. *Three.* And where was I?" He motioned to the room. "This place. Asleep. My fucking father unplugged my phone so he could plug in some neck massager that doesn't even work." Bobby shook his head. "That's rich, isn't it? I'm here keeping a man who doesn't even know me company while my only friend in the world needs me and can't reach me."

"It wasn't your fault, Bobby, what happened." She reached for him, but he pulled away.

"I was supposed to protect him. It was my goddamn job." He leaned against the kitchen counter, gripping it with his fingers until he could feel the cuts on his hand widen. "He knew something was up. Goddamn Kirk Stryker. Benning saw Stryker lift one of his drinking glasses at some merchants association meeting. Put the thing in a plastic bag like he was going to run a DNA test on it or something. Weird shit. And then he recommends this guy, Cranston, for a position at the firm."

"The guy from the news?"

Bobby nodded. "It was clear that Cranston didn't know a thing about tax law. He just kept asking questions and didn't even bother showing up after a week. Marty was sure the guy was spying on him, and then Stryker ends up dead."

"And they arrested Marty."

"It was probably because of the damn glass. Marty thought tailing some of the people in Stryker's office might help, to see if I could find any connection to the murder— or Cranston."

Roxanne nodded. "That's why you were with Eva?"

"Plus, he was worried about Muriel. And now they've arrested the assemblyman's cousin? Marty thought Satriano was a good guy." Bobby turned his face away so she wouldn't see the tears in his eyes. "Whatever. It doesn't matter. Not anymore. He's gone."

Roxanne came closer to him. "You're not alone, Bobby."

"Don't," he said, pulling away. "You had me pegged at the beginning. I'm a fortysomething-year-old man working as a bodyguard for a CPA. Is that even a job? You're better off staying far away from me."

"Well, that's a little impossible since you're all that Gordy talks about—Bobby this, Bobby that."

"You guys are doing just great without me."

"Why don't you let me decide that." Roxanne forced her hand into his palm, which felt soft but firm against his skin.

He picked up the coffee, and they walked back to his father's room. Gordy was sitting on the bed watching television and eating from the old man's cup of peaches with a plastic spoon.

"Hi, Mom! Hi, Bobby!" Gordy chirped when he spotted them. "The movie's over."

"I see that," Roxanne said. She put her hands on his chewing cheeks. "How did you know what room Mr. Chaucer was in?"

"I asked somebody in the theater," Gordy said, taking another mouthful of peaches. "They said Room 352. They said everyone knows Pete Chaucer."

"They said that?" the old man asked with a grin. He had moved over a little bit on the bed to make room for Gordy.

"Yeah, they also said they know to stay away from you," Gordy said.

"Smart kid." The old man patted Gordy on the back. "What were they playing in that rat hole of a theater anyway?"

"*Forrest Gump.*"

"What the hell is that?"

"It's about a guy who thinks he's stupid," Gordy said.

"Oh, that sounds like a good one for you," the old man said to Bobby and cackled. He jabbed his plastic fork into the container that Gordy was holding.

"But, actually," Gordy said, helping the old man spear a peach, "the man is really loved, and he really makes things happen. He just doesn't realize it. He's had a great life. And suddenly he has this son."

"It's a beautiful story," Roxanne said, squeezing Bobby's hand. He had forgotten he was holding it. One of the strands of her blond hair was brushing the side of his face. Her hair was wild today, like a lion's mane. He liked it that way. He planted a soft kiss on her mouth.

"In the red," Gordy whispered to the old man with a smile.

"Yeah, right, kid." The old man wiggled his socked feet. "You know, I used to be a pretty good baseball player in my day. Do you want to hear the story about the time I batted three hundred in my junior year of high school?"

"Really?" Gordy said. "Sure!"

"It's a good one. Hey, buddy," the old man said to Bobby, "did you ever hear this one?"

Bobby smiled. "No," he lied. He sat down and pulled Roxanne onto his lap. "Why don't you tell us?"

59

"**M**ommy?"

Muriel was lying on her bed, running her hand along the threading of her pillowcase. She could still smell Marty's cologne on the soft fabric and almost imagine his arms around her, his warm breath on the nape of her neck. She would never feel that breath again.

"Mommy?" Zack was speaking into the narrow space under her door. She could see his little pinkie finger poking through. "Mommy, the door is locked. Your door is never locked. Are you in there?"

Muriel didn't know if she was, but she got up and opened the door anyway.

Zack was wearing his dressy black pants and white shirt of the suit he had worn to his grandmother's seventieth birthday party. The outfit was already becoming too small for him, the pant legs and shirt sleeves barely reaching the ends of his legs and arms.

"Can I come in?" he asked. "I'm wearing my nice clothes to show I'm sorry that Marty died."

"That's very sweet of you, baby." She ran her hand along his smooth cheek.

Zack stepped into her bedroom and closed the door. He climbed onto the bed, and Muriel sat beside him. He placed his hand on Muriel's knee. "Are you sad, Mommy?"

"Yes." She wiped a tear that was gathering in the corner of her eye.

"I'm sad too," Zack said. "Marty was a nice man." He leaned against her. "But you still have us."

"I know," Muriel said, kissing the top of Zack's head. "And I love you so much." She removed some dust that had gathered on the side of his face from when he was peeking under her door.

"If Marty isn't here, are you going to have Daddy move back here?"

Muriel ran her fingers through his bangs and brushed them aside. "I don't think so, sweetie. I think it's going to be just the three of us for a while."

"Awesome. Three is my lucky number."

They sat there quietly for a little while.

"Is it okay to ask now?" he asked.

"Ask what?"

"What it was."

"What what was?"

"The surprise."

"What surprise?"

Zack furrowed his brow. "Do you know about the surprise? Because I can only talk to you about it if you know already. Those are the rules."

Muriel rubbed her temple. "Sweetie, I can't play this game right now."

"Sorry," he said. "I just wanted to know."

"Know about what?"

"The surprise."

Muriel took a deep breath and let out a long exhale. "But how do I know if I know about it unless you tell me what it is?"

Zack seemed to consider this.

"Can you give me a hint?" she asked.

Zack thought some more. "I guess that's fair," he said. "I'm talking about the surprise that Marty put in the ceiling in the bathroom." Her son's eyes were both serious and wild with excitement.

"The bathroom? What do you mean?"

"Oh, no!" A look of horror appeared on his face. "So you don't know about it?"

"Zack . . ." Muriel lifted up his chin with her finger. "It's all right. Sometimes you have to tell."

"Don't tell Ellie that I didn't keep another secret. She says I'm a baby who can't keep a secret."

"Zack, you're not a baby, which is why I need you to tell me what you mean. It's very important."

"Okay . . ." Zack took in a deep breath and let out an extended exhale, mimicking Muriel's. "One morning I got up early because I had a bad dream. I think there's something wrong with the dream catcher that Marty gave me. It doesn't work." He paused, looking upset. "Your bedroom door was closed, so I opened it, and I saw that the bathroom light was on. You always told me that I should turn the light off if I see it on, so I went into the bathroom to turn it off, and I saw Marty standing on the sink. He was putting something into the ceiling."

"Into the ceiling? What was it?"

"I don't know, but when he saw me he jumped, you

know, like this." Zack got up from the bed and did a little bounce. "He's lucky he didn't fall, right? I don't think he knows you're not supposed to jump when you're standing in high places. Then he put his finger to his lips, like this." Zack pursed his lips and did the *Shhhh* sign. "He said it was a surprise for you and that I shouldn't tell. He said, 'Are you a big boy?' And I am, so I told him yes. And he said, 'Can you keep a secret?' And I said yes. I said—"

"Okay," Muriel interrupted, "slow down a little bit, sweetie . . ."

"All right." He took another big breath, but then continued talking as quickly as he had before. "I asked, 'What is it?' And he said, 'It's a surprise.' 'For mommy?' I asked. And he said yes." Zack smiled at the memory. "And then he said it was okay for me to crawl next to you and sleep there because my dream catcher wasn't working. I think I fell asleep after that. Can we get a new dream catcher? Do you think my dreams are too fast for this one?" His big eyes were looking at her thoughtfully, and then he appeared sad. "Are you mad that I told? About the secret?"

Muriel smiled. "Of course not. Now why don't you go downstairs. I'll be down soon, okay?"

"Okey dokey." Zack wrapped his little arms around Muriel. "I love you, Mommy. Don't be sad. Remember, Marty is with Grandpa Joe and Grandma Freddie. He's not alone. They're waiting for us." When he got to the door, he asked, "Should I lock it again?"

"Just for a little bit," she said, and he pressed the knob's push-in button and closed the door.

Muriel got up from the bed and hurried to the bathroom. She turned on the light and examined the dropped ceiling, wondering what Marty had put up there and why. She didn't see anything out of the ordinary. Maybe he had already taken down whatever it was. She stepped carefully onto the toilet cover and then onto the sink cabinet, reaching up to move one of the panels. She pushed it away from the seam and poked her head through. The displaced dust tickled her nose, and she fanned it away with her hand, shielding her eyes from the bright light. About a foot away, she saw something—a bundle wrapped in plastic. She reached across the panels, stretching as far as she could until her fingertips reached the bubble wrap, and she pulled at it until she could get a firm grip and yank it out. She crept down off the sink and returned to her bedroom.

The package felt heavy. She sat on the edge of her bed and placed it onto her lap. A small patch of Scotch tape was holding the wrap closed, and she ripped it off. Then she unwrapped the item, sheet after sheet, until a large spool of plastic was at her feet and in her hands was a black onyx box.

She ran her hands along its smooth surface, wondering what it could be. Her heart was beating fast. She unclasped the lid and opened it.

The box was empty, except for a piece of spiral notebook paper that had been folded into quarters. She put the box on the bedspread and unfolded the paper, which revealed a handwritten message:

Dear Muriel,

Please forgive the sloppiness of this note. I wrote it quickly and practically in the dark, fearful that one of the kids would wake up and catch me. As you'll be able to tell, it is the first love letter I have ever written, because it's not very good. But I need you to know—as I look at you now asleep in bed—that I never imagined feeling this way about anyone.

You were right that first night at the restaurant. Everything you had heard about me had been true. I'm not proud of it. But it was who I was, not who I wanted to be. And then I met you. Beautiful, smart-alecky you.

You intrigued me. You challenged me. You made me laugh. But, most of all, you gave me a chance. That was a gift. And the last three months have been more than I could have asked for.

Last Sunday, I know I told you I was in New Jersey for some work thing, but I was actually looking at houses for sale on Long Island. A house for us. And the kids.

Am I going too fast? Who knows. I'm in my late forties. Do any of us know how much time we have left? All I know is I'd like to spend the rest of that time with you.

I should probably tell you all this in person, and one day I'm sure I will. I guess I don't want to scare you. Or maybe I don't want to scare myself . . .

I love you.

I just needed you to know. Right now. But you're asleep. And you know how I feel about email. :) So while I still had my nerve I wrote it on a piece of paper I found in the scrap drawer, as you call it, and am hiding this note away in the recesses of this house in Massapequa Park, under the ugliest dropped ceiling I have ever seen. My hope is that you never read it, because by the time it's discovered by the new people who live here, we will be long gone. You and me. Together.

Always, Marty

Deep, powerful sobs welled up in Muriel's throat. She dropped the note and ran toward the bedroom window, slamming it open and gulping in the outside air.

"Mommy?!"

It was Ellie this time. She couldn't remember the last time her daughter had called her *Mommy*.

"Are you okay?" she asked, knocking on the door. The locked doorknob jiggled.

"I'm fine," Muriel called, her voice hoarse and raspy.

"You don't sound fine."

Muriel wiped what tears she could from her face and took a few deep breaths. She walked to the door of her bedroom and pressed against it, her voice quavering. "I'll be down in a minute."

"Please come out," Ellie said.

"I will. I promise. Just give me a couple of minutes."

"Okay." Muriel could tell Ellie was still standing there. The floorboards were creaking as she shifted her weight. "You know," Ellie said, her voice close to the door. "I never realized what it was like to be on this side of a locked bedroom door. It kinda sucks, actually."

"Tell me about it," Muriel said, smiling a little. She unlocked the door and opened it slightly. Ellie was dressed in jeans and a tight navy blue tank top, her hair in that side part she had been wearing. She looked so beautiful and grown up.

"Can I do anything?" Ellie asked. "For you?"

"Maybe . . . can you give me a hug?"

Ellie nodded, her eyes crinkling, and they reached for one another, both of them sobbing into each other's shoulders. Muriel didn't know how long it had been since she held her daughter, but she felt leaner and taller than she remembered.

"I'm so sorry about Marty, Mommy," Ellie said, digging her face into Muriel's neck. "I'm sorry about a lot of things."

"I know." She lifted her daughter's chin up and wiped the tears from her cheeks. "Me too."

"Are you going to come downstairs?" Ellie asked.

Muriel nodded and tucked Ellie's bangs around her ear. "Give me one second, okay?"

Muriel retreated into her bedroom, returned Marty's handwritten note to the onyx box, and rewrapped it in the plastic. Then she put it back into its hiding place above the dropped ceiling in the bathroom. She thought about that person, sometime in the future, who would find the note and wonder about the man who wrote it, and about the woman he loved and the life they had shared together. She hoped it would make them smile.

Ellie was waiting patiently for her at the bedroom door.

"Mommy, are you coming?" Zack called from somewhere below. "I'm hungry."

Ellie rolled her eyes, and Muriel felt a tiny glimmer of contentment bubble to the surface. She reached for her daughter's hand. A part of Muriel would always be locked up in that dropped ceiling with Marty, but so much of her was not. She knew that now. More than ever. As she and Ellie walked together down the stairs, Muriel also knew that happily ever after was not only something real and something worth fighting for, but also something she deserved—and, in so many ways, already had.

ACKNOWLEDGMENTS

I once worked with a magazine editor who said if he ever won an award, he would march up to the podium, grab his trophy, and exclaim, "I would like to thank . . . absolutely nobody." He believed any success he achieved in his career was a product of his own hard work. Maybe it was, who knows. Yet, writing a book is probably the most solitary profession I can think of, and even I've got a boatload of people to thank. Here are a few.

Stonesong's Ellen Scordato, my publishing spiritual leader. Alexis Castellanos for her fabulous cover design—they say a picture is worth a thousand words, but in this case, it's worth a hundred thousand. Pete Romeo of Wooly Head Design for his talent—and patience. Shona, copyeditor extraordinaire. My beta readers, Jessica and Belisa, whose feedback was invaluable and made this book better. Viki, the Roxanne to my Muriel. And, finally, Tommy, who gives me the room to be me; Griffin, my first born and my go-to first reader; Helena, my girl, my light; and Jack, my dancing buddy—there is no me without any of you.

ABOUT THE AUTHOR

Voted one of the best Long Island authors for two consecutive years, Dina Santorelli writes thriller and suspense novels. Her debut novel, *Baby Grand*, the first book in her Baby Grand Trilogy, was a #1 Political Thriller and #1 Kidnapping Thriller on Amazon Kindle and reached the Top 30 in the Paid Kindle Store. Dina has been a freelance writer for more than 20 years and currently serves as the executive editor of *Salute* and *Family* magazines. Over the course of her career, she has interviewed many celebrities, including Maria Shriver, Martina McBride, Sarah McLachlan, Gary Sinise, Kiefer Sutherland, Michael Strahan, Norman Reedus, Vince Vaughn, James Gandolfini, Tim McGraw, Carrie Underwood, and Kevin Bacon. Since 2010, she has collaborated on a variety of nonfiction titles, and her book *Daft Punk: A Trip Inside the Pyramid* has been published in several languages. Dina also lectures for Hofstra University's Continuing Education Department and is a SELF-e Ambassador for the *Library Journal*. For more information about Dina, visit her website at http://dinasantorelli.com.

Follow Dina on social media:

 Facebook: @dinasantorelliwriter

 Twitter: @dinasantorelli

 Instagram: @dinasantorelli

 Goodreads: @dinasantorelli

Join Dina's newsletter and get a free short story titled "*A Baby Grand Story: Bailino,*" a companion piece to the Baby Grand Trilogy! You'll also receive regular updates on Dina's various books and author events, as well her popular 3 Things I Love: http://tinyurl.com/dinasmailinglist

CPSIA information can be obtained
at www.ICGtesting.com
Printed in the USA
JSHW031640200522
26055JS00001B/4